Walking Into The Unknown

October 1867 – October 1868

Book # 10 in The Bregdan Chronicles

Sequel to Always Forward

Ginny Dye

Walking Into The Unknown

Printed in the United States of America

For Linnea. You have brought so much joy to my life. I am so glad you are now my daughter, and I am so very proud of you!

A Note from the Author

My great hope is that *Walking Into The Unknown* will both entertain, challenge you, and give you courage to face all the seasons of your life. I hope you will learn as much as I did during the months of research it took to write this book. I have about decided it is just not possible to cover an entire year in one book anymore but I actually achieved it this time! As I move forward in the series, it seems there is so much going on in so many arenas, and I simply don't want to gloss over them.

When I ended the Civil War in *The Last, Long Night*, I knew virtually nothing about Reconstruction. I have been shocked and mesmerized by all I have learned – not just about the North and the South – but now about the West.

I grew up in the South and lived for eleven years in Richmond, VA. I spent countless hours exploring the plantations that still line the banks of the James River and became fascinated by the history.

But you know, it's not the events that fascinate me so much – it's the people. That's all history is, you know. History is the story of people's lives. History reflects the consequences of their choices and actions – both good and bad. History is what has given you the world you live in today – both good and bad.

This truth is why I named this series The Bregdan Chronicles. Bregdan is a Gaelic term for weaving: Braiding. Every life that has been lived until today is a part of the woven braid of life. It takes every person's story to create history. Your life will help determine the course of history. You may think you don't have much of an impact. You do. Every action you take will reflect in someone else's life. Someone else's decisions. Someone else's future. Both good and bad. That is the **Bregdan Principle**...

**Every life that has been lived until today is a
part of the woven braid of life.
It takes every person's story to
create history.
Your life will help determine the
course of history.
You may think you don't have
much of an impact.
You do.
Every action you take will reflect in
someone else's life.
Someone else's decisions.
Someone else's future.
Both good and bad.**

My great hope as you read this book, and all that will follow, is that you will acknowledge the power you have, every day, to change the world around you by your decisions and actions. Then I will know the research and writing were all worthwhile.

Oh, and I hope you enjoy every moment of it and learn to love the characters as much as I do!

I'm constantly asked how many books will be in this series. I guess that depends on how long I live! My intention is to release two books a year – continuing to weave the lives of my characters into the times they lived. I hate to end a good book as much as anyone – always feeling so sad that I must leave the characters. You shouldn't have to be sad for a long time!

You are now reading the 10th book - # 11 (*Looking To The Future*) will be released in November 2017. If you like what you read, you'll want to make sure you're on my mailing list at www.BregdanChronicles.net. I'll let you know each time a new one comes out so that you can take advantage of all my fun launch events, and you can enjoy my BLOG in between books!

Many more are coming!

Sincerely,
Ginny Dye

Chapter One
October, 1867

Carrie's eyes opened abruptly as she bolted forward in bed. She willed her pounding heart to slow its erratic beat as she leaned closer to the open window, vaguely aware of the crisp air announcing that autumn had finally conquered the searing heat of a Virginia summer. She hated the fear that made her limbs tremble and her breath come in shallow gasps, but she also knew there was no one on Cromwell Plantation that could afford to become complacent. *Especially her...*

Forcing her legs to move against the fear, she pushed back the bed covers, stood, and moved to a position next to the window. She would not leave a silhouette that would make her a target, but neither would she just lie there. Pulling back the curtain just enough to peer out, she scanned every inch of the land illuminated by a half-moon riding high in the sky. The outline of the barn made her pulse jump harder, but she pushed down the moment of terror and forced herself to breathe evenly.

She knew there were at least a dozen men guarding the plantation every night. Somewhere beyond the reach of her gaze, hidden by the darkness of the woods, they waited with loaded guns for any threat that materialized. It had been the same every night since the fateful moment when KKK vigilantes had exploded from the trees and changed her life forever.

Carrie didn't know how long she stood there before she decided there was no threat. She could have been awakened by the sound of a coyote, a neighing horse, or even the hoot of a harmless owl. The silence reigning over the peaceful beauty indicated none of the watchmen shared her concern. She glanced longingly at the opening to the tunnel leading out to the river, but she couldn't afford to stay up all night. The Harvest Festival would start in just a few hours. Carrie already knew it would take all her energy to endure the day she used to love.

Gradually, she became aware she was trembling from the cold. Her nightgown was no match for the cool breeze flowing through the window. She wouldn't be surprised if the first frost of the year would turn the world into glistening diamonds by the time the sun rose. She gave one final glance out the window before she turned away and crawled into bed, wishing for the 153rd time that she could snuggle into Robert's warm body.

She made no attempt to swallow the tears that streamed down her face as she reached out a hand and gently stroked the pillow that should have cradled her husband's head. Abby had warned her the nights would be the hardest, but the warning did nothing to make the reality less painful. Carrie pulled the pillow closer, buried her face in its softness, and allowed the grief to carry her into a restless sleep.

****

Carrie could barely hear the sound of rushing water in the distance. As she pushed through the dense fog that threatened to smother her, the sound pulled her forward. She couldn't identify why it was so important to reach the water... she simply knew she must.

As prickly limbs reached out to grab her, she pushed them aside, vaguely aware that the thorns piercing her flesh resulted in no pain. She paused for a moment, wondering why that was something she wondered about, and then kept on. The water was the only thing she cared about. She must find the water...

"Carrie!"

Carrie paused, impatient when she heard her voice called in the distance. She shook her head and kept moving. Without being able to explain why, she knew the water represented peace. She had to reach the water. A dim glow began to illuminate the fog, allowing her to proceed at a faster pace. As the rushing sound increased to a roar, her heart pounded in response. Everything would be all right if she could only reach the water. She hesitated as she wondered what had to be made right, but she had no answer, only the compulsion to reach the roaring sound in the distance.

The air began to glow a soft blue as the fog continued to dissipate. The beauty of it wrapped around her, giving her the courage to keep moving.

"Carrie!"

This time she stopped, certain she recognized the voice. "Leave me alone," she called. "I have to get to the water."

"Carrie!"

Carrie sucked in her breath as she identified the one calling her. "Robert?"

She didn't understand why her voice was trembling with disbelief. She also couldn't fathom why Robert was trying to keep her from the water. "Come with me," she called, turning back to plunge toward what awaited her.

"Carrie! No!"

Carrie stopped again, certain she could now see Robert's form in the glowing blue light. Why didn't he come join her? Why was he holding her back? "I'm going to the water," she yelled, every particle of her frantic to reach what she realized was a gushing waterfall catching the rays of sun beaming through the fog—splitting the light into every color of the rainbow. She stared in awe as the colors danced in the spray of the water. Calling her... Calling her...

She stepped forward, knowing what she had to do. She had to join in the dance of the colors. She had to merge with the spray of the waterfall.

"Carrie, no!" Robert's voice became more urgent, his desperation cutting through her intense longing.

Once again she stopped, just short of the final step that would send her into the dance of the waterfall. "Why are you stopping me?" she screamed. Everything would be all right if she simply entered the dance.

The form materialized into the man she loved, but it made no sense because Robert was floating over the waterfall. She stared at him, wondering how her husband could float in the glowing air. "I want to come dance with you," she whispered, realizing this was what had pulled her forward. She had known Robert was here...here in the waterfall...here...waiting to dance.

"No," Robert said, his voice quiet now. "It's not time, my love."

"I want to be with you," Carrie breathed. *Never had she wanted anything more.* *"I want to dance with you in the waterfall."*

"You will," Robert replied, in a voice full of more sorrow than she had ever heard. *"But not now, my love. Not now."*

"Why?" Carrie whispered, her heart shattering when she realized Robert was denying her wish. It would take only one step to join the dance.

"It's not time," Robert responded, both hands reaching out to her in a gesture of love. *"I love you, Carrie. I always will. Never forget it."*

"Robert..." Carrie swayed on the edge of the waterfall.

"There are others who need you," Robert continued. *"You can't join me now."* His voice increased in its urgency. *"You must not join me."*

The love in Robert's voice, and the intensity in his eyes, caused Carrie to take a step back from the edge. As she did, the glow began to fade, and Robert's form was made barely visible.

Another step, though everything in her screamed for her to join the dance. Robert's love was forcing her back.

The rainbow colors evaporated, leaving nothing but cold spray that buffeted her fatigued body. Robert was gone.

Carrie sobbed as she took another step.

The roar of the waterfall dissolved into a vague murmur as the fog settled back in, threatening to once again consume her. She thrashed her arms to beat it away. Desperate to return to the dance of the waterfall, no longer caring what Robert had said, she fought to find her way again.

"Carrie!"

Carrie spun around to identify the voice coming from another direction.

"Carrie!"

Her confusion grew. This was not Robert's voice. It was a new one calling her. Loudly. Insistently. Lovingly.

"Carrie! Come back! Please come back!"

Carrie glanced over her shoulder once more, knowing the dance of the waterfall was only steps away, and then she moved toward the new voice. Without another sound coming from the fog, she could feel Robert smiling his approval.

The smile broke her heart.

Abby was gently stroking her hair when Carrie opened her eyes, confused by the bright sunshine flooding into her room.

"The dream?"

Carrie nodded, the stark reality of the dream rushing through her once more. "Will it ever stop?" she whispered. Part of her longed to have the painful memory fade away. Another part—the biggest part—wanted it to continue forever so that Robert always remained close.

Abby read her thoughts. "Do you want it to stop?" she asked tenderly, her gray eyes full of sympathy and understanding.

Carrie considered the question. "Not yet," she admitted.

Abby nodded and continued to stroke her hair. "I dreamed of Charles for more than three years. At some point, it became less frequent than every night, but I discovered I longed for the dream when it didn't come."

"Because you felt close to him in your dreams, even if wasn't real?"

"Yes," Abby said softly. "When they finally stopped, I felt guilty because I was letting him go. I seemed to exchange one regret for another."

Carrie listened closely, knowing her stepmother was offering her wisdom for the future. "How long did it take?" she asked when the silence stretched out too long. She had been having the same dream every night since Robert had been murdered, but the one she had just woken from seemed somehow more real than the others.

"To let go of the regrets?" Abby cocked her head and stared out the window thoughtfully. "I don't know," she finally replied. "One day they were there. Then they weren't. When I realized it, I knew I was going to be able to move on."

Carrie tried to push down the wave of revulsion that threatened to swamp her as she envisioned life without the dreams that kept Robert real to her.

Abby took Carrie's chin and turned it so she could look into her eyes. "It's too soon to even contemplate it, my dear. And there is no timetable. Every person is different. Just live. Life will unfold as it comes."

"Carrie! Carrie!"

Carrie managed a smile as a demanding voice floated in through the window.

Abby motioned for her to stay in bed and then moved to the window, her soft blue dress swirling around her slender form. "Good morning, Amber," she called.

"Good morning, Miss Abby," Amber yelled back brightly. "Why isn't Carrie out in the barn? The sun has been up for a while. She's always out early on Harvest Festival Day!"

Carrie flinched as memories swarmed her mind. She could feel Abby's eyes on her, but she couldn't bring herself to look up. She had been dreading this day ever since she and Abby had boarded the train in Kansas to return home. She had been thrilled to arrive back on the plantation, but had no idea how she was going to endure the day that evoked memories sure to tear her heart apart even more.

"She'll be out soon, dear," Abby replied. "She slept in a little extra today."

"On Tournament Day?" Amber exclaimed, disbelief dripping from her words. Just as suddenly, her tone changed to one of smug victory. "I guess I can understand since I beat her last year. She probably knows it will happen again."

Abby laughed lightly. "I wouldn't count on that victory quite yet, young lady. There is more than one person who intends to take away your crown."

Amber waved her hand as she turned back to the barn. "Let them try! Clint and I are getting all the horses ready. Today is going to be a big day! Mister Mark and Miss Susan are coming, and that Mister Anthony is coming to check out the babies he bought this summer."

Carrie couldn't miss the excitement vibrating in Amber's voice. It pushed the painful, more recent memories back a bit. She could remember her own childish excitement when she had been Amber's age, although it had been different then. When she was a child, she could do nothing more than dream about being able to ride in the tournament, which was exclusively a male domain. Today, Amber would be competing—riding to maintain the title she had won the year before.

Without warning, the pain surged from within and threatened to swallow her again. She bent over double to hold back the groan of agony that wanted to rip her in half. Abby settled down on the bed next to her and engulfed her icy hand in her warm grip.

"Memories?" Abby asked.

Carrie wanted to hold the pain inside, but she had to talk about it. If she had learned nothing in the past five months, she had learned that. "I met him for the first time the night before the Blackwell Tournament," she managed, as images of his tall form riding down the drive filled her mind. "He was quite simply the best-looking man I had ever seen. It was very confusing for me. I had never been interested in a man before."

"You were only eighteen," Abby murmured, "and your father tells me you were not much like your friends."

"That would be putting it mildly. I thought Louisa and all her simpering ways were ridiculous," Carrie said wryly. "It seems decades ago. It's not possible that it has only been seven and a half years."

"Robert won the tournament on Granite," Abby said, inviting her to continue sharing her recollections.

Carrie forced a smile through the tears that clogged her throat. "Yes. He was quite spectacular. The sight of him and Granite thundering toward the rings was something to behold."

"And he crowned you as his queen that night at the Blackwell Ball," Abby prompted.

"I thought Louisa was going to spit nails," Carrie said, filled with awe as she thought about how much had changed. The war had altered her childhood nemesis into a woman she could be friends with, and now they were once again neighbors, as Louisa and Perry fought to bring Blackwell Plantation back to its former glory. "We never know what is going to happen, do we?"

"In life?" Abby mused. "Never." She paused for a long moment. "I used to find that quite distressing. I was certain that if I could only know what was coming, I would be better able to handle the present, and certainly better equipped to handle the future."

Carrie forgot her pain long enough to ask, "You don't feel that way anymore?"

"I don't," Abby agreed.

Carrie knew Abby wouldn't expound without an invitation. "Why not?" Learning the answer was suddenly more important than anything else, because Carrie had spent much of the last months certain she would be able to handle her situation better if she could simply know what was coming in the future.

"It takes the fun out of life," Abby replied gently.

Carrie stared at her silently. "Excuse me?"

"I know you can't comprehend it now," Abby said. "You're hungry for answers because you are trying to make sense of your life, and certainly nothing seems fun now."

Carrie continued to watch her, hoping that, for once, Abby would tell her what she was trying to say. She didn't have the energy to press harder.

"None of us knows what is coming," Abby said. "Life can change as fast as clouds can turn into a thunderstorm. One minute you're enjoying fluffy white beauty—the next you're dodging lightning strikes. If you focus on having to know what the future holds, you will always be unhappy because it simply can't be done."

"So you just dodge lightning strikes your whole life?" Carrie asked. "If you're trying to make me feel better, I'm afraid it's not working."

"Telling you the truth is not necessarily about making you feel better," Abby replied gently. "It's about giving you a foundation to move ahead."

Carrie considered that for a long moment. "I'm listening."

"Most people cling to what they know simply because it is familiar. They might be miserable, but at least it is a memory they understand. It seems safer to embrace what they know, than it is to let it go for fear of the unknown." Abby pressed Carrie's hand firmly. "I learned a long time ago that I have to keep moving forward, even when there seems to be no place to get to. I had to quit trying to see through time, and live what was in front of me."

"And you did that?" Carrie asked, desperate to know the answer.

"I did," Abby answered. "I discovered the greatest adventures of my life occurred when I quit demanding to know all the answers."

"Like what?"

"Like finding you," Abby said gently. "Like meeting Rose and Moses, and having them live with me. Marrying your father. Moving to Richmond. The list is so long... When I met you, I could never have imagined all those things would happen. They were complete unknowns."

Carrie let the words sink into her heart and mind, surprised they brought her a measure of comfort. "You're telling me there are good things ahead in my life." She wanted to believe that, but the pain was still too fresh. Yes, she had decided to still become a doctor, but she had no hope of actual joy in her life again. She would do what she could to help people, with the hope that that would be a large enough purpose for living.

Abby nodded, continuing to hold her hand. "I believe there are, Carrie, but my saying that is not going to mean much to you. You lost Robert in a horrible way, and then Bridget."

Raw pain gripped Carrie when she thought of the little girl she had lost without ever even seeing her curly black hair and rosebud lips. She only knew that much because Abby had held her when she was stillborn.

"You've begun to heal, but it is still going to take time," Abby added. "Deciding you still want to become a doctor is a big step, but now you have to live through each day until things get easier." She paused. "Part of that will be taking every opportunity for joy that you can find."

Carrie absorbed that thought as she tried to remember the last time she had felt joy. "The trip to Philadelphia," she murmured. She could still remember the joy she had felt when she saw Biddy and Faith, discovered Georgia was still alive and living as George, taking part in the grand opening of the factory. It seemed like a different lifetime, but she knew she had actually felt something other than numb pain.

"I know that was the last time you felt joy," Abby agreed. "The factory is doing well, by the way. Other businesses are searching for buildings in order to take advantage of the labor in Moyamensing. More people will be employed before winter hits."

"I'm glad," Carrie said, relieved to know she could at least be sincere in that sentiment. "The people there deserve it."

"And they have you to thank for it," Abby added. She held up her hand to stop Carrie's protest. "I know it took all of us to make it happen, but it took you putting it into action."

The sound of wagons rumbling in the distance dampened Carrie's feeling of satisfaction. She was truly glad for the people of Moyamensing, but she mostly wanted to run through the tunnel and hide along the banks of the river. She glanced at the mirror covering the opening, wondering how much her absence would be noticed.

"I believe Robert would want you to ride."

Carrie spun back to stare at Abby, certain she had heard her wrong. "What?"

Abby met her eyes squarely. "I believe Robert would want you to ride."

"No," Carrie snapped, not bothering to hide the anger the suggestion sparked.

"You could ride in tribute to him," Abby continued, seemingly oblivious to Carrie's anger. "He was so proud of you last year when you and Amber battled it out for the victory."

Carrie had a flashing memory of the laughter and pride in his eyes twelve months earlier. She bit back her groan of pain. "No."

"It would mean the world to Amber," Abby added. Her voice was firm, but her eyes shone with brilliant sympathy.

Carrie felt the cold knot of anger melt away as pain moved in to replace it. "I can't," she whispered.

"I know you don't want to face the memories," Abby pressed, "but sometimes the best way to deal with the pain is to replace it with new things to remember."

"Without Robert?"

"You will never do a thing on Cromwell Plantation without Robert. He is here in everything you do. Every place you go. Every face. Every horse." Abby took a deep breath. "The day we almost lost you, Robert told you to come back. Do you honestly think he meant for you to give up your life—to choose to live without joy? Is that the kind of love he had for you?"

Not too long ago, Carrie would have lashed out in anger if anyone had dared to question her actions. Now she could at least face it and try to honestly respond to the questions. Silence hung in the room for a long time as she struggled with what to do. She knew Abby would give her all the time she needed.

Laughter filtered in the window as early arrivals unloaded their wagons. Annie and Polly had been cooking for days, but every family coming for the tournament had been doing the same. No one would return home hungry that day.

Carrie almost managed a smile as she thought of how fun the Harvest Festival had been the year before. Her smile faltered as she realized anew that she would never see Robert's laughing eyes again. She would never feel his strong arms wrapped around her. She would never hear him telling her how proud he was of her. The last thought stopped her. *Robert had been so proud of her. He had loved her so much.* Truly, if he had asked her to stay, it was only because he believed she could be happy without him. She still very much doubted that would be true, but she understood she had to try. She nodded as she forced words beyond her frozen throat. "I will ride."

*****

Rose was on the porch when Carrie stepped out, clad in breeches. Rose raised her brow. "I'm riding in the tournament," Carrie revealed, understanding the flash of surprise and happiness in her best friend's eyes.

"I'm glad," Rose said. The look on her face revealed what her words did not.

Carrie came to stand beside Rose as more wagons rolled down the road. They were not needed right away. Moses' men were directing everyone where to go as children spilled from the wagons and spread out over the lawn laughing and running. Women headed toward the shade of the red and orange-leafed trees to spread their blankets. The night had been cool, and had indeed deposited a layer of glimmering frost, but it had melted away quickly and the day promised to deliver Indian summer-warmth.

"You've been home two weeks," Rose stated. "I missed you so much while you were away in Kansas."

Carrie reached down to grasp her hand. She knew Rose was really talking about how much she would miss her when they both left the plantation in January to pursue their education. "I'm going to miss you, too."

Rose squeezed her hand. "I'm so excited you are still going to be a doctor, but I think I've been on the plantation so long I'm afraid to leave," she said with her characteristic honesty. "My decision to stay when Robert died was so easy. This decision is much harder."

"Nonsense," Carrie said firmly.

"I'm serious," Rose insisted, her eyes still trained on the arriving wagons.

Carrie knew Rose was afraid to look at her because the tears would come. Now was not the time for the two friends to be sobbing on the porch together. "I know you are, but it is still nonsense," Carrie repeated. "I know you are going to miss me—maybe as much as I'll miss you. You'll miss the plantation. You'll miss everyone you're leaving behind. You'll miss all your students, and all you've accomplished, but you've dreamed of this for years. It's your turn, Rose."

"But what if I'm being selfish?" Rose persisted.

Rose's rigid stance and the tight clench of her hand told Carrie just how scared she was. "Selfish to become the best teacher possible so that you can help more students? How is that selfish?"

"I'm doing that here," Rose said in a trembling voice. "What about all my students? Both black and white?" She turned to Carrie, her eyes burning brightly. "Did you know I am teaching almost one hundred adults two evenings a week? The men are busy in the fields so it is all women." Her voice took on a tone of disbelief. "Black and white women studying together. I never thought I would see such a thing. How can I leave that?"

"Don't," Carrie answered, knowing Rose would continue to argue if she resisted. It was time for another tactic.

Rose stiffened even more. "What do you mean? Don't go? Don't go to college? How can I not go?"

"Who exactly do you need permission from?" Carrie asked, deliberately keeping her voice bland.

Rose read the expression on her face and laughed. "I'm being ridiculous, aren't I?"

"I believe that would be an accurate assessment."

Rose chuckled. "You have always known how to get me back on track."

Carrie's eyes filled with tears as Rose's face crumpled with sadness. She wiped them away. "We are not doing this," she proclaimed. "Neither of us is going anywhere until January. We are not going to cry our way through the next two and a half months." Her voice became almost desperate as she thought about it. "I've cried so many tears..." she murmured.

"I'm so sorry, Carrie. Of course you're right. There will be no tears," she said apologetically. We will celebrate every minute of our time together."

Amber appeared in the door of the barn. "Are you coming, Carrie?" she hollered. "Granite thinks you have forgotten him."

Carrie was cutting short the time she needed to get him ready for the tournament. She gave Rose a hard hug and then stepped back. "I have a tournament to win," she announced. "For Robert."

Chapter Two

Moses was waiting when Simon's wagon pulled into place, followed closely by Perry, Louisa, and Nathan's wagon. Both wagons were stuffed full of blankets and baskets of food. Moses eyed the wagons, and then looked at Louisa and his sister June with a raised brow. "The two of you do all that cooking?"

"God forbid!" Louisa said with a merry laugh. "I made a few things, but mostly I just helped fill the wagons with the cooking all the other women did. The men finished the work around the plantation while the women worked miracles. I don't believe I've ever smelled so many good things at one time!" Her eyes were bright with excitement. "It won't be long before we'll be ready to host a Harvest Festival at Blackwell Plantation. Then we can take turns." The pride in her voice was unmistakable as her blue eyes rested on her husband.

Perry nodded. "She's right." Then he looked south. "The men are riding over in a few minutes. Their wives are not far behind us in another couple wagons. This was the only way to get all the food here. I don't know what in the world will happen to all of it."

Moses smiled, choosing not to comment on the fact that all Simon's men were riding separately so they could take their turns keeping watch for vigilantes. It's not that every single person in attendance didn't know there was a risk—there was just no reason to focus on it. They were here to have a good time, not be afraid of what might happen. "Don't you worry. You won't take one morsel of that back home with you. I've never seen a Harvest Festival when every bite wasn't eaten."

Perry looked dubious. "Then I hope the wagons going back are bigger than the ones coming in because every person is going to go home larger than they came."

"Simon! Nathan!"

Moses laughed as John's shrill cry blasted through the noise surrounding them. "I do believe my son is eager to see his friends."

Simon Jr. and Nathan leapt out of the wagons, Nathan's bright blond hair and fair skin a perfect foil for Simon's glistening black skin and curls. "John!" they yelled simultaneously.

"I swear, that boy gets bigger every time I see him," June exclaimed. "And the last time was only two weeks ago. At this rate, your son will be even bigger than you are."

"That's what Mama says," Moses agreed with a proud grin.

Simon watched the boys run off together, their delight showing in their gleeful laughter. "Being that big isn't always a good thing," he said quietly.

Moses sobered instantly as he thought of all the times his size had done nothing but make him more of a target. He forced himself to take a deep breath, fighting back the fear he battled on a regular basis. "You can't change what is."

Simon was instantly contrite. "I'm sorry, Moses. I shouldn't have said that."

"No sense in not saying something that is true," Moses replied, forcing himself to speak lightly.

Louisa and June moved off in the direction of the other women as Perry walked over to join Thomas, who had just appeared on the porch. Moses and Simon remained where they were, aware this would be the only time all day they would have an opportunity to talk.

"Did you ever think you would see all those women in one place?" Simon asked, his eyes narrowed with something close to disbelief.

"Black and white?" Moses shook his head. "No. I never quit being amazed at what Rose has accomplished. Those women aren't just in the same place—a lot of them have become friends. Learning together seems to have broken down some mighty big walls. But still...I never dreamed I would see this in my lifetime." He watched as the women worked together to lay out blankets and distribute mountains of food on the tables built for the occasion.

"It didn't hurt any that their husbands protected the school from being burned down," Simon observed.

Moses flinched, hating any reminder of the night Robert had been murdered. "Yep," was all he could manage.

Simon changed the subject. "I hear Carrie is back."

"She came home two weeks ago." Moses was glad to leave the topic of Robert's murder.

"June came home saying she has decided to be a doctor after all."

"That's true." Moses knew Simon was leading up to something, but he would have to wait to find out what it was. His friend couldn't be hurried.

"So she is going back to school?"

"Seems to me it is the only way she can become a doctor," Moses said wryly.

Simon's voice grew more serious. "So you and Rose will be leaving soon? It's time for both of you to go to college?"

Moses nodded, pushing back the uncomfortable feeling that clogged his throat. "That's right. We're planning on leaving in early January." He knew Simon had finally brought the conversation around to what he wanted to say.

"Without anyone here to run the place?" Simon asked. "How you gonna do that, Moses?"

Moses wondered the same thing every day. "I have no idea," he said honestly. "But I've seen a lot of things happen in the last seven years that I couldn't ever imagine happening. I figure if we're supposed to go to college, then somebody is going to show up."

Simon watched him closely. "You don't seem real worried."

Moses shrugged again. "I've never known it to help."

"And Rose?"

"She's got her own things to think about. We're both trying to take it one day at a time."

Simon stared off into the woods for a long minute. "What if you don't find anyone?"

Moses watched him but remained silent. He knew there was more his brother-in-law wanted to say.

"You want me to come back?"

Moses stared at him. "What?"

Simon held his gaze. "Do you want me to come back?" he repeated.

"I would never ask you to do that."

"What if you weren't asking?"

"Are you unhappy at Blackwell Plantation, Simon?"

"Not at all," Simon said quickly. "I'm real happy there, and good things are happening."

Moses smiled and put his hand on his friend's shoulder. "Then that is your answer. I appreciate what you are offering to do, Simon, but it's not necessary."

"As far as I can see, it is," Simon observed. "You're supposed to leave in two and a half months, and you can't unless you have someone to run Cromwell Plantation. You're supposed to be a lawyer, and Rose is the finest teacher I've ever seen. This whole country needs what the two of you can do if you go to college. If it takes me coming back here, then I will."

Moses swallowed the knot again. The idea of leaving the plantation made him almost ill. He loved Cromwell, he loved farming, and he loved the people here. He loved knowing a former slave was now part owner of the fields where he had once toiled. There was nothing about going to college that appealed to him anymore, but all the people around him were convinced he was supposed to be a lawyer for his people. "No," he said. "You are happy at Blackwell Plantation. June is happy, and so is Simon Jr. You're making good money, and you are in charge."

"I would be in charge here," Simon observed. "I'd just have to get rid of you first."

Moses chuckled but sobered quickly. "Answer me this, Simon. Do you *want* to leave Blackwell Plantation?"

"If it will..."

Moses raised his hand. "Stop. Don't make this about me and Rose. The question is about you. Do you *want* to leave Blackwell Plantation?"

Simon took a deep breath. "No. Blackwell may never again be as grand as Cromwell, but it feels good to be creating something from nothing."

"Then this conversation is over," Moses said lightly. "If Rose and I are supposed to go to college, the right person will show up. Until then, I'm going to keep running the plantation. Right now that means running a Harvest Festival."

*****

Carrie emerged from Granite's stall, thrilled to see Susan Jones walking into the barn with one of the geldings Robert had purchased just before he was murdered. The thought took her breath away, but she recovered enough to greet her friend. "Susan, I'm so glad to see you. Did you and Mark just arrive?"

"Mark and Catherine," Susan corrected as she engulfed Carrie in a hug. "Mark is madly in love," she said dramatically.

Carrie eyed her friend, unable to read her voice. "Is that a good thing?"

Susan laughed and held up an envelope. "It became a good thing as soon as I received your letter saying you were happy for me to run Cromwell Stables while you are at school. I love Catherine, but I will admit I was feeling a bit out of place."

Carrie smiled, relieved Susan was satisfied with the letter she had sent. She was thrilled for Susan to run Cromwell Stables while she was in school, but she was not ready to even think about Susan's desire to perhaps own the stables one day. Abby had assured her Susan would understand it was too soon to make such a huge decision so close to Robert's death. Evidently, Abby had been right. "I hope you are you here to stay?" Carrie knew she would feel much better about leaving for school if she and Susan could work together until her departure.

"I am!" Susan exclaimed. "We had to bring a larger wagon to accommodate all my things."

"Well, I certainly contributed my fair share."

Carrie looked over Susan's shoulder as an unfamiliar, amused voice sounded through the barn, moving forward with an outstretched hand. "You must be Catherine. Welcome."

"And you have to be the indomitable Carrie," Catherine responded, gripping her hand tightly. "I am so pleased to meet you."

Carrie knew how *not* indomitable she had been for the last six months, but she decided not to point it out. She opted to go with the obvious. "I understand why Mark fell in love with you. You are stunning." Catherine's tall, willowy body, combined with soft blond hair pulled back into a loose bun that framed laughing brown eyes created a delightful picture.

"Oh, he probably doesn't even notice. He only wants to know I can train the new jumpers recently delivered to Oak Meadows."

Carrie was instantly intrigued. "And can you?"

Susan supplied the information. "We have all known each other since we were children growing up in Pennsylvania. She's outridden my brother her whole life. The new horses couldn't be in better hands."

Carrie laughed with delight. "Then you are *very* welcome on Cromwell Plantation, Catherine. But, for the record, I'm quite sure Mark does realize how beautiful you are."

Catherine lowered her head briefly and looked back up with a mischievous glint in her eyes. "He does seem to be coming around nicely," she demurred.

Carrie and Susan burst into laughter.

"When is the wedding?" Carrie asked, pushing aside thoughts of her wedding day with Robert. She refused to be anything but delighted for Mark and his bride-to-be.

Catherine glanced back toward the house. "If my fiancé gets his way, the wedding will be the day after tomorrow."

Carrie gasped. "Day after tomorrow? Here on the plantation?" Her surprise was mixed with something that felt suspiciously like terror.

Susan took Carrie's hand. "We couldn't plan it before I left to come here, and Mark wants me to be at the wedding." Her voice turned anxious. "Is it asking too much, Carrie? I was afraid it might be."

Carrie searched for an answer, but words refused to come.

"It's more than fine if it's too much, Carrie," Catherine added. "I never knew your husband, but I've heard nothing but wonderful things about him. I'm afraid I pushed rather hard for Mark to ask your father if it would be all right. Please forgive me if I overstepped."

Carrie found her voice, praying she sounded surer than she felt. "Nonsense," she said. The whole world wasn't going to stop falling in love just because the one true love of her life had died. She was done with people walking on eggshells because of what had happened. "Of course, it is fine. We are quite accomplished at having weddings here," she said brightly, relieved beyond words that she and Robert had married at her father's house in Richmond during the war. At least there would be one less memory to contend with here on the plantation. "So that explains why you packed so much for this trip, Catherine," she added, determined to turn the conversation away from her. "I'm assuming you and Mark will leave for your honeymoon when you are done here?"

Catherine exchanged an uncertain look with Susan but decided to play the game Carrie's way. "Yes. We're going to the White Sulphur Springs Resort."

"That's in West Virginia, isn't it? I think I've heard my father talk about it." Carrie was glad to leave the topic of weddings.

"Yes," Catherine agreed. "It's just across the border from Virginia. I've heard about it since I was a child, and I've always longed to go."

Carrie searched her memories. "There is a huge hotel there." She frowned. "Wasn't it burned to the ground during the war?"

"Thankfully, it was not. Much of the resort was destroyed by the Union Army when they took it over from the Confederates, but it has reopened and is mostly back to its former grandeur. During the war, the hotel was used either as a hospital or military headquarters for whomever was in charge at the time. I understand it took quite a bit of money to restore it, but people are coming back."

"Are y'all gonna stand there and talk all day? Have all of you forgotten what is going to happen real soon?"

Carrie smiled as Amber's impatient voice broke into the conversation, and then stepped forward to give Catherine a hug. "I'm so glad you're here. I'm also glad you're getting married here. Truly. Now, can we get our horses ready so at least one of us can beat Amber? I refuse to have her gloating over it for another whole year."

Catherine laughed as Susan grabbed Amber in a warm embrace. "Let's do it."

"Are you still riding Eclipse this year?" Susan asked Amber.

"Of course. Why would I change my horse after I beat all of you last year?"

Catherine gazed over at the towering bay stallion with undisguised admiration. "He's the sire of all the yearlings I'm working with now? I heard he was beautiful, but I didn't expect him to be quite this magnificent."

"Yep," Amber boasted. "He's the daddy. He's also the fastest, best horse on the plantation."

Carrie raised a brow as Granite snorted his disdain. "I would beg to differ with you, Amber. And how is All My Heart going to feel about that?"

Amber smiled. "All My Heart is still a baby. When she grows up, *she* will be the fastest, best horse on the plantation. She is just letting Eclipse think it is him for a while longer. Women have to do that, you know."

Laughter rang through the barn as the four females settled in to prepare their horses for the tournament.

*****

Thomas, resplendent in a black suit that marked the importance of the occasion, smiled as he gazed out over the crowd. Carrie felt a surge of pride but pushed aside any thoughts other than the tournament as he began to speak. She could not afford to think of Robert now. She had decided to ride to honor him, but thoughts of him would destroy her concentration, and along with it, any hopes of winning.

"Ladies and gentlemen, it is now time for the *Charge of the Knights*." Thomas' deep voice rang out through the still air. The quiet seemed to grow even deeper as everyone listened intently.

Not so long ago, the closest many of the people in this crowd could have gotten to a tournament was in their role as a slave. To simply be part of the spectators was a momentous occasion, and not one person was taking it lightly. The fact that there were nearly as many white faces in the gathering as black faces made the whole event even more spectacular. Area neighbors had been invited the year before, but not one had lowered themselves to come. This year, thanks to Rose's school, it was a different story.

Carrie gazed around, unable to stop her fierce longing that someone in this crowd could have stopped Robert's murder. She knew his death had united them even more, and she felt some measure of gratitude for that, but she was aware they were still surrounded by the hatred of the Ku Klux Klan vigilantes who had killed her husband. The two men actually responsible for it were in jail, but they had been replaced by other men determined to keep the South they had always known from changing.

Carrie reined her thoughts back in as her father turned to look at the group of twenty competitors gathered below the platform. His eyes rested on her for a moment, warming her with pride and love, and then he smiled at all of them. Out of the corner of her eye, she saw Amber flash him a big grin, confidence radiating from her. Carrie was going to have to concentrate if she expected to beat Amber this year, because the little girl had been practicing diligently.

Carrie couldn't say the same thing. She could only hope her determination to win for Robert would compensate for her lack of practice. Just six months ago, before his death, she and Robert had spent hours competing against each other. She could almost hear their laughter and teasing as they jostled for the winning position each night. Carrie shuddered and pushed the memory away.

"Ladies and gentlemen, you are gathered here today to participate in the most chivalrous and gallant sport known. It has been called the sport of kings, and well it should. It has come down to us from the Crusades, being at that time a very hazardous undertaking," Thomas said solemnly.

Carrie shivered as she felt the years melt away. Her father was speaking the exact same words that Colonel James Benton had spoken every year of the Blackwell Tournament. It was odd to her that so much in the world could change, while other things remained the same. She supposed constancy amidst radical change was a good thing—probably the only thing that held society together.

"The knights of that day rode in full armor, charging down the lists at each other with the intent that the best man would knock his opponent from his horse. It was a rough and dangerous pastime. Many were seriously hurt. Some were killed. But we, in this day, have gotten soft and tender—as well as much smarter, I believe—and have eliminated the danger and roughness of the sport." Laughter rippled through the crowd, but as in years past, no one spoke to mar the seriousness of the charge.

Thomas sobered as he leaned forward to address the riders. "But with all that, it is still a challenging and fascinating sport. One that tests the horsemanship, dexterity, skill, quickness of eye, and steadiness and control of the rider, and the speed, smoothness of gait, and training of the horse. It is an honorable sport, and I do not need to mention that a knight taking any undue advantage of his opponents will be disqualified from the tournament." His eyes bored into each competitor's until he seemed confident he had made his point. "Now, for the rules."

Carrie knew the rules by heart, but she listened attentively, still hardly believing she was going to ride.

"The three ring hangers are spaced twenty yards apart. The start is twenty yards from the first ring—making the total length of the list sixty yards. Any rider taking more than seven seconds from the start to the last ring will be ruled out. Should anything untoward happen during the tilt that would prevent the rider from having a fair try at the rings, he will so indicate by lowering his lance and making no try at the rings. The judges will decide whether he is entitled to another tilt."

Carrie glanced over to where Mark, Perry, June, Louisa and Abby sat, their solemn faces communicating they were well aware of the importance of their role as judges. Matthew had hoped to continue as a judge, but an important assignment from the newspaper had delayed his and Janie's arrival. They would not reach the plantation until late afternoon.

"All rings must be taken off the lances by the judges," Thomas continued. "No others will be counted. The rings on the first tilt will be two inches in diameter; on the second tilt, one and a half; on the third tilt, one; on the fourth tilt, three quarters; and on the fifth and last tilt—if there are any competitors left—one half inch."

Carrie forced her mind to envision her capturing all the rings on every tilt.

Thomas smiled and swept his arm grandly. "All of you are riding not only to win, but to gain the coveted honor of crowning the person of your choice the King or Queen of Love and Beauty at the ball later tonight."

Carrie swallowed hard as she thought of her surprise when Robert had crowned her his queen after the Blackwell Tournament, and then examined the course, imagining the rings sliding onto her lance. A sense of competition had charged the air while Thomas had been talking. The crowd, here for a celebration, seemed to feel the importance of what was about to happen.

Thomas continued. "The seven riders with the next best scores will have the privilege of honoring the person of their choice as royalty-in-waiting for the queen or king. Only the members of the court will participate in the opening dance at the ball tonight. Good luck to you all," Thomas finished. "May the best person win!"

Another mighty blow on the horn announced the beginning of the competition. A rousing cheer rose from the crowd, along with a whoop from all the riders as they guided their horses toward the starting line.

Carrie felt a flurry of nervousness but tamped it down. Granite's confidence and steadiness would come from her. She gripped her lance, ignoring everyone else around her as she stared down the list at the rings, which already seemed impossibly small. She straightened in her saddle and pulled her shoulders back. She had vowed to do this for Robert. She was going to compete, and she was going to win. She looked over to find Rose's eyes fixed on her.

"Good luck," Rose mouthed. "You can do it."

Carrie nodded as some of her nervousness subsided.

"Ladies and gentleman, our first contestant is Knight Earl Camden."

Carrie's full attention was pulled back to the arena as one of Moses' men moved into position. It was just as she had imagined it would be. The crowd and every other competitor seemed to melt away. The only thing that remained real was the list stretched out before her. She was aware of Earl finishing his run, but she was too focused to hear the results. It didn't matter what anyone else did. Her only real competition was the rings dangling from their clasps. She imagined herself capturing them time and again until Thomas' voice broke through her concentration.

"Our next contestant is Knight Carrie Borden," Thomas said, not bothering to hide the pride in his voice.

Carrie moved forward, a steadying hand on Granite's neck. He was excited, but there was no nervousness in him as he waited for her signal. Out of the corner of her eye she saw the wave of the flag. She leaned forward, and Granite shot down the list. Carrie brought her lance up, her eyes focused on the first ring. It was hers! The second ring was captured just as easily. With no time for triumph, she concentrated on the third ring, allowing a smile to split her lips only after it slid onto her lance. Granite settled into an easy trot as they rode toward the judges' table. Before they got there, the next contestant was off.

Only then did Carrie realize Amber was right after her. She watched with excitement as Amber captured all three rings. The girl and Eclipse gazed out over the crowd with triumphant expressions as they trotted over to join Carrie.

"Well done!" Carrie called to Amber as Mark counted her rings.

"You, too!" Amber called back, her face glowing with happiness.

The competition continued. After the first tilt, the field was reduced to ten riders who had been able to capture all three rings. They lined up for the next tilt. Carrie smiled at the group that included Catherine, Moses, Susan and Amber, and then put her entire focus on the list again. She had expected all five of them to make it through the first tilt, but now she had to prepare. The rings were only a half inch smaller, but they seemed much tinier. She breathed evenly, murmuring to Granite while she waited her turn. This time she was fourth in line.

Once again, Granite ran like lightning. Once again, Carrie captured all three rings. She felt a thrill of accomplishment, but her attention was already on the next tilt as she cantered over to the starting line.

In the past, riders had prepared for tournaments with months of practice. None of today's knights, except for Amber, had been able to do that. They had ridden for fun. Now, those who had failed in their quest were lined up along the arena fence, cheering on the remaining competitors.

There were only five riders left now —Earl, Susan, Amber, Catherine and Carrie. Earl looked surprised to still be in the field, but he was clearly eager to win. Carrie shared a grin of triumph with the remaining women competitors, and then turned her attention back to the list. She could almost hear Robert shouting her on to victory. Her mind told her he wasn't in the crowd, but she couldn't stop herself from scanning the faces just to be sure. She swallowed the tears back. Nothing could blur her vision.

"Ladies and gentlemen, the third tilt is about to begin. The rings have been reduced to one inch in size," Thomas called out. "You have before you five very talented knights."

The start flag waved, and Susan tore down the list on Admiral. Carrie couldn't be sure, but it looked like she only got two rings.

"Knight Carrie Borden!" her father called.

Granite and Carrie, linked as a single unit, thundered down the list again. Carrie, her mind calm and focused, watched as all three rings slid onto her lance. She trotted to the judges' table and nodded her acceptance of their congratulations. Her father's voice broke through her concentration.

"What you are seeing here today is the reason women were banned from competition for so long," Thomas said, his face wreathed in a proud smile.

The crowd laughed and clapped loudly. Only then did Carrie look around. Susan, Amber and Catherine were the only other knights still with her. She glanced over and saw Earl joining his family. Her eyes widened with both surprise and delight that this year was going to be almost identical to the year before, with the exception being that she had every intention of winning this year. "May the best female win!"

"May the best female win!" Amber laughed.

"May the best female win!" Susan echoed.

"May the best female win!" Catherine hollered, her fist raised in defiance.

Carrie was not happy to be first in line. All she could do to insure her continuation was to capture all three rings again. She cleared her mind and settled deeper into her saddle. "Good boy, Granite," she cooed. "We're going to do this for Robert. I know he is watching." Granite's ears flicked to show he was listening, but her gelding's entire concentration was on the list stretched out before them, his muscles bunched tightly in anticipation.

Not waiting for her signal, he surged forward the instant the flag swooped down, giving them a precious advantage. Carrie caught her breath, ignoring the fatigue in her arm from holding the lance, and set her eyes on the first ring. They were so minute that she could no longer tell whether she captured any of them. They raced to the end of the tilt before Granite slowed and turned toward the judges' table with no urging from her. Carrie threw back her head with a joyful laugh when she realized all three rings were on her lance.

"Congratulations!" Moses called.

"You did it, Carrie!" Rose yelled, waving wildly.

Carrie grinned at them and nodded to the cheering crowd. When she returned to the starting gate for the final tilt, only Amber was still in the competition.

"It's you and me again!" Amber crowed. "Just like last year."

"That it is," Carrie acknowledged, feeling a twinge of nervousness for the first time as the pressure of her vow to win settled in more heavily. Amber was completely confident in her ability to capture rings of any size, and Eclipse seemed to have a smug look on his face. Granite snorted and bobbed his head. Carrie felt the nervousness dissipate as her horse assured her they could handle whatever was waiting for them. When she closed her eyes she could once again see Robert's face filled with pride. The look of love was undeniable. Every nerve in her body settled into firm confidence. She was not riding to win— she was riding for the husband she adored.

The crowd's noise had died away to a silent hush as the new rings—just a half inch in diameter—were placed on the tilt. Everyone seemed to hold their breath collectively. "Good luck," she murmured to Amber as her father waved for the girl to advance.

"You, too," Amber replied, her eyes staring forward. The flag waved. Eclipse seemed to float down the list.

Carrie was being waved forward before she knew it, and before she had any idea how many rings her competitor had captured. Last year she had lost to Amber by one ring. It would not happen this year. She gripped the lance tightly but kept her touch on the reins very light. "We can do this." she said, and then closed her eyes for a brief moment. "This is for you, Robert," she whispered.

Again, Granite surged forward with no signal from her. Carrie homed in on the rings but wasn't sure if she had captured *any* of them. She had ridden more on instinct than sight. When Granite reached the end and turned to trot over to the judges' table, she couldn't see any rings on the end of her lance. Her heart sank as she realized she had missed them all.

"Two rings!" Mark called out as Amber presented her lance to the judges.

Carrie opened her mouth to call out her congratulations, but Abby stepped forward and pulled two rings off her lance.

"Two rings!" Abby called out, holding them up triumphantly. She leaned close to Carrie and whispered. "My bet is on you and Granite." There was a slight pause before she added, "And on Robert."

Carrie laughed with relief and incredulity as she saw the two glimmering rings in Abby's hand. "It's a repeat of last year," she murmured, straightening. "Only it is going to end differently this time."

"Now this is what I call competition!" Thomas yelled, his voice tight with excitement. "I don't believe I've ever seen tighter competition than this. Well," he added, "not since last year. Knight Carrie and Knight Amber are going to battle it out again." He raised his hand. "May the best female win!"

"May the best female win!" the crowd roared back.

Carrie rode up close to Amber. "You're amazing," she said quietly. "Robert would be so proud of you right now. He loved you so much." She reached out to touch Amber's shoulder. "May the best female win." Just as it had the year before, the simple statement had become the mantra of the day.

"May the best female win," Amber replied in a husky voice. "Robert would be real proud of you, too. We both love you a whole lot."

Carrie smiled, and then focused on the list when Amber was called to the starting line. Once again, Eclipse seemed to float rather than gallop down the list. Amber was but a small speck carrying a very large lance.

Completely relaxed, Carrie advanced to the line. It didn't matter how many rings Amber had captures. She felt embraced by Robert's presence. "Show them what you can do, Granite," she called, letting out a whoop as they sprang forward. It all seemed effortless as she felt, more than saw, the rings slide onto her lance. She allowed the broad grin on her face as she turned and trotted to the judges.

All the judges were standing quietly beside the table as Carrie reached them. She smiled as Abby and Mark approached the final two competitors.

Abby reached for her lance. "Three rings!" she called out with unmistakable pride.

The crowd held its breath as Mark reached for Amber's lance. "Two rings." he called. "You did a fine job, Amber, but Carrie is the winner this year!"

The crowd exploded with applause and cheers.

Carrie turned to wave her appreciation, not caring now that there were tears blurring her vision. "I love you, Robert," she said softly as she raised her lance in triumph.

Thomas' voice broke through her celebration. "Congratulations to Knight Carrie Borden. This evening, she will have the honor of crowning the King of the Ball."

Carrie gasped. The King of the Ball. She hadn't even considered that when she set out to be victorious. Her stomach clenched as she tried to envision even *attending* the ball. How in the world could she crown a king who was not Robert?

Chapter Three

"You did it, boy." Carrie stroked Granite's neck as he munched his grain happily. "You carried Robert to victory, and then you carried me." She could hear sounds of the Harvest Festival floating in through the barn's open doors, but the confines of Granite's stall gave her the sense of privacy and seclusion her heart yearned for. She inhaled deeply, allowing the sweet smell of hay to carry her back to memories of childhood, when life was not the complicated mess it was now. When Granite raised his head to stare into her eyes, Carrie wrapped her arms around his neck and buried her face in his silky mane.

Granite's snort alerted her that someone had invaded her sanctuary. Carrie fully expected to see Amber or Susan when she raised her head.

"Hello, Mrs. Borden."

Carrie blinked her eyes as she fought to pull herself back to the present. Resentment at the intrusion was tempered by surprise. After several long moments, she found her voice. "Hello, Mr. Wallington."

"I'm sorry to intrude," he said.

"You're not intruding," Carrie murmured as she managed a smile, though she was quite sure it didn't reach her eyes. She had liked Anthony Wallington when he purchased all the year's foals in August, but she wanted nothing more than to be alone. Since that was not going to happen, short of her being rude, she chose to examine him more closely. She had been completely oblivious to his appearance two months ago. Anthony was slightly taller than Robert. His slimmer build spoke of wiry strength. He was nowhere near as handsome as Robert, but there was a certain appeal to his flashing green eyes and thick sandy hair.

"I understand you are to be congratulated," Anthony said warmly.

Carrie cocked her head and stared at him.

"The tournament?" Anthony prompted.

"Of course," Carrie replied, embarrassed he had found her in such a distracted state. "I'm sorry. I'm afraid I was thinking of something else."

"I understand," Anthony said, his deep voice managing to sound both powerful and soothing.

Carrie felt a flash of her old resentment. "I'm afraid you don't, but thank you."

Anthony regarded her for a moment, and then smiled sympathetically. "Understand how hard it is to lose the person you love? Understand that any kind of a victory is dulled by the reality it cannot be shared the way you want it to be?" He walked over to cross his muscled arms over the top of Granite's stall door. "I actually do understand that."

Carrie caught her breath. "You lost your wife? I'm so sorry. I didn't know."

"No reason you should have known," Anthony replied in an easy voice. "It's been almost two years now, but it can still hit me at any moment."

Carrie wasn't sure if she should ask the question foremost in her mind, but she couldn't stop herself. "How did she die?" She wondered if the fact that Robert had been murdered somehow made his death more unbearable.

"Victoria died giving birth to our son," Anthony said, his eyes revealing the pain his words brought. "He lived only a few hours before he joined her."

Carrie sucked in her breath. "I'm so sorry," she managed, swallowing back the tears that wanted to come. She tangled her hands into Granite's mane as she fought to regain control of her feelings. She hated talking about Bridget, but she wanted Anthony to know. He was one of the few who could understand. "My daughter was stillborn the same day Robert died."

It was Anthony's turn to take a deep breath. "I didn't know. I'm sorry, Mrs. Borden."

Carrie was relieved to see nothing but compassionate understanding radiating from his face. There was none of the pity she had come to dread. "Do you still miss your son?"

"Every day," Anthony said simply. "I will never forget the feel of his tiny body in my arms. The doctors could not tell me what was wrong with him, but I knew when they first put him in my arms that he wouldn't live long." He paused and stared down at the barn floor. "I was holding Tim when he took his last breath."

Carrie's heart ached for him. She knew the best gift she could give him was understanding. "Bridget died before I could hold her." She fought the deluge of feelings her words brought. "I never saw her. They had to bury her before I regained consciousness."

Silence held the barn in its grasp. There was simply nothing else to say after such heartbreaking revelations.

They were saved from having to come up with words when Amber rushed into the barn.

"Carrie! Have you decided yet?"

Carrie fought to pull her mind back to the present. "Decided what, Amber?"

"Who you are going to crown King of the Ball tonight?" Amber stopped and stood up straighter. "You're Mr. Wallington, aren't you?"

Anthony smiled, as relieved as Carrie to have a respite from their conversation. "I am. And you are the very talented trainer who is taking care of all the foals I bought a few months ago. It's good to see you again, Amber."

Amber smiled brightly. "It's real good to see you, too, but aren't you early? I don't have all of them quite ready for you to view yet." Her face crinkled with concern.

"Not to worry. I was supposed to arrive tomorrow, but I ran into Matthew and Janie Justin at the train station. They insisted I ride out with them today. I'm happy to wait until tomorrow to see the foals."

"Matthew and Janie are here?" Carrie asked, before her eyes narrowed. "How do you know Matthew and Janie?"

"I met Janie a few weeks ago when I was in Philadelphia on business, but I've known Matthew for years." Anthony replied. "I worked with Abby after her first husband's death, and Matthew was watching out for her then. It took both of us to keep her out of trouble sometimes." His eyes glinted mischievously. "She was quite determined to create a stir in the Philadelphia business scene."

"Which she did extraordinarily well."

Carrie spun around when an amused voice boomed through the barn. "Matthew!" she cried. "It's so good to see you!"

"Not as good as it is to see you." Matthew grabbed her in a hug, and then held her back to stare down at her. "You look wonderful."

The last time Carrie had seen her old friend, she had been a grieving mess. His words to her had helped her begin to find the path back to her old self—at least as much of her old self as she would ever be. "I'm better," she said. "Where is Janie?"

"In the house waiting to help you get ready for the ball tonight."

Carrie looked away from the steady warmth in his eyes. He knew how hard this was going to be for her. She both welcomed and hated the sympathy.

"You never answered my question," Amber said impatiently, moving to stand in front of Carrie. "Have you decided who will be King of the Ball tonight?"

Carrie gazed down at her, unable to think of an answer. She couldn't assure Amber she would actually even *be* at the ball. She grasped at an idea that flashed in her mind. "What about *you* doing it?"

"Doing what?" Amber asked, confused.

"*You* choose the King of the Ball tonight," Carrie said, suddenly sure it was the answer she needed. "I really don't know who to choose, and you came in second place. I will relinquish my choice and let you make it."

Amber gazed at her with wide eyes. "I can't do that, Carrie," she said in a very serious voice. "It wouldn't be right."

"Why not?" Carrie pressed, desperate to be freed from the decision.

"I didn't win," Amber said earnestly.

"But—"

"No," Amber said. "It wouldn't be right. You beat me today because you were riding for Robert. No one should choose the king but you."

Carrie didn't bother to ask how the little girl knew she was riding for Robert. Amber always just knew things. "I can't," Carrie finally murmured.

"Because Robert chose you as his queen when the two of you first met?" She reached up to take Carrie's cold hands. "Rose told me about it," she confided. "And Rose told me you wouldn't want to pick a king."

"She's right," Carrie said quietly.

"She might be right," Amber agreed, "but that doesn't make *you* right."

Carrie was caught by the intense expression on Amber's face. "Why not?"

Amber pursed her lips and gazed at Granite for a moment. "I heard my mama talking about you when you were in that real dark place. She said that you weren't even half living. Now you are, but don't you see? You weren't even going to ride today, and then you came out there and beat me." She glanced over at Matthew and Anthony. "That was a real hard thing to do."

Carrie bit back her desire to chuckle, glad to see the two men were listening seriously.

Amber turned back to Carrie. "You can't win just halfway, Carrie. Whoever wins the tournament must pick the king. If you don't want to start half living again, you have to win all the way."

Carrie had no idea where Amber got her wisdom, but she knew the little girl brought Robert back from the brink of death twice. Carrie stared into Amber's eyes for a long moment, and then nodded. "All right," she said.

Amber grinned even more brightly. "Good! Now, who are you going to choose?"

Back to this again. Carrie shook her head. "I don't have an answer yet," she replied. "But I don't have to know until tonight. You're going to have to be satisfied with that for right now, Amber."

"Yep," Amber answered. "I reckon I can be satisfied with that. We're about to start eating. That's the real reason my mama sent me in here." She flashed a satisfied look at Matthew and Anthony, turned, and ran from the barn.

Silence lingered for several moments.

"Is she always like that?" Anthony asked. "What an amazing little girl."

Carrie smiled. "She is certainly amazing. And, yes, she is always like that." She watched through the door as Amber skipped across the yard to the area under the trees where all the food was laid out. "Robert died saving her life," she revealed. "Vigilantes came here to burn the plantation. They tried to shoot Amber when she got in their way. Robert took the bullet meant for her."

Anthony gained points with her when he replied, "Obviously, it was a life worth saving."

"Yes," Carrie answered. Nothing could bring Robert back, but she was so thankful for the opportunity to watch Amber grow up.

*****

Moses settled back on the ground with a satisfied sigh as he patted his stomach. "Now that was a meal."

Rose raised her brow. "I'd say that was a meal for a few men, not just one."

"I'm a big man," Moses protested lazily. "Besides, I've earned the right to eat all that food." His voice became deeply satisfied. "Somehow we managed to break the tobacco production record we set last year. I just heard the news a little while ago."

Thomas was walking by as Moses made his statement. He settled down on the ground next to them. Rose wondered if she would ever stop being astonished that her old Master was not only her half-brother, but also a friend. A lifetime of slavery had not prepared her for this new reality, but she was grateful beyond words.

"The managers at the tobacco warehouse are asking how in the world you managed to send so much tobacco," Thomas said.

"What did you tell them?"

"That there was more coming," Thomas replied with a grin. "I also told them the results of our crop should show the effectiveness of our methods here on Cromwell Plantation."

"And their response?" Rose asked dutifully, though she was certain she already knew the answer.

"That a bumper crop of tobacco didn't justify treating niggers like white folks," Thomas said with disgust. He shook his head. "I know it's going to take a long time for people in the South to change, but since they are so concerned about money, you would think the reality that Cromwell Plantation has had the largest tobacco harvest in the state would show them that change can be good."

"You can't reason with stupid," Moses said flatly. "They want to make money, but they want to do it the old way—

off the backs of slaves." He took a deep breath. "Do you ever think it will change, Thomas? Really?"

Thomas seemed to sense how serious the question was. "In time," he said, "but I'll admit I believe it's going to take a long time. Slavery has existed in America for centuries. The government might force people to change their actions, but that doesn't mean it will change their thinking. You are going to have to fight that for a long time, Moses," he said with a grimace. "I'm sorry."

Moses shrugged. "It's not anything I don't already know."

"It's why we are going to college," Rose said with firm determination. "It's going to take a long time to change the way people think, but we can play our part in helping make that happen. With me as a teacher and Moses as a lawyer, we can help make things better.

Moses nodded his agreement but he couldn't stop the churning in his gut, and he didn't miss the assessing look on Thomas' face.

*****

The sun had set and the bonfire for the dance had been lit, its flames dancing toward the stars and the canopy of gold and red leaves that swayed overhead. Easy conversation swelled around him as Moses gazed out over the field. His worries about what might happen during the Harvest Festival had been unfounded. The day had been a good one. The children were tired from non-stop playing and games, the women were happy from spending time with their friends, and the men were filled with pride for what had been accomplished. Everyone was looking forward to an evening of dancing.

Moses stiffened and surged forward as one of Simon's men emerged from the woods on horseback. He could tell by the set of the man's shoulders that something was wrong. "What is it, King?" He kept his voice deliberately low so no one would become alarmed. He would not ruin the relaxed atmosphere unless it was necessary.

King swung down easily from his mare, his lanky form almost hidden by Moses' massive body as they talked. "A message came back from one of the fellas guardin' the road. He seen four men comin'. They stopped at the entrance to the plantation and talked for a right long time, but then kept on a goin'."

Moses listened carefully. "What's your gut tell you?"

"That they be going for backup," King said. "I reckon they know there be a celebration happenin' here today. They probably figure ain't nobody watchin'." He shook his head. "You figure they be that stupid?"

"They're not smart, King, just mean." Moses thought through the possible scenarios. He didn't want to alarm anyone, but he also didn't want to put anyone in danger. "How many men are out on the road now?"

"Ten," King answered. "I passed three of the men closer to the house and sent them on up to the road."

Moses considered King's answer. Unless someone knew the woods extremely well, an attack from that direction was unlikely, but they were vulnerable in other places. "I want ten men stationed around the barn," he ordered. "It wouldn't be hard to follow the trail that leads in from the school." He pushed aside thoughts of emerging from those same woods to find Robert shot and dying.

King nodded and glanced over his shoulder. "You gonna tell them? My wife and two little girls be over there. I don't want them scared, but I do want them to be ready."

"I agree," Moses said heavily. "Everyone should have a chance to protect their family." Making his decision, he turned and strode into the bright light formed by the bonfire.

"I need everyone's attention, please," he called. It took only moments for complete silence to reign. Not even the tiniest baby's cry marred the stillness. The only sound was the crackling of flames as the bonfire surged higher. Moses briefly explained the situation. "There may not be anything to worry about, but I don't intend on taking any chances." He didn't need to mention what had happened that spring.

Within moments he was surrounded by grim-faced men. The flames revealed an even mixture of black and white. Before Moses could say anything, Rose pushed forward. "What do you want the women and children to do, Moses?" Her voice was calm, and her eyes were steady.

Moses reached down for her hand and squeezed it gratefully. There were close to one hundred women and children staring at him fearfully. He closed his eyes, but it took only a moment to know what needed to be done. "You know these woods better than anyone, Rose." Her years of teaching a secret school before they had escaped slavery were going to be their salvation. "I want you to take everyone into the woods. Go back at least one hundred yards and make sure everyone is behind a tree. Light some fire sticks so everyone can see. You have enough time. But," he added, "make sure all the sticks are ground out into the dirt once everyone is in place. I don't want anything to give away your position if there is a bigger problem than we can handle."

Rose nodded, squeezed his hand once more, and then turned away toward the women and children.

Moses turned back to the men. "If vigilantes are coming, they will either come from the road or they will come through the woods from the school. There are ten men on the road and ten more of Simon's men are taking position in the woods behind the barn." He waved his hand toward a group of white fathers standing at attention. "There are enough of us here to protect both the school and the plantation. You did a fine job of keeping the school from burning this spring. Are you up for doing it again, Alvin?" He spoke directly to the man who had taken the lead on protecting the school before. He didn't need to add that the vigilantes would show the white men no mercy if they found them here at the Harvest Festival.

"It's done," Alvin said. "I'm getting real tired of this, though."

Moses couldn't agree with him more, but now was not the time to think about it. He merely nodded before the white fathers ran for their horses and disappeared into the darkness. He directed ten of the Cromwell workers toward the gate, ordering them to stay back further from the road in case the vigilantes broke through the line of men already there, and then sent another fifteen men to stand guard in the woods around the house.

Thomas appeared suddenly. "I was inside with Carrie. Is there more trouble?"

"I don't know yet," Moses answered. He once again explained the situation. "Rose is taking all the women and children back into the woods." A quick glance showed the small army was already headed into the trees, their arms full of blankets to make sure everyone stayed warm. Each woman carried a fire stick to make sure they could light the way for their family. He had no doubt every one of them would be carefully extinguished. They respected Rose and would do whatever she told them to do.

Moses turned back to Thomas. "They may come, but we are ready for them. I've directed the men closest to the gate to fire if vigilantes put one foot on Cromwell Plantation." He paused. "I told them a warning shot would not be necessary."

"We will protect the people who are here," Thomas agreed in a grim voice. "You've thought of everything but the tobacco barns. They aren't easy to reach, but we're not going to take any chances they will be burned. I'm taking Mark, Matthew, Jeremy, Perry and Anthony down to the barns. We'll shoot anyone who tries to get close to the crop."

Moses nodded and turned toward the barn.

Miles and Clint appeared out of the open door. Clint was leading Moses' gelding, Champ. "We turned all the horses out into the back paddock," Clint said. "If the barn is set on fire, at least we won't lose any of them."

"Thank you." Moses pushed back thoughts of the men who killed Robert while attempting to set fire to the barn that spring. "Did you check to make sure the barn is empty?" He knew he didn't have to explain his question.

"It's empty," Clint replied, "but I can promise you Amber would never make that mistake again. She came in from playing with the kids to check on All My Heart. I sent her and Mama into the house."

"Your daddy is at the front gate," Moses said. He trusted all his men, but he knew Gabe would keep a clear head in any emergency.

"What you want us to do?" Miles asked.

Moses considered his answer. He had plenty of men stationed around the entry points to the plantation, and there were men around the barn, but there was a chance one or more of the vigilantes would break through. "I want you to stay inside here. If anyone gets close, shoot them." Miles and Clint nodded and turned back toward the barn and the rifles waiting just inside the door.

Moses waited until the last woman and child disappeared into the woods. He waited until the last sounds of snapping twigs and crackling leaves had faded, and he watched until the last fire stick had been extinguished. He had done all he could do to keep them safe. He glanced at the house but knew Carrie and Abby would have things under control. He took comfort in the certainty there was an escape route for them if necessary. He longed to move into position with the men at the gate, but he needed to be at the center of the plantation so he could take charge if an attack happened.

He mounted Champ and moved forward to wait in the deep shadows of the big oak tree. The bonfire continued to burn brightly, but its flames would not reveal his position as they shot up into the sky. He listened intently, forcing himself to ignore the wave of frustration filling his mind.

He would face his future later—right now he had to focus on the present danger.

*****

"I shouldn't be glad that the ball has been disrupted, should I?"

Abby rolled her eyes, but even through the concern, Carrie detected amusement. "What happens if they determine there is no danger?" Abby asked. "Everyone is going to want the ball to happen. They look forward to it every year."

"I know," Carrie admitted with a sigh. She and Abby were stationed at the window in her room. Janie and Polly were keeping watch out the back. Susan and Catherine were at one of the side windows, while June and Annie stood guard on the far side of the house. Louisa, Amber and Felicia were watching the younger children. They would not be caught unawares.

"You're really more worried about choosing a king for the dance, than the possibility of an attack?"

"Pathetic, isn't it?" Carrie wasn't going to tell Abby that the mere idea of an attack had caused horrible images to stampede through her mind. It was easier to deal with the dilemma of who she would crown if the ball were to go on. She tried not to be glad that every passing minute made it less likely, but she was failing miserably.

Abby reached for her hand. "I know the idea of choosing a king must make you feel sick inside."

Carrie tried again to push the images of the Blackwell Ball from her mind, but decided talking about it may be better. "Louisa was certain Robert would crown her queen when he won the tournament on Granite seven years ago. She was furious when he chose me, but it was the best night of my life to that point." She closed her eyes as she remembered moving into Robert's arms for the first dance. "It's like we had always danced together. It was magical."

"Robert told me once that he fell in love with you when you cut a lock of your hair for him during the tournament."

Carrie smiled. "Yes. I felt so silly, but it certainly did turn out well."

Abby chuckled. She turned to Carrie for a moment before peering back into the darkness. "Who will you choose if you have to?"

Carrie groaned. "I have no idea."

"What about your father?" Abby asked. "I know he would be honored."

Carrie shook her head. "I thought about him, but the two of you belong together during the first dance." She held up a hand to silence the protest she knew was coming. "I already know it would be fine with you, but it doesn't feel right."

"The same with Matthew, Mark or Jeremy?" Abby guessed.

"Right." Carrie's mind raced as she thought through all the possibilities. Her first solution had been to not attend the dance. Amber's bold words had destroyed that option, but it had not taken her any closer to a decision. She didn't want anything bad to happen tonight, but she also couldn't help hoping the situation would stretch out long enough to eliminate the Harvest Tournament Ball.

"What about Anthony?"

It took several moments before Abby's words registered. "What?"

"What about Anthony? He's not with anyone here. And I happen to know he is a very fine man."

"No."

"Why not?" Abby asked. "It's a dance, Carrie. Nothing more. If it happens, you have to choose someone."

"No." Carrie couldn't explain what was swarming through her heart and mind, but she knew choosing

Anthony was not an option. He did seem like a good man, but it was somehow disloyal to Robert to even think about crowning a single man as the King of the Ball. As she had many times that night, she eyed the mirror that would open into the tunnel that could take her away from all of this. Amber would be so disappointed in her, but the idea of that didn't bother her as much as it had earlier. What they were asking her to do was simply too much.

*****

Gabe rode up beside King. "Anything?" he asked.

"Not yet," King answered, his voice low enough not to be heard over the wind blowing through the trees.

Gabe nodded and settled in to wait, his tall bulk relaxed in the saddle. King and Moses obviously believed something more was going to happen. He hadn't been there when Robert was murdered, but now he would do anything to keep those he loved on the plantation from being harmed in any way. No one would try to shoot his daughter again.

The warmth of the Indian Summer day had been swallowed by a cold front ushered in with brisk winds. He could feel leaves swirling through the air as they dropped from the surrounding trees. Tomorrow morning there would be a vibrant carpet covering the ground. The wind offered protection, but it also meant it would obscure a threat. Since no one could count on noise alerting them, they had to simply watch for any movement in the dark.

Thirty minutes passed slowly as Gabe shivered into his thick coat. "You really believe they will come back?" he asked.

"I think they believe they can do right much damage on a night like tonight." King stiffened and leaned forward.

Gabe saw the movement at the exact moment King did. He laid his hand on his gelding's neck and held his breath, praying there would be enough light from the moon dancing with the clouds to determine if it was friend or foe. He didn't have to wait very long. A sudden burst of wind shoved back a layer of clouds, allowing the glimmer of the moon to provide just enough illumination to identify a band of hooded men trotting down the road with grim purpose, their arms holding long rifles.

"Here they come," King muttered. "Moses was right. They are stupid."

Gabe waited. Moses had been clear. If the vigilantes made one move to enter Cromwell Plantation, they were to fire. He actually hoped they did. The man who had murdered Robert was in jail, but Gabe was certain some of the men riding tonight had taken place in the fateful raid. He wouldn't mind a taste of justice.

The men rode as far as the gate and stopped. Gabe listened carefully, but could hear nothing of the conversation taking place because of the wind. He could tell there was an argument going on by the fact that several of the men were waving their hands, but there was no way to know if the argument was about attacking the plantation or leaving it alone. He glanced around at the thirty men waiting quietly in the cover of the trees. Without exception, these men were all veterans who had served under Moses or Mark Jones. They knew what to do and would not hesitate to do it—especially with their wives and children counting on them for protection.

Gabe cradled his rifle in his hands, ready for what may come. Suddenly, a lull in the wind allowed the conversation to be heard.

"You really think they're going to let us waltz in there?" one man asked.

"Oh, you know how them niggers are," another retorted. "They're so busy dancing, they won't hear us coming until it's too late."

"I ain't so sure," the first man responded. "Ever since that Robert Borden got killed, I suspect they are being real careful."

"What's the problem?" another man snapped. "If you are too scared to do what we came to do, why are you here in the first place?"

Gabe could sense King's body clenched in fury, although he remained still as a statue. Moses had been clear that no shots should be fired unless the vigilantes actually came on Cromwell Plantation. Gabe could only hope all the men waiting in the woods had as much self-control as King did.

"The Ku Klux Klan has made it clear what has to be done if we are going to take back control of the South," the leader continued. "It's not going to be easy, but what choice do we have? The Cromwells and Bordens are under the impression they can do whatever they want...flaunting all the niggers they let act like white people. It stops right here."

His words had the desired effect as the men quit arguing and fell into position. There were ten men in the front line, with another ten following closely behind.

"Let's do this!" a man called.

Gabe remained still until all twenty had ridden onto Cromwell land, and then he raised his rifle. He smiled in grim satisfaction when the explosion of thirty rifles responded to the invasion almost simultaneously. He had hated the senseless deaths during the war, but now that it was the people he loved being attacked, he found himself responding in a far different way.

Not one of the guards said a word. They simply let their rifles do the talking. The vigilantes attacking the plantation would never know who had fired on them. They would be certain, however, that their attack had failed.

Gabe pulled his trigger again, holding back a crow of delight as his bullet tore through someone's arm. The rifle the vigilante held dropped to the ground as the man screamed and grabbed his arm.

Half of the attackers had already slumped onto their saddles, holding on for all they were worth as they looked for a path of hasty retreat. Some were on the ground, wounded or dead. The remaining quickly decided their plan had gone horribly awry.

"Retreat!" one of them yelled. "Retreat!"

They turned and galloped off. Final shots resulted in two more of them being wounded, but they managed to stay on their horses long enough to disappear with the rest, somehow dodging the barrage of bullets surrounding them as they melted into the darkness.

Gabe wondered what would happen to the five men lying wounded on the ground, but Moses' orders had been clear. No one was to be seen or identified. Gabe understood the wisdom of not making anyone more of a target than they already were, but he couldn't stop the twinge of pity he felt for the wounded men who would fight to survive the long night ahead. He doubted the rest of the vigilantes had enough courage to return for them.

"Let's go," King said. "We're done here. They won't be back tonight."

*****

From the plantation gate, Moses could hear the gunshots in the distance, but he had no idea what was happening. As much as he wanted to ride toward the action, he had to stay in position. There was no guarantee more attacks wouldn't come from an additional direction. He had no idea how well prepared the vigilantes were, but he trusted the men guarding the gate could handle whatever came at them. They had experience, and they also had the element of surprise on their side.

As silence descended once more, Moses felt, more than saw, his men arrive. It was Gabe who materialized from the darkness to ride up beside him. "What happened out there?"

Gabe told him the story.

"Do you think they will return?"

"King says no."

Moses nodded. "That's good enough for me." Still, he didn't relax. And he knew he could not make assumptions that another attack might not come. The longer he waited to get people home, the more dangerous it would be. "Simon, are you out there?" he called softly.

"Right here," Simon answered. "The men did well tonight."

"I never doubted they would," Moses responded. "It's too cold to have people who live close by to stay here tonight. We can't put everyone in the house, so we must get them home. I want a guard of men with every wagon. Load them up with as many people as you can. The rest of the wagons can be returned during daylight hours. I just want everyone to get home safely, and we can't assume they won't return. The Harvest Festival is over."

"I'll take care of," Simon said.

"I'll have the women and children out in a minute, Moses."

Moses was not surprised when Rose's voice split the night. He smiled at her as she walked toward him from the woods. "You heard everything?"

"I did," she assured him. "Have your men pull the wagons up next to the trail I took everyone in on. I suspect they're sore and stiff, but they are all right."

Moses turned again to Simon. "Your men's families can stay here tonight. It is too far to return to Blackwell Plantation with vigilantes on the loose. It will be tight, but we'll put everyone in the old cabins. It's not much, but at least there are blankets."

Simon breathed a sigh of relief. "They will be safe. That's all that's important. We'll get them home in the morning when the sun is up."

"I'll make sure of it," Moses promised. "You and your men will accompany the wagons that take everyone else home. That includes all the white families. Their men are still at the schoolhouse. I'll send Jeb through the woods to tell them what we are doing. You'll be driving right past the school, so they can take over for you there. Then you can join the others who will be guarding the rest of the wagons. A strong show of force will make the vigilantes think twice—especially after what happened earlier."

Carrie appeared out of the darkness, her concerned face illuminated by the flames of the bonfire that had only now begun to die down. "We heard the gunshots. What happened?" She raised her hand. "And don't look at me like I'm foolish for being out here. Abby and I saw your men returning down the road. They wouldn't be coming back if there was still danger. We want to know what is going on."

Moses gave her a tired smile. "Of course." He explained briefly, aware he was still needed to help get the wagons loaded.

"Five men were shot?" Carrie asked.

"More were shot, but only five came off their horses," Moses answered.

"What happened to them?"

Moses shrugged. "My men had orders not to reveal themselves. It would be too dangerous if they could be recognized. They left the injured where they were lying." He decided not to mention how little he cared.

Thomas, alerted that the danger had passed, rode up in time to hear Moses' answer. "It was the only thing you could do," he said grimly.

Carrie nodded and turned away.

Moses stared after her, recognizing the set of her shoulders. "Carrie, what are you going to do?"

Carrie whirled around. "I'm going to help those men, of course. We can't let them stay out there all night to suffer and possibly die."

"They would have done that to us," Moses growled.

"Probably," Carrie agreed. "But I would prefer to think we are better than they are," she snapped. She placed a gentle hand on his arm. "I understand how you feel, Moses, but I am a doctor. I have to do what I can to help."

Moses nodded with resignation. "I'll send some men with you."

"I would appreciate that," Carrie replied before she strode away.

Chapter Four

"They're letting us go?" Janie was waiting behind the door when Carrie walked in and told them about the wounded men.

"*Letting* us go? I don't believe I asked permission," Carrie said. "I also don't believe I mentioned you, Abby and Polly would be joining me."

"Of course you didn't," Abby murmured with amusement.

Thomas came in through the kitchen door. "Not that the mention was needed. I knew you wouldn't stay behind. I didn't suspect Janie and Polly would either. But," he added, "Moses has picked five of his men to accompany the wagons."

"I would certainly hope so," Carrie retorted. "We're determined to help, but we still have brains in our heads."

"I'm relieved to hear that, daughter dear," Thomas replied blandly, his eyes twinkling with amusement. "Do you need to go to the clinic first?"

"No. I have always made sure there is a supply of everything at the clinic here in the house. You never know when it might be needed. Polly is pulling it all together now. Still, I may have to take someone to the clinic." She turned to Annie. "Will you please gather blankets for the wagon?"

Annie scowled her displeasure and planted her hands on her ample hips. "There be plenty of people need them blankets right here, Miss Carrie. I don't see no reason to get them all messed up by some men who came here to try and hurt us."

"I know," Carrie said calmly, "but I still would like you to gather the blankets."

"Me and Felicia will help get them," Amber said. Then she paused, an expression of sadness filling her face. "I know what you're doing, Carrie."

Carrie knelt to look in her face. "What am I doing, Amber?"

"You're showing us that we're better than those men who killed Robert when they tried to shoot me," she whispered as her eyes swarmed with tears. "I was real angry for a long time. I bet you were, too, but now we have to prove we aren't like them."

Carrie grabbed her in a fierce hug. "You're exactly right, honey. Help Annie all you can while we're gone. I promise to come find you and let you know how it went."

*****

Carrie was not surprised to find her father, Matthew, Jeremy, Mark, Perry and Anthony mounted beside the carriages when they walked out with their box of supplies and a mountain of blankets. Five of Moses' field hands waited with them. Off to the side she saw a line of wagons filled with women and children, flanked by a steady line of armed guards surrounding them. She didn't detect fear, just a weary resignation.

Carrie put down her box and dashed forward to the first wagon. "I'm so very sorry the Harvest Festival was ruined for you," she said to the people she knew so well, wishing she had not been so childish in her worry over picking the king for the ball. The tired looks and the sadness on the children's faces tore at her heart. A wonderful, fun-filled day had ended by hiding in the dark woods from vigilantes who wanted to kill them. She shoved down the urge to go back into the house and let the injured men suffer the consequences they deserved.

"Moses keeps telling us this gonna be a long battle to be treated equal in this country," one woman responded. "I figure I'll be thankful those vigilantes didn't show up while we were dancing and couldn't hear them coming. It may take a long time for things to change, but they are still better than they used to be." She glanced at her children. "Me and my children all read now. We all go to school. Thanks to your daddy, we have our own land to call home, and my Alfred brings home money of his own. Yep, I reckon we have a lot to thank the good Lord for."

Carrie smiled as a murmur of agreement rose from the other women on the wagon. She reached forward and squeezed Rebecca's hand. "None of us will quit fighting until things are better."

Rebecca narrowed her eyes as she looked at the wagon being loaded with supplies. "Where you headed, Miss Carrie?"

Carrie opted for honesty. "A number of the vigilantes were shot during the attack. We're going to help." She wasn't surprised when she was met with shocked silence. "What they did was terribly wrong, but—"

"But one of them men could have been with the group that killed your husband!" Rebecca hissed.

"I know," Carrie admitted, once again fighting the internal battle she had fought all night. At first she had been happy knowing the vigilantes might die, but ultimately she decided she couldn't fight hate with more hate of her own. She remembered Amber's words. "We're showing them we are better than they are," she said.

Rebecca stared at her and shook her head. "You're for sure a better woman than I am, Miss Carrie. You just be careful out there. Your daddy and the rest of those men going to take you and the others down there?"

"They are. We'll be fine."

*****

Carrie grew tenser as the wagons rolled closer to the gate. She had no idea what to expect. She also hated the doubts assailing her. What right did she have to put the others at risk to help men who had come here to shoot the people she loved? Did it really matter if they died on the ground during the night?

Abby took her hand and gave it a squeeze. "We're doing the right thing."

Janie reached over to take Carrie's other hand. "She's right, Carrie. I don't know how you can do it after Robert's murder, but we're doing the right thing."

"They right, Miss Carrie," Polly said firmly. "One part of me wants to ride right up and shoot all of them for almost killing my little girl, but that's not the right thing."

Carrie took a deep breath. "Do you really believe that, Polly?"

"I wish I could choose *not* to believe it," Polly answered. "Amber has come a long way, but there still be a lot of nights when she cries herself to sleep because she misses Robert so much. I heard what she told you tonight—that we gots to show we are better than them. There be plenty of times I don't want to *be* better, but for tonight I think this be the right thing to do." She paused. "If I'd been with the men guarding the gate, I wouldn't have had no trouble shooting those men, but now that they be helpless, I figure we have to do the right thing."

"I'm sorry if I'm putting any of you into danger," Carrie replied. Polly's words helped her feel better about her decision, but it didn't assuage her worry.

Mark moved his mare closer to the wagon. "Don't worry about that, Carrie. We won't let anything happen."

Carrie couldn't shake the feeling of dread. "What if there are men waiting in the woods, just like our men were waiting? What if they came back to get their friends, and they decide to take it out on us?" She hated the fact she was coming up with dreadful scenarios, but she couldn't stop herself. What had seemed like a good idea back at the house suddenly seemed like a ludicrous idea that would have disastrous consequences.

"Stop it," Janie said.

"Excuse me?"

"I know what you are doing," Janie said. "You have to stop it. I know where your mind is going. Don't let it," she commanded. "There is not a single person with you right now who did not make a choice to join you. Any of us could have said no. We chose to do this because we want to be better than these men, too. What happens, happens. We will deal with whatever it is." Her voice softened. "This is harder for you, Carrie, because Robert was murdered by men like these. That has to be eating at you. Take some deep breaths and focus on what we need to do."

Carrie decided to follow Janie's advice. She took long, deep breaths, allowing the air to fill her lungs and cool her face. Slowly, the panic subsided. She kept breathing until calm replaced the fear that had pulsated through her. "All right," she finally said. "I'm better."

"Good," Abby murmured. "We're almost at the gate."

Carrie leaned forward to look for shapes on the ground. "I don't see anyone," she muttered.

Matthew edged closer to the wagon. "They must still be alive at least. They would have pulled themselves off the road when they heard the other wagons coming. I imagine they are hiding in the woods."

"With guns?" Carrie asked, all her fears returning.

"No," Mark said. "Gabe and the others collected the rifles that had fallen."

Carrie shook her head. "That's not possible. Moses told them they weren't to be seen."

"That's true," Mark chuckled. "But Klansmen are not the only people who know how to hide their identity. Evidently, some of the men's wives made them red hoods to carry when they were guarding. Three of them put them on and gathered all the guns before they disappeared again."

Carrie was disgusted with herself. "I'm sorry," she said contritely. "I'm the reason we're all out here. Y'all shouldn't be having to make me feel better."

"Here's one of them!" Matthew called out. "He's unconscious."

Carrie jumped from the wagon, glad to have activity replace her fears. "We're coming."

"And here is another one," Thomas yelled. "He's not conscious either."

Carrie heard the hiss of matches as the men ignited their fire sticks. The intense darkness became illuminated with golden circles. She pushed aside the uncomfortable realization that the light from the sticks made them a much easier target. There was work to be done.

"I have another one," Mark called. "He's awake, but he's hurt badly and appears to be in shock."

"I found another," Anthony announced in a grim voice. "He won't need any help."

Carrie winced. Four years of war had taught her about death. "There should be one more."

"He won't need help, either," Jeremy declared.

"All right," Carrie answered, as the women reached for their medical bags. "Janie, you take the first man. Polly, take the one my father found. I'll take the one who is still awake."

Carrie walked toward the light provided by Mark's fire stick. One look told her the man was indeed going into shock, but he was aware enough to be absolutely terrified. She knelt beside the man who looked to be in his late twenties. He was thin, and his shaggy black hair was matted to his head by blood. "We're not here to hurt you," she said. "We're here to help."

"Why?" the man mumbled.

"I'm a doctor," Carrie answered. "It's what I do."

The man's eyes widened. The revelation seemed to have revived him. "You're Mrs. Borden?"

"I am." She motioned to Anthony. "Please bring several blankets from the wagon."

"Don't make no sense," the man muttered.

"You're right," Carrie answered. "It's obvious you are aware that vigilantes killed my husband. What was done was horribly wrong, but I don't want to fight hate with hate. If you were my husband, I would want someone to help you. So, I am." She was examining his wounds as she spoke.

Anthony appeared with the blankets. "Can I ask what you are doing?"

"This man is going into shock. The first thing I must do is treat that, then I can treat his wounds. A bullet grazed his head, causing a tremendous amount of blood loss. He's also been shot in his right shoulder. Thankfully, the bullet went straight through. I have to stop the bleeding from his head to save him."

"What can I do?" Anthony asked.

"Roll him over so he is lying flat on his back. Use two of the blankets to elevate his legs and thighs, and then cover him with the rest of them to warm him. His circulatory system is collapsing." Carrie spoke her orders calmly and reached for her bag. She pulled out a large bottle, answering Anthony's question before he asked it. "I suspected we would deal with shock if people were hurt. Polly made a large supply of herbal shock formula while we were waiting for word." She opened the bottle and poured some into a tin cup. "It's a mixture of water, honey, apple cider vinegar and cayenne pepper."

"Cayenne pepper?"

"It's a miracle herb," Carrie answered. "I've never seen anything better for boosting circulation and increasing heart action. It's one of the strongest natural stimulants I know of. I'm giving him this drink because he needs fluids and he'll get some cayenne, but I'm also going to give him cayenne tincture once he has finished this so it will work faster."

Carrie motioned for Mark and Anthony to lift the man enough for her to pass the liquid through his lips. His eyes were confused, but accepting, as he drank the liquid. "Drink all of it," Carrie ordered, waiting until he complied. She had seen it work countless times, so she wasn't going to wait before she treated his head. It was enough that he had swallowed what he needed.

Normally, Carrie would want to treat his head wound in the clinic where it was much more sterile, but if she didn't stop his blood loss, he wouldn't live long enough to get there. She gestured for Mark to move closer with the light. The bullet had grazed a path down the right side of his skull, going almost a quarter of an inch deep. A fraction more to the left, and he would no longer be alive. "You're lucky," she said quietly. "This is going to hurt, though," she warned. "I have to apply enough pressure to stop the bleeding or you are going to die."

The man nodded slightly, his eyes never leaving her.

Carrie took the clean cloth Anthony handed her, tightened her lips, and pressed down on the wound firmly. A groan burst from the man's mouth, and then he went slack. "It's best this way," she said. "His breathing is better, so I know the shock formula is working. It will be better for him if he stays unconscious through the rest of it."

"The rest of it?" Anthony asked faintly.

Carrie glanced over at him with a slight smile. "I have to sew his head wound together and then pack it."

Anthony's eyes widened. "Out here?"

"No. She glanced up at Mark. "I need the two of you to carry him to the wagon. Keep him as immobile as you can. I will maintain pressure to his head until we get him into it. Then you can hold the cloth to his wound. Hold it firmly, but if you push down too hard it will cut off the circulation. Don't move the cloth to see if it is working, because you can disturb the clotting process. If the blood is seeping through the cloth, add another one," she said, holding back a chuckle at the faint look of terror on Mark's face. "Can you do it?" she asked.

Mark took a deep breath. "I can do it."

Carrie looked at him closely and then nodded when she was satisfied with what she saw. "I'm going to go check on the other two. I'm fairly certain we'll be taking all of them to the clinic." She took a deep breath as she considered the ramifications of having three Klansmen in her clinic, but she tightened her lips and headed toward the next patient.

She found Janie bent over an older man with silver hair. His clothes spoke of wealth, but they had not protected him from the bullet that had penetrated his chest. "Janie?"

Janie looked up and shook her head. "He's lost too much blood. He regained consciousness long enough to beg me to tell the Cromwells that he was sorry for being such a fool, and then he passed out again. I can barely feel his pulse now. He won't make it to the clinic, and even if he did, he won't live for long."

Carrie stepped closer. Both of them had experienced enough death during the war to recognize the signs. One look told her Janie's assessment was correct.

"Randal Poston wasn't always a fool," Thomas said heavily. "He lost three sons during the war. I had heard it changed him, but I never would have dreamed he would take part in an attack against the plantation." He looked down sadly. "We were friends once."

Carrie sighed, knowing there was nothing she could say to make sense of what couldn't be made sensible, and then walked over to where Polly and Abby were hunched over a man who appeared to be in his forties. "Polly?"

"His name is Phillip. He woke up when I poured the shock formula in. He passed out again, but not before he swallowed it. His breathing is better. I believe we can save him."

"Wounds?"

"A bullet through his leg that severed a main artery. He was bleeding out but had enough presence of mind to tourniquet his leg."

Carrie calculated the time since he had been shot. "The tourniquet has been on a long time, and his shock would have hurt circulation even more."

Polly met her eyes with understanding. "I doubt you'll be able to save his leg, but I believe you can save his life."

Carrie waved Jeremy and Matthew forward. "Please carry Phillip to the wagon and put him in with the other man." She watched as they picked him up carefully, and then turned back to Janie. They couldn't leave a man out to die alone in the cold, but she wasn't willing to put anyone else at risk.

Janie looked up as she approached. "He's gone," she said softly.

Carrie wanted to scream at all the death caused by irrational hatred, but all she did was clench her fists. "Let's get out of here," she said shortly.

"I'll send someone for the corpses in the morning," Thomas said.

Carrie refused to think of what could happen to the defenseless bodies during the rest of the night. She had to put her focus on the men she could possibly save.

*****

Moses was relieved when he arrived back at the gate without any more sounds of violence. After he had directed all his men to accompany the wagons, he changed his mind about needing guards for the plantation. He had ridden through the woods to the schoolhouse. Alvin reported no threat there, so Moses reallocated the men to make sure all the wagons would still reach home safely. Simon and a small group of others were behind him now and had promised to protect the entry to the plantation until daylight.

"Everything okay here?" he called.

"Three men are dead," Thomas answered from his driver's seat on the wagon. "We're taking these two to the clinic. Carrie believes she can save them."

"If we get there quickly," Carrie interjected. "Is there more trouble, Moses?"

"No," Moses assured her. "I came to check on all of you. I have a group of Simon's men taking their positions in the woods. They'll keep an eye on things until the morning."

"Good," Carrie answered crisply. "We need to be going."

With his hand raised to wave them forward, Moses froze. "Wait," he hissed. There was the unmistakable sound of horse hooves in the distance. "Someone is coming. Get down in the wagon," he ordered. He waited until the four women ducked down and then moved into the darkness of the tree line, relieved when the rest of the men followed him. They couldn't move the wagon without being heard, but there should be enough of them to stop anyone from getting close. He knew Simon was watching and would take action if needed.

Fatigue pressed down on him. He was tired physically, but it was the fatigue in his soul sucking him dry. All he could do was wait and see what this newest threat would be. His concern turned to puzzlement when he realized whoever was coming was not making an effort to be quiet. He grew even more puzzled when he recognized soft singing in the darkness. At least one of the people coming toward them was a woman.

Moses' gut told him whoever was coming was not part of a vigilante band. Regardless of what had transpired that night, this was a public road. His men had been told not to act without a direct signal from him, but he was not willing to take a chance. There had been far too much bloodshed for one night. His decision made, he urged Champ forward to the middle of the road. "Who goes there?" he called.

"Well, if that don't beat all! Moses, what you be doing out here in the middle of the night?"

Moses stared into the night almost certain he recognized the voice, but was not willing to let his guard down. "Who goes there?" he called again sternly.

"It is a bad night when your old friend doesn't even recognize your voice," came a lamented call as the approaching riders rounded the curve a few yards ahead from where Moses waited. "Have you really forgotten me? I guess saving your life didn't put me in your memory bank after all."

Moses frowned. "Franklin?"

"In the flesh," came the cheerful voice. "I know this isn't really a good time to come calling, but we have discovered traveling at night is preferable to daylight hours."

Moses grinned, thrilled to know there was at least one good thing that was going to come from the long night. "Any time is a good time for you to come calling," he replied as the two riders drew closer. "I've got a ton of questions, but we're not going to talk about them out here."

Franklin finally registered the tension in his voice. "Has there been trouble?"

"If you count twenty Klansmen attacking this plantation, and the fact that three of them are lying dead in the woods right now, then I suppose we have had trouble," Moses answered. "Now is not the time to get into it. They could be coming back. I've got men watching from the woods, but we're headed over to the medical clinic to see if we can save two wounded men we have in the wagon." Now was not the time to reveal the wounded were Klansmen. "Come with us, and then we'll talk later."

"We must go," Carrie said urgently. "These men don't have long."

Nothing more was said until they reached the clinic. Moses wondered who the woman was with Franklin, but there would be time to find out.

*****

Both wounded men had been carried into the clinic before Moses finally turned to Franklin. "Talk," he commanded. He was too tired to say more than that.

Franklin was too busy staring at the door to the clinic. "Those were white men."

"You've always been observant," Moses said drily, and then sighed. "They are two of the Klansmen. Fifteen of the twenty were shot during the raid. We were ready for them. Ten of them managed to stay on their horses and disappear. Out of the remaining five, three of them are dead, and those two are here."

"*Klansmen*? Are you crazy?" Franklin's eyes were wide with disbelief.

"Possibly," Moses admitted. "It's a long story. I'll explain it all later, but for now I want to know what in the world you are doing here. And, who the lovely woman with you is." He had not seen any Indians in his life, but he knew one was sitting in the clinic, and he knew she was not far from giving birth.

Franklin nodded. "It's a long story, too."

"We have time," Moses replied. "We're not going anywhere until Carrie, Janie and Polly are ready to leave."

Abby opened the door and walked in, her eyes settling on the young woman with Franklin. She smiled and moved closer. "You are exhausted. There is a bed in the other room. Come in so you can lie down."

The young woman, whose shiny black hair was pulled into a long braid, looked at Franklin with wide eyes.

"You're with friends," he reassured her. "Anyone who is a friend of Moses is a friend of mine," he said. "Even if they're white," he added.

Moses chuckled. "That's part of the long story."

Abby held out her hand. "Come with me, dear."

The young woman ducked her head shyly and then looked up. "My name is Chooli," she said.

"Chooli," Abby repeated. "It's a beautiful name. You speak English."

Chooli smiled slightly. "Not well, but I am learning every day."

"You're doing wonderfully," Abby replied. "But for now you need to rest." Her eyes landed on Chooli's stomach. "When is your baby coming?"

"Soon," Chooli answered. "Very soon." Her eyes revealed how exhausted she was.

Abby nodded. "Come with me." She took Chooli's hand and pulled her to her feet.

Chooli swayed slightly from fatigue and then followed Abby into the room.

Moses watched until the door was closed and then turned back to his friend. "I'd say it's time to start on that long story." Franklin had served under him during the war, had saved his life during one of the endless battles by pulling him out of the way just before a cannonball shattered the wooden wall he was hiding behind, and then disappeared as soon as the war ended. The three of them—Moses, Simon and Franklin—had spent many long nights in intense conversation. A deep friendship had developed.

Franklin continued to watch the door. "Chooli will be all right?"

"She could not be in better hands," he said. "You can trust me on that. Do you remember me telling you about the woman Rose and I lived with when we first escaped the plantation?"

"That's her?"

"That's her. Her name is Abby Cromwell. She will take good care of Chooli."

Franklin turned back to him with a long, searching gaze before he evidently decided to believe him. He sank back against his chair and started talking. "When the war ended, I was at loose ends. I looked for jobs for a while, but not many people are looking for a black man for a real job, and I was right tired of working tobacco."

Moses remembered now that Franklin had worked on a large tobacco plantation in eastern Virginia before he escaped to serve in the Union Army. They had spent many hours discussing farming techniques.

"Anyway," Franklin continued, "I found out about the Buffalo Soldiers and decided to go back to doing what I knew."

"I read something about them. They are black units that were formed as cavalry out in the West."

"That's right. I picked up the horseback riding pretty quick and then went back to fighting." A look of disgust filled his face.

"Fighting who? The war is over."

"One war is," Franklin agreed. "There's another one going on. This one is against the Indians. Doesn't seem to matter what tribe it is—the white people want them gone."

"Chooli?" Moses asked. There were dozens of questions swarming in his mind, but he wanted the most important ones answered first.

"She is my wife," Franklin said proudly. "Chooli is Navajo. I met her when her family was incarcerated at Bosque Redondo, the Navajo reservation in New Mexico."

"Incarcerated?" Moses knew absolutely nothing about Indians.

"Yes," Franklin replied. "There is no other word for it. Her people were attacked and starved into submission. There are thousands of them starving on the very reservation that was supposed to offer them refuge. The rest are slaves throughout New Mexico." His voice was rough with anger. "Chooli started out as my housekeeper. I fell in love with her. When I realized she was pregnant, there was no way I was going to let her stay on the reservation. So I left."

Moses watched him carefully. "You mustered out of the Buffalo Soldiers?"

Franklin met his eyes steadily. "Not exactly." He hesitated. "I just disappeared with Chooli one night."

Moses had opened his mouth to respond when a sudden scream ripped through the clinic.

Chapter Five

Carrie was putting the last stitch into the younger vigilante's head when she heard the scream. She exchanged a startled look with Janie and Polly. "What is it now?"

"Go ahead," Janie said. "Polly and I can finish up here. Call us if you need help."

Carrie tore off her blood-speckled apron, quickly washed her hands, and rushed from the room.

Abby was waiting for her outside the door. "It's Chooli," she said urgently. "She's the wife of Moses' army friend. It seems she has gone into labor."

Carrie took a deep breath. She was beyond exhausted but that didn't matter. She had worked endless shifts at Chimborazo during the war; she would push through this long night that surely must be on the verge of surrendering to dawn. The memory of the morning's dream flashed through her mind. Was it really less than twenty-four hours since she had woken with Abby stroking her hair? It seemed like days. The question was followed by a quick revelation that she could not have helped any of these people if Robert had not sent her back. She couldn't yet say she was glad he had not let her join him, but she was grateful she'd been able to make a difference. That would have to be enough.

"Carrie?" Abby's voice was worried. "Moses and his friend Franklin are getting what you need. Are you sure you can do this?"

Carrie pushed aside the fatigue. "I can do this," she said reassuringly. "Where are the rest of the men?"

"Out front guarding the clinic."

Carrie nodded and slipped in the room, Abby close behind her. "Hello, Chooli," she said gently. "I am Carrie Borden."

"The doctor?" Chooli asked, her face twisted with pain as another labor spasm claimed her slender body.

"That's right," Carrie answered, glad the time was coming soon when she would have the credentials behind her proclamation. She assessed her patient swiftly. "It looks like this baby is right on time. Is it your first?"

"Yes," she gasped.

Carrie smiled soothingly. "I can't say it will be fun, but women were made tough enough to handle the pain. I'll help you through it."

"Franklin knows?" Chooli asked anxiously. "His baby."

"He knows," she assured the girl. "He and Moses are getting the supplies I need." A soft knock at the door signaled their arrival. Once the hot water and rags were in the room, she sprang into action. "Let's see how close this baby is to making its appearance."

Chooli grabbed her hand. "You are a mother?"

Carrie stiffened as memories shot through her body. She knew Chooli was asking her if she understood the pain of birth, but she wasn't going to tell the frightened young woman what had happened with her delivery. "I'm not, but I have brought many little ones into the world," she answered. Carrie swallowed back the tears that threatened to blur her eyes. She would always be Bridget's mother, but right now her only job was to instill confidence.

Abby stepped forward. "You couldn't be in better hands, Chooli," she said warmly.

Chooli relaxed measurably as she locked her eyes on Abby's kind face. "Thank you." Her eyes said she was hiding many secrets, but now was not the time to delve into them.

Carrie completed her examination quickly, relieved beyond words that there didn't seem to be a problem. Perhaps there would be one event in this endless night that wouldn't be full of drama. "Everything looks perfect," she said as she looked into Chooli's determined eyes. "I don't think it will be long."

*****

Moses glanced at the closed door and then turned back to Franklin. "There is nothing we can do but wait. Perhaps you should tell me a little more about why you deserted from the army."

Franklin shrugged. "I couldn't do it anymore. What America is doing to the Indians out West is completely wrong. Especially the Navajo. Bosque Redondo is worse than any place I ever seen. I hated being a slave, but at least I had food and a place to sleep. More than eight thousand Navajo are crowded onto the reservation. Many of them don't even have shelter. There was nothing built for them, and there are no trees to build homes, so they dug pits into the earth and covered them with branches." His eyes narrowed. "The only reason Chooli is not skin and bones is because she was living with me as my housekeeper. My commander didn't know she was pregnant. I made sure she ate, but her family is another matter," he said bitterly. "Her parents and grandparents have barely enough to keep them alive. I got everything to them I could, but it wasn't enough. They knew I was trying, but it was killing me."

Moses listened, letting Franklin tell the story his way.

"When we realized Chooli was pregnant, she told her parents. They insisted she should leave. It almost broke her heart to leave her family behind, but we all knew it was the only way to save her and the baby."

"Was it hard to get away?"

Franklin shrugged. "Navajo were marched almost three hundred miles to the reservation from their tribal homelands. It started four years ago." He shook his head. "It's hard to believe this was going on when we were fighting a war to keep our country together and free the slaves. Anyway," he continued, "hundreds died along the way. Hundreds more women and children were stolen as slaves before they ever reached Bosque Redondo." His eyes flashed with anger. "Chooli has two younger brothers and a sister. They were both stolen by raiding New Mexicans during the march. They are being used as slaves somewhere." Franklin shook his head heavily. "The Navajo tried to make a life there because their homelands were destroyed, but the conditions are horrible, and many have died. In the last year, thousands of them have simply run away. There are not enough soldiers to keep them there."

"So you just left?" Moses tried to absorb what he was hearing.

"That's right," Franklin answered. "Right after a few hundred of the Navajo disappeared into the night, my commander sent a large battalion of soldiers after them. I wasn't chosen for that mission. I took a couple horses, loaded them with all I could, and departed in the middle of the night."

"When?"

Franklin hesitated. "The beginning of April."

Moses stared at him. "Six months? It's taken you six months to get here?"

"It took a little over three months to travel the Santa Fe Trail, and then I didn't have money to take the train. I could have sold the horses, but I figured we might need them. I wanted so much to have Chooli here long before she gave birth," he said with a scowl. "The Santa Fe Trail is bad at any time, but having to travel at night made it harder. We had to watch out for everyone. The soldiers using that trail would have known I was a deserter because I was with Chooli. There was just as much danger from other Indian tribes. There are a lot of them that don't get along too good out there."

Moses shook his head. "I don't know anything about the Indians," he admitted.

Matthew walked in the door in time to hear his statement. "You and most Americans," he commented. "And what they think they know is probably all wrong."

Franklin looked searchingly at Matthew. "You're the red-headed reporter who kept showing up during the war."

Matthew smiled and shook Franklin's hand. "Guilty as charged. My name is Matthew Justin."

Moses explained briefly about Chooli. "Everything all right outside?"

"Yes. Simon came to report that all your men's families got home safely. They took Rose back to the house to be with the children. He is outside with some more of his men to make sure nothing happens."

"I don't think the cowards who left them are coming back," Moses growled. "It's not that I want them to return, but to leave them there to die is harsh."

Matthew nodded. "They don't appear to be a compassionate lot. Besides, we don't know what happened with the other men who were wounded. They could be trying to keep them alive."

"We'll probably never know," Moses growled. "It's all such a waste."

"A waste?" Franklin asked, but his eyes were glued to the door Chooli was sequestered behind.

Moses managed a smile when he saw the look on his friend's face. "Silence is a good thing. If you don't hear screaming and wailing, it means it is probably going to be an easy birth."

Franklin leaned back against his chair. "I know you're right. It's just that Chooli has been through so much during the trip here."

"You made it before she gave birth," Matthew reminded him.

"My sister, June, gave birth to little Simon deep in the woods when I was helping her escape," Moses added. "It was a nightmare. You did good to get her here, Franklin."

Franklin nodded. "I reckon you're right." He forced his eyes away from the door and returned to their earlier conversation. "What is a waste?"

Moses scowled as his anger flared. "All of it. We fought a war that killed huge numbers of men on either side. It's supposed to be over, but it seems we're still fighting. Sure felt like it tonight. We were waging a military campaign. I don't have any reason to believe it is going to end. I'm sick of all of it."

Matthew eyed him with sympathy. "I know how you feel, Moses, but at least you and Rose are going to do something to change things."

"How's that?" Franklin asked.

"Moses is going to college to become a lawyer. Rose is studying to become an educator."

"A *lawyer*?" Franklin asked. "I know Rose been a teacher for a long time, so that makes sense, but we never talked about you being a lawyer. All you could talk about was having a farm of your own someday. Seem to remember that's what kept you going during the war."

Moses sighed. "I know." He did not want to have this conversation.

Franklin didn't share his feelings. "Why a lawyer?"

Moses shrugged. "So I can help make things better for my people." He tried to remember all the reasons he had thought this was a good idea. "It's going to take educated blacks to change things. We have to fight to change the laws if things are going to be different."

"I hope you don't mind me saying so, but you don't seem real excited about that."

"I didn't realize excitement was a requirement," Moses snapped as his exhaustion caught up with him. He held up a hand in apology. "I'm sorry."

"No problem," Franklin said.

"You can't leave until you find someone to run the plantation anyway," Matthew offered.

"You run Cromwell Plantation?" Franklin asked.

Moses took a deep breath. "I own half of it," he revealed. "Rose is Thomas Cromwell's half-sister. He gave me half the plantation not too long after the war ended. Thomas and Abby own a factory in Richmond, while I handle operations out here."

Franklin sat back and stared at him. "You *own* half of Cromwell Plantation?" His voice was one of stunned disbelief. "You expect me to believe that?"

"I don't really care if you do or not," Moses replied wearily.

Franklin turned to look at Matthew.

"He's telling the truth," Matthew assured him. "A lot has changed in the last couple years."

Franklin swung back to stare at Moses. "That why the Ku Klux Klan did what they did tonight? They can't be too happy with the way things be around here."

"They're not," Moses said, gazing at the closed door. "Carrie Borden—the woman helping Chooli right now—is Thomas Cromwell's daughter. Her husband, Robert, was killed here on the plantation by KKK vigilantes this spring. This is the first time they have come back."

He was saved from having to say any more when Janie and Polly stepped into the room.

"The two men will survive," Janie said quietly.

Moses remained silent, not wanting to reveal that he would have been perfectly all right with hearing both had died.

Matthew's question revealed he felt the same way. "How long before they can ride back to wherever they came from?"

Polly stared at him. "Put them men on a horse and they'll be dead before they get very far."

Moses reluctantly accepted they were his responsibility. "Can we put them in a wagon and have a group of the white fathers take them home? Are they conscious?"

"Neither are conscious," Janie answered. "I don't know how long before they will be. I'm not happy about it either, but we're stuck with them for at least two days. By then, if they have woken up and told us where they live, we can have a wagon transport them home. If," she added, "it seems safe to do that. The KKK is not any happier with the white men than they are with you. There has been enough bloodshed."

Once she had made her pronouncement, she inclined her head toward the other closed door. "The woman?"

Moses nodded. "Her name is Chooli. She is giving birth."

Polly smiled. "Death and birth, all on the same night. My mama told me that be a good sign. It shows that the cycle of life never changes. No matter how bad things get, we just got to wait for a new beginning. Babies be God's way of saying He ain't given up on the world quite yet."

"Chooli," Janie murmured tiredly. "That's a beautiful name."

Moses smiled and answered her unspoken question. "Chooli is Navajo." A lusty cry from behind the closed door saved him from a lengthy explanation.

Franklin leapt up and moved closer to the door. "Is that my child?" he asked hoarsely.

Janie smiled. "I do believe it is." She walked to the door. "I'll let you know something soon."

*****

Carrie glanced up with a weary smile as Janie walked in the door. She finished cutting the umbilical cord and then handed the infant to her friend. "Will you clean her up?"

Janie reached for the baby eagerly.

Carrie turned to Abby. "Will you tell everyone there is a new little girl in the world? And that she has a very brave mother?"

"Absolutely. I'm glad something good has come from this tragic night," Abby replied.

Chooli smiled tenderly as Abby left the room, not removing her eyes from her daughter as Janie cleaned her with warm water and rags. "She is healthy?"

"She's perfect," Carrie said. Knowing she had helped bring this beautiful little girl into the world somewhat eased the pain of Bridget's death. She knew now that she had not been responsible for her daughter's death, but successfully delivering Chooli's baby provided a measure of redemption. "Have you decided on a name?"

Chooli nodded. "Franklin say all right I give her a Navajo name." She frowned slightly. "It will make things harder for her."

"There's time to worry about that later," Carrie said. "What is her name?"

"Ajei," Chooli answered. She reached out to draw her daughter close to her bosom after Janie had finished wrapping her in a blanket. "Her name is Ajei," she crooned. "*My heart.*" She gazed down lovingly. "Hello, Ajei. You are here. You are my heart."

Carrie blinked back tears. "Ajei. It's a beautiful name, Chooli. And now it's time to get some rest," she added with a warm smile. "You definitely earned some sleep."

Chooli shook her head. "Franklin see daughter."

As if on cue, the door opened. Franklin gazed into the room, Moses and Matthew pressed close behind him.

"Franklin!" Chooli cried. "Come see. We have child."

Franklin, his face filled with awe, walked to the bed. He stared down a moment and then held out his arms. Chooli lifted the girl and placed her in his waiting arms. "Hello, little one," he said gruffly. He carefully inspected her dark face and curly black hair. He pulled back the blanket to count all her fingers and toes. Finally, he looked up. "She's perfect," he whispered. "The trip didn't hurt her."

"We Navajo women are strong," Chooli said proudly. "I told you it be all right."

Moses didn't miss the flash of pain that darkened her already black eyes, but she had a smile on her face again when Franklin looked down. He knew without asking that Chooli was missing her family back in New Mexico.

*****

Moses had only slept for a couple hours, but he was up and mounted on Champ before the sun had topped the trees. The shimmering rays caused the oaks and maples s to burst into even more brilliant red, yellow and orange. A light layer of frost glistened over everything, as a low mist danced across the treetops. Vibrant patches of goldenrod blended with purple aster. He took in deep breaths, loving the feel of being up on such a peaceful morning. He closed his eyes as he thought about having to leave, and then forced them open again. He was not going to dwell on what was coming. They were sending the final shipment of tobacco today. That was enough to occupy his thoughts.

Distant sounds reminded him the families from Blackwell Plantation were still down in the cabins first lived in by his own men. Seasonal field hands occupied most of them now, but there had been enough empty ones to provide crowded shelter for everyone. Wood smoke wafted through the air, the smell of bacon not far behind.

His men would soon arrive at the tobacco barns to load the last shipment into the wagons. Moses wasn't going to take any chances with the delivery. Normally, he would send each wagon with two drivers and then go about his business with no concerns the tobacco would make it to its destination. This morning, the eight wagons going into Richmond would be surrounded by all but a handful of his men, who would be left behind to guard the plantation. He hated how easily he planned each day as if it were a military campaign, but he had no choice. Everyone would be exhausted by the end of another grueling day, but he also suspected his men would be eagerly waiting for him at the tobacco barns.

"You want some company?" Franklin strode out on the porch behind him. He smiled at Moses. "I never slept in a white man's house before," he drawled. "I left Chooli and Ajei sleeping peacefully. I heard you get up and figured now would be a good time to talk to you."

"I'm heading out. You want to join me?"

"Give me a few minutes to get Chancellor ready."

Moses nodded, thinking through the day while he waited for Franklin to saddle his gray gelding. The horse probably wasn't the finest the army had, but he imagined they had been more than aware that the gelding and the tall chestnut mare Chooli had ridden in on were missing. They would have been less than pleased, especially if they figured out what had happened. They rode for several minutes before Moses spoke. "You finally going to tell me what you are doing here?"

"You didn't consider I might just drop by since I was in the area?"

Moses stared at him pointedly.

Franklin smiled. "I was heading here when I left New Mexico."

"Why?"

"I figured you would be doing what you are doing. Raising tobacco."

Every word was only confusing Moses more, so he was just going to wait and see where this conversation was headed. He continued to trot evenly down the road that split the tobacco fields. It was always odd to see an empty expanse stretching as far as the eye could see after a long summer of watching the tobacco grow, but he knew the results would once again alter his financial situation.

"How does it feel owning half of Cromwell Plantation?" Franklin asked. "I can tell you had a bumper crop."

"It feels surreal," Moses admitted, "but good." He eyed Franklin. "How can you tell it was a bumper crop?"

Franklin shrugged. "The dirt is still dark and fertile-looking, so it had to grow some mighty big tobacco. The plants are close together, and the stalks are thick. You pulled a lot of tobacco off these fields."

Moses nodded and met his friend's eyes. "What are you doing here, Franklin?"

"I came for a job. I didn't have no idea you would own half this place, but I heard through the grapevine that you were here."

"You became a Buffalo Soldier because you didn't want to work in the tobacco fields anymore," Moses reminded him, not surprised at the effectiveness of the grapevine. It was the only way slaves had communicated for generations.

"That's true, but all my time in a tobacco field been as a slave. I wanted to get as far away from any reminder of that as I could." Franklin paused. "The thing is, I missed it every minute I was out West. Oh, it's pretty enough out there, but I missed the green, and I missed making things grow. When I decided to leave Bosque Redondo, I knew I wanted to come back to Virginia. I decided I was going to find you and try to get a job. I know it is the end of the growing season, but I got me a little money from the army. I could have bought train tickets, but I figured Chooli and I might need it to live for a while."

Moses listened carefully, remembering his long conversations with Franklin during the endless nights between battles. Franklin had known as much as Moses did about farming tobacco. "It's not easy living around here right now."

"Best I can tell, it ain't easy living as a black man anywhere in this country."

"That's true," Moses agreed, still watching his friend. "It will probably be harder having an Indian wife."

"I thought you didn't know nothing about Indians."

"I don't, but people don't seem to like anyone that is different. Combine a black man and an Indian woman? It might be harder, is all."

Franklin shrugged. "Harder is all I've ever known. If I can at least do what I want to do while I'm living harder, then I guess it will even out."

Moses couldn't argue with that; it was the same conclusion he had come to many times. The tobacco barns came into view. "We'll finish this conversation later. Right now I have to get this shipment moving."

Franklin eyed all the men. "They're up early, too."

"They get a percentage of the crop. They're not going to take any chance of something going wrong."

Franklin whistled his disbelief. "A percentage of the crop?"

Moses glanced at him, certain he saw nothing but approval. "We find having a stake in the success of the tobacco yield makes everyone work harder. Even with the workers getting a percentage, we all make more money."

"Makes sense." It was all Franklin had time to say before they arrived at the barn.

"That be you, Franklin?"

"Where in the world did you come from, man?"

Moses watched as his men clustered around Franklin. They had all respected him during the war. Two and a half years of being apart didn't seem to have changed that any.

His eyes narrowed as he watched the easy laughter and banter.

After a few minutes, Franklin edged away. "I hear tell y'all got a shipment to get moving. How can I help?"

Within an hour, all eight wagons were loaded with great bundles of dried tobacco. Moses watched as the wagons, surrounded by well-armed guards, rolled down the drive toward the gate. The departure of the wagons announced the official end to the 1867 harvest. Now would begin the hard work of preparing for winter and the coming spring.

"You're looking sad, Moses," Franklin observed.

Moses waited until the last wagon had rolled out of sight before he responded. "Leaving the plantation will be hard. At one point I was excited about going to college..." His voice trailed off.

"But now you're not?"

"I don't really know what I feel about it anymore, I just know I don't want to leave the plantation."

"Then why are you?"

"Because Rose deserves her chance to go to school. She's waited for a long time, always putting others' needs before her own. This is her turn." He briefly explained about Carrie. "Now that Carrie is going back to school, Rose can leave. I would never do anything to get in her way." He answered the question he saw in Franklin's eyes. "And I would never let her go by herself. The war kept us apart far too long. She's given up a lot for me. Now it's my turn to give up something for her."

"I see," Franklin murmured.

Moses appreciated that there was no judgment in his voice. "I watched you with the men this morning."

"They're good men," Franklin replied. "It's clear how much they respect you."

"It's also clear how much they respect *you*," Moses answered. "Do you really want to grow tobacco again?" He had watched as Franklin inspected the crop, nodded his approval of the drying barns, and pitched in to help with loading the bundles.

"More than anything," Franklin answered. "You saying I got a job here, Moses?"

Moses took a deep breath. "I'm saying I may have the person who can run things here while I'm gone."

Franklin pulled Chancellor up short and stared at Moses for a long moment. "What you say?"

Moses smiled, suddenly more certain than ever that he was right. "I remember our long talks. You know tobacco. The men respect you. I can teach you what else you need to know before I leave in January. There is a nice cabin down in the old quarters that will be perfect for your family." He could tell Franklin was searching for words. "I'll give you time to think about it."

Franklin found his voice. "I don't need no time to think about it, Moses. I just couldn't figure out how to make my mouth work to form words."

Moses chuckled. "Should I assume the words are going to mean yes?"

"Yes," Franklin managed. "Yes," he repeated, shaking his head. "You really figure I can run a fancy place like this?"

"Maybe not today," Moses replied, "but you'll be ready by the time I leave. As long as your head can handle all I'm going to cram inside it. I sure am glad I taught you and Simon how to read during the war." He hesitated. "I do have one question..."

Franklin read the expression on his face accurately. "The army has no idea where I am, Moses. I didn't talk to nobody before I left. I promise you ain't nobody going to come looking."

Moses peered into his eyes and then nodded. "I trust you." He thought about how difficult it would be to leave the plantation. "I don't really know when I'll be back." He refused to say *if* he would be back. He didn't know what the future was going to hold, but he couldn't imagine it wouldn't have him back on Cromwell Plantation at some point.

"Not knowing ain't no problem for me," Franklin assured him. "I had no clue what was going to happen when I left the reservation. I still didn't have no clue this morning. Now I got me a clue, but I don't have to know what's coming out there in the future. I figure I'm going to live today. I been doing that for the last six months, and it seems to be working out right well."

Moses chuckled and pushed Champ into an easy canter. "I don't know about you, but I'm starving. Let's go have breakfast and check on our families." Franklin fell into place beside him. Until now, Moses didn't realize how much he had missed Simon when he left for Blackwell Plantation. He liked all the men who worked for him, but Simon had been like a brother. He hoped he could have something like that with Franklin for the months he would still be here. It would fill some of the void left by Simon's departure and Robert's death.

Chapter Six

Carrie inhaled the crisp air as she walked toward the barn. The only way she was going to make it through today was by first losing herself in the horses. A filmy layer of fog hovered over the ground, and the sun was nothing more than a pink glimmer on the horizon. The surrounding trees, silenced into autumnal statues by the fog, seemed to reach out to her with sympathy.

Carrie stopped, crossed her arms over the board fence, and watched as the foals—most of them at least five months old now—cavorted in the fields. She loved to watch them prance around the pasture, their tails waving like flags as their heads bobbed with youthful pride. One in particular always brought her great joy. As if called by her thoughts, Sable shot across the field, bucking her joy as she raced up the fence line. She snorted, hopped to a stiff-legged stop, and lifted her head to stare at Carrie.

"Hello, girl," Carrie murmured. She never tired of watching the leggy, solid-black filly. Robert had taken an instant liking to her, telling Carrie that Sable was the finest of this year's crop of horses. Her conformation was perfection, she was fast, and her eyes glimmered with both spirit and kindness. All the horses were intelligent, but Sable had an edge on them, catching on a little more quickly and always performing just a little better.

"I still believe you should have included her in our sales agreement."

Carrie was startled when Anthony's voice sounded next to her, but she kept her gaze on Sable. Robert had decided when she was just weeks old that the filly would stay here on the plantation to improve the breeding program. "I'm sure you do."

"And you feel absolutely no remorse, do you?"

"Not a bit," Carrie retorted. She didn't want the interruption, but she would not be ungracious. "You're up early this morning."

"Weddings do that to me," Anthony replied.

"Excuse me?"

"I've known Mark and Catherine all my life. I'm truly happy for them, and I'm glad your father agreed for them to marry here today, but any wedding really does nothing more than remind me of what I've lost," Anthony said.

Carrie took a deep breath. He had spoken her thoughts. "I understand."

"I'm sure you do," Anthony replied. "Did Robert's death interfere with the breeding program for next year?"

"Not a bit," Carrie said quickly, grateful for the change in subject he was offering. "Clint was more than qualified to handle it. We had only bought a few more mares before Robert..."

Anthony saved her from having to say it. "Are all the mares in foal?"

"All that were here in May," Carrie answered. "Clint and I purchased thirty more mares this summer, but they will not be bred to Eclipse until next spring. Robert believed it is best for all the foals to be born as close to each other as possible, and he wanted them to be older before winter struck. Next year's crop will be larger than this one, but the following year will be even better," she added.

Anthony gazed at her, interpreting her expression. "It's going to be hard to leave to finish school," he said perceptively, his eyes kind.

"Perhaps no harder than staying," Carrie said softly. As much as she savored every memory of Robert, she sometimes wondered what life would be like if every moment wasn't filled with painful remembrances. She had experienced a taste of it during her trip to Kansas, but being back in Philadelphia would be far different.

*****

Carrie sat next to her father and Abby while Mark and Catherine exchanged their vows. She had stayed busy in the barn until there was just enough time to change into a ruby-red gown that reflected the leaves glistening overhead. Her father's shining eyes said she looked lovely, but it was not really important to her.

The heavens had delivered a perfect day. A slight breeze rustled its music through the trees as red-tailed hawks screeched their agreement. Carrie watched as three red cardinals glided in to perch on the limb over the couple's head.

Against her will, her mind traveled back to the spring day when she had given her oath to Robert. She thought of the single magnolia bloom her father had picked for her—a spot of beauty in a war-torn city. She and Robert had shared so many hopes and dreams. To have survived so much only to lose him to the bullet of a fellow southerner was still more than she could comprehend.

Carrie blinked back hot tears and focused on the words being spoken by the minister her father had somehow secured in time for the wedding. She smiled as Mark, his face glowing with joy, leaned down to kiss his bride. She wished for them nothing but happiness, but she knew life could steal anything away in a moment's breath.

*****

"Carrie!"

Carrie was jolted from her thoughts. "Yes, Amber?"

"I said your name three times before you heard me," Amber accused.

"I'm sorry, honey. I was thinking about something else."

Amber locked eyes with her. "I know what you were thinking about."

She was sure Amber was right, but talking about it would do nothing but make this day harder. "Do you want something, honey?"

"I want to ask you if you're coming to the dance. Since everyone had to miss the Harvest Ball, this wedding dance will have to do."

Carrie's breath caught and her mind raced. It had been hard enough to attend the ceremony. She was no more ready for a wedding dance than she had been for the Harvest Ball.

"Well, are you?" Amber demanded.

"She can't."

Amber turned on Anthony as he walked up behind her. "And why not?"

"Because she promised to show me around the plantation," Anthony said gravely. "I'm leaving tomorrow and this is the only time she can do it. Since I am a very important client, she feels she has to."

Carrie felt a rush of both relief and amusement as she watched doubt flicker in Amber's eyes.

"Is that right, Carrie?"

Carrie grasped on to the rope Anthony presented. At this point, she couldn't have cared less what was true. All she knew was that she was confident she would not survive a wedding dance. "Yes, honey." She struggled to keep her voice appropriately regretful. "I promised Anthony before I knew there would be a wedding. This is really very important. You want Cromwell Stables to keep selling the babies, don't you?"

Amber nodded reluctantly, but then turned to Anthony with a flash of her usual defiance. "It seems to me a wedding dance is more important than riding around the plantation, though."

Anthony smiled. "I promise you Mark and Catherine won't miss us. I have to go home tomorrow, and this is our only chance. It seems important for me to be able to tell potential buyers about the wonderful plantation the horses are coming from," he added persuasively.

Amber considered his words before flashing a bright smile. "I guess that's makes sense," she acquiesced. Then she spun toward Carrie. "Do you remember the dress I wore for last year's Harvest Ball when I won the tournament?"

"The creamy white gown that made you look like a queen? Of course I remember."

Amber's eyes grew serious. "Do you think it's all right if I wear that dress again?" she asked uncertainly.

Carrie saw past Amber's words to her real question. "Who is the boy you are trying to impress?"

"Wade," Amber admitted, her eyes dropping from shyness. "His daddy started working here this spring. He's the first boy I've ever liked, I reckon."

"He's a lucky boy," Anthony said warmly.

Amber's eyes shot up. "Do you really think so?"

"I know so," Anthony said. "You are beautiful, you are smart, and you are a great horse trainer. Wade should be the one trying to impress *you*."

Carrie felt a surge of gratitude when Amber giggled. Intense sadness followed close behind. Robert should have been the one encouraging Amber. Carrie knew how much it would have meant to him to learn the little girl he loved as a daughter was finally noticing boys. He would have made her feel like a princess.

*****

Carrie began to relax as soon as she and Anthony rounded the last curve. A final glance over her shoulder told her the plantation house was no longer in view. Despite her decision not to attend the dance, she had struggled with guilt as she saddled Granite. She doubted anyone else would notice, but her mother would have been appalled at her lack of courtesy. The thought made her chuckle.

Anthony, looking completely at home on Eclipse, raised a brow. "Care to share?"

"I was thinking about my mother," Carrie admitted. "How she would disapprove of my not attending the dance. Then I imagined the look on her face if she could see me riding away from it in breeches and a coat." She saw no need to mention it was Robert's old jacket. There were days in the hot summer that she had worn it just to make him feel closer. She was thankful for the crisp days that now made it part of her necessary attire. It had not been washed since his death, so it still carried his smell—or at least she imagined it did.

"You and your mother didn't see eye to eye, I take it," Anthony observed.

Carrie smiled. "My mother was a very traditional Southern woman. I was her cross to bear," she said cheerfully. "We found peace during the last days before her death, but for most of my life, she was intent on changing me."

"I'm glad she failed," Anthony said sincerely.

Carrie tensed but saw nothing except a casual friendliness in Anthony's eyes. "I believe in the end she was, too." A gust of wind created a swirl of leaves that danced through the air and unleashed the band that had tightened around her heart and throat during the long day. She leaned forward. "Let's see if you can catch up," she called. The constriction fell away as Granite leapt forward into a gallop, his long strides swallowing the road.

She was aware of Eclipse falling into place beside her, but Carrie was content to let the wind whip through her hair. She lay low over Granite's neck and let him run. It wasn't until he began to slow down on his own that she straightened and reined him down to an easy walk. "That was fun!" she called.

Anthony laughed. "Indeed it was. I've been wanting to ride Eclipse ever since I laid eyes on him. I never dreamed of being able to race him."

Carrie smiled. "Don't worry, I know Eclipse could probably beat Granite now in speed, but there is no other horse on the plantation quite like mine," she said loyally. "There are plenty of horses that have speed, but not all of them have such great hearts."

"I couldn't agree more," Anthony said. "Mark has told me about you and Granite."

Carrie laughed. "I bet he has. He'll never forget how we got away from his men during the war."

"Escaping his soldiers and the plantation, and then jumping a high fence after you had been shot was quite memorable," he said dryly.

Carrie grinned. Mark knew the secret of her escape, but it was not something they shared with most people. It was time to change the subject. "You're headed back to Philadelphia tomorrow?"

"I don't actually live in Philadelphia anymore. I have moved to Richmond."

Carrie raised a brow and waited for him to continue.

"After spending many years in the garment industry, it was a relief to work with horse buyers. It took me back to my roots. During the war it was not possible to come south to make deals, so Philadelphia was the best choice. Horse breeders are just now starting to rebound south of the Mason-Dixon Line, but I have decided being here to build relationships is worth the financial risk. Besides," he added, "I would prefer never to live through another Philadelphia winter."

"I understand that feeling," Carrie replied. "Have you found a home there? The city is rebuilding from the destruction of the war, but I'm afraid it will take quite some time to ever regain its former glory."

"I have," Anthony replied, his voice taking on a slight hesitancy as if he wasn't sure how she would respond to his next words. "I will be living with your father and Abby for the foreseeable future. I travel quite a bit so they have assured me I will not be an inconvenience."

"I see," Carrie murmured. She felt another twinge of uneasiness that she chose to push away.

"You don't have to worry, Carrie."

Carrie looked at Anthony expectantly. "Worry?"

"That I will want to court you," he said directly. "You are quite an attractive woman, but my heart still belongs to my wife. I also know it will be some time before your heart is ready to consider *any* man." He smiled gently. "I can be a good friend if you have any interest."

Carrie smiled, welcoming his open honesty. It was another thing she liked about Northern men. They did not seem to be bound by the Southern tradition of hypocritical courtesy. "I would like that," she said. She could tell by the look in his eyes that he appreciated her quick acceptance. "You will find I don't have time for the games most women play."

"I would say *most* women on both sides of the Mason-Dixon Line have been taught to play those games," Anthony chuckled. "I find it singularly exhausting. Thank you for being different." He laughed. "Not that I would have expected anything else. I still tell people about how easily you played all three of us when we came to look at the colts and fillies in August. You did Abby proud."

It was Carrie's turn to laugh. "I loved the look on all your faces when you realized you would be negotiating with me."

"Negotiating? There was not one thought of a negotiation. I know when I have been out-maneuvered. I simply made the highest offer I had been authorized to make because I knew you were in the control of the whole situation."

"Was I?" Carrie asked demurely, and then burst into laughter.

Chapter Seven

Janie stepped gratefully into her home, stopping for a moment to appreciate the warmth rushing toward her. She hoped the light snow falling outside was not an early harbinger of a brutally cold winter. Every time snow fell in Philadelphia she found herself longing to be back in the relative warmth of the South. As she hung her thick coat on the hook by the door she wondered if the plantation was getting snow. At least there the blanket of white was beautiful. A sound coming from the kitchen startled her. "Matthew?" she called.

"Janie!" Matthew pushed open the kitchen door and peered out, his bright blue eyes alight with joy. "You're home early."

"As are you," Janie replied. "What are you doing here?" An early arrival usually meant there was new trouble in the country, but she didn't want to always assume the worst.

Matthew grinned at her and waved a sheet of paper. "I had to come home so you could see this!"

Janie relaxed as she eyed the paper, realizing it must be special to have brought a gleam of joy to her husband's eyes. "It must be good news."

"News I thought I would never hear," Matthew agreed.

Janie's curiosity was growing. "What in the world is it?"

Matthew waved it in the air and began backing into the kitchen. "Wouldn't you like to read it over some hot tea and biscuits?"

Janie grinned. "*Hot* biscuits?"

"And strawberry preserves," Matthew offered temptingly. "Annie sent them back with us after the Harvest Festival."

Janie's grin grew. "I'll follow you anywhere for hot tea and biscuits with Annie's preserves."

She waited until Matthew had put her plate in front of her, along with a steaming cup of tea, and then reached eagerly for the letter. It took only a few seconds for her eyes to widen with surprise. "Harold? Your brother?" Her breath caught. "I thought he was dead."

Matthew's grin matched hers. "I thought the same thing." He shook his head in wonder. "I had to read the letter a few times before I even believed it was real."

Janie continued to read. "He's living in Buffalo, New York." Her eyes grew wider. "He's a reporter for the *Buffalo Evening Courier*?"

"Seems to be," Matthew replied.

"Both of you are *reporters*?" Janie asked. "You have never said much about him other than to tell me you had a brother who died. What does he look like?"

Matthew hesitated. "He looks like me."

Janie cocked her head, hearing something unusual in his voice. "It's not unusual for brothers to look alike."

Matthew met her eyes. "We are identical twins."

Janie inhaled sharply and placed the letter on the table. "Twins?" she asked. "You never told me that." Somehow, the fact they were twins was much more important than merely brothers.

"Talking about Harold was never a favorite thing." Matthew took a sip of his tea before continuing. "We were close growing up, but then we left home to go to college and things changed. I went to the University of Pennsylvania in Philadelphia. He went to Madison University in Hamilton, New York." He stared unseeingly out the window for several moments. "We grew apart," he finally said.

Janie could tell the memories were painful, but she sensed he needed to talk about it. "Why?" she asked softly, grateful for the cocoon of comfort the kitchen created as the snow swirled against windows fogged by steam from the kettle.

Matthew continued to gaze out the window. "Manifest Destiny," he replied.

Janie shook her head. "I'm afraid I'm not following you." Matthew swung away from the window and fastened his gaze on her. Janie could tell he was trying to center himself. She held his eyes, realizing that despite how joyful he was to hear from Harold, the memories of what had torn them apart were still painful.

"Manifest Destiny is a phrase coined in the 1840s to support the belief that as Americans we are meant to expand across North America. According to this belief, American settlers have special virtues that make it our mission to remake North America in the image of the United States. We are meant to spread from coast to coast. Whether we want to or not, it is our destiny under God to subjugate anything that stands in the way of that."

Janie stared at him, her mind whirling. "That sounds rather arrogant."

Matthew managed a chuckle. "That would be putting it mildly, my dear. The belief in Manifest Destiny was used in the forties to justify war with Mexico. In 1846, it was used to take back a large part of land in the Oregon territory that had been claimed by the British. It was used in 1845 to annex the Texas Territory. The government agreed to assume a lot of its massive debts when they annexed the state. It wasn't until the Compromise of 1850 that the debts were fully paid."

Janie raised a brow. "I never knew any of this," she murmured. "How did the Compromise relieve the debt?"

"The government gave Texas ten million dollars. In return, they ceded a very large portion of Texas-claimed territory to the United States." Matthew frowned. "The same Manifest Destiny belief is being used to take land away from the Indians now. It's what is happening to Chooli's people."

As fascinating as Janie found all this, it still didn't answer the question that had started the conversation. "How did Manifest Destiny tear you and Harold apart?"

Matthew shook his head heavily. "He believed in Manifest Destiny. I did not."

"Enough to tear you apart?"

"Manifest Destiny has been disagreed on since the beginning. There were people who certainly endorsed it, but there were many, including Lincoln and Grant, who rejected it. They saw America's moral mission as one of democratic example rather than one of conquest. They did not believe we should just take what we wanted because of some kind of divine mandate. Obviously, Harold and I felt differently. I tried to understand his position, but he treated me as if I was an evil barrier standing in the way of what America was meant to accomplish."

"I'm assuming there was money involved?"

Matthew smiled bitterly. "Isn't there always? Harold wanted to be a part of the railroad industry. He had visions of becoming a millionaire. He knew the only way that could happen was for the railroads to stretch coast to coast. He was for anything that would assure that reality. Nothing could stand in the way of the profits that could be created."

Janie frowned. She knew such an attitude would have infuriated her fair-minded husband. She could imagine the fight that had split the brothers. She was just as intrigued that somehow he and Robert had managed a friendship even when they were on opposite sides during the war. To have remained friends with Robert, yet lose his brother, must have been a bitter pill to swallow.

Matthew read her thoughts. "I tried to find a way to bridge the gap. Although Robert fought for the South during the war, we still had mutual respect and love for each other. Harold let greed take him over completely. There was nowhere in the middle to find common ground." He shook his head. "It was Harold who told me he never wanted to see me again. That was ten years ago." He closed his eyes. "I was able to discover he was fighting during the war so I kept an eye out on all the casualty reports. The reports told me he was killed during the Battle of Gettysburg."

"You've thought he was dead for more than four years," Janie murmured, her soft blue eyes darkened with pain. Then she thought of the joy she had seen on Matthew's face. "You looked so happy when I came in. I know you're thrilled he is alive, but have things changed?"

Matthew's eyes cleared of the memories. "*Harold* has changed," he answered. "I have to let the past go and focus on what he has become." He pointed at the letter. "Go ahead and finish reading."

Janie reached for the letter again. As she read, a huge smile spread across her face.

> *I'm hoping you can forgive me for being a*
> *fool. The War taught me there is so much*
> *more to life than money. I watched people*
> *die all around me. I'm still amazed I came*

out alive. I've seen all the death and destruction I hope to ever see.

During the long nights, I thought back to all the conversations we had before I threw you out of my life. It took almost dying more times than I can count to realize it was greed that brought America to war, and that I was as greedy as any of them. I asked God for forgiveness, and now I'm asking you.

You are my only brother, and I want you in my life. I am living in Buffalo, New York. I know I am asking a lot, but if you can find your way to forgive me, I would like to see you again. I can come to Philadelphia, or you can come to Buffalo. I have read every article you have written. I'm proud of you. I hope to be as good a journalist as you are, but I have some catching up to do.

Is there any chance to bridge this gap, brother? You talked to me so many times about bridging the gap between our beliefs. I refused then. I'm hoping there is still a way that can happen.

Your brother,

Harold

Janie smiled when she laid the letter down. "That's wonderful, Matthew. We should go to Buffalo for Christmas."

"Christmas?" Matthew looked confused. "But this might be our last Christmas on the plantation with everyone. I want to see Harold, but I don't want to miss that."

Janie thought quickly. "What if we could do both things?"

"Have you discovered a way to be in two places at the same time?"

"No," Janie replied with a chuckle, "but I have an idea. What if we were to leave here on December seventeenth to go to Buffalo? We could spend three days with Harold, and then catch a train back to Richmond in time to get to the plantation in time for Christmas. I'm done with school on December fifteenth. We could make this work." The more she talked, the more she became confident of her plan.

Matthew considered her words for a moment. "I'm so very glad I married a brilliant woman. It might be a little tight, but it's a perfect solution." He picked up the letter and read it again, a glad light in his eyes. "Let's finish our tea and biscuits. Then I'm going to write Harold a letter. We're going to Buffalo!"

*****

Carrie reined in Granite to give him a breather after a race with Susan and Silver Wings. Susan's tall, black Thoroughbred mare with the glistening white star on her forehead had arrived by train several days earlier. As much as Carrie wanted to claim Granite the victor, the truth was they had been neck and neck the whole way. Neither one could get an edge on the other.

"That was fun!" Susan called, tossing back her long braid.

"Granite was going easy on Silver Wings because he has a crush," Carrie replied. "I never felt him open up all the way."

Susan snorted. "Silver Wings was the one taking it easy. She seems to know male ego is weak. How can she expect to win Granite's heart if she leaves him in the dust?"

"As if she has a chance," Carrie protested. She burst into laughter. "You're right—it was great fun!"

The two friends laughed and chatted as they rode along at a ground-swallowing walk. Mid-November had swept the brilliant fall foliage from the trees. Their color still created a vivid carpet, but the gray limbs, unencumbered by the leaves, clattered freely. What had been a soft breeze when they left the barn had turned into a brisk wind that made Carrie pull her coat tighter.

"There is a cold front coming in," Susan observed.

"Winter is on the way," Carrie agreed. "I hope they have fires going in the house when we get home."

"Home," Susan echoed. "It's strange, but it already feels that way to me." She smiled at Carrie. "You've made it so easy for me to fit in here. Thank you."

"You're welcome," Carrie replied, "but I haven't had to do anything. You have fit in from the day you arrived. I love having you here."

"The day I arrived..." Susan cocked her head. "That was a day to remember."

"I think I would prefer to forget it," Carrie retorted. "I was quite certain it was never going to end."

"You never found out what happened with those two men?

"They were there when I left the clinic the night of the Harvest Festival. I suppose I should say the next day since it was almost dawn when we left. We were all exhausted and needed some rest. They seemed stable when I checked on them so I told everyone to go home and get some rest, including the guards." Carrie shook her head. "When I got there later that day they were gone. The Klansmen must have been watching from the woods. When we left, they broke in and rescued their friends."

"Rescued them or carried them to their death?"

"We'll probably never know," Carrie answered, not wanting to ruin a wonderful day by thinking about it anymore. She had done what she could to save the men. They were no longer her responsibility. "I'm grateful they didn't do damage to the clinic, though. I suppose that was their way of saying thank you for saving their friends." She pushed Granite into a trot, hoping Susan would catch the hint that she didn't want to say anything else.

Susan edged up to ride beside her again. She was not done asking questions, but at least she had changed the topic. "And you're really all right with me taking over Cromwell Stables?"

"I'm perfectly fine with you running things because I know you'll do a great job."

Susan had a worried pucker between her brows. "There is something you're not saying. Is something wrong?"

"No," Carrie insisted. "It's just...I don't want to leave." There. She had finally said it. Rose knew how she felt, but she hadn't wanted to admit it to anyone else.

"You've changed your mind about being a doctor?" Susan asked.

"No," Carrie said. "I know I want to be a doctor. I just don't want to go back to school. The idea of being in Philadelphia again is suffocating." She didn't need to add that even though there were times she longed to be away from all the memories, leaving the place she had lost Robert was making it even more difficult. It was no secret that working with the horses Robert had loved and raised was a big part of what had brought Carrie back to life.

"Do you have to go?" Susan asked.

"If I want to be a doctor. I know I can do it, and I'm looking forward to seeing my friends again, but I'm sad to leave the plantation."

"How long before you are an accredited doctor?"

"One more year of study." Carrie craned her head back so she could watch the clouds swirling in the stiff breeze. She watched as one solid mass danced away into a multitude of shapes. Her eyes suddenly sharpened as they gazed farther. "Look!"

Susan's eyes followed hers toward the thick mass of dark gray clouds gathering on the horizon. "Miles said it was coming. He was right."

Carrie shook her head. "I didn't think it was possible this morning."

"I thought you were the one who told me Miles is always right when he forecasts snow."

"I did say that, but it's been a very long time since we had snow in early November." Carrie sighed. "I love a snowy winter on the plantation, but Philadelphia in the snow is miserable because it just turns into soot-covered mounds that clog the streets."

"Well," Susan said, "you still have two months on the plantation. How about we enjoy the time we have?"

"Yes, Rose," Carrie said, smiling. "Do you realize how much you sound like her?"

"Do you realize how lucky you are to have two people who can talk sense into you?" Susan retorted. She urged Silver Wings into a gentle canter. "I don't know about you, but I would love some hot tea about now. Let's get home."

Carrie laughed when Granite sprang forward to canter beside his new girlfriend without any urging. At least he wouldn't be lonely while Carrie was gone.

The thought was sobering.

*****

Carrie smiled when she found Chooli sitting in the rocking chair in front of the fireplace with Ajei snuggled into her shoulder. Franklin's new cabin was still being prepared for his family so Carrie had insisted they stay in the house until it was ready. They would be settling into their new home the next day. There had been little chance for conversation with the shy young woman, but Carrie intended to change that.

"Hello, Chooli."

Chooli looked up with a gentle smile. "Hello, Carrie. Hello, Susan."

Annie appeared at the door with a tray full of hot tea and ham biscuits. "I saw you girls comin'. Those coats you two took weren't enough to keep you warm. I figured you be ready for something hot since you didn't heed Miles' warnin' about the snow comin' tonight," she said sternly.

"And you did?" Carrie protested. "It was a perfect fall morning when we left."

"I've done learned Miles knows what he be talkin' about," Annie retorted.

"Or maybe you're just so sweet on him you'll believe anything he says," Susan teased.

Annie put the tray down and planted her fists on her hips. She glared at Susan, before turning to Carrie. "Ain't you gonna put her in her place?"

Carrie grinned. "Because you have a problem with the truth, Annie? Isn't it about time you admitted you have fallen for Miles?"

"I don't know what you be talkin' about," Annie sputtered.

Carrie looked at her silently.

Several moments passed before Annie removed her hands from her hips. "Well, I reckon maybe he ain't so bad."

Carrie remained quiet.

A slight smile creased Annie's face. "You don't think I be too old for such nonsense?"

Carrie smiled. "Sarah used to tell me you're never too old for love. I think you should do us all a favor and put Miles out of his misery. It hurts me to see how hard he tries to get your attention. Will you please let him know you are interested?"

Annie glared at her again. "Miss Carrie, at my age, I ain't got no time to be *interested.*"

Chooli giggled. It was the first time any of them had heard her laugh.

Annie whirled around and looked at her. "You got somethin' to add to this, Chooli?"

Carrie knew that if any of the rest of them had spoken to Chooli that way, the young woman would probably have melted into a puddle.

Chooli merely smiled at Annie. "My grandmother taught me love has no age. Navajo women are very strong. When they find what they want, they go after it."

"Like you went after Franklin?" Annie guessed.

Chooli smiled demurely. "Franklin and I love." She lowered her head briefly before she looked up again with a glint in her eyes. "I was not *just* his housekeeper for long."

The room erupted in laughter. Carrie was delighted when she saw life leap into Chooli's eyes. She could only imagine how lonely it must have been for the Navajo woman with no other females in her life.

Annie turned back toward the kitchen. "I got me a lot of work to do."

"But you're going to put Miles out of his misery?" Carrie pressed. "My old friend is smitten with you. Please don't make him suffer any longer."

Annie paused but didn't turn around. "I might just take something to eat out to the barn," she replied before disappearing into the kitchen.

Carrie was satisfied. She sank down into the last of the three chairs pulled in front of the fire. "I'm so glad to find you here, Chooli. I would like very much to get to know you better. Do you mind if I ask you some questions?"

Chooli shook her head. "I don't mind."

The few minutes of talk and laughter seemed to have erased the shuttered look from her eyes. She was never anything but gracious, but Chooli had kept a very definite distance from everyone in the house. Carrie suspected the shyness was nothing more than a protective layer for a young lady who had left behind everyone she knew and everything she loved. "I know nothing about the Navajo. Will you tell me more about your people?"

The expression of love and loss that filled Chooli's eyes almost broke Carrie's heart. "I'm sorry I asked," she said apologetically. "I don't want to cause you more pain."

Chooli brushed away the tears from her eyes and forced a brave smile. "It's all right, Carrie. I miss my family, and

I miss my people." She snuggled Ajei closer to her. "I will tell you because I promised my mother I would never forget where I come from. I can tell all of you here are good people. What is happening to my people is wrong."

"I want to know," Carrie said softly.

"So do I," Susan added.

The three women sat silently for a few minutes, the only sound the crackling of wood in the fireplace.

The cozy warmth embraced them and seemed to infuse Chooli with courage. "My people are Navajo," she began, "but we are also called Diné. It means *'the people.'* Our homeland lies between the four sacred mountains."

"In New Mexico?" Carrie asked. "Hold on," she commanded. "I want to get something." She hurried over to the library bookshelves and reached for a large rolled document. Moments later she had it spread out on the floor in front of the fire. "Will you show me where you are from?"

Chooli stared at the map. "What is that?"

"It's a map," Carrie explained. "It shows what our country looks like." She pointed to the large free-standing sphere in the corner of the room. "That is a globe. It shows the whole world."

Chooli, still holding Ajei firmly to her shoulder, slipped down onto the floor to kneel in front of the map. She traced the drawings with her forefinger reverently.

Carrie knelt beside her and pointed. "This is Virginia. It is where you are now." She ran her finger west on the map. "This is New Mexico. Where the reservation is." She understood when Chooli's black eyes became even darker. "Where is your homeland?" she asked in order to distract her.

It worked. Chooli looked at where Carrie's finger was on the map, and then traced it farther west. "Here," she said. "This is where the four sacred mountains are."

Felicia had come in during their discussion. She watched as Chooli showed them where she was from. "I know about your people," she said. "At least a little," she added. "Your homeland is in parts of the Arizona, New Mexico and Utah Territories."

Carrie stared at the girl, but she was not surprised. She interpreted the look on Chooli's face. "Felicia knows more than all of us combined about what is going on in this country."

"And in the world," Felicia said smugly.

"That's true," Carrie answered with a laugh. "Why else do you think we keep you around?" she teased. "You keep us from being ignorant about current affairs."

Felicia turned to Chooli. "I know so little about the Navajo, though. Why did you have to leave your homeland?"

Chooli gazed at her. "You know where my homeland is, so you have read more. What do your papers tell you about my people?"

Felicia looked uncomfortable. "I don't know if it's true."

"It probably is not," Chooli replied, "but I believe I would like to know what is written. Then I tell you the real story. Truth is good."

Felicia nodded. "It was good when people learned the truth about how my mama and daddy died."

"They are dead?" Chooli's eyes were soft with sympathy.

"Moses and Rose aren't my real parents. They took me in as part of their family when my mama and daddy died. They were killed during a riot in Memphis two years ago," Felicia said, her voice quavering slightly. "Because they were black."

Chooli locked eyes with the girl. "And my people are being killed because they are Navajo. I'm very sorry for you."

"And I'm sorry for you," Felicia said. She reached out and grabbed Chooli's hand. "Why are they killing your people?"

"Because they want what we have." Chooli's eyes sparked with anger. "And because the white man believes he can take anything he wants." The anger faded into anguished grief. "My people had much. Many sheep and horses. We had homes. We grew our food for animals and people. Then the white man came. My people did not want to give away their land, so many fought the white man. Then they came and stole away many of our women and children to be slaves in their fancy houses."

"Slaves?" Felicia gasped. "My mama and daddy used to be slaves. So did Moses and Rose. And Annie. And all the workers you see on the plantation."

"I am sorry," Chooli said gently. "I know that pain. My two brothers and my sister were stolen during the march. I have not seen them since they were taken."

Carrie watched and listened as Felicia and Chooli bonded over similar experiences.

"What march are you talking about?" Felicia asked.

Chooli shook her head. "I'll tell soon. First, I want you to know about my homeland. There is no more beautiful place in the world. My heart will always be there. We fought off many who wanted to take it away from us. They finally won. They had many more guns and soldiers. We signed a treaty, but it did not protect us, because they wanted what we had."

"Kit Carson," Felicia said sadly.

"Kit Carson?" Chooli asked in a puzzled voice.

"I read about it," Felicia revealed. "They put things in the papers here about the Indian Wars out West. The army was having a very hard time keeping your people from fighting so they decided to send the Navajo to a reservation."

"Bosque Redondo," Chooli hissed.

"Yes. They had the place, but they couldn't get your people to go there. So they sent in a soldier who is well known for fighting Indians."

"Kit Carson?" Chooli gazed at Felicia intently.

"Yes," Felicia agreed. "While we were fighting the war here, Kit Carson was fighting a war against your people." She shook her head. "What I read sounded terrible. It was like what General Sherman did in Georgia during our war. He sent his troops through your homeland to do as much destruction as they could. He burned your crops, destroyed your villages and homes, and killed your livestock so your people would starve."

"It worked," Chooli said in a flat voice. "My people were starving. I watched people die during the cold winter because there was no food. Our homes had been burnt so we were hiding in the caves in the mountains above the valleys, but the old and the young were not strong enough to survive." Her voice faltered. "We finally had no choice. This Kit Carson told us we would be safe and have food at Bosque Redondo. We walked over three hundred miles to get there."

Carrie gasped. "*Three hundred miles?* You walked three hundred miles?"

"We walked," Chooli repeated. "Many died along the way. My brothers and sister were stolen during an attack. I remained safe only because I had gone to get water down in a gully. They did not see me. We kept walking because we believed we were going to a place we would be safe. We knew it would not be a better place, because no place is better than the homeland given to us by the Holy People, but we believed them when they said we would be safe."

"Like the Cherokee and the other tribes," Susan said, pain radiating in her voice.

Carrie looked at her. "Who?" She hated her ignorance, but what she had heard so far convinced her she would never be ignorant again. She understood that when people didn't care enough to know the truth, terrible things could happen.

"The Cherokee Indians lived mostly in North Carolina and Georgia," Susan explained. "There were already whites that wanted them gone, but then they discovered gold on their land in northern Georgia. The whites who were still supporting them turned against them because they wanted the gold. The government ultimately decided it was time for the Cherokee to be removed."

Carrie felt sick. "What happened?"

"President Andrew Jackson happened," Susan replied. "Cherokees saved his life during the Battle of Horseshoe Bend in 1814. Jackson repaid them by authorizing the Indian Removal Act sixteen years later. He believed the only way to deal with the Indians in our country was to get rid of them."

"They were here first!" Carrie cried.

"Yes," Susan agreed, "but that doesn't seem to have had much impact on our way of thinking. The Indians didn't open their arms to us when we wanted to take their land, so we decided the problem had to be dealt with." Sarcasm dripped from her words.

Carrie gazed at Susan. Until now, she hadn't realized her friend was so knowledgeable.

Susan read her thoughts. "I had a Cherokee woman when I was growing up who was like a grandmother to me," she explained. "Her name was Nina—it is Cherokee for '*strong.*' She told me the stories before she died. The

Georgia courts supported the Cherokee claim to the land, and affirmed Cherokee sovereignty. President Jackson arrogantly decided he was above the law and ordered the removal anyway." Her eyes sparkled with anger. "They were forced out of their home by soldiers, rounded up in the summer of 1838, and loaded onto boats that traveled several rivers into Indian Territory. Many were held in prison camps while they awaited their fate." She took a deep breath. "About four thousand died from hunger, exposure and disease. The ones who lived are on the reservation in Oklahoma."

Carrie thought about what she was hearing. "Did Nina keep from being taken?"

"No," Susan said bitterly. "She watched her husband and children die on the trail. Just before they reached the reservation, she managed to escape. Somehow she made her way back east to the only home she knew." She shook her head. "She would never tell me those stories—they were too painful.

"She almost died getting back to Georgia, and when she finally made it, she discovered her home had been destroyed. So she headed north, and eventually came to work for my family in Pennsylvania." Susan smiled slightly. "Nina had hated the flatlands of the Midwest. She said what was left of her soul would have died without the mountains. We didn't have mountains like she had in Georgia, but it was enough for her. Even though she could never return to her home, it was enough for her to know she had fought for her freedom, rather than simply going where she was told."

Chooli had been listening carefully. "I am not glad others suffered, but I am glad to know I do not stand alone."

Susan smiled sadly. "You are definitely not alone, Chooli. Many tribes have been forced off their land and onto reservations. They have been driven to the Oklahoma Indian Territory from Georgia, Florida, Mississippi, Louisiana, Wisconsin, Illinois, and many other places." She glanced at Carrie and answered the question in her eyes. "I don't think any of us has the freedom to be ignorant in our country. I love America, but there are many wrong things happening. I can't do anything about them if I don't know about it. My relationship with Nina certainly started my desire to understand, but everything I have learned only makes me hungry to know more."

"What is Bosque Redondo like, Chooli?" Felicia asked.

Chooli looked at Felicia sadly. "It is horrible. More than nine thousand of my people were forced there. We did not all come at once, though. There have been many walks. Many groups of my people were ripped from their homeland when they realized they could no longer survive. They were not told where they were going or why they were being taken from their homes. They did not know how long it would take to get where they were going. They just started walking."

"That's horrible!" Felicia cried.

"I had a friend on my march," Chooli continued. "She was with child. Her husband was killed during the raids by your Kit Carson. She tried so hard to keep up with everyone, but she could not. She was very tired and weak as she got closer to her time. Her parents begged the soldiers to stop long enough for her to have her baby." Her voice grew harsh. "The soldiers refused. They said that my friend would not survive anyway. Sooner or later she was going to die." Chooli's voice thickened as she continued. "Takoda begged her parents to keep going without her. Somehow she convinced them she would be all right..."

"What happened?" Felicia asked fearfully.

"Her family was not far down the trail when they heard the bang. The soldiers shot her," Chooli said flatly. "They said it was better than letting the animals kill her."

A heavy silence fell over the room. The crackling flames were now competing with the stiff wind blowing outside. No one noticed the first snowflakes of the season fall. The fire danced off the walls and mirrors as they all thought of the horror of that girl's death.

"I'm so sorry," Carrie murmured. She knew her words were not enough to soothe the pain in Chooli's eyes.

Chooli continued. "When we finally got to Bosque Redondo, we realized the soldiers had lied to us all along. Many of my people were already there—thousands of them. No one had homes; there was nothing to build with. We dug pits in the ground and laid limbs across them to try to keep some of the weather out. Many were sickened by the water from the nearby river. There was no wood for fires, so we would walk long distances to find some. I'm sure many of my people are still being killed by other Indians while they are out searching for wood."

Carrie knew by the look on Chooli's face that she was telling them only a tiny portion of the horror.

"My people are starving," Chooli said. "The soil there is no good for crops. There are insects that we never saw before, the river floods without warning, and hail comes from the sky. For three years, the crop has failed. Right before I left, the fields had been planted again, but no one has hope. They know it will fail."

"How will they live?" Carrie asked.

"Will they live at all is a better question," Chooli shot back, and then looked contrite. "I'm sor—"

Carrie held up a hand. "Please do not apologize. I can only imagine how terrible this has been for you."

Chooli looked around with a small smile. "I have so much now. My family..." Her voice trailed off as she shook her head. "I don't know if my grandparents and parents are still alive. My mother was so sick when I left. I didn't want to go, but Shima, my mother, told me I must. She told me Franklin is a good man and that I must leave to give my child a chance to live. I miss all of them every day." She gazed down into Ajei's face. "I hope someday my little girl will meet her family."

Carrie decided to keep Chooli talking so she wouldn't have to dwell on being apart from those she loved. "Were there many of your people that were sick?"

"Yes," Chooli answered immediately. "There are many diseases we have never seen. Many people are sick. We do not know how to help them. The medicine men do their best, but without the herbs for their chants, many are dying." Her eyes lit with pride. "My grandfather is a great medicine man. He has saved many lives. He does more rituals than anyone." She looked at Carrie. "Our rituals are very hard to learn. They take a long time."

"I would love to know more," Carrie said. She could tell, though, that Chooli was growing fatigued. She was still regaining her strength after her long months on the road. Carrie had more questions, but they would have to wait for another time.

Ajei stirred and began to whimper. Chooli looked down with a tender smile. "My Ajei is hungry."

"And you are tired," Carrie replied. "Thank you for all you have told us. I would like to learn more another time."

Chooli nodded. "I will tell you." She stood with great dignity and walked up the stairs to her room.

Chapter Eight

Rose looked up from the stack of papers she was sorting through. "Hello, husband."

Moses looked at the thick stack. "Dare I ask what you are doing?"

"Choosing our college," Rose replied happily.

Moses smiled at the look of joy on her face. Even amid his own inner turmoil, he was truly excited Rose was finally going to obtain what she had dreamed of for so long. "And have we made a decision?"

Rose cocked her head and regarded him for a long moment. "You really don't care where we go?"

Moses hesitated. He probably *should* care but that didn't change the reality that he didn't. His days were spent teaching Franklin all he needed to know to run the plantation. They were working closely with the men to prepare the plantation and fields for winter. The early November snow had been all the warning Moses needed that it would be a harsh winter. The snow had receded with the more moderate temperatures that followed, but he had the men laying in an even bigger supply of firewood. They had spent days hauling in downed trees from the woods and were now cutting and chopping them. He was sending everyone home early enough to make sure they had daylight to cut wood for their own families as well.

"Moses?" Rose pressed.

"I'm sorry," Moses responded. "I was thinking about what else I need to teach Franklin before we leave. No, I really don't care where we go. I know you won't choose a school where we both can't study what we need. Where it is doesn't seem important."

"Even if it is in the North?"

Moses thought of the brutal winter in Philadelphia. "How far north?"

"Ohio."

Moses thought through what he knew about colleges in the United States that accepted both black students and female students. "Oberlin?"

"That would be the one." Rose put down the sheaf of documents she was holding. "It will be colder even than Philadelphia."

Moses had no idea what the weather would be like in northern Ohio up near Lake Erie, but he suspected it would indeed be frigid. He and Miles had talked about the cold in Canada. Oberlin College wasn't quite that far north, but far enough to make a Virginia winter seem mild by comparison. "You believe it's the best place?"

Rose nodded her head firmly. "I do." She met his eyes. "I don't think I want to take our family into any city in the South right now. I don't want Felicia to have to live in fear again, and I don't want to have to worry about John and Hope while we are in class."

Moses heard beyond the calmness in her voice and suddenly had a much deeper understanding of how painful the last months had been for her. She lived with fear every day because the school she had built was always in danger of being attacked or burned to the ground. Wanting his wife to finally have a time when she felt safe completely overrode his nebulous feelings about going to college. She had made so many sacrifices—now it was his turn. His smile was warm and sincere. "Oberlin sounds perfect."

Rose sighed with relief. "You mean it? Don't you want to know more?"

"Yes, I mean it. And, yes, of course I want to know more. I'm assuming you have a plethora of things to tell me."

Rose raised a brow. "Plethora?"

"A plethora," Moses repeated smugly. "It means a large or excessive amount."

"I know what it means," Rose retorted. "I just didn't realize it was part of your vocabulary."

"What? You think you're the only one preparing to go to college?" Moses loved the look of surprised admiration on his wife's face. "If I'm going to be a lawyer, I have to speak as well as those fancy white ones or I won't be able to make a difference for our people."

Rose laughed as she rushed forward to engulf him in a hug. "You're really all right with this?" She stepped back. "Don't even pretend you haven't been struggling with our decision to leave. I know how much you love this plantation. I know you don't really care that much about being a lawyer, and I know you could be happy farming this land for the rest of your life."

Moses stared down at her. He should have known Rose would see through his attempts to hide his feelings. What surprised him was how long she had waited to confront him. That, more than anything, said how eager she was to leave. She was only challenging him now because she would feel guilty if she didn't. He felt his love for her expand. "What you haven't mentioned is that I love my wife more than I love farming and Cromwell Plantation. The plantation isn't going anywhere." He spoke the words he had been telling himself every day. "There may come a day when we return. If not, I will still have had the chance to do what I love, and I will still be half owner of the finest plantation in Virginia. That's not an insignificant thing. I predict there will be a *plethora* of men who will be quite jealous."

Rose laughed and grabbed him in another fierce embrace. "I love you, Moses Samuels."

"And I love you, Rose Samuels," Moses said huskily. He kissed his wife soundly and then stepped back, remembering what had brought him inside in the first place. "Did I see Carrie in the carriage? Where is she headed?"

"Richmond."

Moses was surprised. "What is in Richmond? I wasn't aware of any plans for her to go."

"A messenger came out today with a letter from Dr. Hobson. Carrie said that if it was important enough for Abby to send it out via a special courier, then she had to go immediately to satisfy her curiosity. Miles told her the weather should hold, so Jeb is driving her in."

Moses cast a now-practiced eye on the sky outside their window. "She'll get there," he predicted. "But she might have trouble getting home."

"I don't think she'll mind," Rose said. "She took enough clothes for a week. Now that she is so close to going back to school, I think she is eager for some time with Thomas and Abby. And with Jeremy and Marietta," she added.

*****

Carrie was torn between curiosity about the letter that had her moving down the road toward Richmond, and sheer pleasure at the reality she was going. Rose had rightly guessed that watching the calendar turn to December had made Carrie realize just how soon she would be heading for Philadelphia. She was ready to finish school, but she was not eager to leave the plantation...and she was not eager to be so far away from those she loved. She sobered as she reflected on the months since Robert's death. She knew she would not have gotten through the trauma without all the people who had surrounded her, refusing to let her give in to her grief and anger. They had loved her despite how horribly she had treated them.

She pushed aside her memories and thought about the letter from Dr. Hobson. It had been very brief, but intriguing. He had requested she come to Richmond at her convenience to discuss her future in relation to some communication he had received from Dr. Strikener. She was quite certain Hobson had been deliberately vague, knowing her curiosity would bring her quickly. She smiled in admiration at how correct he had been. Her smile faded as another thought crossed her mind. "Jeb, are you quite sure everyone will be safe on the plantation?"

"You worried about Miss Susan being the only white folk there while you gone, Miss Carrie?" he asked good-naturedly.

"Oh, nonsense!" Carrie retorted. "I'm more concerned that the vigilantes will attack the plantation while I'm away. I've been practicing and have become quite a good shot."

"I heard that," Jeb said approvingly. "I reckon we don't ever know when they might come after us again, but we done learned our lesson good back in the spring. There is not a night goes by that there aren't men guarding the plantation house and the barn. The white men keep an eye on the school. It ain't full force, but it wouldn't take long to scare up all the men we needed. That's why we were able to stop them so easy at the Harvest Festival.

There be plenty of us to take care of things," he said confidently.

Carrie frowned. "That makes for very long and cold nights," she mused.

"Yep," Jeb agreed. "But we ain't just protecting your home, Miss Carrie. We be protecting our own homes and the plantation. We ain't gonna let nobody come in here and try to destroy what all of us are working to build. Why, I made me enough money last harvest to add on to my home and buy a plow for my fields," he said proudly. "A few years back I couldn't have even dreamed of being able to do such a thing. My kids and wife are all in school, and my wife is teaching me how to read at night. I ain't gonna let no ignorant vigilante mess that up for me and my family." He paused. "I got one of the men who lives on the plantation keeping an eye on my family while I be gone, and my Bessie be a real good shot. Just like you," he said.

Carrie hated that she knew how necessary it was for everyone on the plantation to assume the worst would happen. "I wonder if it will ever change?" She was talking to herself but realized she had spoken out loud when Jeb answered.

"I reckon it get better someday, Miss Carrie, but it ain't gonna happen soon."

"How would you define soon, Jeb?"

Jeb kept his eyes on the road as he considered her question. "Ain't gonna be for some years," he said finally. "Things be better around here 'cause Miss Rose opened up her school to all them white folks, but most of the South ain't like that at all. Moses is right that there be an awful lot of hate in people. That kind of hate don't go away easy."

Carrie didn't bother to argue with him. He was right. Instead of dwelling on it, she focused on the country they were passing through. There were still some brown leaves hanging on the massive oak trees, but strong storms the past two weeks had denuded most of the branches. "Is this winter going to be as cold and snowy as I think?"

"Reckon so," Jeb agreed. "All the signs be there."

Carrie thought of all Miles and her father had taught her through the years. "The geese and the ducks have already migrated farther south."

"Yep. And I saw me a Snowy owl just last night. They don't usually show up until later in the year."

"Moses told me the corn husks are thicker than normal this year."

"They are," Jeb replied. "My wife done told me a couple months back when she was shucking corn that it was gonna be a real hard winter. Me and my boy chopped up a lot of wood. But the real sign was the caterpillar my daughter done brought me. My daddy taught me about that when I was a boy. The woollybear caterpillar gets real fat and fuzzy when there is gonna be a snowy winter, and it gets a narrow orange band right around the middle."

Carrie sighed. He wasn't telling her anything she didn't know. She knew their winter was going to be extra hard. At least she could be grateful that no one she loved would be fighting battles in the snow. She shuddered as she thought of the thousands of hands and feet that had been amputated from frostbite during the long siege to take Richmond the last winter of the war. She knew the image would never disappear from her mind.

*****

Carrie fidgeted uneasily in the carriage seat. "Can we go any faster?"

Jeb looked back with a laugh. "Only if you know how to pick this here thing up and make it fly. There be an awful lot of folks out today.

Carrie scowled as she eyed the almost total gridlock. "These people ought to be at home."

"They probably be thinking the same thing about you, Miss Carrie."

Carrie shifted impatiently and sighed. "I know you're right. It always takes time to get used to so many people when I come off the plantation."

"I bet it ain't as bad as Philadelphia," Jeb observed.

Carrie eyed the crowds. "I don't know. There are so many people coming into Richmond now that the war is over. It doesn't look much better than Philadelphia. I don't know where they are putting everyone."

"I'd say it's a might crowded," Jeb agreed.

Carrie knew Richmond was also a very tense city. She had talked late into the night with her father, Abby,

Jeremy and Marietta the night before. It was coming back from the long years of war, but there were still empty lots testifying to the burned buildings that had been cleared away, and there were still signs of wear and poverty everywhere she looked. The city air was thick with refinery smoke. The people she passed had looks of tired determination on their faces. It would be a long time before Richmond resembled the beloved city of her youth, but at least the guns had stopped booming, and people felt hope.

"It finally be moving," Jeb announced.

Carrie breathed a sigh of relief as the carriage rolled forward. It took only a few minutes to reach Dr. Hobson's office once the traffic started moving. The sun shone weakly through a layer of high clouds as they pulled in front of the stately brick house that had been converted into the doctor's homeopathic clinic.

Jeb had just pulled the carriage to a stop when Dr. Hobson appeared on the porch and started down the walk. Carrie smiled when she saw the man who was just as tall and vibrant as she remembered him from the year before. There seemed to be a little more gray in his beard, but his thick hair was still a lush brown, and his eyes still shone with brilliant life.

"Carrie Borden!"

Carrie stepped from the carriage and reached out to clasp his extended hands. "Dr. Hobson. It is so wonderful to see you again." Dr. Hobson held her hands tightly and gazed into her face. Carrie knew he was looking for the grief that had consumed her. She held his eyes, content to let him see whatever he saw. She would never be the same person she had been before Robert's murder, but she was ready to move on with her life.

"And it is wonderful to see you," Dr. Hobson murmured. He glanced at Jeb. "Please pull the carriage around back. There is hot coffee and biscuits in the kitchen for you."

"Yes, sir," Jeb answered. "Thank you."

Dr. Hobson nodded but was already leading Carrie up the brick walkway to his office. "I didn't expect you so quickly."

"And I didn't expect such a vague letter," Carrie retorted. "You knew my curiosity would get me here right away."

"I merely hoped," Dr. Hobson said mildly, his eyes twinkling with fun.

Carrie laughed as she stepped into his house and moved into the office. "I am not known for being a patient woman. Now that I am here, I expect some answers."

"You haven't changed." Dr. Hobson laughed, but then sobered immediately. "Excuse me for saying that. I know you have changed greatly since I last saw you. I am so sorry for your loss."

Carrie had no desire to talk about Robert. "Thank you. May I ask about the communication you received from Dr. Strikener?"

An elderly lady with silver hair and a plump face appeared at the door. "Your tea is ready, Doctor."

Dr. Hobson looked up with a warm smile. "Thank you, Victoria. I would like to introduce you to Mrs. Carrie Borden."

Victoria smiled brightly. "Hello, Mrs. Borden. How would you like your tea?"

"Just a little cream, thank you, Victoria," Carrie answered. Her impatience was growing. She would appreciate the hot tea, but she wanted so much to know why she was in Richmond.

Dr. Hobson waved her toward one of the chairs next to the crackling fire. He waited until she sat down and then chose the one across from her. "I will not keep you in suspense. I understand you are ready to continue your pursuit of becoming a doctor."

"That's right." Carrie didn't want to discuss the long months she had stayed mired in the belief she had been responsible for both Robert and Bridget's deaths – convinced she would never be a doctor.

"Abby told me you saved her life in Kansas. Her life, and the lives of three children."

"Actually, it was the medicines she brought along from you that saved their lives," Carrie corrected, once again feeling the gratitude that had swept through her when she realized she had what she needed to help the critically ill patients. "Thank you."

"You knew what to do with them," Dr. Hobson responded.

When he took a deep breath, Carrie hoped he was ready to discuss the real reason she was here. The serious look on his face gave her a quick flash of alarm. Had she done something wrong? Was she to be refused entry to school? Was her career over before it could even be resumed? There had been nothing in the letter to give her that feeling, but then there had been nothing to give her an indication of *anything*. All she could do was wait to hear whatever he had to say. She clasped her hands together and watched him closely.

"I have been communicating with Dr. Strikener," Dr. Hobson began.

Carrie remained quiet. Her mentor at the College of Homeopathy in Philadelphia had been nothing but supportive and encouraging, but she may have pushed him past his tolerance with her long silence.

"He and I agree you do not need more schooling at the college."

Carrie froze for several long moments. "I'm afraid I don't understand," she finally managed. "Am I not going to be allowed to return to Philadelphia?"

"Oh, you will be allowed, but I don't think it will be your best course of action."

Carrie shook her head. "Excuse me if I'm confused."

"I'm not doing a good job with this. I'm afraid I have no experience with telling a medical student that they are so far advanced in experience that we believe we have nothing more to teach you." Dr. Hobson paused. "You've read every book that I sent you home with last year, haven't you?"

Carrie nodded. Most had been read before Robert's death. The rest she had devoured upon her return from Kansas, putting much of it to use in her clinic.

"I suspected as much. Carrie, Dr. Strikener and I would like to suggest a different path for you to obtain your medical license."

"I won't have to return to Philadelphia?" Carrie asked, her head spinning with the direction the conversation was taking.

"Would that make you happy?"

Carrie cocked her head. "That depends. You might want me to go somewhere worse."

Dr. Hobson laughed. "What if it were *your* choice what you did?" He held up a hand. "Both Dr. Strikener and I believe you need one final experience that will test your medical abilities before we grant your license, but we don't believe sitting in classes will benefit you."

Carrie stared at him. "Is this normal?"

"Hardly. But then you aren't exactly normal, Mrs. Carrie Borden. I have seldom met anyone, of any gender, who has such an immediate grasp of medical issues, or who has such a hunger to help their patients." He leaned back in his chair. "You are here so we can decide what internship you would like to do during the next eight months. At the end of the internship, if we believe you have accomplished what we believe you are capable of, we will grant your medical license from the Homeopathic Medical College."

Carrie shook her head and gazed into the flames. "I was not expecting anything like this," she murmured.

"Do you have any ideas of what you would like to do? You are more than welcome to do your internship here at my office, but you are free to make another choice."

Carrie held her breath as a wild idea sprang into her mind. Her thoughts raced as she considered what she was about to suggest. There were far more questions than answers, and she was not at all certain how she felt about her own idea, but once it had sprung into her thoughts it refused to go away.

"You have something in mind," Dr. Hobson observed. "What is it?"

Carrie continued to stare into the flames, uncertain of how to communicate what she was thinking. It was ludicrous, and yet...

"Please, tell me. It may not be as crazy as your expression tells me you believe it is."

Carrie finally looked at the doctor. "Have you ever heard of Bosque Redondo?" His blank look answered her question. "It is a Navajo Indian Reservation in New Mexico. Right now there are more than eight thousand Indians there who have been torn from their homeland." Her voice grew passionate as she thought about all she had learned from Chooli in the past weeks. "People are dying from diseases they have no treatment for because they no longer have access to the herbs of their homeland that they have always used." She paused as she searched for what to say next.

Dr. Hobson's eyes revealed his confusion.

"I want to go there," Carrie blurted out. "I want to take a few medical students with me, and I want to go there to help those people. I want to learn the herbs and plants in the Southwest that heal, and I want to take enough of our homeopathic medicines to help the Navajo that are dying."

It was Dr. Hobson's turn to stare. "In New Mexico?"

"Yes," Carrie said. Now that she had actually put the idea into words, it had taken on even greater appeal.

"How will you get there?" Dr. Hobson asked faintly, his expression saying he had no idea how to respond.

Carrie smiled, certain she would find a way. "I don't know, but those people need help. If I'm being given a choice of what I want to do, that is my choice."

"Do you realize how far it is to New Mexico?"

Carrie nodded, suddenly realizing her talks with Chooli and Franklin had revealed exactly how she would get there. "We will take the train into Independence, Missouri," she answered. "From there, it will take close to three months of travel to reach the reservation in New Mexico." Her mind spun as she talked. "I can write a book that documents all I learn. It will be of great use to anyone who comes after me. The students with me will learn quite a lot, and they will have the satisfaction of saving lives."

Dr. Hobson continued to stare at her, obviously at a loss for words. "You are certainly not normal, Mrs. Carrie Borden."

Carrie laughed cheerfully, feeling suddenly that she was about to embark on a grand adventure. She wouldn't have to return to the confines of Philadelphia, but she would also have a chance to move forward without constant remembrances of all she had lost when Robert died. She had no idea of what would be waiting for her when she returned, but none of that seemed important right now.

"We have a young lady living on the plantation who is Navajo, Dr. Hobson. Chooli is quite remarkable. Her grandfather is a revered medicine man in the Navajo tribe. I have been teaching her the herbs and medicines I use, and she is teaching me about the native medicines. I'm sure she would love to join us, but her daughter is only six weeks old." She chose to not mention that Chooli had escaped the reservation. "Chooli can teach me even more of what I need to know before I get there, and I know communication from her will open doors of trust with her people." Every word she spoke told Carrie this was the right thing to do, but she hesitated. "Is this not the type of internship you had in mind?" she asked. "Might it not meet the requirements you have set?"

Dr. Hobson laughed and shook his head. "It is far larger than anything Dr. Strikener and I could have possibly imagined." His face grew more serious. "This is a large endeavor. I'm sure your father will never agree to this unless he is assured of your safety, but I will only approve it if I can be assured of the other students' safety, as well. And, of course, you have to convince someone that this is a good idea."

Carrie nodded. "I'm certain I can." Her mind whirled. She had no idea how to accomplish what she was proposing, but there must be a way. "I will do some research and then I'll be back to talk to you."

Dr. Hobson reached for his tea and took a long swallow. "I am confident you will."

Carrie laughed brightly. "You have given me such a gift, Dr. Hobson. I will find the answers, and I will not disappoint you."

Dr. Hobson eyed her over his cup. "Do you know anything about the Santa Fe Trail? I know there is no railroad out there."

"No railroad," Carrie agreed. She thought about what Franklin had told her. "We would travel by wagon train for twelve hundred miles. It can normally be done in about sixty days, but the reality of winter might make it take a little longer."

"Winter?" The doctor put down his cup carefully.

"You said my internship will be for eight months. I imagine it will take until early February to have everything in place that we will need." Her mind worked as she talked. "I will go to Philadelphia to select the students who will join me."

"Select? Do you suppose you will have more that will want to go than you will have room for?" Dr. Hobson asked skeptically.

Carrie was certain of that very thing. "Why, yes, of course. This is a wonderful opportunity to do things most medical students could never dream of. Besides," she added with a grin, "who doesn't want to leave Philadelphia in the wintertime?"

"To travel the Santa Fe Trail in a covered wagon? I suspect there will be many that prefer the snow-clogged streets of Philadelphia."

Carrie waved her hand. "I only need a few. If they are trained correctly, we will be able to help with almost all the diseases killing the Navajo." She sobered instantly. She was treating this as a grand lark, but the truth was that many lives were at stake. She leaned forward. "I have to try, Dr. Hobson. The Navajo are a proud and wonderful people. What is being done to them is wrong. I can't stand by and do nothing if I have an opportunity to help them." She sat back. "I will return to my father's house and find out just what it will take to turn this wild idea into reality. Then I will come back to talk to you. You can tell me then if my plans meet your approval." Carrie stood and held out her hand, eager to begin right away.

Dr. Hobson rose and clasped her hand firmly. "You do that, Carrie. I will be most eager to hear what you discover."

Chapter Nine

Rose looked up from her papers when she heard a noise at the door. Felicia was staring at her intently, but had not said a word. Rose smiled and set aside the papers on Oberlin. "Hello, Felicia. Do you need something?" Her daughter had come so far in the two years since her parents' brutal murders, but Felicia seldom sought her out.

"I want to do a Kinaalda."

Rose blinked. "A what?"

Felicia smiled slightly before moving into the room. Evidently blurting out her intention for being here had freed her enough to pursue it. "I want to do a Kinaalda," she repeated.

"I heard that part," Rose said. "I don't know what it is, but I'm listening."

"Chooli didn't tell you about it?"

"Evidently not, but I'm intrigued. What is a Kinaalda?"

"It's the Navajo rite of passage for women," Felicia explained. "Girls do it when they turn thirteen. I turn thirteen next month. I want to do a Kinaalda."

Rose knew from the anxious look in Felicia's eyes, and the abrupt sentences she was speaking with, just how much this meant to her daughter. "That seems like a reasonable request," she said.

Felicia stared at her. "It does?"

Rose nodded, memories flooding her mind. "My mama used to talk about the rite of passage she did when she was a girl in Africa. There weren't many things she told me about her life there, but that one was important to her."

"Did you do a rite of passage, too?" Felicia asked eagerly.

Rose shook her head. "I was still a slave. We weren't allowed to do things like that. I'm sure it was mostly because it would have taken us away from the work we were meant to do, but it was also because the Cromwells believed we needed to be separated from anything that would remind us of our old life and culture."

"Thomas did that?" Felicia asked in an appalled voice. "*Our* Thomas?"

"Thomas has changed quite a bit," Rose reminded her. "He used to do things the way his daddy did them, and the way his granddaddy did them. It took Carrie, and a long war, to help him change the way he thought." She took Felicia's hand. "He is the man you know him to be now. There are many people who have very wrong beliefs until they meet someone who puts a face to those wrong beliefs."

"Like you."

"Learning I was his half-sister certainly played a part in it," Rose agreed, "but Carrie was the biggest reason he changed. It took him a long time to understand her love for black people. It took him a longer time to understand the need for equality for all people, but he finally did. It took a lot of courage for him to do that. Don't feel badly that he used to believe differently. All of us have wrong beliefs about *something* that we need to change. Only people who are truly courageous find the way to do that."

"Oh, I know Thomas is a great man," Felicia answered. "I had to change, too," she said earnestly.

Rose gazed at the girl. "How did you have to change?"

"I hated everyone that was white when my mama and daddy were killed. The only thing I knew about white people was that they made my parents be slaves, and then they killed them." Her eyes burned with the memory. "I hated them all..." Felicia's voice faded away, but she looked up with a smile. "Until I came here. Carrie and Robert were different. And then I met Thomas and Abby. I could tell they were good people, so I had to change how I thought about white people." She paused thoughtfully. "I suppose I've learned there are good and bad people everywhere. There are good and bad people of all colors. None of what is on the outside matters at all—it's only what is on the inside." She closed her eyes for a moment. "And then you made me change."

"And how did I do that?" Rose asked, amazed at the depth of this little girl.

"I had to change when you let white students come to our school. At first I hated it. I never said anything because I knew how much it meant to you, but there were some of them that were real mean to me."

"I'm sorry for that," Rose said softly. She had been completely aware, but had known she had to let Felicia handle it herself.

"Oh, it's okay," Felicia said intently. "I thought *they* were as stupid as they thought *I* was. I just decided to prove I was smarter than any white student there." She smiled. "I still think I'm smarter than anyone there, but I learned there are some very smart white students, too. Some of the ones who were real mean to me are now friends. Anyway," she added, "I had to change, so I understand people needing to change. I also realized I can't change other people, but I can change me."

Rose pulled her into a warm embrace. "You are extraordinary," she whispered. "I love you."

Felicia leaned back but didn't break the embrace. "I love you too, Mama. Does that mean I get to do the Kinaalda?"

Rose laughed. "Tell me about it."

"It's the Navajo rite of passage for girls who are thirteen. It's what they do to become a woman," Felicia began. "Chooli told me all about it."

"What do they do?" Rose was not sure this was the best way for Felicia to enter womanhood, but she was certainly curious to know more. Ultimately, it would be her daughter's choice.

"Kinaalda lasts for four days. During that time, the girl learns how important the Earth is to her life. Chooli says her people have many rituals to maintain *hozho. Hozho* is everything that is good and happy and beautiful." Her eyes shone. "The rituals must be done correctly to be effective," Felicia said seriously. "Chooli's grandfather is a great medicine man so she knows all about it."

Rose listened intently, eager to learn all she could.

"The girl doing Kinaalda learns that the universe must be kept in perfect order. I learn that I have to take care of the Earth, and that all the animals and plants must be valued. The Earth is the mother of all life!" Felicia grew more serious. "There are a lot of regulations and taboos. I can only eat certain things; I can't touch my own skin, or comb and wash my hair; and I can't dress or undress myself. Everyone will listen to what I say to make sure I don't say anything negative because that is not allowed."

Rose hoped the look on her face was not revealing the thoughts racing through her mind.

"I will have to grind corn, make a special cake called *alkaan*, and I will have to do a lot of racing."

"Racing?" Rose asked. "As in running?" It took all she had to get Felicia out of the library, where she spent her days buried in books, journals and newspapers. Rose couldn't pull up an image of the girl running around the plantation.

"I can do it for four days," Felicia said impatiently. "Someone will have to mold my body..."

"Mold your body?" Rose interrupted. "What does that mean?"

Felicia hesitated as she thought about the question, and then finally shrugged. "I don't know, but Chooli said it is important. I'm sure she will explain it more thoroughly. Anyway, someone also has to teach me the proper behavior for being a woman. That person is the one who washes my hair and dresses me. They will also paint my body with white clay and put many shells on me." She paused to take a breath. "And there are more things."

"I see," Rose murmured, though in truth she didn't see at all. "Did Chooli tell you that you should do a Kinaalda?"

"No," Felicia admitted. "She told me it was only for Navajo women."

Rose bit back her sigh of relief. "Yet you want to do one?"

Felicia lifted her hands in a helpless gesture. "I want to do *something*. The Kinaalda is the only rite of passage I know about." She walked over to stare out the window, and then swung back around. "I don't know why I think it is so important, but I do. Life is getting ready to change a whole lot again when we leave here. Since I am going to be a woman, I want to do something that will make me ready for it."

Rose nodded. "I understand. How about we come up with a rite of passage just for you?" She smiled at her daughter. "I was sad when I didn't get to have my own rite of passage. My mama told me it was all right, but I know she was sad, too. She did, however, make a very special dinner for me when I started my menstrual cycle. She said it was important to celebrate moving from one stage of life to another. It meant a lot to me."

"Why?" Felicia pressed.

Rose considered the question. "I suppose because it made me feel like my life was meant to be more than simply moving from day to day as a slave. I was a woman. I was thirteen, but I started thinking about how I could do things with my life after that. I felt like I was part of something bigger than myself."

Felica nodded. "I feel the same way! It would mean a lot to me, Mama, if we could do something." She paused. "There is something else..." Her voice trailed off uncertainly.

"You can ask or tell me anything," Rose said quietly.

"I know we're going to Oberlin soon, but I want to do whatever we are going to do before then because there are women here I want to be a part of it."

"Who?"

"Carrie, of course, but I also want Abby, and Grandma Annie, and Polly. I want Janie and Marietta to be here, and I also want Chooli here. And Susan." Felicia hesitated. "I love Daddy and Thomas, but I don't want them to be there. It should only be women."

"I agree," Rose replied, delighted when she saw Felicia's eyes ignite with joy. She thought for several moments and then reached out to touch the girl's cheek. "Will you trust me to create the rite of passage for you?"

"Yes," Felicia said immediately, "but when will it be?"

"I propose New Year's Day. We will be leaving several days later, but all of us should still be here."

"New Year's Day," Felicia repeated. Then she grinned. "That is perfect!"

*****

Moses shrugged off his thick coat, sank down in the wingback chair pulled next to the roaring fire, and reached gratefully for the steaming mug of coffee Rose held out to him. "Thank you," he murmured, content to merely hold the cup and let it warm his huge hands.

"I knew you would be freezing," Rose replied. "Jeb had enough blankets in the carriage to keep me warm on the ride home, but the woodstove could barely heat the school today. Every student had to keep their coat on."

"I knew this winter was going to be brutal," Moses said as he took his first sip and closed his eyes in ecstasy. "As long as I can come home at night, I'll make it through."

"Everyone has enough firewood?"

Moses nodded, but kept his eyes closed as he took another drink. "They do. All the signs were there, so we made sure there was enough stockpiled. Everyone will be warm, and everyone has enough food."

"Which, in today's America, is more than a lot of people can say," Rose said sadly.

Moses opened his eyes, obviously hearing the pain in her voice. "The white families?"

Rose sighed heavily. "Many are struggling. I can tell some of my students are only warm when they are in school. There is so much talk about what the freed slaves are going through, but as far as I can tell, most of the whites are hurting just as badly. The world we live in here on the plantation is not the world most people live in. I talk to the wives. Their husbands feel they have been completely forgotten now that the war is over. They don't have jobs, many of them are disabled..."

"It's going to mean even more trouble," Moses said grimly.

Rose nodded. "There is so much anger and hopelessness. It has to have an outlet." She stared into the fire for a long moment and then swung around to stare at her husband. "Are we making a mistake? Are all these people going to be all right if we leave? Can Franklin really run the plantation the way you would? Do I have a right to leave the school? They tell me they are sending a new teacher down, but what if my students don't trust her? What if they refuse to come to school?"

"That's a lot of questions." Moses needed to give himself time to think through Rose's outburst. He couldn't deny her questions had given him a spark of hope that they might stay on Cromwell, but his heart told him it wasn't the solution.

"I know you don't want to go!" Rose cried. She stood abruptly and began to pace. "What if our people need us *here* more than they need us to go to school?"

"Sounds to me like you are borrowing trouble, Rose."

Rose whirled around to glare at him. "Don't quote my mama to me, Moses Samuels. I'm not borrowing trouble. I'm acknowledging the reality of the situation. It doesn't make any sense to go where we can't do anything about what is going on here. So many people count on us." Her voice was frantic.

Moses took a deep breath. It had been noble of him to make it about wanting Rose to be happy, but it was only because he had refused to truly understand the bigger picture. "That is exactly why we *must* go," Moses said firmly. He nodded his head toward the chair. "Sit back down, please."

Rose sat, but the wild look in her eyes did not abate.

Moses considered his words carefully. "Things are happening in America faster than most people can keep up with." He reached into his pocket and pulled out the letter he'd stood on the porch to read. He'd wanted to read it, and have time to ponder it, before he came in the house. Rose eyed the letter, but waited for him to speak. "It is certain Congress will try to impeach President Johnson this spring. He has lost all political sway in the country, and he has burned too many bridges with people."

Rose shrugged, obviously not impressed that this could have anything to do with their situation.

Moses continued to pick his words. "The amendment to the Kansas constitution that Abby and Carrie fought so hard to get passed, failed. Women all over the country are disheartened."

"If you're trying to make me feel better, you are failing."

"I'm not trying to make you feel better," Moses replied as he picked up the letter. "The results of the constitutional conventions are coming in. Virginia's just began on December third, but there are enough results from other states to give us a clear indication of what is happening." He watched Rose carefully, aware of the moment he finally had her complete attention. "All the constitutions are guaranteeing our civil and political rights."

"Go ahead and tell me the 'but,'" Rose muttered. "I know one is coming."

"There is," Moses agreed. "The conventions are clear about a commitment to equal rights and a new South, but that seems to be about all they can agree on. They are united on general principles, but not on how to implement them." He held up the letter. "Thomas just sent this."

"Is Carrie coming home soon?" Rose demanded.

Moses knew how much his wife missed her best friend. "According to this letter, she should be home tomorrow."

"Good," Rose said shortly. She took a deep breath. "Please continue."

Moses took it as a good sign, but he didn't believe what he was going to tell her would make her feel better. He regretted that he didn't have better news, but she had to know so she could understand why they must go to school. "It seems the constitutions agreed on public education for everyone, but they can't agree on whether the schools should be racially segregated. They agree on civil and political rights for blacks, but they can't agree on *social* equality." Rose scowled but remained silent. "They want democracy to expand, but they don't want to allow black domination of local or state governments."

"I'm sure," Rose retorted.

"There are other more minor positions, but the overall outcome seems to be that they can't agree whether they should try to forge a political majority by striving to serve the interests of blacks and poor whites, or whether their prime concern should be attracting respectable whites and outside capital to rebuild the South."

"And they can't manage to do both?" Rose snapped. "It sounds to me like more selfish men concerned with only their personal agendas."

Moses could not have agreed with her more. "Which is exactly why we have to go to school." He could tell by the look on her face that he had not said enough to persuade her. "North Carolina is a good example."

Rose raised a brow. "North Carolina?"

"It seems there aren't many people—either black *or* white—who believe integrated education can work, but the black delegates are quite adamant that no constitution should *require* racial segregation. There is a man down in North Carolina by the name of James Hood."

"I know of him," Rose replied. "He's from Delaware so he was never a slave, and he has been a pastor in North Carolina for four years. He has formed several churches, but he has also worked hard to make sure blacks receive an education."

"That's him," Moses confirmed. "He says he favors separate education because all white teachers have been taught to view black children as naturally inferior," he said disdainfully. "He wouldn't let them write segregated education into the constitution, though. He said that if it became law, the white children would all have good schools, but the black children would have none. He believes the threat of integration will force states to provide blacks with good schools of their own."

Rose nodded. "That makes sense."

"Which is why you have to go to school," Moses said persistently. "If black students are to have good schools, they have to have good teachers who believe they are not naturally inferior. Public education is going to be free, and at some point all the states will make it mandatory. If there aren't enough black educators, they will put white teachers in our schools who believe black children can't learn."

Rose was listening intently now. "And what about you?"

"You're right that I haven't wanted to leave," Moses admitted. He picked up the letter again. This time he read out loud.

> *There may never be a time in history when it is more important for you and Rose to be a voice for your people. Blacks have gained the right to vote, but it will take educated men and women who know how to speak and write to turn the tide. Your people are intelligent—now they must be given true opportunity to become educated. It is going to take great courage to choose a route that ensures enmity among the majority, but society changes only when there are those who will step up to do so.*

Moses put the letter back down. "If my decision was just about me, I would choose to stay here on the plantation, but it's not. One minute I am sure I want to go. The next minute I just want to live my life and plant tobacco. I don't particularly want to live in a time where I must be courageous and go against people that will hate me," he said, "but I don't know that anyone who has stood up to change things for our people wanted that. They simply made a choice to do what they believed was the right thing." He turned away from the fire and gazed at Rose. "I believe Franklin is ready to run the plantation, but the people here are being called to fight their own battles. They know how to protect themselves and this land. If the students in your school truly want to learn, they will learn no matter how bad their teacher is. You've taught the parents, too, so they will be able to help their children."

"And when we are done in four years?" Rose asked, her eyes locked on his.

Moses managed to laugh lightly. "Wife, I can barely manage to imagine life in one month. I have no idea what four years will bring." He placed a hand on her cheek. "The only thing I am certain of is that we will face the future together. For now, that is enough for me."

"I learned something about Oberlin College today," Rose said by way of an answer. "The first black woman to receive a bachelor's degree in America graduated from Oberlin. Her name is Mary Jane Patterson. Right now she is teaching in Philadelphia at the Institute for Colored Youths."

Moses listened, knowing there was more his wife wanted to say.

"I met her," Rose said softly. "My teacher had her come to the Quaker School when I was there, before I went to the contraband camp to teach. I remember thinking I wanted to be just like her. She never said where she went to school, but I knew it must be a special place."

"And now we will be there," Moses replied. "Like it or not, we are alive in a time when we have the unique privilege of being a voice for our people."

Rose grasped his hand. "Oberlin College, here we come."

*****

"Would you like to repeat that?" Rose shook her head in stunned disbelief.

Carrie smiled patiently. "I am not going back to school in Philadelphia. I am taking a team of medical students to

Bosque Redondo. When I return home, if I've done well, I will receive my medical degree."

"When?"

Carrie was confused. "When will I receive my medical degree?"

"When are you *leaving*?" Rose shook her head again. "I'm having a hard time comprehending this, Carrie. You're going to New Mexico? On the Santa Fe Trail?"

"Evidently," Carrie replied with a laugh. "I'm still trying to comprehend it myself."

Rose eyed her for a long moment, and then raised her voice. "Chooli, will you come in here, please?"

Carrie was delighted. "Chooli is here? I thought she would be down at her cabin."

"She came up for her cooking class with Annie."

Carrie blinked. "Her cooking class?"

Rose laughed. "Chooli and Annie have become good friends. Annie is teaching her how to make good southern food so Franklin will be happy." She scowled. "You changed the subject. When are you leaving?"

Carrie hesitated. She was certain Rose would not be any more impressed than her father and Abby had been with her decision.

Chooli breezed into the room. "Carrie! You're home. It's good to see you."

Carrie had only been gone a week, but the young Navajo woman seemed to be blooming. Every day the light seemed to gleam more brightly in her eyes. The private tutoring she was receiving from Rose and Felicia had given her a grasp of English far faster than Carrie could have imagined. "It's good to see you, too, Chooli." She could hardly wait to tell her the news.

"Answer the question, Carrie," Rose pressed, a tinge of frustration in her words.

"February first," Carrie said reluctantly.

"What is February first?" Chooli asked, obviously feeling the tension between the two friends as she looked back and forth between them.

Carrie saw Rose open her mouth but wasn't going to allow her to share the news. "I'm going to Bosque Redondo, Chooli!"

Chooli stared at her and then sank down into the chair behind her. "Bosque Redondo? Why?"

Carrie explained what had transpired in Richmond. "I'm going to Philadelphia the first week of January to select students who will join me. I'm writing a letter to many of them this week so that we will be ready to leave by February first. We will take the train out to Independence, Missouri, and then go on from there."

Chooli was still staring at her with an open mouth. "You would do such a big thing for my people?" She shook her head with disbelief, but a smile was beginning to tug at her mouth. "You will take letters to my family?"

"Of course," Carrie said. "I'm counting on you to write letters that will encourage your people to trust me so that I can help them most effectively."

"You're taking medicines to make their sickness go away?"

"I am," Carrie assured her. "We are taking a large number of homeopathic remedies, but you and Polly and I will be working hard until then to also make as many herbal remedies as we can. I'm eager to find the plants in the Southwest that have healing properties, too." She explained about the book that was to be one of the results of the trip.

Rose looked only slightly mollified by Chooli's grateful response. "But February?" She turned to Chooli. "What is the Santa Fe Trail like in February?" she demanded.

Chooli looked uneasy, obviously torn between telling the truth and not wanting to discourage Carrie from going to help her people. "You will be with others?"

"Yes," Carrie assured her, glad to be able to share this part of the plan with Rose. "Actually, we will be with a contingent of soldiers who are going to the reservation."

"Soldiers?" Rose asked. "How did you manage that?"

"I have Anthony Wallington and Mark Jones to thank. Anthony came in during dinner the night I was trying to convince Father and Abby that my idea was doable."

"I can imagine how thrilled your father was," Rose said wryly.

Carrie made a face. "I will always be his little girl," she admitted. "Anyway, Anthony listened all the way through, and then told me Mark had met him for dinner the night before in Philadelphia. Both were there on business. They were talking about Chooli, and Mark had mentioned some friends who had just been deployed to the reservation.

Anthony telegraphed Mark, and the confirmation came through yesterday afternoon that we could ride out with the soldiers. Evidently, Captain Jones still carries a lot of influence. And my father is going to buy two wagons for the team, and for all the supplies." She grinned at Rose. "Does that make you feel better?"

"I haven't decided yet," Rose retorted, though her mouth was no longer a straight line of displeasure. She turned on Chooli. "What is that trail like in February? And I want the truth," she added.

"It will be hard," Chooli admitted. "There will be snow in February and maybe some in March. Wagons can be hard in the snow." She looked at Carrie apologetically. "And the winds can blow very hard. You will be cold."

Carrie shrugged. It wasn't anything she hadn't already thought of or been warned of. "I've been cold before," she said blithely.

"For months on end with no hope of warmth or a hot bath?" Rose shot back. "I don't think so."

Carrie sighed. "I know it will be very difficult, Rose, but whatever I will suffer is nothing compared to what the Navajo are suffering."

Rose sighed with resignation. "You have me on that one."

"And as hard as it may be, at least I won't be stuck in Philadelphia for the winter." Carrie grinned again. "I am choosing to see it as a grand adventure—one where I will be doing a lot of good."

"I wish I could go with you," Chooli said sadly. She gazed down at the baby nestled in the crook of her arm. "I would love for my family to see Ajei."

"I know," Carrie said gently. "I wish you could go, too. You've already learned so much, and you would be such a help. But Ajei is too young, and if you were to return, they would never let you leave again."

"You're right," Chooli agreed.

Carrie ached at the gaping sadness in Chooli's eyes. Perhaps changing the topic would help. "Will you teach me everything I need to know about the Santa Fe Trail?"

Chooli managed a faint smile. "I will teach you what I know, but I'm afraid it might not be much help. Franklin and I traveled at night, and we were often not on the actual trail. We kept it in sight, but we had to make our own way. Franklin will be able to tell you much more."

Carrie had a sudden insight into how difficult the trip must have been. She might be cold during the time it took to reach New Mexico, but at least she would have a wagon, and she would travel in daylight. She was also uncomfortably aware that she had not mentioned the conversation she'd had with Anthony that first evening he'd arrived in Richmond. He had warned her about the ever-present threat of Indian attacks. Though the soldiers would be a strong deterrent, the number of violent attacks on wagon trains had increased greatly.

Carrie had thanked him for the information, but she had decided on her course of action. She believed it was the right thing. She would handle whatever came.

Chapter Ten

Janie shivered into her thick winter coat, yearning to step within the warmth of the train waiting on the tracks. She knew the two hundred or so travelers clustered around her felt the same way. She gazed at the eight wooden cars pulled by a large engine. Four were passenger cars; four were baggage cars. Windows down every side would make keeping it warm in winter difficult, but she knew the pot-bellied stove would be working hard. She pushed aside a feeling of uneasiness that had been dogging her since she had woken that day. Surely it was just because of the early hour.

Matthew wrapped his arm around her to pull her close. "Only a few more minutes," he promised.

Janie smiled. "I'm fine, but I'm certainly going to tell Rose and Moses that winter in northern Ohio is much colder than what they experienced in Philadelphia. Home feels rather balmy in comparison," she joked. A last-minute assignment for Matthew had delivered them to Cleveland for a day, and now they were waiting to board the 6:40 a.m. *New York Express* that would take them to Buffalo, New York. Icy winds blowing off Lake Erie made the pre-dawn darkness at Union Station even colder. The cavernous station would be warmer later in the day, when all the stoves could heat it, but the morning cold was too intense for the struggling stoves to make much difference. She was no longer certain her feet were attached to her legs, and her hands were growing numb.

Matthew frowned as he scanned the crowd. "You've never been on an express train," he said worriedly. "It won't be like the sleeper car we rode to come here from Philadelphia. I didn't have another choice to get us to Buffalo today, though. I'm afraid express trains are rather rugged."

Janie shrugged. "How bad can it be?" She was determined to be cheerful and make the best of it, though she had read enough about express trains to know she would probably be very happy to reach Buffalo.

"All aboard!"

"Stay close," Matthew ordered. "I'm going to make sure you are in one of the best seats. We've suffered through getting here early in order to be as comfortable as possible for the long ride ahead."

Janie clung to his arm, sighing with relief when they boarded the next-to-last car. Matthew wound his way to the middle of the car, three rows away from the pot-bellied stove that was already belching heat. They would be traveling up the east side of Lake Erie with the icy wind buffeting the train the entire trip. Matthew grabbed the satchel stuffed full of gaily wrapped packages for his brother Harold, and slid it onto the rack over their seat. Their luggage was in the baggage car, but Janie hadn't wanted to take a chance the gifts would be harmed.

Matthew sank down into the thickly upholstered seat next to her. Train travel was bumpy and uncomfortable, but the cars had been made as accommodating as possible. "This is the best place to sit on a train like this. If you were to sit closer to the stove, you would be sweating and miserable, but if you sit much farther away, you're going to be pounding your feet on the floor to feel them. Especially on a day like today."

Janie smiled gamely but couldn't help the feeling of revulsion as she looked around. "Does everyone spit tobacco on the floors?" she whispered.

Matthew scowled. "It's against railroad rules, but the conductors don't have time to police it." His frown deepened. "I'm sorry, Janie. I know it is rather disgusting."

Janie wouldn't deny that the pools of yellow tobacco spit were vile, and she tried her best not to notice the streams of spit running down the walls. Still, she didn't want Matthew to feel badly. There had been no other option. Besides, he endured these conditions on a regular basis as he traveled for the newspaper. "It's an adventure," she said bravely, forcing a cheerful smile even though she was quite sure it didn't reach her eyes.

Matthew's expression confirmed her suspicion, but he chose to play along. "You truly don't mind that I'm on assignment during this trip?"

"Not at all. You always create stories in your head for every person you see anyway. You might as well get paid for talking to them." She pulled out a copy of *Harper's Weekly.* "I will keep myself happy reading until I am awake enough to care about meeting some of the people around me."

Matthew smiled as she stifled a yawn. "We have almost six hours before we arrive in Buffalo. You can take a nap."

"I will at some point," Janie responded. "For now, I'm happy to read and wonder about the people around me." She waved him away. "Go do your journalist job."

Janie leaned back in her seat and watched Matthew weave his way down the aisle. She could tell he had already picked someone out to talk to from the crowded car. He could never explain why he felt drawn to certain people, but he always came away with a fascinating story. She was sure he would regale her and Harold with tales when they made it to his brother's house later that night. She watched as he stopped to talk to a man close to her age. Moments later, Matthew had taken what seemed to be the last seat beside the man.

Janie stared out at the flat, colorless landscape for a few minutes but quickly realized there was nothing other than blowing snow to hold her attention. They would leave Ohio soon and then travel the countryside of western Pennsylvania before they reached a stop at Erie. She turned the page on her magazine and was soon lost in an article.

*****

"Mind if I sit next to you?" Matthew asked courteously. The man he had chosen looked to be in his mid-twenties. There was nothing remarkable about him, but the tension on his face invited discovery.

The young man with unruly dark hair and light blue eyes glanced up at him. "You're welcome to the seat," he said before he turned back to the book he was attempting to read.

Matthew was somehow sure the words were not being seen. He settled into the seat, hoping Janie was comfortable. "My name is Matthew Justin."

The man, startled out of his thoughts again, looked up. "Josiah Hayward," he said shortly.

Matthew nodded pleasantly and then let silence reign for a few minutes, certain he must handle the situation carefully if he wanted to know what had put the anxious gleam in Josiah's eyes. When he felt enough time had passed, he cleared his throat. "Are you stopping in Buffalo or moving on?"

"Buffalo. It's a business trip."

"What kind of business are you in?" Matthew kept his voice casual. He didn't know how long Josiah had been traveling. He might be too exhausted after two or more days on the train to be willing to engage in any conversation. That could also be the explanation for the tension on his face.

"I work for the railroad," Josiah revealed.

"That must be interesting," Matthew responded. "I am a reporter for the *Philadelphia Inquirer*." His last statement seemed to capture Josiah's attention.

"Are you writing about the dangerous conditions of railroad travel during the winter?" Josiah snapped. He immediately looked contrite. "I'm sorry. That wasn't necessary."

"No need to be sorry, but no, I'm not. There seem to be plenty of publications that cover that issue. My job on this trip is only to interview some people on the train."

Josiah's eyes narrowed. "And you chose me? Why?"

Matthew knew honesty was always the best course of action. "Because you seem to be very tense. I'm wondering about what, though if it's private, it's certainly none of my business."

Josiah met his eyes squarely. "There is a bad one coming," he said bluntly.

There was something about the directness of his gaze that made Matthew uncomfortable. This was not a man who had lost touch with reality, but he did seem to be troubled. "A bad what?"

"A bad wreck," Josiah answered in a voice that managed to be both tense and flat.

Matthew was intrigued. "How do you know?" Josiah hesitated for so long that Matthew suspected he was not going to say more.

"I had a dream," Josiah blurted. "You can think I'm crazy, but I know what I know."

Whether Matthew thought he was crazy had yet to be determined; what he knew for certain was that he had discovered a great story. "Will you tell me your dream?" There was another long silence, but finally Josiah nodded. Matthew leaned forward to hear him over the train racket.

"I had the dream six months ago," Josiah began. "It looked like I was in the desert. I was about to explore when I heard a very loud crash. It sounded like the gates of Hell had been unlocked. I turned around to look and saw a very bright light." His eyes grew wide. "The light seemed to reach to the heavens. And then I heard it..."

Matthew waited for several moments. "You heard what?" he prompted.

Josiah turned to stare at him, almost as if he had forgotten he was there. "The screams," he said quietly. "So many screams. Dozens of them." His voice thickened. "They sounded so hopeless." He shook his head as if to clear the vision. "Then I saw the monk."

"The monk?" Matthew was careful to keep his voice calm, but he was indeed beginning to believe there was something wrong with the young man's mind.

"Yes. I don't know that he was a monk, but he was dressed like one. I asked him where the screams were coming from. He told me they were from Hell." Josiah shuddered. "I asked him what it meant, and he told me I must instantly die."

"You're still here," Matthew replied, shaking off the uneasy feeling Josiah's words were giving him.

"I begged the monk for more time." Josiah took a deep breath. "He told me I might have six more months before I died. My wife woke me then. She said I had been thrashing wildly in my sleep."

Matthew thought about what the young man had said. "Six more months?"

Josiah nodded. "I had the dream six months ago. Today."

"And you believe it could be true?" Matthew struggled not to sound skeptical.

"I believe it enough that I bought three thousand dollars' worth of life insurance before I got on the train. And now, if you don't mind, I would rather not talk anymore."

"Of course," Matthew murmured. He had gotten a good story, but he pushed aside the idea that it might indeed be prophetic. "Thank you for talking to me."

Josiah stared at him. "Do you believe me?"

"I don't disbelieve you," Matthew said carefully, "but is it all right if I hope you are wrong?"

Josiah managed a brief smile before he turned back to his book.

*****

Janie smiled at the young woman two seats over. "You have your hands full."

Tired brown eyes turned to her. "We left Minnesota yesterday morning. It's been a long trip."

Janie gazed at the swaddled bundle in her arms. "How old is your baby?"

"Minnie was born nine months ago. I don't know what made me think bringing a baby to a wedding on a train was a good idea, but it's too late to turn back now." The baby whimpered but quieted when Emma cooed at her.

"The wedding must be very important." Janie smiled. "My name is Janie Justin."

"I'm Emma Fisher." She inclined her head toward the man sleeping next to her. "My brother-in-law is getting married. My husband couldn't leave their business, so I decided I would come along instead."

"I imagine it's been a rough trip," Janie said sympathetically. She couldn't imagine being on this train for more than twenty-four hours with an infant. Emma looked exhausted. Her hands and face were covered with a grimy film of soot, smoke and grease. It was easy to tell the young lady with blond hair was lovely, but it was well concealed by the evidence of long travel.

"Yes," Emma replied. "I want to get to Buffalo, but I'm already dreading the trip back home. If there was any other way to return, I would never put Minnie through this again. I'm glad she's too young to remember how I'm torturing her," she added ruefully.

Janie grinned, impressed Emma still had a sense of humor. "Babies are resilient."

"Much more than their mothers," Emma retorted.

"You're lucky to be getting off in Buffalo," another woman broke in.

Janie looked toward the woman, a few years her senior, who had spoken. "How far are you going?"

"Too far," the woman said wearily. She looked at Emma. "I'm from Minnesota, too. I'm taking my children to make a new home in Vermont." She nodded toward the two children sleeping beside her. "James is twelve. Mary is just ten. My name is Christiana Lang," she added.

"Vermont is a long way from Minnesota," Emma remarked. "I would cry if I thought I had to go that far."

"I'm going back to where I grew up," Christiana replied. "My children have had nothing but trouble the last few years."

"Are you traveling alone?" Janie asked. At least Emma had her brother-in-law.

"Yes. My husband died a few years ago in Boston. I thought we would make a new start in Minnesota last year." Agony filled her eyes. "I had three children then. My Anna died a few months ago from the flu."

"I'm so sorry," Janie whispered. She reached out to put a hand on Christiana's arm. The grief-stricken mother looked grateful for the human touch. Janie could only imagine how lonely she must be feeling. "Do you have family in Vermont?"

"Yes." A glimmer of hope ignited in her eyes. "I should have gone to Vermont last year, but I believed the reports that Minnesota was the new paradise of the West. It was pretty enough, but I didn't know anyone there. Annie got the flu, and it took her in just a few days. James and Mary got sick, too, but they pulled through." She let her eyes rest on her sleeping children. "I'm going back where we won't feel so alone. It's time something good happened for them."

*****

Matthew was wondering what to do next when he spotted someone he thought he recognized. He stood, balanced himself against the rocking train, and made his way to the back of the car. A glance showed him Janie was deep in conversation with two women. He smiled as he watched her reach out and touch one of them. He was lucky to have someone like Janie to love him, and he knew it.

As he drew closer to the man he had glimpsed, he knew he was right. "John Chapman!"

The man glanced up. A broad smile lit the brown eyes crowned by gleaming brown hair. "Matthew Justin? What in the world are you doing on a train in Ohio?" He raised a hand. "Don't bother to answer that question. There probably isn't a train in this country you *haven't* been on. How goes the reporting life?"

Matthew laughed easily. "As busy as ever, but this happens to be a personal trip. My wife and I are on our way to visit my brother in Buffalo."

"You're married? That's wonderful! Who is the lucky lady?"

"I'm the lucky one," Matthew replied. He pointed a few rows up to where Janie's blue bonnet stood out in the dim light filtering in through the windows. "That is Janie in the blue hat."

"The back of her head looks lovely," John said, his eyes gleaming with amusement.

"I'll introduce you at the next stop," Matthew returned. "The rest of her is as lovely as the back of her head."

"Then I really don't know how you managed to get her to marry you," John quipped.

The passenger seated next to John stood. "Take my seat," he invited. "I'm going to the bathroom, and then I'm going to stand for a while. It might help my aching back."

Matthew smiled his gratitude and slipped into the newly emptied seat. "It's been years since I was assigned to cover one of your trials. I don't even remember what it was about." John Chapman was a well-regarded Boston attorney. He had been only twenty-seven when he was assigned a big enough case that it captured the attention of the *Philadelphia Inquirer*. Matthew had been assigned to do an in-depth interview with the young attorney. The two had hit it off, sharing many meals in area restaurants, but the war years had separated them.

"There have been too many trials to keep track of," John said lightly. He grew more serious. "I'm glad to see you made it through the war. I imagine you were on some of the battlefields."

Matthew pushed back the memories he was certain would never quit haunting him. "Just one was too many."

"I've read your work since the war," John continued. "I was appalled—as was the rest of the nation—with the riots in Memphis and New Orleans. Your coverage created quite a stir and managed to change the political influence in this country."

Matthew gazed at him, not sure if he heard approval or censure. "I simply told the truth."

"A truth that was greatly needed," John said. "It opened our country's eyes to doing the right thing. Well done, man."

Matthew smiled. "Thank you. How is Agnes?" He remembered a vivacious young woman who had joined them for a few meals.

John frowned. "Agnes died several years back."

"I'm sorry, John. I hadn't heard."

"No reason you should have. I'm hardly that important." John's expression warmed. "She gave me two fine sons, though. Walter and Willie. They are at home waiting for me to return."

"Where are you headed?"

John smiled. "I actually found a second woman who will take a chance on me. I'm getting married."

"That's wonderful news!" Matthew exclaimed. "Who is your bride-to-be?"

John hesitated a moment. "Clara Green."

"She is indeed fortunate," Matthew replied, wondering about the hesitancy.

John nodded but watched Matthew closely. "You don't know who she is?"

"Should I?"

"Most journalists in this country seem to have made it a point to know everything about her," John revealed.

Matthew shook his head. "I'm afraid I'm not one of them. Of course, I suspect that is a good thing in your estimation." He saw no reason to go into the fact that most of his time was spent working on his book.

John nodded. "That would be true. I can't believe I'm about to tell you the story, but you're a friend, not just a journalist." He hesitated again. "Are you on assignment?"

"Not when I'm talking to you," Matthew promised, glad when John looked relieved. He obviously needed to talk to someone who didn't have an agenda.

"Have you ever heard of the Malden murder?"

Matthew frowned. "I seem to remember hearing something, but I know none of the details. It was during the second year of the war? I believe I was a guest of Libby Prison in Richmond during that time."

"What?" John exclaimed.

Matthew held up his hand. "That is a story for another time. Tell me about the Malden murder."

"It was in 1863 that a postmaster in Malden, Massachusetts decided to rob a bank. His name was Edward Green. He has the honor of having committed the first armed bank robbery in American history. He had a bad drinking habit and was heavily in debt. Anyway, he went into the bank one day to get change and discovered there was only one clerk on duty. Frank Converse was the bank president's seventeen-year-old son." John sighed heavily. "Green saw his chance. He went home, got his gun, and went back to the bank. Converse was still alone. Green shot him in the head at point blank range, and then went into the bank vault and helped himself to five thousand dollars in cash."

Matthew was horrified. "What happened to Green?"

"The case went unsolved for a while, but people began to wonder how he was paying off his debts. They arrested him about a year later. He confessed everything when they questioned him. They hanged him in April of '66"

"Yes, I do I remember hearing about that," Matthew acknowledged. "I just didn't remember the name. What's all this got to do with you?"

John looked him steadily in the eye. "I'm marrying his widow."

Matthew whistled.

"Clara was only twenty-three when Green murdered the boy. She was nine months pregnant and had no idea what her husband had done. When he was arrested, she still couldn't believe he would do such a thing, but she gradually realized the truth. Their daughter was three when her father was hanged. She just turned four."

John took another deep, steadying breath. "Clara is also Agnes' sister. We fell in love after Agnes died. The coverage has been merciless. The newspapers have named her the 'Wife of the Malden Murderer'."

"Ouch," Matthew murmured. "And now you are about to become even more of a public person by extension."

John nodded. "I'm hoping that getting her away from Malden will help. In time, the fact that she no longer has Green's last name may make it fade away. But regardless," he said firmly, "I love her and want to marry her."

"Then I'll repeat what I said before. She is a lucky woman."

*****

Harold Justin paced the platform, scowling at the clock. He walked over to the ticket office again. "Any word, Davison?"

The manager of the ticket office nodded his head. "I got a wire a few minutes ago. They should be passing through Angola soon. Should be here in about an hour."

Harold glared at his friend. "They are late."

"This train and most every other train," Davison said imperturbably. "Look, my friend, it's coming. That is the most I can tell you right now. Train travel is notorious for not being on time. Combine that fact with winter weather, and you may as well count on it."

"Did you make it late because I beat you in poker last night?" Harold asked suspiciously, his blue eyes glaring out from under red hair.

"Not even I have that kind of power," Davison responded with a laugh. "Besides, it's about time you won. I was getting tired of taking your money." He cocked his head. "It's your brother on that train, isn't it?"

Harold nodded. "Matthew and his wife are coming. I haven't seen him in ten years."

"Then two and a half hours shouldn't bother you," Davison observed. "Go over to the diner and get something hot to drink. You'll hear the whistle blow when the train is approaching."

Harold nodded but hesitated. "Did you feel it this morning?"

"The earthquake? Everybody who isn't dead felt it. It wasn't as big as some I've read about, but it woke me."

Harold had felt the earthquake, but it had not alarmed him. Too much had happened during the war for a mild shaking of the ground to bother him. He started to turn away again but something held him. "Feel anything else?"

Davison eyed him. "What's wrong with you today? Did I feel what?"

Harold shook his head. "I just have a weird feeling. Like something isn't right. I don't know what it is."

Davison smiled. "You and most of Buffalo. The earthquake shook people up. That and the uncommon cold snap, and people are a little edgy. Don't worry about it. Your brother and his wife will be here soon."

*****

Janie woke from a deep sleep when Matthew settled into the seat next to her. "Hello," she murmured, rolling her shoulders to relieve the stiffness, and raising her arms to stretch. "To what do I owe the honor?"

Matthew smiled. "You've been asleep for a while now. We should be arriving in Buffalo in an hour. We're about to pass through the town of Angola."

Janie yawned. "I didn't think it was possible to sleep being so uncomfortable." She glanced toward her new friends. Both Emma and Christiana were sleeping soundly. Minnie was snuggled into her mother, and Christiana's children leaned against her shoulders. "Emma will be glad to disembark in Buffalo, and Christiana and the children will be glad to get off the train for a while. They disembarked in Erie to let the children run around outside the station, but this trip must seem endless to them."

"I'm sure," Matthew commented. "I learned our two-and-a-half-hour delay in Erie was caused by a mechanical breakdown with another train. Thankfully, we should be there soon. I hope they were able to wire ahead so Harold knows why we are late." A sudden stir at the front of the car caught his attention. His eyes widened as he saw who was making his way to the middle of the train. He laughed and rose to his feet. "Thaddeus Culligan!"

"Matthew Justin!" A large man with uncommonly wide shoulders reached over to shake hands. "If you're not a sight for sore eyes." He grinned. "And I would thank you to call me *Doctor* Culligan."

"They gave someone like you a medical degree?" Matthew asked with an answering grin. "Medical education must be going downhill in this country." He turned to his wife. "Janie, please meet *Doctor* Thaddeus Culligan. He went to college with Robert and me. We shared a suite for one term before he decided he was too good for us and left." He turned to his friend. "Meet my wife, Janie Justin."

"Well, the medical establishment might be going downhill, but we should all be questioning the intelligence of beautiful women if this one agreed to be your wife."

Janie laughed with delight, immediately liking the gregarious man with sparkling blue eyes. "It's a pleasure to meet you, Dr. Culligan." She pushed aside the concern that the doctor standing in front of her might share the same disdain for homeopathy that the majority of medical practitioners had. He was Matthew's friend and that's all that was important.

"You must call me Thaddeus," he said. "Dr. Culligan is only meant for my inferiors." He laughed again heartily. "Now, the two of you must come up to the next car with me. My wife, Susannah, will want to meet you. The two people who were seated next to us left the train back in State Line."

Matthew exchanged a look with Janie before nodding. "We would be delighted. How did you know I was here?"

"John Chapman warned me. He came wandering through the car and told me had talked to you, and also met Janie at the stop in Erie."

Matthew pulled Janie to her feet. "Do you want to bring the gifts with us?"

Janie shook her head. "No. I'll want to come back and say good-bye to my new friends. I can get them then."

Thaddeus took her hand warmly and leaned in close. "You really married this mountain man?" he whispered theatrically.

"You may find this *mountain man* knows more about life than you do, Dr. Culligan," Janie said sweetly. "I would tread carefully."

Thaddeus' laugh boomed through the car, causing heads to turn from every direction. "You did well, mountain man. You did well."

Matthew grinned. "You don't know the half of it, my friend."

"Ten minutes until Angola! Ten minutes until Angola."

Matthew barely registered the call that rang through the car. As they made their way down the aisle, he nodded at John, smiled at Josiah, and then locked eyes with three other young men he had interviewed. Young professionals, they were all on their way to New York City to celebrate Christmas. He had enjoyed his talk with them, and believed his editor would be pleased with the stories he had gathered.

Moments later, he and Janie were settled in their new seats next to Thaddeus and his wife Susannah.

Thaddeus turned to Janie. "So this big mountain man is a famous newspaper reporter. Do you roam the country with him?"

Janie smiled. "Not usually. I am a student at the Homeopathic College in Philadelphia. I graduate next year." She waited for his reaction.

Thaddeus raised a brow, while Susannah smiled brightly and leaned forward to respond. "How wonderful! How did you get involved in medicine?"

"I served in Chimborazo Hospital during the war," Janie replied, watching Thaddeus. He was surprised, but she saw none of the disdainful judgement she had seen on many doctors' faces. "I worked under my best friend, Carrie Borden, who served as a doctor there. She will finish her degree this year, as well."

Thaddeus continued to stare. "That was quite an undertaking," he murmured.

Matthew smiled. "Are you still the same old-fashioned man you were when we graduated, Thaddeus? If so, prepare to have your world shaken. My wife is just one of a group of powerful women who aren't content to let us men go along with outdated thoughts."

"I'll remember that," Thaddeus murmured with something that was not quite amusement. "You said Carrie Borden. Any relation to Robert? What is the old man doing now anyway?"

Matthew saved Janie the pain of an explanation. "Robert is dead, Thaddeus. Carrie was his wife."

Sadness filled Thaddeus' eyes. "The war?"

Matthew shook his head. "He was murdered on Cromwell Plantation this spring by Ku Klux Klan vigilantes," he said. "He managed to live through the war, but was killed by a fellow veteran."

Susannah gasped and covered her mouth. "How horrible!"

Matthew could tell the moment Janie's pain overtook her politeness. There were moments she was almost philosophical about Robert's death, but the pain could still overwhelm her quickly. Her sensitivity made her feel Carrie's pain as strongly as she felt her own. Combined with the long hours on a crowded, dirty train, she had reached her limit.

Janie stood abruptly. "I hope you will excuse me for a few minutes," she said, a polite smile plastered on her face. "I realized I forgot to give little Mary's doll back to her." She turned and threaded her way back to the car behind them.

A deep silence followed her.

Matthew smiled slightly, wishing he could follow her to make sure she was all right. "Mary is the daughter of a woman Janie made friends with on this journey. I imagine Janie stored her doll in with my brother's gifts while the little girl was sleeping." Matthew really had no idea where Janie was headed, and he could tell his companions saw through the excuse. "Robert's widow, Carrie, is Janie's best friend," he admitted. "Janie was also very close to Robert."

"The poor dear," Susannah murmured. "I can tell by the kindness in Janie's eyes that Robert's death must have been so difficult. Do you want to go to her? We can connect when we get to Buffalo."

Matthew wanted nothing more than that, but he felt compelled to stay in his seat. "I'll go back in a few minutes if she doesn't return."

Thaddeus was regarding him somberly. "Robert was your best friend. How are *you* handling his death, Matthew?"

Matthew drew a deep breath. "I learned during the war to handle death, but Robert's murder was so senseless that it has made it even more difficult to comprehend. I miss him every day." Memories of times with his friend swarmed through his mind. He forced himself back to the present. "I'm angry, but I promised Robert I would take care of Carrie, so most of the time I'm able to swallow those feelings." He shook his head. "To know the political climate in our country is going to do nothing but increase these types of violent killings…" His voice trailed off.

"Then all the stories about the vigilantes in the South are true?" Thaddeus asked. "I was hopeful that it was more media sensationalism at work."

Matthew opened his mouth to reply but was interrupted by a sudden lurch that jolted them all forward in their seats.

"What was that?" someone called. All talking ceased as anxious looks were exchanged.

Matthew tensed, knowing that what he had just felt was far from common. The jolt had been powerful, and felt very much like the release of a car coupling, which could only mean one of the rear cars had derailed and detached from the train. He locked eyes with Thaddeus, his friend's grim expression saying he suspected the same thing.

He stood to reach for the rope dangling close to his head, but someone had beat him to it. A clanging bell cut through the afternoon air as he looked out the window and realized they were crossing a high bridge. As he strained to see further back, his blood froze.

"Janie!" Matthew leapt up just as another strong jolt threw him off his feet headlong into the aisle. His head cracked against the side of a wooden seat, and he struggled to regain his footing before darkness swallowed him.

Chapter Eleven

Janie had just handed Mary her doll when a strong jolt knocked her back into her seat.

"What was that?" Emma cried as she clutched Minnie close to her chest.

Janie shook her head and stood again. "I don't know." All she was certain of was that she wanted to be with Matthew. Her earlier feeling of uneasiness had instantly turned into full-blown panic. "I need to go to my husband."

Another jolt knocked her off her feet. A bell began clanging as she struggled to push herself free of her seat again. A scrambling sound from the rear of the train made her look back in time to see several people rush through the door from the rear car.

"The train is derailing!" one man hollered, his eyes wide with fright.

And then the screams began.

Janie gasped as she leaned over to look out the window. "No!" Her scream rose to join the rest of the horrified passengers as she watched the rear car sway precipitously and then begin a slow roll from the high bridge they were flying across.

"God help us!"

"Oh, dear God!"

"Mama!"

"Hold on!"

Screams and cries for help from the rear car faded and then disappeared, but rose in volume all around Janie. She looked toward the door that led to Matthew, but the swaying of the car made it impossible to see through the crush of people being tossed around.

This is how it would end? Separated from Matthew and everyone she loved? She would die alone?

The seconds that passed felt like minutes as the scene unfolded around her. Mothers clasped their children. Husbands grabbed their wives to hold them close.

"Stop the momentum of the swaying!" Somehow the scream cut through the confusion. A young man shouted from the aisle. "Every time the train sways we have to throw our weight the other direction to keep it on the tracks," he hollered. As the train swayed to the right, he lunged at the left side of the car and pushed against the siding. Several men jumped up to help him, their determined shouts mixing with the screams and the clanging bell.

Janie watched as the men rushed from one side of the train to the other, but she knew the truth. It was too little, too late.

The screams rose around her as she felt the train car tip, and then fall from the track.

Janie grabbed the seatback in front of her and held on with all her strength as the car hung suspended for a moment. "Matthew..." she whispered as the train began its rushing freefall.

******

Matthew came to, his head spinning. "What happened?" Thaddeus and Susannah were both looking at him with stricken expressions. Suddenly, the continued clanging of the bell cut through the fog. "Janie!" He bolted forward, ignoring the pain in his head. "Janie!"

Thaddeus grabbed him. "Matthew..."

The raw pain in his voice cut through the rest of Matthew's fog. He glanced back at the cluster of people in the rear of the car. "What is it? What happened?" Everything was confusion. "Tell me!"

Susannah was the one to reach forward, her soft eyes blurred with pain. "The last two cars came off the train." She opened her mouth to say more, but no words came out. Finally, she shook her head. "I'm... so ... sorry."

Matthew had a flash of memory. They had been crossing a high bridge coming out of Angola. "The bridge?" he ground out. He had another flash of the rear car tumbling through the air.

Thaddeus nodded. "Both cars went off the bridge," he said in a voice of stunned disbelief.

Matthew stared blankly at him, trying to make sense of what he was hearing. "Off the bridge? Janie's car?"

Thaddeus returned his gaze but said nothing more. The pain and shock in his eyes were more eloquent than any words could be.

Matthew doubled over as agony ripped through his entire being. He cursed and leapt to his feet. "I have to get to her!"

Thaddeus continued to grasp his arm. "The train is stopping." He reached for the bag Susannah was handing him. "As soon as we are stopped, we'll go."

Matthew's eyes locked on the medical bag in his friend's hand. "Janie," he murmured as visions swarmed through his mind. It took no imagination at all to picture people tossed like ragdolls as the train cars rolled from the tracks. All it took was memories of other wrecks to understand that hot coals from the pot-bellied stoves were also being spread through the wrecked cars.

*****

Janie prayed as she held tight to the seatback in front of her, her feet shoved against the same seat to hold her secure. Her prayers had no words or coherent thought. They were simply cries of her heart as she prepared to die. "I love you, Matthew."

She was dimly aware of bodies and a sundry assortment of belongings flying around her as the car tumbled through the air for what seemed like an eternity. It crashed into something solid and her face slammed into the seatback. Shards of glass filled the air as the train car tumbled along the ground, and splinters of wood from walls and floorboards mixed with the bodies and the screams. A sudden burst of light shot through the car as the roof split apart. The light was extinguished quickly as the roof parts crashed back together.

Janie looked up, horrified to see a man's body dangling from between the cleft roof. Determined to see no more horror before her death, she closed her eyes and waited for the movement to stop—waited to take her last breath.

Finally, the rolling and tumbling ceased. There was a moment of stunned silence before the cries and groans became audible to her.

Janie opened her eyes, shocked to discover she was still alive. She looked around slowly, trying to make sense of what had happened. She knew the car had come off the track, and that they had fallen from the bridge. As her head cleared, she realized the car was lying on its side, snow pushing in through the missing window frames. Her death grip on the seat frame had left her hanging almost suspended in air. It was the only thing that kept her apart from the crush of people piled on the side of the car below her.

"Mama..."

"I'm hurt..."

"What happened?"

"We're all going to die..."

The voices and groans rose from below her.

Janie took a deep breath, still shocked to realize death had not claimed her. The cries for help began to filter through the shock. She moved carefully, checking for injuries. Her head and face hurt, but she didn't feel any cuts or blood. She was aching all over, but she didn't seem to have any broken bones.

She was alive.

Matthew! What had happened to the rest of the train? Had every car derailed on the bridge? Was he still alive?

*****

The main engine had traveled more than a thousand feet past the end of the bridge before it managed to slow and stop. Matthew and Thaddeus were among the first men off the train.

Matthew was running as soon as his feet hit the ground. He was terrified at what he would find, but all he could think about was reaching Janie. He pushed aside images of what derailment from a bridge would do to a wooden train car. His breath came in gasps, frozen air floating behind him as he ran.

He could hear the wreckage before he saw it. He was vaguely aware of a swarm of men coming from the other side of the bridge—residents of Angola responding to the tragedy. Matthew gritted his teeth as his innate reporter's sense ripped through his terror. Derailment from a bridge could be nothing less than tragedy.

Groans and screams lofted into the frigid twilight.

Matthew slowed as he approached the end of the bridge. He took a deep breath and forced himself to gaze over the right side. His breathing stopped as he quickly identified the last train car, emblazoned with the word *Toledo*. His quick assessment showed the train was crushed almost flat in many areas. It was standing on its end, leaning against the northern embankment of the bridge. He could hear cries and moans, but there was another more ominous sound. He heard the crackling of fire and watched as the first flame, ignited by sparks from the stoves, licked from a window.

He watched only a moment before he leapt to the other side of the bridge to locate Janie's car. There were already people heading down the slope toward the *Toledo*, but his only thought was to find his wife.

Thaddeus' voice sounded behind him. "Is that Janie's car?"

Matthew nodded, but could not force words past his lips. Within moments, he was carefully working his way down the slippery slope. It would do Janie no good for him to fall; he could only help her if he could reach her.

The *Erie* had landed only partway down the steep incline to the river below. It lay on one side, the snow littered with belongings...and bodies.

Matthew grasped hold of small trees and brush as he half walked, half slid toward the wreckage. "Janie!" he hollered in a cracked voice that he almost didn't recognize as his own. "Janie!" He was dimly aware that Thaddeus, his medical bag draped over his back, was following his course of descent. The only sound coming up to him from the wreckage was piteous cries.

*****

Janie, convinced she was not critically injured, began to look for a way to escape. She must find out what had happened to Matthew. If she could release her position on the seat she was wedged in, she would drop down into the tangle of crushed people. She forced her eyes to skim the bodies as she looked for a path to work her way out of the mangled car. She wished briefly for her medical bag, but her thoughts refused to stray from Matthew. What if he was in another car in need of medical care? The thought drove her forward.

Janie squeezed her eyes closed when she glimpsed a woman who had been completely scalped during the fall. The skin of her head and her hair, drenched in blood, were attached to her skull by a slight web of tissue. The only blessing was that the woman was obviously dead.

A young married couple that Janie had met briefly were lying close together, their bodies blackened by bruises sustained during the crash. The woman had vomited a pool of blood.

Janie blanched and turned away. She had seen horrific wounds during the war, but this was a different situation. These were innocent travelers who just minutes before had been merrily headed toward a Christmas celebration, a wedding, or the beginning of a new life. She scanned the floor carefully for Emma and Minnie, or Christiana and her two children.

"Emma!" she cried as her eyes settled on a prostrate form. She couldn't tell if Emma was dead or not, but she quickly realized her daughter was no longer clasped in the arms that hung loosely at Emma's sides. "Minnie!"

The only answer was the continuous crying and moaning.

"Help me..."

"Please..."

"Where is my husband?"

Janie bit back her cry of despair. Suddenly, she noticed passengers who were still conscious swatting at something. Her terror increased as she realized they were batting at sparks and coals from the overturned pot-bellied stoves.

Fire!

She had to find a way out of the train car before the sparks created an inferno. A shift in the air told her there was an opening not too far in front of her. Twilight was quickly swallowing any available light. Janie edged forward, allowing her body to drop until her feet were on the floor. Picking her way carefully, holding tight to the seats above her, she made her way toward the back of the train. Her hope soared as she saw a man in front of her slip through a narrow opening in the rear of the car.

Janie moved as fast as she could, hoping help was on the way for the piteously wounded passengers.

"Matthew," she whispered.

"Janie! Janie!"

Janie gasped and held her breath. Was the voice real, or was she hallucinating?

"Janie!"

Janie released her breath in a gush and began to move faster. "Matthew!" she cried.

"Janie! I'm here! Can you get out?"

Janie reached the opening she had seen the man go through and stared. How had he made it through? A creaking, splitting noise told her the wooden car was collapsing in on itself even more. She gritted her teeth and leapt forward, biting back her cry as she used her feet to propel her way through the opening. Her arms and head were barely through when she felt someone grasp her arms and pull her out. Moments later, she was cradled in Matthew's arms.

Janie collapsed into his embrace. "You're alive. You're alive..." she murmured. She reached up to touch his face. Her hand, when she withdrew it, was wet with his tears.

Thaddeus' face loomed in her vision. "People are alive in there. How badly are they hurt?"

Janie stared at him. "It's bad," she said. Safe in the shelter of Matthew's arms she was suddenly able to think as a doctor again. "But some of them can be helped."

The grim look on the men's faces told her they had correctly interpreted that many more were probably dead.

*****

Harold was enjoying a steaming cup of coffee when he heard the bell jingle on the diner door. He waited until the gust of cold air was swallowed by the warm heat, and then lifted the cup again.

"Harold Justin?"

Harold looked up, eyeing the gangly teenage boy calling his name. "That would be me. What can I do for you?" The boy eyed him, a strange sympathy in his gaze.

"Davison sent me to get you. Said you need to come over to the station."

"Is the train coming in early?" Harold asked. He hadn't heard a whistle announcing the approach.

The boy shook his head. "Davison just said to come get you."

Harold pushed aside his uneasiness, pulled out a coin to pay for his coffee, and then left the diner. The unsettled feeling he had fought all day was back in full force. He strode across the snow-covered road and climbed the steps to the station. One look at Davison's face made the knot in his stomach grow larger. "What is it?"

Davison gazed at him for a moment. "There has been an accident," he said carefully.

Harold froze, waiting for whatever Davison had to say.

"The *New York Express* lost two of its cars."

"Lost them?" Harold asked, not able to make sense of what he was hearing.

Davison nodded reluctantly. "They derailed just outside of Angola." He paused, the expression on his face saying he wished he was anywhere but standing in front of his friend. "The last two cars went off the bridge."

Harold stared at him, still trying to make sense of the words. "Derailed? Off the bridge?" His thoughts spun. The bridge just outside Angola was nearly fifty feet above Big Sister Creek.

Davison nodded. "That's all we know now. They wired for a relief train, and..." His voice trailed off.

"And what?" Harold demanded hoarsely.

"And all the doctors we can send," Davison finished hoarsely. He forced a note of confidence in his voice. "There were two passenger cars that stayed on the track. Your brother and his wife could be in one of those cars."

Harold heard the words, but they didn't register. He had pushed his brother out of his life ten years ago because of pride and greed. Was this the price he would pay? To never see his brother again?

"Harold? Harold!"

Harold jerked his eyes up, realizing Davison must have said something else he hadn't heard above the roaring in his head. "What?" he asked impatiently.

"They are taking reporters on the train."

Men begin to appear from the deepening dusk to give what help they could. Thick coats and hats could not mask the grim set of their bodies and faces. Janie had seen some of them come from beneath the bridge. "The other car?" she called. "How are the passengers?" She felt Matthew's body tense. The agony on his face when she peered up at him told her all she needed to know, but something in her needed to hear the words. "Are there any survivors?"

Matthew swallowed hard. "I don't know," he said quietly.

"There were a few who got out before it started burning," one man said, his face twisted with pain. His haunted eyes roamed over the second car. "At least this one's not burning yet."

The wind shifted, bringing with it screams and terrified shrieks Janie had not heard before. She shuddered and shrunk into Matthew's broad chest. "All those people are burning to death?" The thought was more than she could comprehend as she envisioned the excited faces she had seen on the train platform in Cleveland that morning. Matthew's only answer was to hold her closer. Janie pushed away from him. She could feel all the horror she wanted to later, but right now, there were lives to be saved.

"Janie?"

Janie pushed to her feet, ignoring the pain every movement shot through her bruised and aching body. She was alive. No bones were broken. She was not burning to death. "There is work to be done," she said. She motioned to the men. "There are many people still alive in this car." She didn't add that at least there were when she crawled out. The cries and groans had diminished in the few minutes she had been free from the crushed coffin.

Several of the men pushed forward with axes and began to chop at one of the walls. The collapsing car had closed off all escape routes, so they would have to create one.

Janie turned to Thaddeus. "Whatever you think of the Homeopathic College, I have had quite a lot of experience with trauma during the war. I can help."

Thaddeus nodded with no hesitation. "We'll need all the help we can get. I'm sure the station has wired for a relief train to bring doctors, but I imagine it will be at least an hour before they arrive. It will be up to us to keep people alive until we can get them somewhere warm and safe." He motioned to the men gathered around. "We need to get as many people out of that car as possible. It could start burning at any minute. Bring the live ones first."

Matthew moved forward to help with the rescue effort. As the hole widened in the wall of the crushed car, the cries for help grew louder.

Janie gestured to several of the men who had just arrived from Angola. "The injured will need something to lie on. Please gather all the clothing scattered in the wreckage and make beds from it. It will be better than nothing."

The men hurried to do her bidding. By the time the injured began to appear in the opening, there were makeshift beds waiting for them.

"Look for more clothing inside," Janie ordered. "We must cover them the best we can. Most of them will be in shock." She grabbed the man closest to her. "Are you from Angola?"

"Yes, ma'am."

"How far is the nearest house?"

The man crinkled his brow. "Not very far, I reckon."

"I want you to go there and get some things for me," Janie said. "I need water, apple cider vinegar and honey. As much as they have. And cayenne pepper if they have it. I also need jars or glasses." She sighed impatiently as the man stared at her without moving. "I am a doctor," she snapped. "Will you go get the supplies, or do I need to find someone else?"

Thaddeus stepped closer. "Do what Dr. Justin has asked you," he ordered.

The man looked between the two of them and then nodded abruptly. "I'll be back quick," he promised.

"I'm here to help."

Janie and Thaddeus turned toward the new voice.

"And you are?" Thaddeus asked as he leaned over a young boy with what looked to be a badly broken leg.

"Dr. Romaine Curtiss. Years of serving in the military has given me more experience than I wish I had. I'm the doctor in Angola."

Thaddeus nodded as Janie sighed with relief. "I suggest you take charge, Dr. Curtiss. These people will be staying here in your town, and you know your citizens. We are here to help *you* any way we can."

Dr. Curtiss nodded his acceptance, though Janie could not miss the haunted look in his eyes. She had seen that same expression on countless other doctors treating the wounded during the war. This man had seen more than he should have. She also saw his lips tighten with resolve, and she guessed he would do whatever was needed to care for the victims of the wreck.

He turned to the growing crowd of rescuers. "These people are going to have to get out of the cold." He looked around. "Jack Southwick," he barked. "Your house is the closest. May we start to take people there?" He waited for the nod and then continued to give orders. "Getting these people up the slope is going to be hard. We need to make stretchers out of anything we can find—siding, pieces of wood, tree boughs, metal from the roof. Be creative. Gather whatever you believe will do the job. As we release the patients, your job is to carry them to Jack's house."

He glanced around again. "His house won't hold all these people. What house is the next closest?"

"Doug Griffith's place," a man offered.

Dr. Curtiss nodded. "That's where we'll take those with the most minor injuries."

Janie was aware of the conversation, but she was already bending over the body of Christiana Lang. Her new friend was barely conscious, with glazed eyes robbed of any awareness. Janie murmured softly as she checked her pulse and ran her hands over her limbs and skull. Janie's lips tightened as she located the deep gash in Christiana's head. From how quickly the woman was going into shock, Janie also suspected internal injuries. She reached for the gauze in Thaddeus' bag and wound it tightly around the head wound to staunch the bleeding. There was nothing more she could do with no supplies. She willed the relief train to arrive quickly as she gestured some of the men forward with their makeshift stretcher. "Handle her carefully?" she asked softly. "She is a friend."

"We'll do the best we can, ma'am," one of the men replied. "We'll get her out of the cold as fast as possible."

She managed a slight smile when she recognized two conscious forms staring at her. "If Christiana wakes, please tell her that her children are all right. I will send them up on the stretchers once we have cared for the most critically injured."

The four men lifted the wood panel they had ripped from the train car and began to make their way up the slippery slope. They held tightly to one corner of the stretcher while they grasped trees and bushes to pull themselves forward. They moved slowly to keep from jostling Christiana, but still there were groans of pain. Janie was relieved when the groans stopped. Unconsciousness was a blessing. If her friend lived through the night, there would be time for her to absorb the tragedy.

Janie moved over to James and Mary. Both stared up at her with frightened eyes.

"Is Mommy dead?" Mary asked in a trembling voice.

Janie ached for the little girl who had first lost her father, and then her little sister just a year before. "No," she assured her as she took her hand. She was relieved when a quick assessment revealed both children had cuts and abrasions, but there did not seem to be any major injuries. "Your mommy was hurt, but we are going to take good care of her." She understood the skeptical look on Mary's face as her eyes tracked the halting progress of Christiana's stretcher as the men carried her up the slope.

"When can we go be with her?" James asked, his eyes also locked on the ascent.

"Soon," Janie promised. "First we have to take care of the people who are hurt worse than you two. You were very lucky," she said. "Can you be patient while we help these other people?" She smiled when the two children nodded bravely and then turned back to her job of treating the wounded.

Janie was relieved when the screams of agony echoing under the bridge faded into silence, only because she knew that the suffering had finally ended. She forced her mind away from the torture the people had to have endured. There was nothing she could do for them. She had to put her focus on the wounded who were still living.

Thankfully, it seemed that most of the people in her car had survived the brutal crash.

Matthew and others were busy scooping huge mounds of snow into the wreckage. They were making certain there was no chance fire would turn a second car into an inferno of death.

*****

Harold was as silent as the rest of the group on the relief train as they chugged as close to the bridge as they could get. Everyone was intent on helping, but they had all silently accepted the worst-case scenario they believed they might find. The train was full of doctors, railroad maintenance crewmen, and a handful of reporters. Harold had received immediate approval from his editor when it was discovered his brother and sister-in-law were on the train. One moment he was glad; the next he did not want to be the one to discover his brother's body.

"You have a brother on this train?" a doctor asked as they waited to come to a full stop.

"Yes," Harold answered. "I haven't seen him in ten years." He tried to calm his pounding heart as he viewed the plumes of smoke rising from beneath the bridge. The final wire before they pulled out of Buffalo had indicated they should expect a high death toll.

"Good luck," the doctor said tersely as he stepped off the platform into the snow.

Harold followed him, almost gagging as he took his first deep breath. "What...?"

A railroad maintenance worker disembarked behind him. "That would be the smell of burning flesh," he said grimly. "You never get used to it."

Harold stood numbly for a moment as the worker hurried off. He knew he was here on assignment, but all he really cared about was finding Matthew and Janie. He joined a group of men looking over the right side of the bridge. He stared in horror at the twisted, charred remains of what had once been a railroad car. Dark lumps were scattered across the snow.

"Those are bodies," a man said hoarsely. "The poor beggars never had a chance."

Harold shuddered and stepped back. He may have to examine those corpses in time, but surely there had to be some who had lived through the wreck. Determined not to focus on the worst, he moved toward the two passenger cars that had not derailed. He could see faces plastered to the windows as they waited for whatever would come next.

Harold boarded the train, noticing the somber silence as people tried to absorb both the tragedy unfolding behind them, and the realization they had been spared from a horrible death. He walked quickly through both cars, sickened to discover Matthew was not on either one. He turned and wove his way to the back, knowing he had to continue looking.

"Excuse me," a woman said urgently.

Harold paused. "Yes."

"Do you have a brother?"

Harold stiffened. "Yes. A twin. His name is Matthew Justin. Do you know him?"

The woman reached out to grasp his hand. "My name is Susannah Culligan. Your brother was sitting with me and my husband when the cars derailed. They have gone down to help." Her grip tightened. "Your brother is alive."

Harold sagged with relief, but then hesitated. "His wife? Janie?"

Susannah's eyes filled with sadness. "She was in the second car that went over the bridge. I've not heard anything since Matthew and my husband left. My husband is a doctor," she explained.

Harold took a deep breath. "Thank you for letting me know." He turned and hurried out of the train, headed for the left side of the bridge. He knew the second car, the *Erie*, had gone over on that side. As he approached the ravine, he saw groups of men struggling up from the bottom, carrying makeshift stretchers with wounded people. "Have you seen Matthew Justin?" he asked each group. They responded to his frantic question with sympathetic gazes, but shook their heads wearily.

Harold gazed down at the wreckage barely visible in the encroaching darkness and then began to slide down. There was only one way to discover what he had come for. The descent was slow, but at least there were fires burning below to provide illumination as the wounded were cared for. When he finally reached the bottom, he felt both relief and trepidation. Would his first meeting with his brother in ten years revolve around his wife's death?

*****

Matthew wasn't sure what ached more, his body or his heart. His hands were raw from ripping away wood and metal to free trapped bodies. His shoulders ached from lifting heavy debris, including the hot pot-bellied stove he had strained to lift off a man who was trapped. The man was alive when he had rescued him, but just barely. He'd had no time to go check on the status of the increasing number of people laid out on the snow, but occasional glances told him the number was diminishing.

His body would heal quickly, but his heart was another matter. All but one of the men he had interviewed for his story had been killed in the crash. When he found his friend John Chapman, his anguished eyes had gazed at him for just a moment before they closed forever. Matthew could do nothing other than set his lips and move on to the next person crying for help.

The grief would come when the world got quiet again.

He had recoiled in horror when he looked up at the roof straight into Josiah Haywood's bulging eyes. He had no idea how his body had been caught between pieces of the roof, but he hoped the man's death had been instantaneous. Matthew's mind traveled back to the dream Josiah had related to him. The young man had been given six months. Not a day more.

Matthew had been almost relieved when the cries for help continued. At least there were living people to help. He knew others had been given the grisly job of collecting the dead.

The three college boys he had interviewed for almost two hours had been under the crush of people when the train rolled and landed on its side. One of them was pulled from the wreckage still breathing. Matthew had closed the eyes of the other two, who would not continue their education nor celebrate Christmas in New York City.

Now he stood in the middle of the wreckage and gazed around. All the bodies had been removed either to the triage area, or to the waiting sleds that took the dead to the building at the train station. The wounded would be transported when they could be moved. The dead would follow in another train. Some had been identified, but he knew from the muted voices around him that too many were charred caricatures of humans. It would be a miracle if some of them could be identified.

A miracle...

Matthew yearned for one. He was grateful so many had lived through the wreck. He was thankful beyond words that Janie was alive and well, though he knew how exhausted and heartsick she must be. He had gone to check on her, but she had simply shaken her head and returned to her work of caring for the wounded. He had never been more proud of her, but he had also never hurt so much for her. He loved his wife's tender heart and respected her strength, but he also knew her tenderness made her so susceptible to heartbreak. Taking care of soldiers was one thing. Taking care of mangled, carefree travelers whose lives had been forever altered in a moment was another.

A miracle...

Was it too much to hope for? One bright spot of the pure miraculous in a night full of darkness, pain and suffering?

Matthew took one more look around, but the late hour had obscured almost everything. Here and there the flames leaping from the fires outside glinted off a watch or a piece of jewelry, but the rest simply looked like a pile of refuse—hardly the treasured belongings of humans on their way to celebrate the holidays. There was nothing more to be done inside. Articles would be gathered in the morning. He wondered where the presents for his brother had landed. It hardly seemed important, except for the reminder that Harold must be frantic with worry. Perhaps he could ask someone to send a message through the telegraph. He certainly wasn't going to leave the ravine until Janie was ready to go.

A miracle...

His thoughts returned to his futile hope. One step from the train and his nostrils filled with the smell of death and charred flesh. There were no miracles on a night like tonight. He swung his gaze over the tramped down snow, looking for Janie. The glow from the fires reflected off her exhausted face. For the first time he noticed the bruising and swelling that had risen while she worked.

As he hurried forward he heard it.

Matthew stopped. He had heard something—something that seemed out of place in the chaotic night—but he couldn't identify it. He wanted to move on, but something held him in place.

The noise cut through the night air again.

Everyone in the ravine grew quiet. They turned as one to hear the sound.

Matthew strained his eyes. He was positive he had heard a cry, but it had not come from any of the people lying on the ground. Of that he was certain. He waited, willing the sound to come again.

In response to his thoughts, another pitiful cry rose into the air.

Matthew launched himself toward a bundle on the ground. He reached down, picked up the pile of what looked like clothing, and pulled back the fabric.

And looked down at his miracle.

Janie appeared at his side. "Matthew?"

Matthew grinned and held up the bundle. "It's a baby," he said, pulling the infant close to his chest. "A baby," he whispered reverently. "It's alive."

Janie gasped and reached for the little girl who was crying but unharmed. "Minnie!"

"Minnie?"

"This is Emma's little girl," Janie cried happily. "She was thrown from her arms when the wreck happened. No one could find her. Where…?"

Matthew felt the joy of one good thing. "She was lying there in the snow all wrapped up."

The miracle of a small baby defying the odds seemed to infuse hope and life into everyone at the bottom of the ravine. There was a long minute of silence before everyone turned back to their work. They would celebrate the miracle later, but right now there were people still to be tended to.

"Leave it to my brother to find the baby."

Matthew whirled at the voice he had not heard for over a decade. "Harold?" His eyes strained to see beyond the illumination of the fire.

"I was already going to be glad to see you, but knowing you survived a train wreck certainly takes it to a new level." Harold moved forward and engulfed Matthew in a hard embrace. He stepped back as his voice took on a new hesitancy. "Janie? Did she...?"

"She did," Janie answered, stepping forward to take Harold's hand. "I am Janie. I'm so happy to meet you."

Harold sagged with relief. "You both made it through this wreck?"

Minnie began to cry harder.

Janie laughed, sheer relief giving her energy to continue through this endless day. "I'm going to let you and Matthew talk. I have a baby to care for. I will see you when we're done here tonight." She pulled Minnie to her chest and moved closer to the fire to examine the child more thoroughly.

Matthew turned back to his brother. "This was not how I imagined our reunion."

"And I never dreamed I would spend the entire afternoon wondering if I had been too late to find you again," Harold said hoarsely, his eyes bright with emotion. "Even covered with black soot and blood, you look good."

Matthew grabbed him in another bear hug. "The paper sent you to cover the wreck?"

"More like I told the paper I was going to find my brother," Harold quipped. "I suppose I'll be able to write some of what I've seen, but mostly I've just been looking for you." He stepped back and stared at him harder. "You're really all right?"

Matthew nodded, though this was one more thing he was not certain his heart would ever heal from. How many traumas could the heart endure? Why did he always seem to be in the middle of so many tragedies?

Harold spoke his thoughts. "You always seem to be in the center of the action," he said. "Do you think you could spread it around a little?"

"I would be more than happy to," Matthew admitted. Suddenly he was more fatigued than he could remember ever being.

Harold noticed immediately. He stepped forward and wrapped a strong arm around Matthew's waist. "I've got you, mountain man."

And just like that, Matthew was transported back to carefree days with his twin, growing up in the mountains of West Virginia. They had spent countless hours hunting, fishing, and exploring the hills they called home. They had always been there for each other.

Matthew took a deep breath. "I missed you," he said quietly.

"I know," Harold replied. "I know."

*****

Janie turned to Dr. Curtiss as the last patient was carried up the icy slope. Minnie was being taken directly to her mother. She hoped Emma was awake to enjoy the reunion. "Which house do you want me to go to, Doctor?"

"Neither," Dr. Curtiss responded. "You have done magnificent work, Mrs. Justin, but you need rest."

"I don't," Janie protested, speaking past the fatigue that clogged her throat and blurred her eyes. "There are so many people who need help."

"And they will need you in the morning," Dr. Curtiss responded. He stepped back and viewed Janie's face. "Someone told me you were in the *Erie* when it went off the tracks. Your face is bruised and swollen. It's time to take care of yourself," he said. "One of the men will take you and your husband to their house so you can rest. If you feel up to it in the morning, I will gladly accept your help. By the way, what was in that mixture you gave everyone? I have never seen people come out of shock so quickly."

Janie smiled. "Apple cider vinegar, water, honey, and cayenne pepper." She understood the look of skepticism on his face. "I'll explain more fully when I can put more than a few words together," she promised.

"You have a deal," Dr. Curtiss replied. "But only if you promise to get some rest."

"She promises, and I will make sure she holds to that promise." Matthew appeared from the shadows.

"Good," Dr. Curtiss said. He waved a man forward. "Please take the Justins to your house. They have earned a break."

Matthew nodded his thanks and then turned to the man waiting for them. "Do you have room for three

Justins? My brother arrived on the relief train. He will be staying the night as well."

The man nodded. "We have plenty of room," he replied. "The name is Andrew McCullough. My wife and I welcome you."

Janie had been willing to continue working, but now that a reprieve was on the horizon, she realized just how exhausted she was. She looked up at the hill, wondering if she had the strength left to climb out of the ravine.

"Harold and I will help you," Matthew said quietly. "Your day is over, my love."

Janie collapsed into his arms with a smile. "That sounds nice," she admitted.

As they climbed from the ravine, the snow that had threatened all day began to fall in huge swirling flakes.

Chapter Twelve

"You sure you want to come with me?" Harold asked. "I think you should stay here and get some sleep with Janie."

"So do I," Matthew admitted wearily, "but my editor will be less than pleased if he discovers I wasn't hurt and still didn't get a story from the first night."

The McCullough's farm was about half a mile out of town. They had been received into the cozy cottage with warm hospitality. Hot bowls of soup and thick pieces of bread slathered with butter were placed in front of them as soon as they arrived. Matthew and Harold inhaled three bowls, while Janie had fallen asleep after a few bites, her head sagging back against her chair. Matthew had carried her to bed before coming back out to talk to their hosts. When Andrew had revealed the dead were laid out in the building next to the train station, Matthew and Harold knew they had to go discover what they could. Bolstered by the soup and bread, they were now headed into town.

"Do you ever get tired of it?" Harold asked as they walked the snow-covered road.

Matthew didn't pretend to not understand. "Constantly covering bad news and tragedies? All the time," he responded.

"How do you do it?"

Matthew pondered the question. "I would like to tell you it gets easier, but it doesn't. Sometimes I feel numb. Other times..."

"Other times?" Harold prompted when the silence stretched out.

Matthew shrugged. "Other times the pain is so bad I think it will rip me apart. The battlefields... The riots... the murders ... It's enough to make you want to give up on humanity."

"And have you?" Harold questioned.

"No," Matthew said quickly. He knew Harold was struggling and looking for answers. He hardly felt qualified to help, but he was the only one who was standing there. He pushed through his fatigue to figure out what to say. "There have certainly been times when I wished I could remain ignorant about what has happened. I see people around me who choose to remain unaware. I have to admit there are times those people seem happier than I am."

"Sometimes I think they have it right," Harold said brusquely.

"I think so, too," Matthew agreed. "Until I *really* think about it. Once I get past the hurt and the pain, I realize I would rather know."

"Why?" Harold asked.

"Because knowledge gives me the power to act," Matthew said. "I hated being in the riots in Memphis and New Orleans, but I'm glad the articles I wrote helped change the civil rights issues in our country. I still have nightmares about the explosion of the *Sultana* on the Mississippi, but I'm glad I could expose the greed that made it happen. If there is enough exposure, things like the *Sultana* won't happen again." He paused for a long moment. "Knowledge is power. The pain of knowing is sometimes more than I can handle, but I think it is better than getting to the end of my life with the knowledge that my selfishness was part of the reason bad things continued to happen."

Harold nodded his head thoughtfully, but Matthew could still see the rampage of emotions on his face. "What happened?" he asked. There was so much he didn't know about his brother's last ten years.

Harold stayed silent for long moments but finally looked into Matthew's eyes. "I was married."

Matthew stopped walking and faced Harold on the dark road, barely aware of the snowflakes swirling around them. "I didn't know."

"I figured I would tell you when we saw each other," Harold replied. "My wife died of cholera two years ago." He took a deep breath. "So did my two daughters."

"What?" Matthew stepped forward and took Harold's hand, reeling from what he had heard. "All of them were taken by cholera?" He wrapped his brother in a warm embrace. "I'm so sorry. So sorry." Grief constricted his throat. He was sorry for his brother, and he was also sorry for all the lost years that meant he had never known his sister-in-law, or his nieces. "What were their names?"

"Beth was my wife. Martha Ann was four. Nancy was three." Harold took a shaky breath. "Beth was pregnant with our third when she died. I'd only been back from the war a few months."

Matthew knew there were no words for the kind of pain his brother was feeling, but he began to understand the depth of the changes in his life. "You realized everything you were working for didn't really matter."

Harold nodded. "I thought reporting the news would help me make a difference."

The brothers stood silently while the thick snow mounded around their feet.

"I'm glad Janie didn't die," Harold said, staring off into the distance.

Matthew searched his heart to come up with something that would make sense to a man who had lost so much. He thought of all the people he had seen die. He thought of Robert, and then of Carrie. "I can only tell you what helps me," he began. "I came to the point when I was finally able to accept that bad things were always going to happen. My being angry or depressed wasn't going to change that reality." He took a deep breath. "Once I realized anger or depression wasn't an option I wanted to live with, I had to make conscious choices to feel differently about my experiences. The most important thing for me was to realize I had to take action to make things change." His voice grew stronger as his emotions settled. "It makes me feel good to do those things, so I choose to put my focus there."

"How do you do it?" Harold pressed. "What actions help you make sense of it?"

"Writing for the paper is one thing, but it isn't enough, so I'm writing a book," Matthew revealed. "It's called *Glimmers of Change*. For the last year or so I have been interviewing people who are doing good things, or who have overcome terrible things. It's given me hope for our country and for all humanity."

"Do you have a publisher?" Harold asked.

"I do. I'm scheduled to be finished with the book this spring."

"But you are still a reporter?"

Matthew shrugged. "I tell the stories I want to tell."

"Or the ones that fall in your lap," Harold replied ruefully.

Matthew wanted to learn more about Beth and his nieces, but he sensed now was not the time to press that issue. He decided to change the subject. "I have hopes this crash will be the tipping point for the railroad industry."

"The tipping point?"

Matthew nodded. "The railroads have grown quickly since the war. More and more people of all types are riding them. Before the war, it was mostly men who rode the trains. You saw the train today—there were as many women and children as there were men. Railroad travel has gotten cheaper, so more people are able to use it, but," he added, "it has not become safer. In fact, it has become more dangerous." He was glad they were not close enough to the bridge to smell the lingering odor of death.

Harold nodded. "I wrote an article last month about the use of kerosene lamps and candles for lighting. I learned just how dangerous the stoves are. We saw that first-hand today," he said bitterly. "There are unreliable signaling mechanisms, and the rails are flawed and unpredictable. The couplers are outdated on far too many trains. Every time you get on a train you are putting your life into someone else's hands."

"Hands that shouldn't be responsible for them," Matthew agreed. He felt a surge of guilt that he had allowed Janie to ride the train at all. His decision had almost cost her life. "I'm going to do my best to make things change," he vowed.

"By using your articles to reveal the truth."

"Yes. If enough people are aware of the problem, and they demand change, the railroads will have no other choice. I'm going to make sure readers all over the country know how horrific this crash was. It must be the worst train wreck in the history of America. People are going to want details, and if people are too afraid to ride, the railroad's profits will drop."

"And money always speaks louder than anything," Harold stated.

"Always. They will have to change." Matthew nodded toward town. "We've got to keep walking if we're going to get there."

Harold fell in step with him. "Need any help with that book of yours?" he asked casually.

Matthew eyed him. "Are you offering?"

Harold nodded. "I think I would enjoy putting my focus on something other than pain and suffering for a while." A vulnerable look flashed across his face. "I know I'm asking a lot. I haven't exactly been a great brother, and—"

"Nothing would make me happier," Matthew said.

Harold stopped again and swung to face him. "Really?"

Matthew nodded. "I've missed you. And besides, we would make a great team. The first book is close to being finished, but my publisher has already told me they want as many as I can write. Evidently, the people of America are starving for good news that will give them more than feelings of despair." A smile formed on his lips as he thought of working with his twin. A few weeks ago he had believed Harold to be dead. Now they would be working together. The smile stretched into a grin. "We start tonight," he added.

"Tonight," Harold whispered. "Thank you. This is the first real feeling of hope I have had in a long time. I was still trying to make sense of the war when Beth and the girls died. Since then, it's been impossible to make sense of anything."

"You're welcome," Matthew replied. His thoughts were churning as he put words to them. "We are going to use the papers we write for to expose just how horrible this wreck was so that we force change. At the same time, we are going to interview the residents of Angola. I was watching the men down at the wreck. I've never seen such compassion and caring from total strangers. The scenes of train wrecks are notorious for crime, but I saw none of that. Nothing was stolen. Nothing was taken away as a souvenir to sell later. Those people, like the McCulloughs, simply wanted to help."

"And America needs to know about these people," Harold said eagerly.

"Just as much as they need to know about the wreck. Probably more." Matthew slowed as they reached the edge of town where the train station perched next to the tracks. The smell of burned flesh and death once more filled the air. "But first we must do the part we will both hate."

*****

Matthew was numb as he moved through the frigid station freight house. He had ceased to feel as soon as he had stepped through the doors and seen the rows of ravaged corpses laid out on the frozen ground.

"Dear God," Harold ground out.

Matthew remained silent as he gazed upon the horrific scene. Some of the corpses could be recognized as people. Bodies were intact and still semi-clad in woolens and flannels. His eyes rested for a brief moment on faces he recognized from his walk through the rear train cars in search of interviews. It was almost impossible to comprehend the gaping hole these deaths would leave in families.

Finally, when he could no longer avoid it, his gaze turned to the other forms on the ground. If they had not been situated next to the other victims, it would have been almost impossible to identify them as humans. Blackened bodies were curled into a fetal position from the searing heat of the fire that had consumed them. Most of them were without arms or legs. Matthew wanted to turn away, he wanted to run from the building and never look back, but he forced himself to look. He forced himself to confront the horror so he could effectively report it, and so he could tell a story that would help force change in the railroad industry.

He forced himself to consider the last moments of these people's lives—the terror they felt when they realized the flames were reaching their bodies; the pain when their clothes and skin ignited; the shrieks that would have come from their mouths as they screamed until the force of life that gave them the ability to scream departed.

When Matthew had absorbed all he could, he walked out of the freight building, turned into a darkened corner, and threw up everything he had eaten for dinner. He leaned against the wall and took in shallow gasps of the frozen air, ignoring the burning in his lungs.

Harold found him there minutes later.

The brothers exchanged a wordless look and then walked back down the road they had come up just thirty minutes earlier.

Matthew wanted nothing more than to climb into bed next to Janie. He grieved that Harold would not receive the same comfort.

*****

Janie was confused when she awoke late the next morning. She didn't recognize the strange room, or the strange bed, or the strange voices she heard coming from the other side of the door. She lay quietly for several minutes before memories began to filter through the fog. As soon as they did, she wished with all her heart that she could make them stop. Sounds of shrieks, screams and cries filled her mind.

Bolting upward, Janie grabbed her pounding head as her legs swung over the side of the bed. She couldn't stop the groan that escaped her lips.

The voices went silent and moments later the door opened, letting in a gush of warm air scented with the odor of biscuits and bacon.

"Janie!"

Janie looked up with gratitude when Matthew rushed to her side. "I didn't dream it," she whispered. "You are alive."

Matthew lowered his head to capture her lips tenderly. "I am alive," he assured her. He raised a finger to trail it down her face. "Your face has to hurt terribly."

"My face?" Janie asked in puzzlement. She reached up a hand to touch it, wincing from the pain.

"You must have smashed it into something during the wreck," Matthew said. "You have two black eyes, and your whole face is swollen." His voice reflected his agony. "I can't believe you spent hours caring for everyone last night."

Janie vaguely remembered crashing into the seat when the train landed hard in the snow. "The others were hurt far more than I," she murmured, warmed by the expression in her husband's eyes. "I must look quite attractive with two black eyes."

"You're the most beautiful thing I've ever seen," Matthew responded.

"I'm glad you are biased," Janie murmured softly. She looked up when a stout woman with curly brown hair and kind blue eyes appeared in the doorway. "You're Hannah."

"That I am," the woman replied. "I'm surprised you remember anything from last night."

Janie frowned. "I'm afraid I remember more than I wish I did."

"It was a terrible night," Hannah said sympathetically. "I'm thinking a hot bath will make you feel much better."

Janie almost groaned from pure pleasure. She was filthy, and she ached all over. "A bath?"

Hannah smiled. "I have one almost ready for you in the other room. I suspected you would wake up soon. You've been out for twelve hours, but I figured your stomach would demand attention about now."

Janie felt the hunger the minute Hannah mentioned it, but there were questions rampaging through her mind. "The patients? Has there been word?"

"Yes," Hannah answered. "But I'll not tell you a bit of it until you have had your bath and you are seated in front of hot food."

Janie smiled through her pain. She could tell Hannah was not a woman to be trifled with. She and Annie had much in common. "Yes, ma'am," she said meekly.

Hannah snorted as she put her fists on her hips, her eyes shining with admiration. "I heard what you did out there last night, Mrs. Justin. I know you're not the type of woman to order around, but someone has to take care of you, too."

A young girl appeared at the door. "Momma, the bath is ready. I just poured the rest of the hot water in the tub."

"Janie is ready, too," Matthew replied. Without asking, he moved forward to scoop her into his arms.

Janie wanted to protest, but chose instead to snuggle into her husband's chest. Perhaps she would feel like herself after a long hot bath had washed away the worst of the grime and memories.

*****

It was late afternoon before Andrew McCullough drove Janie and Matthew to the Southwick home that was now operating as a hospital. She had learned that most of the injured had been transferred by train to Buffalo hospitals early in the morning, but Emma, too injured to move, was still at the house.

Emma locked eyes on Matthew as soon as they walked into her room. "You're the man who saved my Minnie," she said weakly. "Thank you."

"I hardly saved her," Matthew protested. "I simply found her in the snow."

"She would have died..." Emma's voice trailed away weakly.

"Hush," Janie said as she took her friend's hand, but she knew Emma was right. Minnie would not have lived through the cold night if Matthew had not found her. She shuddered at the idea of the beautiful little girl freezing to death. "The important thing is that she is all right."

Janie had pumped Dr. Curtiss for information and knew Emma had sustained serious internal injuries, but the doctor believed she would recover in time. Her brother-in-law, Alexander, had not been so fortunate. He had escaped the train and gone for help for his sister-in-law and niece. He reached a house and managed to gasp out the information before he collapsed in a heap, evidently dead before he reached the ground. Janie had realized, as Dr. Curtiss told the story, that it must have been Alexander who had shown her the way out of the train.

"I have some good news for you, Emma."

Emma locked her eyes on Janie's face. "My husband?" she asked hopefully.

Janie nodded. "A wire came through a little while ago. He arrived in Buffalo this afternoon, and he will catch the next train to Angola."

"Alexander..." Emma murmured.

"Yes," Janie said sadly. "He will grieve his brother, but he still has his wife and his daughter. I'm sure he knows he is a lucky man."

Emma gazed into her eyes for a long moment. "Thank you," she whispered as her eyes fluttered closed.

Janie continued to hold her hand for several minutes, knowing Emma needed rest more than anything. When she was confident Emma was asleep, Janie looked around the room and then moved into the hallway. She stopped a village lady bustling by with a pail of warm water. "Where is Minnie?"

"The little angel girl?" the woman said tenderly. Her eyes were tired, but her face radiated kindness. "A friend of mine who recently had a son is nursing little Minnie until Emma can do it again."

Janie smiled. "What a wonderful thing for her to do."

"Our village knows how to care for its own," the woman said. "Since all you folks dropped off our bridge, you are our own to care for, too."

"Thank you," Janie whispered. She watched the woman hurry off, and then turned to Matthew.

"Are you ready now?"

"Yes." Janie knew that Christiana and her children had been taken to Buffalo earlier that day. The train that would take the three Justins to Buffalo would be arriving soon. She couldn't quite imagine getting on that train and rolling across the bridge, but there was no other way to reach their destination, and she knew Matthew would hold her until they were on the other side. "I'm ready," she said bravely.

Chapter Thirteen

Abby looked up when Thomas walked into the bedroom. She was putting the final things into their luggage before they left for the plantation. "Hello, dear," she said. A good look at his face dimmed her smile. "What is wrong?"

"Why don't you come downstairs," Thomas invited. "May has some hot tea waiting for us."

Abby followed him silently. A hot cup of tea would be welcome if she was about to hear bad news. She pushed aside images of what the news could pertain to. She would know soon enough—there was no point in making something up.

Thomas waited until May had served their tea and departed, glancing over her shoulder in concern.

"What has happened, Thomas?"

Thomas sighed and handed her a copy of the *Philadelphia Inquirer*. "This came today."

Abby's eyes caught on the headline, *"The Angola Horror,"* before she realized the article was written by Matthew. She gazed at Thomas for a moment and began to read. Her face whitened as the details of the wreck unfolded in the article. "My God..." She gasped. "*Matthew* was on the train? Matthew and *Janie*? Are they all right?"

Thomas handed her a telegram.

"Janie and I were on the train that wrecked in Angola. Janie's car derailed, but by a miracle she is unharmed. We are on our way to Richmond now with my twin brother. We will all be there for Christmas."

Abby stared at the telegram. "Janie's car went over the bridge?" She shuddered as the images brought to life by the article spun through her mind. "She's alive?"

"Matthew said they were on the way to Richmond," Thomas reminded her. "That must mean she is more than alive. She must truly be all right."

Abby shook her head, her eyes catching on the other part of the telegram. "Did you know Matthew has a brother? A twin?" She frowned. "I've known Matthew for ten years. How could I not know he has a twin brother?"

"I'm sure we'll have answers to all our questions in time," Thomas said.

"How soon?"

Thomas smiled. "Their train arrives in one hour. We'll all leave for the plantation together in the morning."

"I need to let May know we will have more for dinner," Abby said.

"I already got more food goin' in the oven!"

Abby smiled when May's voice floated in from the kitchen. "I should have known she would hear every word."

"'Course I do," May retorted. "How you think I keep on top of things 'round here?"

Abby laughed but grew grim as she read the article again. "Thomas, this is horrible. Those poor people! Train travel seems to have gotten more dangerous. I thought it would get better, but it seems to only get worse."

"I believe it will start to change now," Thomas replied gravely.

Abby looked for a paragraph she had already read. "Matthew believes the train wreck in Angola must become the tipping point for the railroads to make improvements."

"He's right," Thomas agreed. "It's wrong that it so often takes a great tragedy to create change, but I believe this wreck may become the rallying cry that will transform how the railroads operate. People are changing how they see things," he said thoughtfully.

Abby cocked a brow.

"The war years changed our nation in so many ways. Before the war, I believe most Americans would have accepted the Angola wreck simply as the mysterious workings of an unseen force—the providence of God. Now, more people are beginning to believe they should know *why* and *how* things are happening. They want answers and solutions."

"As they should," Abby retorted. "It's ridiculous not to understand there are scientific and mechanical explanations for accidents like this. But explanations are not enough—there must be accountability."

"Spoken like a successful businesswoman," Thomas said admiringly. "If everyone in our country had your mind, change would come much sooner. Until people clamor for change, though, wrecks like this will only happen over and over."

Abby held up the paper. "I suspect Matthew is not going to allow that to happen."

"I suspect you're right," Thomas said with a nod. "Matthew's article was one of the first to hit the major papers. It will take weeks, perhaps months, for the news to spread across the country, but already there are other writers demanding accountability and change. It seems this will truly be the tipping point Matthew proclaimed."

Abby shook her head sadly. "I suspect that is no consolation for the families who have lost loved ones."

*****

Carrie was waiting eagerly on the porch when the carriages arrived. "You're here!" She ran laughing down the steps when they pulled to a stop.

Rose, Moses, Annie and Susan stepped out onto the porch behind her. "Welcome!" they cried in unison.

Carrie hugged her father and Abby first. It felt like much more than ten days had passed since she had returned from Richmond. Knowing this might be the last Christmas all of them would be together made it even more special than usual.

She turned to embrace Janie and stopped abruptly, stepping back in shock. "Janie! What happened to you?"

Janie turned to Matthew. "You told me it looked better," she accused.

"It does," Matthew assured her, a gleam of amusement shining in his eyes. "But I don't recall saying it looked *good.*"

"What happened to you?" Carrie's blood chilled. "Did someone attack you?" Anger blurred her eyes as she envisioned opponents of women medical students beating her friend. She whirled on Matthew. "Did you find them?"

Janie managed a laugh. "I was not attacked, Carrie."

The whole group fell silent as they waited for Janie's explanation.

"I was in a train wreck," Janie said quietly. "The car I was riding in came off the tracks while we were crossing a bridge."

Carrie stared, certain she had not heard what she thought she was hearing. "I'm afraid I need you to repeat that."

Abby stepped between them. "You'll get the whole story inside," she said. She reached behind her and pulled a man forward. "I would like all of you to meet Harold. He is Matthew's brother."

All eyes left Janie to inspect the man standing before them.

"You have a twin brother?" Carrie asked in a stunned voice. She spun and stared at Matthew. "A twin brother? Why do none of us know about him?" She turned back to Harold. "Where have you been?"

"That's a rather long story," Harold said with an easy smile. "I'm afraid I was stupid enough ten years ago to push Matthew out of my life. It took a war and losing my family to bring me to my senses." He glanced over at Matthew. "Thankfully, he was willing to let me back into his good graces."

Carrie gazed at him and then turned back to Matthew. His look of happiness told her all she needed to know. She rushed forward to give him a hug, and then warmly welcome Harold, before embracing Jeremy and Marietta. "Everyone is here," she announced. "Let's get this holiday started."

*****

Carrie was standing by the fire when Harold came over to join her.

"Your home is beautiful."

Carrie smiled and looked around. Greenery adorned every window frame and encased every door. Cedar boughs, interspersed with bright red holly, lined the hearth over the fireplace that leapt with flames. Candles flickered in the windows, competing with the soft light from the kerosene sconces decorating the walls. A huge tree, cut fresh the day before, stood guard in the corner. Felicia, Amber and John had worked tirelessly all day to decorate it with the items Carrie had hauled from the storage room. "Thank you," she said quietly. "I have so many memories of Christmas on the plantation, but I believe this one will be the most special."

"Why?"

Carrie looked up at Harold, once again feeling the strangeness of looking at someone who was almost a replica of Matthew. His hair was longer, and his beard was a little fuller, but everything else was identical, including the kindness in his eyes. "Because I suspect this may be the last Christmas we are all here together. Some of us were separated during the war, but now it will be choices that take us apart." Saying the words created a wave of sadness that swept through her.

"I know about choices," Harold said.

Carrie examined his eyes. "What happened with you and Matthew?"

"I thought that being right was more important than having a brother."

Carrie had only just met Harold, but the resemblance made it seem she had known him long enough for her to be intrusive. "How?"

Harold shrugged. "I won't go into the whole story. Let me just say we had a political difference that I couldn't seem to move beyond." He paused. "*Wouldn't* move beyond is probably more the truth. Matthew very accurately pointed out that my belief was based on pure and simple greed. His position wasn't political," he mused. "It was a core moral issue for him. I wasn't willing to accept the truth at the time because what I wanted was the most important thing to me. I hated that his observations made me feel guilty, however, so I told him I never wanted to see him again." His lips twisted with self-loathing. "I was an idiot."

Carrie listened quietly.

Harold looked down at her, waiting. "Aren't you going to tell me I wasn't an idiot?"

"Why would I do that?" Carrie asked. "You *were* an idiot." She softened her words with a smile. "Our country just finished a war that decimated both sides because leaders couldn't find a way to make choices for our country as a whole. Political decisions were made that were based solely on personal agendas and greed. I believe all of them forgot they are *Americans* and not only a political party or a belief."

Harold continued to penetrate her with his blue eyes. "You believe the war could have been avoided? Do you believe slavery could have been ended any other way?"

Carrie considered his question. "We can never know for certain, but I do believe *whatever* has to be done in the future to prevent such a thing from happening again, must be done. We have to learn from our mistakes or there is no value in making them."

Harold nodded. "I understand why Matthew thinks so much of you."

Carrie smiled. "I love your brother. He helped me tremendously when my husband was murdered this spring." Sadness swamped her as she thought of how much Robert had loved Christmas. Memories of the last Christmas they had spent together almost overwhelmed her.

"My wife and daughters died two years ago," Harold said, only his eyes revealing the depth of his agony. "From cholera."

Carrie reached out to grip his arm. "I'm so very sorry." It was heartbreaking to know she could probably have saved all of them with the same homeopathic remedies she had used in Philadelphia. Her determination to become a doctor solidified even more as she read the pain in Harold's eyes. "And I understand."

"I know. Matthew told me about Robert and Bridget."

Carrie felt her breath catch.

"I try to focus on being grateful that I had them for as long as I did," Harold said, shaking his head. "Enough of this kind of talk. It's Christmas." He turned to look out the window. "Those are beautiful horses out there. Even with their thick winter coats, I can tell all of them are special."

"Those horses were Robert's dream," Carrie replied. "He poured everything he had into them." She followed his gaze to where Granite galloped around the pasture, his head and tail held high. Several of the yearlings were chasing him in wild pursuit, their snorts hanging in the air as frozen clouds. The sight made her laugh. "Would you like to go see them?"

"Very much," Harold answered. "Might I go for a ride while I'm here?"

"Of course," Carrie promised.

*****

Janie was waiting on the porch when Carrie returned to the house. She had left Harold to talk horses and breeding with Clint. Matthew rode well, but his brother was obviously a horseman through and through.

"When were you going to tell me?" Janie demanded.

Carrie chose ignorance. The anger shooting from Janie's blackened eyes was disconcerting. "Tell you what?"

"Don't even try that with me, Carrie Borden," Janie snapped. "You're not coming back to school?" She stepped closer. "You are going to New Mexico? What are you thinking?"

Carrie sighed, realizing she wasn't going to avoid this conversation. "The Navajo on Bosque Redondo need me," she responded. She prepared herself for an argument, though she was not at all certain why they were even having one. She had honestly believed Janie would be excited for her. "Janie, I..." As she looked more closely at her friend, she saw the tears. She stepped forward and grabbed Janie's hands. "What is it?"

Janie's tears dissolved into sobs that shook her slender shoulders.

"Janie!" Carrie pulled her friend into her arms. The cold air wrapped around them as she let Janie cry. The why of it would come out soon enough. The only important thing now was to be with her. Carrie had heard enough about the train wreck since their arrival to know Janie had been deeply traumatized. Matthew had revealed there were terrifying nightmares every night.

"I'm... sorry," Janie finally gasped.

Carrie allowed her to step back, but she didn't release her hands. "Tell me," she invited.

"I know the Navajo need you," Janie managed, "but..." Her voice trailed off as her eyes filled with shame. "I do, too," she finally murmured. "I've been counting on you being in Philadelphia."

Carrie battled with the guilt Janie's words created. She knew how hard it had been for Janie to admit how she felt. She gazed at her friend, torn about what she was to do. Everything in her said to go to Bosque Redondo, but was her determination based more on the fact that she didn't want to be in Philadelphia again, or was she really being called to New Mexico? Suddenly, Carrie wasn't sure. Janie had always been there for her. How could she not be here for her friend when she needed it? The questions rampaged through her head.

*****

"You're quiet," Matthew said as he snuggled with Janie later that night. The crackling flames in their bedroom fireplace created a cozy cocoon against the cold wind rattling the windowpanes.

"I know," Janie admitted.

Matthew frowned at the fatigue he heard in her voice. He felt the tension in every part of her body. He recognized the signs of trauma. They were the same signs he had seen in so many soldiers during the war. "Can I help?"

"Carrie is not coming to Philadelphia. She is going to New Mexico. She will finish her degree by completing an internship helping the Navajo on the Bosque Redondo Reservation."

Matthew absorbed the news quietly, pained by Janie's emotionless, flat voice. "How did you find out?"

"Rose told me. She thought I should know. I talked to Carrie and she believes she must go, though I know I made her feel guilty."

Matthew ached at the sadness in Janie's voice. "You need her to be in Philadelphia."

Janie stiffened as if she was going to protest his observation, and then she slumped against him. "Yes." The single word was clogged with raw emotion. "I don't know that I've ever felt this way, Matthew."

"You haven't," Matthew assured her, praying he would say the right words. "Carrie reached her breaking point this spring when Robert was murdered. You reached your breaking point when your train car flew off a bridge. The fact that you lived is amazing. Instead of being cared for, along with everyone else on the train, you chose to take care of them."

"I had—"

Matthew held a finger to her lips. "I know you had to, because it's who you are. But all of us have a breaking point. We reach a point where we simply can't take another blow. It makes everything seem overwhelming."

Janie listened as she stared into the flames that shot dancing shadows around the room and then sighed. "What do I do? I can't pretend the train wreck comes close to Carrie losing Robert, but I don't want to close down and shut anyone out. She and I have talked so much about the regrets she has from doing that. I just don't know what to do," she said.

Matthew had felt a plan formulate as he waited for her to respond. It sounded completely crazy - and it sounded completely right. He pushed himself up in bed so he could lie across Janie and see her face. He wanted to see her immediate reaction, rather than give her time to formulate one she thought might be appropriate. "Let's go to New Mexico with Carrie." Janie's eyes widened with surprise, but Matthew did not miss the immediate rush of relief he saw swim into them.

"New Mexico?" Janie gasped. "Go to New Mexico? We can't do that."

"Why not?" Matthew asked. He had seen what he needed to see. Now he just needed to give her mind time to reach the conclusion her heart had already reached.

Janie stared at him. "I have school. You have the paper. We can't walk away from our commitments."

"Why not?" Matthew repeated. "Carrie is looking for homeopathy students to join her, and Dr. Strikener has given her approval if she can find anyone who wants to go." He saw the flicker of hope in Janie's eyes before she shook her head stubbornly.

"You have your work. You can't just walk away from it."

"Can't I? I believe the paper will be interested in articles about Bosque Redondo. It will also give me time to finish the book, and also start on the next one." Matthew waited for that to sink in before he pressed forward. "You need a break, my love. I know you are strong enough to push down all your feelings and continue with your studies, but I don't believe you have to." He also very much doubted she had enough left in her to push down her feelings, but he wasn't going to tell her that. "It would mean the world to Carrie to share this experience with you, and the two of you together can do so much good for the Navajo. The stories I tell will make Navajo problems real for the rest of the country. School will be waiting for you when you get back."

Janie turned to stare at the window casting their reflection back into the room. The winds were growing more intense. The snow Miles had forecast would probably be coating the ground when they woke.

Matthew saw the instant she quit fighting. He reached for her hands as she turned to him.

"New Mexico..." It was no longer a question as Janie murmured the words, her eyes beginning to shine.

"New Mexico," Matthew said firmly. Now that she was no longer resisting the idea, he decided to press his advantage. "You can help Carrie recruit a few more students to join the team, and you'll also be there to help gather all the medicines and supplies you will need."

Janie jumped up and began to pace around the room, her flannel nightgown flowing behind her. "New Mexico!" she exclaimed. She turned and leapt back onto the bed. "We can really do this?"

"We can really do this," Matthew replied with a smile. "Personally, I am quite excited about it. I've not done any travel out west. I never quite envisioned heading out there in a wagon train, but it might be my last chance. It won't be long before the railroads stretch coast to coast. Wagon trains will not always be a possibility."

Fear crept into Janie's eyes. "We have to take a train as far as Independence, Missouri," she said hesitantly.

"Yes," Matthew admitted. He wasn't going to be hypocritical and tell her it would be fine, because they both knew the truth. If there were any other way to navigate the first part of the trip, he would do it. "I will be there with you for every moment," he promised. He knew his next words were risky, but he didn't want Janie's fear to stop her from taking advantage of a great opportunity. "Isn't two days on a train better than a whole winter in Philadelphia without Carrie?"

Janie narrowed her eyes. "You do know how to put things in perspective, don't you?"

Matthew waited, knowing she had to come to her own conclusion. He watched the play of emotions over her face, hoping she had enough spirit left in her to walk through her fears. He sagged against the bed when she nodded her head.

"Let's go to New Mexico."

Matthew grinned. "You mean it?"

Janie eyed him. "You're really excited about this, aren't you?"

Matthew nodded easily. "I am. I was being truthful when I said I always wanted to travel out west. Just think what a great story it will make for our children when we tell them we were on a wagon train on the Santa Fe Trail."

*****

Carrie was up early. Her fire had died down during the night, leaving her room like a cold tomb. She jumped out of bed, pulled on slippers, and shrugged into the thick robe lying across the end of the bed. She glanced at the stack of wood and kindling next to the fireplace, and then dashed to the window. A wide smile spread across her face when she saw the line of saddled horses tied to the fence posts. Miles and Clint had gotten up extra early to do as she had asked.

Carrie dashed into the hallway. "Everybody get out of bed!" she called. "You have a Christmas surprise waiting!" She clapped her hands loudly. "Get out of bed!" She laughed and ran back into her room to put on layers of warm clothing.

Thomas and Abby were the first to walk into the kitchen to join her, their eyes still sleepy. Susan trailed them, rubbing her eyes.

"This better be good," Thomas muttered. Abby remained silent as she reached eagerly for the hot cup of coffee Annie held out to her.

Susan grabbed a cup of coffee and settled into one of the rocking chairs in front of the fire. "Wake me again when everyone is here," she said wearily. Her head slumped against the back as her eyes closed.

Matthew and Janie pushed in through the door next.

Matthew glared at Annie. "Do you know what is going on?" he demanded. "I know better than to ask the woman who jousted me out of a solid sleep. I'll probably say something I might regret later."

Annie shrugged. "I ain't tellin' nothin' I know. Once Miss Carrie told me I didn't have to do the nonsense she has planned, I just did my part."

"And what is your part?" Jeremy growled as he and Marietta joined the group. He turned to Carrie. "You know I love you, but snowy mornings like this are meant for sleep."

"No, they're not!" Amber yelled as she ran in through the back door, letting in a blast of cold that made all of them edge closer to the roaring fire. "It's meant for riding!" Her eyes were wide with excitement as she danced in front of them. "We have horses ready for everyone. Me, Clint and Miles started working as soon as it was light."

Harold walked in at the same time Rose and Moses did. "Horseback riding?" he asked. "I looked outside and saw the snow on the woods out back. I was hoping to go riding."

"Are we all going?" Moses asked, his eyes glowing with pleasure as he pulled Rose close to his side.

Carrie grinned. "Well, I couldn't talk Annie or Polly into it, but they convinced me they would be more appreciated if they have a hot meal waiting for us when we return."

The door to the kitchen flew open again as John bounded in. "Me, too! I'm going riding, too!"

Rose looked at Carrie and raised a brow.

Carrie nodded. "This is a *family* Christmas outing. John and Patches will be fine."

John nodded hard. "Patches can keep up with those big horses," he boasted. He looked up at Moses. "Tell them, Daddy!"

Moses smiled proudly as he scooped John into his arms. "He's right. He rides the plantation with me most days. If Patches can't keep up at some point, John can handle him just fine."

Carrie felt emotion swell in her as she looked at the group gathered in the kitchen. She pushed aside the surge of sorrow that Robert wasn't there, determined to focus on creating good memories. The people she loved most in the world were all right here for Christmas. Her blessings far outweighed her sorrow.

"What about Felicia?" Thomas asked.

"She's in the barn already," Amber answered.

All eyes turned to her. "Excuse me?" Rose murmured. "Did you say my daughter is in the barn saddling horses on a cold, snowy morning? I think you must have her confused with someone else."

Amber giggled. "It's Felicia," she insisted. She smiled slyly. "I told her it was part of her cocooning time, and that she didn't have a choice."

"Her what?" Marietta asked.

Rose smiled. "I'll explain it later. You're going to be part of it." Her smile grew broader when others stared at her. "Felicia wanted to have a rite of passage like my mama and Chooli had. She told me I could create one for her." She shrugged. "I have. And all the women standing in this room are going to be part of it."

"But you ain't talkin' about it now," Annie said, ending the discussion. She handed each person a hot ham biscuit wrapped in a cloth. "The only way you're gonna get the feast me and Polly are fixin' is to get out of this house and go for a ride in that cold, frozen world out there." She shuddered as she opened the door. "Now get out of my kitchen, eat that biscuit, put on enough clothes so you don't freeze to death, and leave me be."

*****

Seventeen horses were lined up at the fence, watching with great expectancy as the group emerged from the house. Their breath hung suspended in air as they stomped their feet and swished their tails.

"What a marvelous idea!"

Carrie smiled at Janie when she walked up, glad to see the dark sorrow had lifted from her friend's eyes. She had struggled all night with her decision to go to Bosque Redondo, but she still believed she was doing the right thing. "I'm glad you think so. I want to create as many memories as possible this year."

Janie eyed her as they moved toward their horses. "Because you think this is our last Christmas together?"

Carrie sighed. "I don't know what to expect about anything anymore," she admitted. "Every day I feel like I am walking into the complete unknown. Rose and Moses are leaving with their kids. I don't know what I'm going to do when I get back from New Mexico, and I have no idea where you and Matthew will be."

Janie smiled slightly. "I can tell you where we will be until late summer."

Carrie stopped walking, caught by something in Janie's eyes. "Where?"

"I hear the weather is wonderful in New Mexico," Janie said quietly.

Carrie stared at her. "New Mexico?" she stammered. "What are you saying?"

Matthew walked up. "My wife is saying we have decided to go to Bosque Redondo with you."

Carrie continued to stare at them, at a loss for words. She finally made her lips move. "You're coming to Bosque Redondo as part of the team?"

"We are," Janie answered. She hesitated then, a flash of vulnerability in her eyes. "If you want us, of course."

Carrie laughed and sprang forward to embrace her friend. "There is nothing I would like more," she cried. "How did you...?"

"Now, Miss Carrie, you can talk to Miss Janie later."

Miles' scolding voice broke through the questions swarming in Carrie's mind.

"You told us to get up early to get these here horses ready for ever'body. We done did it. It be too cold to stand around and talk." He walked over to his Cleveland Bay mare, Chelsea, and mounted easily.

Carrie smiled. "You're right." The look she gave Janie told her they would talk later, but excitement coursed through her body as she thought of Janie and Matthew being on the trip with her.

She quickly directed everyone to the horses selected for them, and then mounted Granite, making no effort to stop his playful prancing. She laughed as snow powdered around his flashing hooves. "Let's go!"

Happy chatter filled the air for the first thirty minutes of the ride, and then it was as if a blanket of silence settled over the group. Even Amber and John fell silent. The only sound was the crunching of snow under horse hooves as they rode across white expanses bordered by gray trees and interspersed with pines and cedar. Flashes of red and blue appeared, as cardinals and blue jays darted among the branches. The silence deepened when a red fox darted from the woods, froze into a statue as it stared at them, and then vanished as quickly as it had appeared.

Carrie took deep breaths, content to let the silence wrap around her. Harold rode beside her. She could tell by his face that he was entranced by the plantation. The towering bay gelding he rode was a perfect fit for his tall slender body. His blue eyes snapped with life when he turned to smile at her. Carrie returned the smile, but the odd feeling that she was riding with Matthew continued. She did not know this man, but she felt very much like she did. She wondered if he had his brother's depth of character.

Harold grinned. "Is galloping allowed?"

Carrie glanced back at John proudly riding Patches between Moses and Rose. There were only a couple inches of snow on the ground, so the horse's legs were not in danger.

Moses interpreted the question in her eyes. "Go," he mouthed.

Carrie looked at Harold, but her only answer was to grin and lean forward slightly. Granite had been waiting for the signal since they had left the barn. He went from a sedate walk to a ground-swallowing gallop in a few seconds. Carrie heard the calls behind her, but all she cared about was the wind rushing through her hair and blasting her face. With Eclipse still stalled in the barn, and with Silver Wings being treated for a swollen fetlock, there was not a horse that could come close to catching Granite. She laughed with delight, and for just a moment...

Carrie caught her breath and listened to the wind.

*For just a moment...*she heard Robert laughing back.

Chapter Fourteen

Rose stood at the end of the table and looked at the women who had assembled. The ride was over, and the feast Annie and Polly prepared had been consumed. When the last bite was eaten, Rose had excused all the men from the table. They had left willingly, though with puzzled expressions. Rose smiled at Felicia who was seated next to her, and then gazed around at the women surrounding the table, expectant looks on their faces. Felicia had wanted Carrie, Janie, Abby, Marietta, Chooli, Susan, Annie and Polly to share this time in her life. Felicia had gotten her wish, though she was still horrified at how close Janie had come to not being there. She pushed aside that thought, and began.

"Ladies, you have all been invited to be a part of the Cocooning Rite for Miss Felicia Samuels," Rose said gravely. "My mother often shared with me how important her rite of passage was when she moved into adulthood at age thirteen in Africa. Slavery robbed young black people of that important moment in their lives. Freedom has given it back. Felicia has requested her own rite of passage." She paused. "Since none of the rites I know about seemed to be appropriate for Felicia, she asked me if I would create one for her. I have done that."

A murmur of approval rose around the table.

"How wonderful," Abby said softly.

Chooli remained silent, but her eyes glowed with delight.

Rose laid her hand on Felicia's shoulder. "We are calling it the Cocooning Rite." She had considered having Felicia explain it but ultimately decided it should be her, since Felicia had asked her to create it. "As Felicia and I talked, she mentioned that the thing she found most fascinating in nature was just how a caterpillar turns into a butterfly. We discussed why she found this so fascinating, and she raised many wonderful questions."

Rose was excited they had discovered the perfect symbol for Felicia's rite of passage. "I've always been enthralled by the caterpillar, as well. It will never cease to amaze me that a caterpillar has the ability to transform into a butterfly or moth capable of flight. It's a strong testimony to the power of God, and also to the power of nature. I believe Felicia, as a young woman, is transforming from a child into a woman capable of anything she desires. As we talked about that transformation, she asked some significant questions." Rose smiled as she remembered her amazement at the quality of questions Felicia had raised. "She wonders if the wormy caterpillar can really envision what it will become someday. She asked if they are aware of what is happening when they are enclosed in a cocoon that must surely seem like a pretty tomb. She wonders if they have any clue that this dark, scary time is actually the prelude to the most wonderful time of their life."

Rose smiled at all the women clustered around the table, leaning forward with intense concentration. "It's crucial to the success of the Cocooning Rite that the women who are important to Felicia be part of it. She requested all of you who are here at this table because you mean so much to her. I am excited to have you all here because every woman at this table has something special and unique to offer my daughter as she moves into womanhood." Pride and pleasure filled all their eyes. "Many rites of passage last for weeks or months, but we don't have that kind of time. Besides the fact that we are leaving for Ohio in a few weeks, this will be the only opportunity for Felicia to be with all of you. The final Cocooning Rite will be held on New Year's Day—marking the beginning of her new life. I would ask that each of you find time in the next nine days to talk privately with Felicia. Let her ask you questions, but most importantly, Felicia would like to know what you believe is the most important thing she should know as a woman."

Rose looked down when Felicia rested her hand on her arm. "Yes, Felicia?"

"May I speak, please?"

"You may," Rose said formally. She knew *how* the rite was performed was as important as the rite itself. She wanted her daughter to always remember this as a sacred, special time in her life.

Felicia let her eyes sweep the table. "I appreciate each of you being here. I realize I am becoming a woman at a very vital time in our country. I will not have a life where I can choose not to be strong. As a black woman, I will have to be very strong." Her voice grew more earnest. "I want to be strong. I want to be like all of you. I'm so glad I have been able to watch how all of you live, but I'm also eager to hear what you have to say to me." She took a deep breath. "I only ask that you be honest, even if you think it will be hard for me to hear. I already know these are very scary times. I have already lost my parents, and I know there are many people who would be very happy if I was dead. I don't intend to give them that satisfaction." She lifted her head proudly. "I already know that I'm smart— it would be silly to pretend otherwise—but I'm learning I must become wise, as well. If I can learn wisdom from each of you that will keep me from making the mistakes you made, then I will be able to help my people much sooner."

Stunned silence followed her words.

Rose understood. She had never known a thirteen-year-old with Felicia's maturity, but that was all the more reason the young girl on the threshold of womanhood needed these women around the table.

"The second phase of the Cocooning Rite has begun," Rose said gravely. "Felicia will wait for all of you to approach her when the time is right."

*****

"Do you know what they are doing?" Matthew asked as he glanced at the closed door to the dining room.

Moses shrugged. "Being women," he answered lamely. "Rose wouldn't tell me anything about it. She said it was a rite of passage for Felicia, and that Felicia had asked for all the women here to be a part of it."

"Only women?" Harold asked with a raised brow.

"I asked more questions, but she told me I wasn't allowed to know because I am a man." He looked over at

Thomas, who had settled with the newspaper into his favorite armchair in front of the fire. "You don't seem to care."

"When you're as old as me, you won't care either," Thomas said, flattening the paper so he could read it better. "Women are a mystery to me most of the time, but I know I can't live without them. If they have some kind of ritual thing going, I'm all for it. I'm probably not intelligent enough to be part of it, so I would rather be left out. It's less embarrassing that way." He grinned and then pointed to an article in the paper, changing the subject. "I understand things are rough for the blacks at the Virginia Constitutional Convention in Richmond, Jeremy. Is that true? I've been so busy with the factory lately that I haven't been able to keep up."

"It's true," Jeremy said, his eyes flaring beneath his blond hair. "The black delegates are being laughed at and humiliated in the papers, mostly because of their speech, but they are not letting that stop them from fighting for the rights of those that elected them."

"I understand a lot of the whites refused to take part in the convention elections back in October," Harold said.

Jeremy nodded. "It seems to be happening all through the South. Blacks had the chance to vote here in Virginia for the first time in October. Since many whites refused to take part in it as a way of protest, the whites who were elected are Radical Republicans, and there were twenty-four black delegates elected. Some of them were free before the war, but many of them were slaves. What they lack in education, they more than make up for with passion and political savviness. They know what they are fighting for, and I predict they will fight hard."

Thomas held up the paper he was reading. "The results show that voter registration was about equal for blacks and whites, but that ninety-two percent of blacks voted, while only sixty-two percent of whites voted."

"Blacks aren't going to sit around and wait for somebody to rescue them," Moses said in a tight voice. "This shows what people will do when they feel an ownership of the political process. The newspapers can laugh at how they speak, but they are doing the right thing to have power to change this country."

"There are whites determined to fight back, though," Jeremy said. "There was a large group of white men who met in Richmond on December eleventh and twelfth. They formed a new political party."

Thomas raised a brow. "A new political party? And I wasn't invited?"

Jeremy snorted with laughter. "Sorry, brother, but I think your record shows you would not be sympathetic to their platform."

"Which is?" Thomas asked, all pretense at humor gone.

"They call it the Conservative Party," Jeremy explained. "They are springing up around the South. It's a union of the Democratic and Whig parties that existed before the war. Basically, they oppose everything the Radical Republicans stand for. They oppose black suffrage, black office-holding, and equality in general. They are recruiting members that agree with them."

Matthew eyed him. "And how did you discover this so quickly?"

Jeremy grinned. "I remembered the story you told me about you and Robert sneaking into a secret meeting at the convention down in Charleston before the war. I heard the rumor something was happening, so Marcus and I found a window open in the building where they met. We were already there, hiding in the balcony, when they arrived. They never suspected a thing."

Matthew and Harold hooted with laughter.

"There is always a way to get information if you really want it," Harold agreed.

Thomas smiled. "Has your brother told you about going to the Ku Klux Klan Convention in Nashville this spring in disguise?"

Harold's eyes widened as he regarded his brother. "You did?"

Matthew nodded. "It seemed important at the time." He knew his voice was bitter.

Harold cocked his head. "At the time?"

"We didn't discover anything that was helpful enough to derail their agenda. The power of the Klan is growing, and no one seems to realize it. At least not anyone who is willing to do what it takes to stop it," he said angrily. "Just a few weeks after the convention in Nashville, they decided who they wanted as their Grand Wizard." He hesitated, knowing how Moses would respond when he heard the news. Matthew had not been back on the plantation since his discovery of the Grand Wizard's identity, and he had avoided telling Moses.

Moses caught his hesitation and narrowed his eyes. "Who is it, Matthew?"

"Nathan Bedford Forrest," Matthew revealed reluctantly.

Moses tensed with fury.

Thomas frowned. "I know he was a Confederate general, but I'm not familiar with his record."

"He was far more than that," Moses snapped. "Did you never hear about the Fort Pillow Massacre?"

Thomas watched him carefully. "Evidently, I didn't." He turned to Matthew. "Would one of you enlighten me, though I have a feeling I would rather not know."

"Everyone should know," Moses growled. "There is a monster in charge of the KKK now." His eyes were fiery with anger and something very close to desperation.

Matthew ached for him but at some point he would have to learn the truth about just how bad it was going to get in the South. "The Battle of Fort Pillow was fought in April, 1864. The fort was on the Mississippi River. A few weeks earlier, Forrest had launched a month-long cavalry raid into Tennessee and Kentucky. He sent about two thousand men to attack Fort Pillow once he discovered there were only five hundred soldiers holding it. He needed the horses and supplies there, and thought it would be an easy target." He took a deep breath. "About half the men were black. They were some of the first black soldiers in the war. They fought courageously, but they were badly outnumbered. When they realized they could not hope to win, they surrendered."

"They *tried* to surrender," Moses interrupted. "And they were all massacred," he said bitterly. "Forrest was there. His soldiers went in and murdered them in cold blood. Out of four hundred black soldiers, along with their officers, only twenty survived. Twenty!" He turned agonized eyes to Matthew. "And this is the man who is now in charge of the Klan?"

Matthew gazed at him steadily, wishing it were not true. "I'm sorry."

"Tell me all of it," Moses demanded.

Matthew was glad all the women were still in the dining room. They would know everything before long, but if he could hold it from them until after Christmas he would...though he doubted Rose wouldn't demand to know the truth once she saw her husband's face. "He was the perfect pick," he said honestly. "The Klan no doubt appreciates his reputation. He was a wealthy man when the war started, and he had nothing when it ended. So he relates to the anger fueling the vigilantes. He has also started a new career as an insurance representative and railroad promoter. He is in the perfect position to recruit members and grow the Klan throughout the South."

"Dear God," Thomas muttered.

Matthew pushed on. "The Klan is becoming more visible, and they are becoming much bolder. Continued instability and fear in our country is playing into the hands of those who want to make the Klan bigger and more powerful. Things got worse after the vote in August. The Klan hoped that the push by the Conservatives—" He paused when he caught Thomas' look. "Yes, the same party that just formed here in Richmond. Anyway, the Conservatives told the black voters that their former masters were still their best friends and had their genuine interests at heart. They encouraged them to vote the Conservative ticket."

Moses snorted his disdain.

Matthew nodded. "The black voters there felt the same way. The Republicans had a resounding victory at the polls, and the Conservatives immediately attributed blame to the Union League."

Harold interrupted. "The Union League came down here to register blacks to vote and teach them how the ballot box worked."

"And to tell them to vote Republican," Jeremy added. "But all the blacks I know were already going to do that."

"That's all true," Matthew responded. "The Conservatives refuse to accept reality. They have a ridiculous belief that blacks voted Republican simply because they were told to. The Conservatives believe that if there was no influence from the North, then the blacks would all go back to being the 'good slaves' they were before the war and follow the dictates of their former masters." His voice showed his disgust. "They are idiots."

"Dangerous idiots," Thomas said soberly.

"Yes," Matthew agreed. "Anyway, the Klan sprang into action after the Tennessee vote four months ago. They paraded and recruited boldly. Their numbers grew impressively."

"Go on," Moses prodded. "I want to know it all."

"A couple months ago they started a series of organized raids on blacks and on the white teachers of black schools. There has been an alarming increase in murders, assaults, rapes and arsons aimed at blacks. It is all attributed to the KKK." He looked Moses squarely in the eyes. "The KKK is becoming an army. Their numbers are growing all over the South. Their agenda is a reign of terror that will keep blacks from the polls so they can regain control of the life they once knew."

"And nothing is being done?" Jeremy demanded. "What good is martial law if the military is allowing this to happen?"

"I ask myself the same question every day," Matthew replied. "The army seems to be doing a good job in the larger cities, but it is just not possible to control what is happening in the rural South. There are not enough soldiers to protect an area that large."

"So it just continues?" Moses asked. "Everyone turns a blind eye while black people are murdered and tortured?" He stood and stalked over to the window. "What is the use of freedom if we are never free? If we continue to be killed?" His voice was full of agony and pain.

Thomas moved over next to him. Matthew, Harold and Jeremy joined him.

"You are not alone," Thomas promised. "There is not a white man in this room who will not fight for your right to freedom. You going to school to become a lawyer is more important now than ever."

"If I live through it!" Moses exclaimed. "What will happen to my family?"

"It's good that you are going to Oberlin," Thomas repled. "There is probably nowhere in the South that is truly safe right now, but you have picked a college in a town known for civil rights and equality for everyone. You will be safe there."

"Safe." Moses almost spat the word. "While my people are being murdered, I will be *safe*."

"Long enough to become what your people need," Thomas said firmly. "You already knew this was going to be a long fight."

Matthew watched, knowing Thomas was trying to lift Moses from his despair. "Change is coming, Moses," he added, "but it's going to take a long time. People are going to die," he said. "One war has ended, but another has begun. You fought the last war with everything you had. You have the opportunity to do the same thing now."

Moses finally turned from the window and gazed at his friends. "There are times when I would give anything in the world to be white," he admitted, "but I'm not. I'm a black man." He squared his shoulders. "I'm a black man who is going to go to his grave fighting for what I believe is right."

Matthew, his thoughts full of Robert, hoped with all his heart that Moses was not being prophetic.

Chapter Fifteen

Abby was waiting in the parlor with a cup of hot tea when Felicia slipped through on her way to the library. "Good morning, Felicia."

Felicia jolted to a stop. "Miss Abby! You scared me. What are you doing up so early?" She looked around with frightened eyes. "Is something wrong?"

Abby smiled. "You're not the only one who can get up before the sun, my dear. Rose told me you are usually in the library reading before anyone else is up. I decided to find out if she was right."

"Why? Have I done something wrong?"

"Of course not," Abby answered, "but I do believe we are to spend time together before New Year's Day."

Felicia relaxed. "That's right! I just wasn't expecting anyone else to be up at five thirty in the morning."

"It's not my preferred rising time," Abby admitted, "but I wanted to be sure we had a quiet time to talk."

"I'm real glad," Felicia said earnestly. She curled into the other soft chair in front of the fire, and pulled a gaily-colored quilt over her. "May I ask you a question, Miss Abby?"

"Anything."

"You're a very successful businesswoman, and you also fought for many years for abolition. What is the most important thing you can tell me about being like you?"

Abby laughed softly. "I've been trying to answer that question for myself ever since Rose told us to be thinking about it. I could probably talk for days, but trying to narrow everything down to just one thing is rather daunting."

"You know I have to talk to everyone," Felicia reminded her hesitantly.

Abby chuckled. "I know, dear. Don't worry, I'm not going to talk to you for days." She bit back another laugh at the obvious relief on Felicia's face. "I've thought about what you are facing as you become a woman. You have the freedom so many people worked so hard to achieve for you. It is a great privilege, but it is also a great responsibility."

Felicia stared back, listening intently.

"As I thought about what I wanted to tell you, I realized the most important thing is to never take anything for granted. When my husband died and I took over the business, I worked hard and faced many dangers."

"Dangers?"

Abby nodded. "Dangers. There were many people threatened by what I chose to do because it was out of the norm for women. I was intimidated, accosted by men who had been sent to frighten me, and I faced obstacles of all kinds as I fought to get business in a man's world."

"*Men*," Felicia murmured. "They do seem to make things hard on women."

Abby smiled. "Yes, most of them were men, but there were women, too."

"Women?" Felicia's eyes were wide with disbelief. "Why would women want to make it hard for you?"

"Because I threatened them, as well. I was choosing a route they didn't wish to take, or didn't believe they could. They thought I was stepping out of the proper role for women and should be brought back in line. They chose angry words and sneers to let me know just how they felt."

"That was dumb."

"It didn't work," Abby agreed, "but there were so many times I got tired of fighting." She paused. "There are still times I get tired of fighting."

Felicia's eyes narrowed. "You are one of the most successful businesswomen in Richmond and Philadelphia—probably on the whole east coast. Why are you still fighting?"

"I will always fight," Abby said. "That's what I meant about not taking things for granted. It's easy to believe that once you have accomplished something you can sit back and rest on your laurels. That's not true. If you do, you will see your accomplishments slip away." She thought for a minute. "Have you ever played with a hoop before?"

"Rolled a hoop? Of course! My daddy and I used to do it in Memphis."

"Have you ever rolled a hoop up a hill?"

Felicia nodded. "There was a big hill not too far from where I lived."

"What happened if you started up the hill with the hoop and then quit pushing it?"

Felicia looked at her with something akin to pity. "You can't quit pushing the hoop when you're going uphill, Miss Abby."

"Really? Why not?"

"Because if you do," Felicia said patiently, "it will start to roll back downhill."

Abby let Felicia's response hang in the air, recognizing the moment the girl understood her point.

"That's what you mean by not taking things for granted," she exclaimed. "You can't ever stop fighting for what you want." She stared into the fire, deep in thought. "Is that true for everyone or just for women?"

"The principle is true for everyone," Abby responded, "but it is truer for women because there are so many people that want to see us fail."

"That's not right!" Felicia cried.

"Right or not, that is the way it is," Abby said. "It's hard for me as a woman, and it's going to be harder for you as a black woman. There are many times you are going to be very tired. You're going to want to quit fighting and take a seat, but you can't..."

"...Because I will go downhill and lose what I worked so hard for."

Silence reigned in the room for several minutes as Felicia absorbed what she had heard. "What keeps you fighting, Miss Abby? When you're real tired and want to stop, what keeps you going?"

Abby smiled. "You do, Felicia. You, and all the other girls in America who deserve a better life. You can only fight for so long if you're fighting for yourself, but if you're fighting for something much bigger, you find the energy to keep going." She held Felicia's gaze. "You fight because it matters."

"Because it matters," Felicia murmured.

Abby leaned forward and took her hands. "It's going to matter so much for you, Felicia. You are fighting for you, but you are also fighting for the first generation of black girls and women who have ever been free, and then for the next generation who will follow. You'll fight for your children, and you'll fight for your grandchildren. You'll fight for other's children and grandchildren."

Abby watched the play of emotions on Felicia's face and felt sorrow for what she was certain the little girl would have to endure. "I'm sorry it has to be so hard, my dear. I wish it were different for you. I believe you are a very special girl—soon to be a woman—who is going to do powerful things for your people, but I also know what a huge responsibility you are going to carry."

Felicia continued to stare into the fire. "I made myself a promise when I came here," she said quietly.

"A promise?"

Felicia nodded. "When my mama and daddy were murdered, I promised them I would do everything I could to make sure things like that didn't continue to happen. Then I came here and discovered the library. I realized I had all the knowledge to become who I needed to be. That's why I'm always in here. There is so much to learn, and I believe the more I know, the more I will be able to help my people." She paused for a long moment. "I know Rose and Moses worry about me because I spend so much time in here, even though they say it's all right. They think I should act like a child more." Her face grew very serious. "I quit being a child the moment I saw my parents murdered. I may be young, but I'm not a child."

"I know," Abby replied. "I know, Felicia."

Felicia searched her face. "Do you? Do you really?"

"I do, and even though Moses and Rose want you to have more of a childhood, they never had one either. Slavery robbed them of that opportunity. All parents want their children to have better than what they had, but that doesn't mean they don't understand."

"We're going to Oberlin," Felicia said. "Rose said I'm going to like it there."

"You're going to *love* it there," Abby replied.

"Will I? I'm a little scared to be in a town," she admitted.

"Oberlin, Ohio is nothing like Memphis," Abby told her. "You are going to be safe there, but more importantly, you are going to learn even more, and you're going to make friends with other black women who want to know as much as you do."

Felicia smiled. "I never thought about it that way, but I suppose that is true." Her worried look disappeared. "Thank you." She gazed deeply into Abby's eyes. "I promise to never take anything for granted."

Abby smiled. "If you start to forget, I'll be sure to remind you."

*****

Thomas had just stepped out on the porch when Carrie appeared at the barn door. He waved and waited for her to join him. "You look happy," he said fondly.

Carrie thought about his comment and was surprised to find he was correct. "I actually *feel* happy right now." The realization instantly made her uncomfortable.

Thomas read her thoughts. "It's natural, honey. I thought I would never be happy again after your mother died, but almost despite myself, I found moments and days when I was not miserable. I struggled with the guilt over that when I realized it."

Carrie held his gaze for a moment before she looked away. "I still feel guilty," she admitted.

"Would you want Robert to feel guilty if you were the one who died?" Thomas asked.

"Why do people always ask that?" Carrie asked, irritated. "How in the world could I know what I would want if I were the one who had been brutally murdered? I wasn't! I can imagine what I might *want* to feel like, but that is the best I can do."

"All right," Thomas responded calmly. "How would you *want* to feel?"

Carrie laughed, the irritation dissolving as quickly as it had come. "You always did know how to handle me."

"I stopped trying to *handle* you a long time ago, my dear. It's actually a very good question. I've also wondered before why people say it. I think the truth is that all the questions we ask, and all the things we say, are nothing more than our attempt to make sense out of a world that doesn't usually make sense."

Carrie slipped her arm through her father's. "As long as I still have you, I will keep finding a way to make sense of it."

Thomas kissed the top of her head. They stood silently and watched the horses cavorting in the field. The snow had stopped, but the frigid temperatures kept it from melting. Miles was predicting more that night.

Carrie thought about the happiness swirling in her mind. "Robert would be so proud of what he created."

"He would be, and he would have every right to be. He took the opportunity Abby offered him, and he went so far in such a short period of time."

Clint strode from the barn, leading Eclipse. The towering Thoroughbred held his head proudly, snorting as he watched the progeny he had spawned.

"Clint has done a magnificent job," Carrie murmured.

"Because of Robert," Thomas replied. "Not many Southern white men would have given such a responsible job to a young black man. Robert recognized talent and passion, and he saw beyond the color, just like he did with Amber. Only with her, he also had to see beyond her age." He smiled as Amber's filly, All My Heart, broke free from the group to race along the fence next to where Eclipse stood.

Carrie laughed. "All My Heart is showing off for her daddy." She turned her attention back to her father. "Amber is one of the finest natural trainers I've ever seen." She frowned suddenly.

"Why the frown?"

Carrie shook her head and stayed quiet for a moment. "I wonder what the future holds for her," she admitted. "The KKK tried to kill her once already. What will happen to her as she grows older and has to work within a horse world dominated by white men? It's hard enough for Clint, but it will be harder for her as a black woman."

"What would Sarah tell you?"

Carrie turned to stare at him. "What?"

"I obviously never knew Sarah the way you did, but I've heard enough of her wisdom from you and Rose to know she would have had sound advice for you. What would it have been?"

Carrie looked over the fields, her gaze fixed on the horizon. "She would have told me *I be borrowin' trouble* 'fore it be dere." She smiled softly as she envisioned the tiny black woman who had taught her the most important lessons about life. "She would have told me *dat dere ain't been no black folk eber born dat don't have a passel of trouble. But dat black folk be strong 'nuff to fight battles white folks ain't got no idea how to fight 'cause dey been fightin' dere whole life.*" Saying the words made her feel better.

"Amber knows," Thomas said.

"Knows?"

"She already knows she is going to have to fight battles."

Carrie swung her eyes back to him. "Did she tell you?"

Thomas nodded, his eyes full of love when he saw Amber exit the barn leading one of the colts she was training. "That little girl is something," he murmured. "She told me that she knew working with horses was going to be a challenge when she grew up, but that she was going to do whatever it took to make Robert proud of her. She is determined to make Cromwell Stables the best stables in the country. I told her I would be satisfied if it was just the best stables in Virginia, but she said that wasn't good enough because Robert had wanted more."

Carrie swallowed the tears that threatened to come. She watched as the colt Amber was leading pulled back on the rope and threatened to rear. She couldn't hear what the little girl whispered, but the colt relaxed as soon as Amber put her hand on his neck. He dipped his head to listen, nudged her gently, and then fell back into an easy walk. "She has a magical way with them," she said.

"She certainly does," Thomas agreed. "Of course, you did, too. Miles used to brag about you to me all the time."

Carrie grinned. "We made a great team." She sometimes could still hardly believe her childhood mentor had returned to work at the plantation.

Thomas changed the subject. "How are things going with Susan?"

"It couldn't be better," Carrie said enthusiastically. "She's fit right into the stables. She knows she will be running things, but she has complete respect for Miles, Clint and Amber. She also has great ideas for the breeding program. I saw the papers for the mares she is planning on buying in the next few weeks."

"You approve?" Thomas asked keenly.

"More than approve," Carrie answered. "Abby and I have also been working with her on her negotiation skills. She will make us all proud."

Thomas nodded but remained silent for several minutes.

Carrie was happy for the silence. She loved having the house full of guests for Christmas, but it was times like these that she was also reminded how much she craved solitude and silence.

"You haven't changed your mind?" Thomas asked.

Carrie hid her smile at his careful tone. She was aware how difficult her decision to go to New Mexico was for him, but this was one time when she *could* imagine how she would feel if she was the parent. "I haven't changed my mind."

Thomas nodded. "I suspected as much, but a father holds on to hope." He smiled ruefully. "I heard from Anthony before we came out."

Carrie waited for whatever he had to say. Anthony had gone north to be with family for Christmas, but he had been working to finalize plans for her trip out with the army unit.

"They leave on February second. There will be one hundred men in the unit, enough to make sure you are safe. He sent the money I gave him to a connection in Independence. Two wagons have been purchased and are already waiting for you."

Carrie laughed and hugged him. "Thank you! I know you are less than excited about my decision."

"It certainly isn't the first time," Thomas said. "I'm quite certain it won't be the last." He shook his head. "For a while I had the crazy idea that as you got older you would make fewer decisions like this."

"Did you now?" Carrie asked, a smile twitching her lips.

"Abby assured me you would never change," he revealed. "That you would probably get bolder as you aged. She convinced me I shouldn't count on you being different."

"Poor Father," Carrie murmured, her eyes dancing with laughter.

Thomas chuckled. "I'm not thrilled about you going to New Mexico, but I could not be prouder of you," he said.

"Would it make you feel better if you knew Matthew and Janie were coming along?" She had been waiting to tell him until they were alone.

Thomas turned to stare at her. "What?"

Carrie nodded. "They have decided to join me." She grew serious. "I suspect the train wreck was much harder for Janie than she has admitted. I can tell Matthew is worried about her. I'm certain he was the one who suggested the trip."

Thomas looked skeptical. "And a trip on a wagon train in the midst of winter is supposed to help? Does she have any idea what she is getting herself into?"

Carrie shrugged. "None of us do, but Janie told me it would be better than another winter in Philadelphia."

Thomas smiled but still looked doubtful.

*****

Marietta found Felicia in the kitchen making biscuits with Annie. She cocked a brow. "I don't believe I've ever seen you cook before."

Felicia looked up from the flour mix she was carefully stirring. "There is a science to good biscuits," she said.

Marietta nodded, trying not to notice Annie rolling her eyes. "I see," she said. "Would you care to share? I keep trying to make biscuits like Annie, but they are never quite the same. I think Jeremy despairs of me ever achieving it."

Felicia giggled. "It's not so hard. I read all about it."

Annie couldn't hold back the snort. "Can't nobody learn how to make biscuits in no book."

Felicia looked at her with pity. "You can learn anything in a book, Grandma."

"Let's just see how them biscuits turn out," Annie retorted.

Marietta settled down on the chair next to the counter, pushing back the long red hair she had been in no mood to tame into a bun. Her blue eyes danced merrily. "I want the secrets," she demanded.

Felicia smiled. "Most people mix their biscuit dough too much." She carefully added the lard to the flour mix she had already stirred. "But first you have to snap the lard," she explained.

Annie leaned forward at the same time Marietta did. "What you say about snappin'?" she demanded.

Felicia nodded. "You are supposed to pinch the flour and lard together like you are snapping your fingers. It keeps your biscuits real soft."

"Ain't never heard of such a thing, but at least you be makin' it look like I do," Annie said grudgingly.

Marietta watched carefully. She had never taken the time to read about baking biscuits. She was more than happy to learn from Felicia. She had tried to learn from Annie, but the old cook just told her to watch and learn. Annie moved so fast in the kitchen it was almost impossible to keep up with her, much less copy her technique.

"Once you have the lard snapped," Felicia continued, "you add in the cream and the buttermilk. Most people mess up their biscuits at this step because they stir too much." She stirred carefully, leaving the batter very lumpy.

"That lumpy?" Marietta asked. "I always make sure mine is smooth."

"That be your problem," Annie grunted. "You mix too much and you end up with tough biscuits that ain't be worth eatin'."

"You never told me that," Marietta protested.

"Ain't never asked me 'bout it."

"But you were supposed to be teaching me how to make biscuits like yours for Jeremy," Marietta argued. She had suspected all along that Annie was holding back on her. Now she knew it was true.

Annie looked her over carefully. "I ain't found me a white woman yet that can make a good southern biscuit."

Felicia laughed at Marietta's outraged expression. "You'll be able to make them now, Miss Marietta. Just snap the lard, and don't overmix them. Jeremy is going to be very happy."

Annie looked displeased. "You ain't supposed to tell all our secrets, Felicia. I wouldn't a let you in my kitchen if I'd known you were gonna tell them."

"You didn't tell me either, Grandma. My mama told me that you don't want anyone else to know how to make good biscuits, so you make it seem like some big secret. I made sure I read about it before I came in here."

Annie planted her fists on her hips and glared at the little girl. "You think you be real smart, don't you?"

"I *am* real smart," Felicia said smugly. "Smart enough to be glad I can take making biscuits off my list now that I've made them. I'm more than happy to let you bake them all from now on. I'll stay in the library!"

Annie couldn't stop the deep chuckle. "I done got me a real smart granddaughter," she said proudly. "But we still gots to see how them biscuits look when they come out the oven."

*****

Ten minutes later, their plates full of perfect, tender biscuits slathered with melted butter and preserves, Marietta and Felicia headed for the library. Marietta had already let everyone know to steer clear so she could have her Cocooning Rite time with the girl.

They pulled up chairs in front of the window, covered themselves with warm quilts, and sat quietly while they enjoyed their treat. "These are wonderful," Marietta sighed. "And you really believe I can make them like this for Jeremy?" After so many dismal failures, she was almost afraid to try again. Jeremy was always gracious, but she could tell he was losing hope.

Felicia arched a brow. "If Jeremy wants them so badly, why doesn't he learn to make them himself?" she asked. "Is there some rule that says only women can make biscuits?"

Marietta almost choked as she laughed helplessly. Once she had herself under control, she reached out and took Felicia's hand. "There is hope for women in the future as long as the world is full of girls like you."

"I'm serious," Felicia replied. "I keep hearing about rules. Rules about how women are supposed to dress. Or how they are supposed to act. I read that women should make sure men believe they are smarter than them." She rolled her eyes. "Who comes up with these rules? And why in the world do women think they have to live by them?"

"Where did you hear about the rules?"

"Mama suggested I should read some women's magazines, so I read some issues of *Godey's Lady's Book* and *Harper's Bazaar*." She rolled her eyes. "There were a few good articles, but most of what I read made me wish I had been born a man." She shook her head in disgust.

"What magazines do you enjoy?"

Felicia's eyes lit up. "I love *The American Freedman*, and the *American Journal of Science*. I've also read every issue Thomas had of *The Knickerbocker*, but they quit publishing it two years ago." She shook her head. "It was a huge loss when they quit publishing. I've learned about so many things in that magazine, but I also learned a lot about the area where Carrie, Janie and Matthew will be in New Mexico, and I've learned a lot about Chooli's people."

Marietta eyed her thoughtfully. "I am going to make sure my children have the same hunger for knowledge that you do, Felicia. Because you know so much, you are able to cut through the nonsense to what is true or false."

"It's not really that difficult," Felicia replied. "Why *do* people simply go along with the rules other people make? I've been thinking about that a lot. Don't they realize they should be the ones to make the rules for their own lives?"

"Evidently not," Marietta said dryly. She picked up her last biscuit, watching as the first flakes from the coming snowstorm began to dance against the massive oak towering over the three-storied home. After growing up in the city, being on the plantation always felt like being in a fairytale. She never grew tired of it.

"Miss Marietta?"

"Yes?" Marietta pulled her thoughts back to the library. She was not here to indulge in fantasy, though she couldn't imagine what she could add to this extraordinary girl's life.

"Are you afraid?"

Marietta gazed at her, surprised by the question. "Afraid of what?"

Felicia hesitated. "Afraid of the KKK," she finally said, a slight quaver to her voice. "The KKK hates black people, but from what I read they hate white teachers about as much."

Marietta took a deep breath, remembering Felicia's plea for honesty at the initial meeting. "Yes," she admitted. "I'm afraid every day. I'm afraid for myself. I'm afraid for Jeremy. I'm afraid for my students, and I'm afraid for everyone I love."

Felicia stared at her. "I'm afraid, too," she said. "I'm afraid to leave the plantation."

Marietta thought about the attacks already made on the plantation, but fear of the unknown was usually stronger than fear of what you knew. "I understand how you feel, honey, but I can promise you will be much safer in Oberlin."

"That's what Mama told me, too," Felicia said, although her voice and eyes were full of doubt.

"You don't believe her?" Marietta understood fear far too well. "What have you read about Oberlin?" she asked. She wasn't going to repeat platitudes the girl had probably already heard. She hoped facts would help soothe her fears.

"Oberlin was founded by two Presbyterian ministers who were friends. They didn't like how things were going in America so they decided to start both a community and a college that would change it," Felicia answered. "In the beginning, tuition was free because all the students were expected to contribute by building the community. It's not that way anymore because it didn't turn out to be very efficient, but it started Oberlin."

"Go on," Marietta encouraged.

"When they were two years old, there were only a few hundred residents, but they started sending out abolitionist missionaries across the country to fight against slavery." Felicia's eyes took on a shine. "And lots of black folks, both free and runaway slaves, started moving there. They were the first college to admit both men and women of all colors."

Marietta had done her own research on Oberlin when she discovered Rose and Moses were going there with their family. "Weren't they part of the Underground Railroad?"

"Yes," Felicia answered eagerly. "There were thousands of my people who went through Oberlin when they escaped. Even when the government passed the Fugitive Slave Law, the people there kept helping the slaves go free. Instead of helping them settle in Ohio, they took them all the way up to Canada."

"I believe Frederick Douglass called it the 'Gibraltar of Freedom,'" Marietta added.

Felicia's eyes widened. "You know a lot about Oberlin, don't you?"

"I do."

"Why have you learned about it?"

Marietta hesitated, but spurred on by Felicia's plea for the truth, answered honestly. "Because I've been afraid for your family here in Virginia. Things are going to get worse, Felicia. I don't want any of you to be harmed. If I were to pick one place in the whole country for you to be, I would choose Oberlin, Ohio."

Felicia absorbed the statement. "Do you think that is why Mama chose Oberlin?"

"No," Marietta admitted. "Your mama would not have let fear stop her if she believed she and your father would get a better education somewhere else. The fact that Oberlin is safe is just a bonus. A bonus I'm very grateful for."

"What about you?"

"Me?"

"You said you were afraid for you and Jeremy. What are you doing about that?"

Marietta took a deep breath. She had known they would come back to that. "I'm choosing to not let fear stop me," she said. She leaned forward for emphasis. "Felicia, there are always things to be afraid of. You are going to be safe in Oberlin, but I don't believe all of you will stay there. Your parents are getting an education so they can make a difference—that won't include staying in Oberlin. They may settle in the North, or they may return to the South. You may end up staying there until you graduate from college yourself, but the odds are that you won't remain there for the rest of your life. And John and Hope could end up anywhere," Marietta added, and then continued, speaking softly to make the words easier to hear. "Things are going to be hard for blacks in America for a very long time. You are free, but you are not safe."

"I know," Felicia said tremulously.

"But that does not mean you need to *act* afraid," Marietta said. "I was honest when I told you I am afraid every day, but I do not act afraid. I do the things I believe are right, and I say the things I believe are right. I teach because black children deserve an education. Doing so puts my life in danger every day, and I know it, but I won't let that knowledge stop me."

Felicia was watching her closely. "You feel afraid, but you don't act afraid," she repeated. "Is it hard?"

"Sometimes," Marietta admitted. "But it can also be fun."

"Fun?" Felicia asked skeptically.

"Fun," Marietta repeated. "Remember those rules you were talking about? There are *rules* that say women are the weaker sex. Most people tend to believe them. They are always caught off guard when a woman doesn't act like the weaker sex. It gives us the advantage sometimes because people aren't expecting us to act strong." She grinned. "I love seeing the surprised looks when I don't behave the way people believe I am supposed to."

Felicia returned her grin. "Are your mama and grandma strong like you?"

"Stronger," Marietta replied. "They have been my role models for my entire life."

"Are they scared to have you down here in the South, and married to a man who is half-black? I read that the Klan hates people like Jeremy almost as much as me."

There was the crux of the issue, Marietta acknowledged. "My family worries about me, but they support my decisions."

Felicia considered that for a moment. "Can I ask you a real personal question?"

Marietta almost laughed. Had Felicia not already been asking personal questions? "Go ahead."

"What are you going to do if you have a baby that looks black?"

Marietta ran possibilities of answers through her mind. She and Jeremy had discussed the possibility when they chose to marry almost a year ago. She opted for the truth. "I don't know."

"Will it bother you to have a black baby?"

"Absolutely not," Marietta said. "I will love that baby with all my heart."

"Will you stay here?"

Again, Marietta chose the truth. "I don't know."

Chapter Sixteen

January 1, 1868

Carrie was already dressed and ready when the knock came. She had been sitting by the window, watching the moon play over the glimmering snow. A barn owl had glided silently out of the woods as she watched, skimming low over the ground in search of prey. A six-point buck and doe had emerged from the woods and stood as still as regal statues for several long minutes before they bounded off.

Carrie opened the door to her room and slipped out quietly, avoiding the creaking boards she had discovered long ago as a child. "Good morning," she whispered.

"Good morning," Rose whispered back, but she didn't start moving down the hall. Instead, she pointed to Carrie's room.

Puzzled, Carrie pushed the door back open and walked in with Rose. "Is something wrong?" She had been looking forward to their tradition for months. She had missed getting up for the New Year's sunrise the year before because she had been so ill with morning sickness. The memory caused a flash of pain. That was the day she had discovered she was pregnant with Bridget. She shook her head, not wanting to remember.

Rose, sensitive to her every mood, took her hand. "Nothing is wrong. It's just cold out there."

Carrie raised a brow. "Certainly you're not going to let a little snow keep us from what may be our last New Year's Day sunrise."

"I can't bear to think of it that way." Rose frowned. "But no, I'm not going to let a little snow stop me, but I'm thinking that perhaps we can change the place we actually watch the sunrise."

"Why? We've gone to the same rock every year since we were children."

"True, but isn't the important thing that we are together?"

Carrie was the one to frown now. "What are you trying to say, Rose? Where do you want to go?"

Rose smiled. "There is a perfectly lovely log on the bank of the river that faces east for the sunrise."

Carrie grinned. "Are you getting old?"

Rose stuck out her tongue. "I'm getting wiser," she protested. "Why should we tramp through a foot of snow in the dark when we can walk down a perfectly dry tunnel lit by the candles we hold? A sunrise is a sunrise," she insisted.

Carrie laughed. "It's a wonderful idea. And since we won't be tramping through a foot of snow, we can also carry thick quilts to keep us even warmer." She opened the lid to her cedar chest and grabbed two colorful quilts. She tossed one to Rose and then tucked another under her arm before she walked to the mirror and pulled the handle that would reveal the tunnel her ancestors had built. As she lit the candles she laughed softly. "Wiser. Definitely wiser."

*****

The sky was scattered with cumulus clouds when the sun began to shimmer far below the horizon.

Rose sat, her heart and mind full as she watched a new year unfold. She clasped Carrie's hand as the clouds began to glow a soft gray while they floated across the sky. Moments later, they took on a pink hue that seemed to dance through the gray, slowly transforming it to a startling orange as the sun continued its ascent. The water of the James River went from steel black to coal gray, to a glowing coral as it reflected the clouds hovering above.

The wind picked up a little, causing a ripple across the water that made the coral color dip and sway in time with the wind. A fish leapt, its silvery form hanging in the air for what seemed an impossibly long time before it landed with a splash. An eagle swooped from the sky, dove for the river, and departed with a fish wriggling in its talons.

Rose let the beauty explode through her soul. Carrie's look of delight told her she was feeling the exact same thing. When the sun finally peeked its way over the horizon, the clouds framing it were alive with pink, orange and purple—a kaleidoscope of ever-changing colors.

"Hello, 1868," Carrie whispered.

"Hello, 1868," Rose repeated.

The two friends rose for their annual tradition. When the sun was fully above the horizon they both began to dance, twirling and spinning as they welcomed the new year. After a few minutes, they began to laugh hysterically, and then finally collapsed onto the log again.

"Happy New Year!" Carrie shouted.

"Happy New Year!"

They stared at each other for a long moment before grabbing each other into an embrace.

Rose was suddenly certain she would never be able to let go. How could she? How could she leave? Going to college was what she had always wanted, but the reality was something else.

"You're doing it again," Carrie chided.

"Doing it?" Rose asked, pretending she didn't understand.

"You're trying to come up with reasons why you shouldn't go to college."

Rose sighed. "Not reasons why I shouldn't go to college," she protested. "Reasons why I shouldn't leave the plantation."

"Your mama would skin you good if she could hear you," Carrie scolded.

Rose shook her head. "No, she wouldn't. She would tell me to go, but she would understand what it means for me to leave here." She looked around. "With the exception of the war years, this has always been home. First, I was a slave here. Now I'm free. Cromwell Plantation is home."

Carrie sobered. "I know," she said gently. "I do understand."

Rose met her eyes. "Do you?"

"I think so. I haven't experienced it the same way you have, and I've been gone for school already, but I knew that every time I came back, the people I loved most would be here." Carrie took a deep breath. "That is no longer going to be true," she said sadly. "You and Moses won't be here. Felicia, John and Hope won't be here. Nothing will ever be the same."

Rose didn't try to correct her because she knew it was true. "We always knew this time would come," she said.

"That doesn't make it any easier."

"No. It doesn't." Rose fell silent, watching as the sun continued its upward arc. The clouds gradually surrendered their colors and turned soft white. The sky became a startling blue that reflected in the river flowing at their feet.

"Are we wiser now?" Carrie demanded.

Rose smiled, remembering the conversation they'd had by her mama's grave earlier that year. "Wisdom comes from great suffering," she murmured.

"So are we wise yet?"

"You are both certainly wiser than you were."

Rose and Carrie almost fell off the log when the voice sounded behind them.

Rose was the first to find her voice. "Abby! How did you find us?"

Abby smiled. "I hope you don't mind."

"Never!" they answered in unison.

Abby looked at Carrie. "Thomas began to worry when you weren't back for brunch. He was afraid you had fallen in the river, or..." she hesitated briefly before she continued, "that something else had happened."

Rose exchanged a look with Carrie. No one needed to expound on what that *something else* might have been, but her thoughts were on something else entirely. "What time is it? We've never missed a New Year's Day Brunch!"

Abby smiled and pulled out the bag she had been holding behind her back. "I had a suspicion where you would be because it really is too cold for you to have walked through the snow and then sat down on a rock for this long. I confirmed the tunnel door was open, told your father not to worry, and then talked Annie into putting some of the feast into the bag."

Carrie frowned. "But we have to get back!"

"Why?" Abby asked. "Carrie, you have created one amazing memory after another during the last ten days. Now it's time for you and Rose to create one more special memory just for the two of you." She held out the bag. "I'm not going to stay. I just wanted to make sure you don't starve."

Carrie glanced at Rose, saw the answer she expected, and then patted an empty place on the log. "Please don't leave. It will make it even more special if you join us, and it might help us from turning even more melancholy."

"I am honored," Abby replied, sinking down onto the spot Carrie had indicated.

The three women sat quietly, watching as the day continued to unfold. A gaggle of geese flew overhead, their loud honking celebrating the new year. The wind had completely died down, and the mirror-like surface of the James River reflected the clouds, while the sun beamed off the snow mounded on the bank and the clumps that clung to the branches arching over the water.

Abby was the first to break the silence. "Every time I come here I wonder how in the world I can bring myself to return to the city." She sighed. "It gets harder every time."

Carrie eyed her. "Haven't you always lived in the city?"

"For all my adult life," Abby agreed. "It's where I needed to be to run the business, but I grew up in the country. My heart feels most at home here."

"Mine, too," Rose said.

"It's very difficult for you to leave." Abby's statement was not a question.

Rose nodded. "I want to go. I want to stay."

"It's hard when you want to be in two places at one time," Abby agreed.

Rose waited for her to say more, to give advice that would make her departure easier, but nothing broke the morning silence. "Aren't you going to say anything else?" she finally asked.

Abby raised a brow. "What would you like me to say?"

Rose stared at her. "You always have a kernel of wisdom that makes things easier."

Abby considered the statement. "What would you tell Felicia?"

Rose sighed, knowing what Abby was doing. "Could I just repeat whatever you tell me?"

Abby chuckled. "When I came out of the tunnel, I heard the two of you talking about whether you had gotten wiser in the last year. I assured you that you had. So, what would you tell Felicia?"

Rose shifted uncomfortably. "I've told her walking into the unknown is always difficult." Abby waited for her to continue. As hard as it was to admit, Rose had nothing more to add.

"Nothing else?" Abby queried gently.

"I know I should have said more," Rose admitted, "but I couldn't seem to find words. I have too many questions and fears exploding in my own mind."

"I see," Abby murmured, but there was no judgement in her eyes. She turned to Carrie. "What would you say?"

Carrie met her eyes before she turned to gaze at the placid water. "I have been walking into the unknown all year. I suppose I would tell her that she will survive whatever is coming."

"How encouraging," Abby said drolly.

Rose was embarrassed, but too desperate to care much about it. "I'm tired of it!" she burst out. When Abby raised a brow again, she forced herself to explain. "It seems my whole life has been about walking into the unknown. I'm tired of never having a clue what is going to happen next. When does it get easier?"

Abby seemed to hear the desperation in her voice. "When you change how you think about it," she said, her voice tender but firm.

Rose looked at her as another long silence stretched out. "Would you care to be a little more specific?"

"Both of you are afraid of walking into the unknown because you think it is scary. You are afraid of what will happen when you do."

"Seems reasonable," Carrie mumbled.

"It's not," Abby assured her. "My life changed when I began to see life as a grand adventure."

Rose absorbed the words, knowing by the look on Abby's face that she was imparting a very important lesson. "A grand adventure..."

"Yes," Abby said. "We have all talked about this before, but I know the step both of you are getting ready to take is bigger than either of you has taken before. You are so lucky!"

"Lucky?" Rose murmured, but she was caught by the light in Abby's eyes. "You mean that, don't you?"

"Indeed, I do." Abby reached a hand out to touch each of their shoulders. "Change used to terrify me, and I got too weary of never knowing what to expect, but now I get excited about it. When I have absolutely no idea what I'm doing—when I am getting ready to walk into the unknown—I have decided to view it as a grand adventure that is going to lead me to amazing places." She paused and smoothed the folds of her skirt. "As I look back over my life, I see that the most wonderful things happened when I had no idea what I was doing or where I was going. I just kept doing the things I thought felt right at the time. Somehow they all worked out, and now here I am," she exclaimed. "I am married to Thomas. I have a family I adore." She reached down to squeeze both their hands. "Slaves are free. I have five factories in two cities that are doing well." She shook her head. "I could never have dreamed all this on my own. I just kept walking forward."

"We don't really have a choice about that, though," Carrie murmured with a touch of resigned bitterness.

"Oh, but you do," Abby argued. "I watch people every day who simply stay exactly where they are, insisting that they continue to do exactly what they have always done. Change scares them, so they refuse to change. They allow themselves to become trapped in their lives."

Rose thought about what Abby was saying, hoping it would bring relief but her insides were still churning.

Abby turned to her. "When you told us about Felicia's Cocooning Rite, you said she had some important questions. She wonders if the wormy caterpillar can really envision what it will become someday. She asked if they are aware of what is happening when they are enclosed in a cocoon. She wonders if they have any clue that this dark, scary time is the prelude to the most wonderful time of their life."

"Yes," Rose murmured with a frown. "I haven't known what to say to her."

"The answer is simple," Abby replied. "It's *no.*"

"No?"

"How could a caterpillar possibly know it would become a butterfly when it chooses to be encased by a cocoon? How could it know that by enclosing itself into what must seem like a tomb that it will emerge as a winged creature able to fly?"

Rose shrugged, concerned that she was disappointing Abby with her lack of answers, but too honest to pretend otherwise.

"It can't know," Abby pressed. "That caterpillar is simply doing what it was designed to do. Every caterpillar spins a cocoon; it's not just special ones. It's not just some. *Every* caterpillar does what it is designed to do," she repeated. "Some come out as small moths, while others come out as big yellow swallowtails, or bright blue ones, or any number of glorious colors." Her eyes were shining. "The difference with humans is that we do have a choice. We choose whether we are willing to walk into the darkness and have our lives transformed."

Carrie was listening intently. "And because we live longer..." she mused.

"Exactly," Abby replied. "Because we live longer, we are given the opportunity to choose the cocoon more than once!" She smiled. "The glorious thing is that the more we make that choice, the easier it becomes because we have learned how magnificent the result is."

Rose managed a smile. "And you know this because you are older, and because you have chosen the cocoon more times than we have."

"There have to be some benefits to getting older, my dear," Abby quipped. "I can at least be sure there is a purpose by making walking into the unknown a little easier for those I love most." She paused for a moment and then faced Rose squarely. "Don't forget what happened in New York."

Rose caught her breath. "Sojourner Truth," she said softly. She had to admit there were times she wished she could forget, but it wasn't possible.

"Tell me what happened that day," Abby commanded.

"You already know. So does Carrie."

"Tell me again."

Rose knew she was being asked to remember, to put into words what had transpired. She remembered the feeling of awe she had as she watched the elderly woman stand on the stage, a beacon of light to every black person who had ever dreamed of freedom, and to every woman who dreamed of the right to vote. Sojourner Truth had fought what must have seemed like a losing battle for decades, simply refusing to give up. Yet the scourge of slavery had been abolished, and she was now fighting for women's rights.

"She passed the baton to me," she finally murmured, some part of her still wishing it weren't true.

"And you accepted," Abby said.

Rose nodded. When Sojourner Truth had finished speaking, Rose knew that in the span of sixty minutes she had become a changed woman, ready to do whatever it took to make things better for her people, and for all women in general. She had no idea how it was going to play out in her life, and she had no idea what it would require of her, but she was determined to live with the same passion, dedication and perseverance as Sojourner Truth. How had she so easily let that feeling of certainty go? The answer followed on the heels of the question. *Fear.*

Rose stared out at the river for a long time as she let the memories wash over her. They strengthened her resolve but didn't change the sorrow gripping her heart. "I wish we didn't have to leave everything behind to crawl into the cocoon," she said sadly.

Carrie squeezed her hand. "That is the hardest part," she agreed. "It's still hard for me to believe you are moving to Ohio, and that in one month I will be in Independence, Missouri, waiting to embark on the Santa Fe Trail."

"You both are about to start grand adventures," Abby said.

Rose heard something in Abby's voice that didn't ring true with the words she was saying. She met Abby's eyes, probing for what she was suddenly certain was there. "This is almost as hard for you as it is for us, isn't it?"

Abby sighed but didn't look away. "Every bit as hard," she admitted. "You and Carrie are the daughters I never had. The last two and a half years, since the end of the war, have been some of the best of my life. There have certainly been hard times, but having the two of you has made it all worthwhile. I would never stand in the way of either of you moving forward, and I'm happy for both of you, but I will miss you so much it will hurt."

Rose didn't miss the shine of tears in her eyes.

Neither did Carrie. "Leaving you is one of the hardest things," she said. "I'll be home by fall, but after the war years, I know how heartbreaking it is to be separated from both of you. I'm all for having new adventures, but I wish

I could take all the people I care about with me." Her voice clogged with emotion.

"Me, too," Rose said.

"Me, three," Abby added.

*****

The men had all been sequestered in the parlor when Rose pulled the door to the library tightly shut. The furniture had been pushed out of the way to make room for the circle formed with pillows. Chooli had assured her the circle was very important. Every pillow was occupied by the women Felicia had requested for her Cocooning Rite. There was no talking as everyone looked at her expectantly.

The oil lanterns had been extinguished. Dozens of candles created a warm, flickering light that spoke of sacred mystery.

Rose moved into the center of the circle. "We are here tonight for the Cocooning Rite for Felicia Samuels." She smiled at her daughter, who looked beautiful in a long, soft-blue gown, with a wreath of greenery adorning her head. Carrie had woven dried strands of the most powerful healing herbs through the greenery, signifying connection with the Earth. Felicia returned the smile with an endearing mixture of shyness and confidence. Rose felt her heart swell with even more love as she gazed at the almost-young-woman who had become part of her family only two years before. She could never have guessed what a blessing the shattered girl would become.

"We meet here in a circle tonight because the Great Circle of Life, which comes from the Navajo teachings, is the circle of unity with all things in the Universe, including our Creator, about which all life revolves."

Rose let her eyes rest on Chooli. The lovely woman was glowing with passion and vibrancy. Chooli was thrilled that Felicia had chosen to have her own rite of passage after they talked about the Navajo ways. Rose had depended on Chooli greatly as she crafted the Cocooning Rite. "Life is a circle of birth, maturity, decay and death. All living things follow this circle in the same cycle. From birth, each of us begins our journey. Life is the path we walk. True wisdom comes when we stop merely looking for it and start *living* the life the Creator intended for us."

Rose's eyes traveled to Carrie as she spoke more of the Navajo beliefs. "When we live our life on Mother Earth, we always walk softly because we know the faces of future generations are looking up at us from the ground beneath us." She had thought immediately of the Bregdan Principle Biddy had shared with Carrie. Truly, no person could take action that would not have repercussions throughout history.

As her gaze swept the rest of the group, she thought of how fortunate Felicia was to have these women in her life. Her heart caught at the idea of taking her daughter away from them, but then she remembered Abby's words. Felicia was also walking her path into the unknown. There would be new women waiting for her in Oberlin who would become part of her circle and part of the transformation that was about to occur in their lives.

"Felicia now stands on the threshold of adulthood. She is becoming a woman."

Rose's words rang through the room, absorbed by the light of the candles, and then reflected back into the mind and heart of every woman present. The words, spoken for her daughter, were coming full circle to everyone.

"While the Navajo teachings are important to the Cocooning Rite, it is also important to Felicia to incorporate her African roots. During her reading she learned of an African word that symbolizes the life she yearns to live." Rose had been thrilled when Felicia had come to her with the information. "The word is *ubuntu*. The core of *ubuntu* is that a person is a person through other people." Rose let the words resonate and settle in everyone's mind. She watched as eyes ignited with understanding. "We create each other. We belong to each other." Rose paused, her eyes settling on Felicia, who was watching her intently. "You are because *we* are."

Felicia grinned. "*Ubuntu*," she mouthed silently.

Rose returned the grin and motioned for her daughter to join her. "I have asked Felicia to share what she has learned from her time with all of you over the last ten days. I also asked her to create something that would be a blessing to others. I did not give her any direction, rather, the decision was completely hers." She turned and gave Felicia a warm hug. "I am so very proud of my daughter."

Felicia waited until Rose had taken a seat in the circle, and then smiled tentatively. "The last ten days have been the most powerful days of my life," she began. "When Chooli first told me about Kinaalda, the Navajo rite of passage, I knew I wanted to do something to mark becoming a woman. Just five days ago I discovered the term *ubuntu*. I understood it immediately because I'd already had five days with the women who have made me what I am." Her eyes grew sad. "Except my mama, who was murdered. Even though she is dead, I remember everything she ever said to me. Perhaps I will remember it more because she died." Her voice faltered for a moment. "The thing I most remember is watching her and Daddy being gunned down outside our house during the Memphis riot just for being black. As I watched her die from where I was hiding, I made her a promise that I would do everything I could to make the world safe for all black people."

Rose's heart broke as the pain suffused Felicia's face, but a swell of fierce pride followed as she watched her daughter's shoulders straighten with resolve. She saw the same emotions on the faces of every woman in the room. Each of them had known great loss and sorrow. Each of them had made their own choices to live with courage and resolve. Her heart surged with gratitude for these women in the circle that surrounded Felicia.

"I believe my mama is watching," Felicia said. "I can still feel her, and I believe she knows I am becoming a woman. I also believe she knows how each of you have helped me over the last ten days." Her smile this time was strong and genuine. "All of you have taught me to be a strong woman. I've thought so much about what I have learned, and I can't possibly communicate it all tonight, but I'm going to do my best."

The silence in the room was palpable. The only sound was the crackling of the flames in the fireplace and the hiss of damp wood.

"I've learned that many women don't want to be powerful because they are afraid of the responsibility. They want someone else to take care of them, even if that means giving up who they are. That is an expected part of this culture, but I'm grateful that I know women who are breaking that mold. My generation has a long way to go, but I'm going to help make it better." Felicia paused for a long moment. "I've learned it's all right to be afraid, but I don't have to *act* afraid. I can choose every day to do the things I believe are right, even if I have to fight through the fear."

Rose watched as Felicia locked eyes with Marietta, who was giving her a warm smile. She acknowledged that her daughter's words spoke to her, as well. She could be afraid, but she didn't have to *act* afraid. She tucked that truth away for further contemplation.

"I've also learned I have to accept life is going to be hard as a black woman." She smiled slightly as she gazed at her Grandma Annie. "I didn't like this one, but I know it is true. If I expect anything else, I'm going to be disappointed my whole life. If I accept it now, then I'm ready for it. That means I have to work harder than most other people to be who I want to be." She shrugged. "I will."

Her pronouncement rang through the room with blunt clarity.

"I've also learned that I don't have to conform to any rules," she said defiantly. "I think it's horrible how many rules there are for people—not just women, but all people. Who in the world made up all these rules? They do nothing but imprison people with ridiculous expectations." She lifted her head. "I'm not going to let any rules define me."

Rose watched as the other women lifted their heads, too. She knew, as it was true for her, that every woman in the room was being challenged. It was one thing to know the truth, but it was another to live it on a daily basis. To be reminded by a thirteen-year-old was both humbling and empowering, and a beautiful reminder of the power of women.

"I've also learned I have to create my own opportunities." Her voice grew very serious. "I know I'm going to have many opportunities when we get to Oberlin, but I have to take advantage of them. Mama and Daddy have waited a long time to be able to go to college. They have put people, including me, before their opportunity to go to school, but it is finally their turn. I also know they don't regret any decisions they've made."

Rose felt tears well in her eyes as Felicia communicated what they had talked about that afternoon. She had finally found words to share with her daughter.

Felicia paused and her voice became even more grave. "Blacks have opportunities right now because the government is down here making the South give them to us. But everything I'm learning says that might not always be the case. Things might stay better for blacks for a long time, but I wouldn't count on it. The government is working to protect us right now because it makes political sense, but it probably won't stay that way."

Rose felt the atmosphere in the room change as Felicia stated what she believed. As much as she wanted to discount her daughter's words, her intuition told her to listen closely.

Felicia's voice remained firm. "I have to take advantage of every opportunity I have now because they may not always be there." Her voice softened. "I'm sorry. I know that is probably hard to believe coming from someone my age, but—"

"It's not hard to believe coming from you, Felicia," Abby said quickly, speaking the hearts of every woman in the room. "I hope you are wrong, but I'm afraid you might be right."

That acknowledgement seemed to be enough for Felicia. Her smile bloomed again. "I've also learned I should search for joy in every place I can. Life will always have hard times, but there will also be times of great joy. I need to embrace every one of them. If you fill your heart up with joy, it makes the hard times easier to bear."

"I've also learned I need to always surround myself with women like all of you. Women are weak when they stand alone, but we can do anything when we do it together." She paused. "I've seen that. It was mostly women that helped free my people. Men passed the laws, but it was women that made them sit up and take notice. It was women that wouldn't back down. We're going to do the same thing for women's right to vote. We have to refuse to ever back down because America will never be what it is supposed to be if it doesn't have the women's voice."

Rose had to repeatedly remind herself she was listening to a young girl of only thirteen. She already knew how extraordinary Felicia was, but the girl's knowledge and her ability to communicate it far surpassed any other young woman Rose knew, including those far older. It was a blessing, but it would also make life difficult for her.

"I learned during the last ten days that my being smart will sometimes make things harder for me. I'm young, I'm smart, and I'm black." She shrugged. "I can't change that, but I know there are people who will want to put me in my place. They will be threatened by who I am so they will try to diminish me. I can't stop it from happening, but I can refuse to believe what they tell me." Her gaze swept the room again. "I'm counting on all of you to remind me."

A murmur of ascent filled the room.

Felicia sighed. "There is so much more, but it's not possible to say it all. I want all of you to know you changed my life during the last ten days. I expected good things when I told Mama I wanted to talk to all of you, but I didn't really understand how much it would mean to me. Thank you all," she said.

Rose stood and stepped forward. "I know there are things all of you want to say, but it's not time yet. I asked Felicia to do a project that would help someone, and I will be learning of it for the first time tonight, along with the rest of you." She sat back down and waited expectantly.

Felicia walked to one of the shelves in the library and took down a thick, leather-bound book. Rose had seen her writing in it over the last week but didn't know what it contained.

Felicia held the book carefully. "I asked Thomas to bring this to me when he came from Richmond," she began. She looked at Carrie, then Janie, and finally Chooli. "Chooli was the one who gave me the idea for the rite of passage, so I wanted to do something to help her people. I can't go out to New Mexico with Carrie and Janie, but I could create something that would help them." She held up the book. "I've done a lot of studying about the Navajo, about the Santa Fe Trail, and about New Mexico since Chooli got here, and especially since Carrie decided to go out there. I've written down everything I believe will be helpful in this book."

Carrie and Janie both inhaled sharply. Chooli clasped her hands together, her eyes shining with pride and delight.

Felicia presented the book to Carrie. "You can read it before you leave, but you should take it with you on the Santa Fe Trail. It will help you with what you experience and with how to work with the Navajo so you can make the most difference."

Carrie jumped up and pulled Felicia into a fierce hug. "Thank you," she cried. "This is perfect!"

Felicia looked down shyly until Chooli took her hands.

"You are my sister," Chooli said. "You are now a woman, but you have long been a woman because of what you have suffered. We have both watched as horrible things happened to our people. You have done a great thing that will help the Navajo. I will always be grateful for you, Felicia."

Felicia threw her arms around Chooli. "I love you. I'm going to miss you when we leave."

A somberness spread through the room in the wake of Felicia's statement. Their departure had been pushed to the background, but now there it was in stark reality. Rose stepped forward, grateful beyond words for the time she had spent with Carrie and Abby that morning. "Leaving all of you will be one of the hardest things we have ever done. I thought this afternoon about the day Moses and I escaped the plantation through the Underground Railroad. I was so happy to be free, but it tore my heart in two to leave Carrie. Still, we both knew we had to take the opportunity while we had it." She smiled at her best friend. "I could never have dreamed that someday we would all be living on the plantation together as free people, or that I would have three beautiful children, and that Moses would own the place where we were once slaves. I have a vivid imagination, but I would have been certain I was hallucinating if I had envisioned such a thing." She smiled softly as she remembered. "The point is that I could never have imagined the outcome when we left that day. I walked into the unknown and did what I believed was the right thing for us at that moment. No one in this room can imagine what is waiting for all of us in the future. We have been brought together with a bond stronger than anything we could have imagined. Our lives may change, but we will always be a part of each other."

Rose cleared her throat and brought the evening back to Felicia. "We are not done with the Cocooning Rite yet."

She smiled at Felicia, beckoning her daughter to join her in the middle of the circle. "This is everyone's opportunity to welcome Felicia into womanhood." She waved her arm around the room. "Into the Circle of Women, and especially the women in this room tonight who have helped lay the foundation for Felicia's life." She slipped her arm around the girl's slender waist, noticing how her body was blooming into womanhood. "I will begin."

Rose turned to her daughter, releasing her waist as she grasped both her hands. "Felicia, you have been a gift from the moment you stepped into my life. It has been one of the greatest privileges of my life to be your mama. Perhaps more importantly, it has been one of the greatest joys of my life." She smiled tenderly as a sheen of tears appeared in Felicia's eyes. "There have been so many times I have felt inadequate to be your mama because you are so extraordinary, but we have learned together and grown into a family. Your daddy and I could not be prouder of you, or love you more, if you were our flesh and blood daughter. You will forever be ours, and we both know you are going to do amazing things with your life. As you become a woman, I want you to know you will always be our little girl, and we will always be here for you." She hugged Felicia to her tightly, and then moved to her place in the circle and sat down.

She beckoned to Abby. "Please go next. Carrie will follow you, and then we will continue until we have gone around the circle."

The rest of the Cocooning Rite passed with words of encouragement, challenges, laughter, tears, and incalculable love. The fire burned strongly as the first snowstorm of 1868 battered the windows with wind and hard, icy flakes.

Rose watched, her heart swelling with so much emotion she feared she could not contain it. The women in this room would always be the most important people in her world. Her family was moving into a new season of life that would bring different experiences and people, but no one could ever replace what was already hers. The women in this room had lived through a war, and were now taking bold actions to rebuild a shattered America into a country they could be proud of.

When Janie, the last one in the circle, finished speaking, Rose stood and took her place by Felicia again. She reached into her pocket and pulled out a long, narrow white box. As Felicia watched wide-eyed, she pulled the cover off the box and slipped out a lovely sterling silver necklace. Dangling from the silver strand was a star set with a tiny diamond that caught the light of the fire and sent it shooting through the room.

Felicia gasped and put her hand over her mouth. "For me?" she whispered.

Rose smiled gently and placed the necklace around her daughter's neck. "All the women in this room got together for this necklace. It is from Tiffany's in New York City. Abby received it in the mail from a friend the day before she came to the plantation. We chose a star because you are such a bright light in our lives, but also because we know you are going to be a glittering light in the world." She turned Felicia to face everyone in the circle, and then closed the clasp on the necklace. She stepped back to leave Felicia standing alone. "Felicia Samuels, you are now a woman."

Applause filled the room as Felicia stood tall and proud, her eyes glistening while a radiant smile lit her face.

*****

"And now I think the men are waiting for us to join them," Rose said when silence had fallen on the room again.

"Actually..." Felicia raised a hand, a shy, hesitant smile replacing the radiant one. "We're not quite done here."

Rose raised a brow. "Did I forget something?"

Felicia shook her head quickly. "No, mama. You don't know about this." The same smile flashed again. "When you told me I needed to do a project to help someone, you didn't tell me I could only do one."

"That's true," Rose agreed.

"So," Felicia rushed on, "I decided to do something for Grandma Annie."

"What you say, girl?" Annie exclaimed. "What you be up to? I ain't got nothin' I need."

"That's not true!" Felicia objected.

Rose saw Felicia exchange a look with Chooli. The Navajo woman who had become like a sister to her daughter, grinned and nodded.

"You just tell me what I be needin'," Annie demanded.

"You need a husband," Felicia said firmly.

Rose's eyes widened as she suddenly understood what was going on, but a quick look at Annie revealed her mother-in-law had not caught on yet.

Felicia walked over to kneel in front of her grandmother. "You know you love Miles, Grandma Annie. Miles knows you love him. You should be married."

"What nonsense!" Annie sputtered. "Women don't get married at my age."

Felicia shook her head. "We've had this conversation already," Felicia said patiently. "You're never too old for love, and you are in love with Miles." She took a deep breath. "Miles is waiting outside in the parlor to marry you." Felicia's words hung in the room for a long moment before Annie made sense of them.

"What you say?" Annie's voice was tremulous now. "What did you do?"

Felicia continued, her voice hesitant now. "You know you love Miles, Grandma Annie. It's not right that y'all shouldn't be together. Mama said I should do something to help someone. I made the book for Carrie, Janie and Chooli, but I also wanted to do something for you." She reached out to grasp Annie's hands. "I've never had a grandma. I love you." Her voice took on an imploring tone. "Please let me do this for you. And for Miles," she added. "He loves you so much, Grandma Annie. He wants to marry you."

"Why didn't that fool ask me himself?" Annie snapped, her eyes full of something like surprised pleasure.

"Because he knew you would say no," Chooli replied calmly.

Annie's head whipped around. "You a part of this nonsense?"

"It's not nonsense," Chooli answered. "And you already know you want it. You're just having a hard time doing something for yourself because you are so used to just giving."

Rose laughed softly. "They're right, Annie. You need to put Miles out of his misery, and you deserve to be with someone who loves you."

Choruses of approval sounded from around the room.

Rose turned to Felicia. "What is waiting out there?"

Felicia grinned, her hesitancy gone. "Miles is waiting."

"Who gonna marry us?" Annie demanded, obviously believing she had found a way out of the situation. "Can't be married without no preacher."

"I know," Felicia answered, and then smiled slyly. "I bet you didn't know that Franklin was ordained as a preacher during the war, did you?"

Annie's mouth dropped open. "Franklin be a preacher?"

Felicia nodded vigorously. "He's waiting with everyone out there now."

Annie stared at her, but couldn't seem to find any more words.

Felicia suddenly looked uncertain. "Was I wrong, Grandma Annie? Maybe you don't really love Miles..." Her voice faltered.

Annie's expression changed to one of concern for her granddaughter. "Of course I love that old man," she stated in a voice that brooked no nonsense. "I just didn't figure on gettin' married again."

"But you want to?" Felicia pressed in a hopeful voice.

Rose bit back her laugh. She didn't know if she should be impressed or dismayed that Felicia was so skillfully manipulating her grandmother into submission.

Annie sighed. "Yep," she finally muttered. Then her shoulders straightened. "All y'all get on out of this room. You send that Miles in here. I ain't marryin' no one that ain't asked me proper."

Felicia jumped up and beckoned everyone toward the door. "Yes, ma'am." Then she leaned down and kissed Annie's plump cheek. "You're going to make a beautiful bride."

Annie glared at her, and then looked down at her plain dress with sadness. "I don't reckon it matter what I be wearing when I get hitched."

Felicia grinned again. "There is a dress hanging behind the big mirror. Chooli made it for you!"

Annie raised her hands to her cheeks, her eyes shining with tears.

Chooli dashed over and pulled the dress down from where it had been hidden. The soft blue color glowed in the firelight. "I'm sure it will fit, Annie."

"It's beautiful!" Rose exclaimed.

"It's perfect," Abby said happily. "We'll send Miles in, and then we'll come back to help you get ready."

"I certainly don't need the bunch of you to get me dressed," Annie growled, but her face was glowing.

"No," Rose agreed, "but it will probably take all of us to get you through the door into the parlor once you are."

Miles must have said the right things, because he emerged from the library after only a few minutes, a satisfied smile on his face. "Y'all can go on in now," he said happily.

*****

The wedding ceremony was simple and brief, but Rose had never seen her mother-in-law's face exhibit so much happiness. Her head had been held high with pride when Moses had walked her to where Franklin had waited beside the fireplace, and her voice had resounded with joy as she declared her vows. Miles had fairly glowed with delight as he promised to love his wife. Rose was confident Annie was in good hands. She knew the two would make each other happy for however long they had left.

Felicia's celebration food turned into a wedding reception as laughter rang through the house late into the night.

Rose slipped up beside Felicia when she caught her standing alone beside the window. "I'm so proud of you," she said softly as she slipped an arm around her waist.

Felicia leaned into her. "I love seeing Grandma Annie so happy."

"And you?" Rose asked.

"I'm going to like being a woman," Felicia admitted as she turned and threw her arms around her. "Thank you for my Cocooning Rite, Mama!"

Chapter Seventeen

Carrie stood with Rose and Moses on the Broad Street Station platform, the raucous noises of Richmond swelling around them. Carriages clattered on cobblestone; train whistles blew at the same time wheels screeched against metal; conductors and ticket agents called out instructions as people began to board the trains. Felicia sat with Hope and John on a bench within sight.

Carrie stared at the two people who were such an integral part of her life. "I...I don't know how to do this."

Rose and Moses shook their heads, their eyes revealing the same dilemma.

"How to say good-bye again?" Carrie murmured, her heart already aching. She knew the separation was because of choices they were all making, but that knowledge did nothing to make her feel better. Her mind searched for a way to make it easier.

"You can't you know," Rose stated.

"Can't?" Carrie asked. "Can't what?"

"You can't make this easier," her friend replied. "We are all going to get on that train and shed tears for what we are leaving behind. We are going to miss each other terribly, and we are going to wonder if we are doing the right thing." Rose paused. "And then we are going to turn our eyes to what comes next in life. The missing will not be easier, but we are all walking the path we are meant to walk."

Moses nodded his head. "Just like when we rode away with you the day we escaped with Mike O'Leary. We wanted to be free, but we didn't want to say good-bye to you. It's the same right now. We want to go to school, and you want to go to New Mexico, but we don't want to say good-bye." He sighed heavily. "Just like before, we have to."

Carrie knew he was right. Oh, they didn't *have* to leave each other. They could all make the choice to stay on the plantation together, but then they wouldn't be fulfilling the purpose of their lives, and they would end up feeling dissatisfied. She summoned her courage. "There is no war this time. We can write letters, and we can visit."

"Once you get back from your grand adventure in New Mexico," Rose reminded her. "I don't imagine you'll pass many post offices on the Santa Fe Trail."

Carrie frowned. "I will at least send you a telegraph from Santa Fe when I arrive in New Mexico," she promised. "And I still have almost four weeks before I leave."

"All Aboard to Philadelphia!"

Carrie flashed a look toward the train on the other side of the station. She grabbed Moses in a fierce hug, feeling his breath catch. "I love you," she whispered as she leaned back to stare up into his face.

"And I love you, Carrie Borden," Moses answered in a husky voice, his face tight with emotion.

Carrie took a deep breath, and then turned to Rose. They had decided together to never say good-bye again. Their life was going to be a series of separations now that they were adults, but they were not going to say good-bye. Carrie raised her hand and laid it on Rose's cheek. "See you later."

"See you later," Rose replied, her voice steady, though tears were quivering on her eyelids. "I love you."

Carrie threw her arms around her best friend and clung tightly. "I love you!"

"Last call for Philadelphia. All Aboard!"

Rose pulled away, brushed aside her tears and nudged Carrie. "Go. You can't miss this train."

Carrie gulped back the sobs that were threatening, grabbed the satchel she was carrying, and dashed across the platform. She leapt up the stairs, mindless of what anyone thought of a proper young woman running wildly through a train station, and then turned back to wave at her friends. Rose, Moses, Felicia, John and Hope, standing together as a family, were watching her. They all waved madly. Carrie locked eyes with Rose for a long moment before she turned and disappeared into her car.

*****

Carrie stared at Janie with delight. "Really? You're serious?"

"Do you think I would make this up?" Janie demanded, her eyes dancing with fun.

Carrie sat back and stared at her. "Four students have signed up to go on the wagon train..." The words trailed off as she realized her dream of going to New Mexico was actually going to happen.

Janie nodded. "Dr. Strikener posted the notice you sent him on the bulletin boards before he left for Christmas. When he returned several days ago, there were letters waiting from four students. They are thrilled for the opportunity."

Carrie's eyes narrowed when she heard Janie hesitate at the end. "What aren't you telling me?"

Janie shrugged. "It's nothing important. I don't want you to have too big of an opinion of yourself," she said playfully.

"Excuse me? What are you talking about?"

"All four students said they wanted to do anything *you* are a part of because they know how much they will *learn*," Janie proclaimed dramatically.

"That's nonsense," Carrie sputtered. "That is not true."

Matthew walked in the door then. "Actually, it is completely true," he said. "You have a fan in Dr. Strikener. He seems to believe that saving the lives of hundreds in Moyamensing was a rather important thing. I hear he added a personal note to your notice. It seemed to have done the trick."

Carrie flushed. "I did what anyone would do." She knew that was not true since few students had been willing to enter the poor Irish section of town during the cholera epidemic, but the only thing that mattered was how many lives had been saved. "I'm just thrilled to know we have an entire team for the trip." She paused as she thought of her father's question when he discovered Matthew and Janie were going. "Do they have any idea what they are getting into?"

Janie raised a brow. "Do any of us? Learning how to deal with life as it is thrown at you is not something you can learn in a textbook or a class."

Carrie knew she was referring to the train crash, but that was something Janie was rarely willing to talk about. "That's true," she said softly. Janie had given her all the time she needed to come back to life after Robert's murder, and had not once pushed her to talk. She would return the favor. "Tell me about them," she invited.

"You already know one of them," Janie answered, her eyes dancing again. "Do you remember Carolyn Blakely?"

"Carolyn? Of course I do!" Carrie cried. "She was the first person I met at the Homeopathic College, and she helped me in Moyamensing." Her head spun as she envisioned the compassionate woman with salt and pepper hair that crowned soothing, light blue eyes. "She is going with us?"

"She signed up as soon as she saw the notice," Janie assured her. "We will be meeting her in two days."

Carrie shook her head. "It will be so wonderful to have her with us." Then she hesitated.

"You're thinking Carolyn might be a little old for the wagon train," Janie guessed. "She suspected you might worry. She asked me to remind you that we're riding in the wagons, not walking behind them, and that we will have the protection of the US Army. She also asked me to remind you that your father would probably fill the wagons he bought with plenty of food and supplies."

Carrie laughed. "Carolyn learned quickly how to banish any doubts I had." This time her smile was without reservation. "She will be a valuable part of the team. Who else is joining us?"

"I don't believe you know the other three. There is another young woman who is a first-year student from Massachusetts. Her name is Melissa Whiteside. She is young, but she worked for years with her father who is a homeopathic physician. She brings quite a bit of experience, but is looking forward to learning new things."

Carrie was pleased. "Who else?"

"Randall Bremerton served in the Union Army under Dr. Strikener for the duration of the war. He, too, was disenchanted with traditional medicine. He will finish his education in another year after we return from New Mexico. He is much like you, Carrie. He functioned as a surgeon for years, but also believes in the power of homeopathy."

Carrie's delight was growing. "And the fourth?"

Janie's smile was wider this time. "Nathan Gaffney. He had only just completed his first term when he saw the notice. When he realized who was leading the mission, he insisted on being part of it."

"Why?" Carrie had never heard the name Nathan Gaffney.

"Because both his parents are alive because of your efforts in Moyamensing," Janie explained. "You saved them from cholera. He received a scholarship to the college because he is determined to help people like you have."

Carrie stared at her for a long moment, her brain sifting through faces. "The Gaffneys," she murmured. "I remember them now. They were a couple in their forties who had only been here from Ireland for a few years." She frowned. "Their two youngest children died before I started dispensing the remedy. I don't remember an older child."

"Nathan is twenty. He was working on a merchant ship during the outbreak. When he returned home, he found out what had happened. He came to the school to thank you, but found out you had not returned for the term. Dr. Strikener took an immediate liking to him and decided to give him a scholarship." Janie smiled. "You will like him."

"I know I will," Carrie replied, but her thoughts had already turned in a new direction with the talk of Moyamensing. "Were you able to secure a carriage for me so I can visit Biddy and Faith? I know we have a lot of work to do, but I won't miss this opportunity to see them."

Matthew nodded. "I finalized everything for you today. I also sent Biddy and Faith a letter to let them know you are coming. I received Biddy's response today. They can hardly wait for your visit." He grinned. "Faith is making Irish Oatmeal cookies. Enough for you to bring some back here."

Carrie smiled. "How have the two of you managed to get so much done so quickly? You only left the plantation two days before I did."

"Superior ability," Janie said loftily, and then laughed. "We are so excited about this trip we can hardly sleep at night. I've already talked to everyone joining us and secured a room for our meeting in two days. I gave Dr. Strikener the list we made of homeopathic treatments we want to take with us, and he has the contact information for Abby's attorney so he can transfer payment." She paused. "He said he wasn't a bit surprised that Abby and your father were going to pay for all the medication you are taking along."

Carrie nodded. "I realize how fortunate we are to have the resources to take everything we need. My only concern is whether we will take enough. We have two wagons, but we also have seven people and supplies for a few months on the trail."

Matthew nodded. "Not to worry. Anthony has finagled a wagon from the army to carry nothing but medical supplies for the Navajo. It will all get there."

Carrie stared at him. "When did that happen?"

"Anthony was in Philadelphia over Christmas with family. Mark and Catherine Jones were here, as well. They met with some old army friends who have some connections."

"It's all in who you know," Carrie murmured, pleased beyond words that everything was coming together so smoothly. She hoped it was an indication of how easily the three months on the Santa Fe Trail would go, but something inside her told her to prepare for challenges.

*****

Philadelphia skies were a brilliant blue, but the gray soot covering towering mounds of snow seemed to absorb every ray of the sun. Carrie gazed up and shivered under her thick layer of blankets. The sun could shine only weakly through the smoke from all the industrial chimneys that choked the air. Sidewalks were piled high with snow, while the roads were clogged with carriages and wagons fighting for the clear lanes available. Indignant voices and angry calls rose above the sound of wagon wheels on the cobblestone streets.

"Only five days," Carrie muttered.

"Excuse me, miss?"

Carrie glanced up at the driver who had arrived for her an hour ago, only then realizing she had spoken out loud. She was embarrassed but opted for honesty. "I said I'm only going to be in Philadelphia for five days. I have discovered that is the most I can take during the winter."

The driver nodded. "You're lucky to have a way out."

Carrie caught the accent. "You're Irish." She saw the flash of anger in his eyes, but his face remained stoic. Obviously, he had been the recipient of Philadelphia's virulent anti-Irish sentiment.

"That I am," he responded. "I miss the green hills of Ireland most every day." His voice deepened with pride and something like regret.

"It must have been so hard to leave your beautiful country," Carrie said sympathetically.

The driver looked back at her with surprise. "You don't be thinking my kind be the scourge of America?" he asked.

"I most certainly do not," Carrie said. "Are you familiar with the Cromwell Factory in Moyamensing?"

"Certainly, I am," the driver responded. "Me mother has a job there. It's been open not a year, but it has already grown." He looked at her curiously. "How do you be knowing about the factory?"

Carrie smiled. "I'm Carrie Borden. My parents, Thomas and Abby Cromwell, own the factory."

The driver grinned broadly and pulled out the sheet of paper containing the instructions to where he was taking her. "Well, I'll be jiggered. I knew we were going to Moyamensing, but I hadn't paid close attention to the address yet. You're the lass going to visit my Biddy."

"*Your* Biddy?"

The driver nodded. "My name is Angus McCormick. I am the best mate of Biddy Flannagan's grandson."

"Arden!" Carrie exclaimed, vividly recalling the night the hospital had been set on fire in Moyamensing. Arden had saved her, Janie and the rest of their housemates at the time. "How is he?"

"He's doing more than fair," Angus answered. "He has a job at the factory, he has a new wife, and he has a wee son born just a few months ago."

"That's wonderful!" Carrie exclaimed. "And how is our Biddy?" She caught the slight hesitation before Angus answered.

"Our Biddy is doing fair well."

Carrie waited for him to say more, but he was suddenly intent on the road. "What is wrong with Biddy?" she asked, leaning close to make sure she could hear over the street noise. "And don't make up something. I can tell you're not telling me the truth."

Angus sighed, navigated his way around a delivery wagon stuck in a snow bank, and then answered. "Our Biddy is old."

"She's been old for a long time," Carrie retorted, suddenly afraid of what she was going to find.

"But she be acting old now," Angus said sadly. "She still has the same stout heart, but her spirit seems to be failing some."

Carrie absorbed the words, very glad she had made the trip to Philadelphia. "Are we almost there?" she asked, though she knew they were still at least thirty minutes away. After countless trips into Moyamensing for cholera treatments, she knew the way well. "Don't bother to answer," she said with resignation. "I know you'll get me there as soon as you can."

"That I will," Angus promised. "And now that I know who you be, it will be a sight faster. I can promise you that."

Carrie tried to distract herself by planning details of the upcoming trip, but her thoughts were never far from the tiny, wrinkled woman with silvery hair, dancing blue eyes, and a heavy Irish brogue. For once, she was glad the weather was too cold for the children to be out on the streets. As much as she loved seeing all the children she had grown close to, she was more eager to get to Biddy and Faith.

She breathed a deep sigh of relief when Angus pulled the carriage up in front of the largest home in Moyamensing. Once the center of her family's estate, the home had been slowly swallowed by the expansion of the Irish community in Philadelphia. Biddy had made it her life's work to make the Irish existence easier, but there was still a long way to go.

"I'll be waiting in the pub," Angus promised. "There will be someone who stops by the house that you can send for me. There is always a stream of people coming to visit." He paused. "Mostly to claim some of Faith's famous Irish oatmeal cookies." He shook his head. "Every Irish woman in Moyamensing makes those cookies, but Faith's have something fair special about them. Not a person has been able to figure out her secret."

Carrie remained silent. Faith had made her promise to never reveal the secret before she had sent the recipe home to Annie. She had decided a plantation in Virginia was far enough separated to protect the legacy passed down from her own great-grandmother. Carrie smiled to herself as she remembered the regular smell of Faith's cookies wafting through Cromwell Plantation. There were many that had asked for the recipe, but Annie protected it with the same ferocity Faith did.

She waited until the carriage came to a stop before she stepped down and ran up the steps to the house. The front door flung open almost immediately.

"Well, if you're not a sight for sore eyes!"

Carrie laughed and reached her arms around Faith. The elderly black woman was thirty years younger than Biddy, but the two had been best friends and housemates for more than three decades. She was almost seventy, but vibrant life still shone in her eyes.

"I am so happy to see you!" Carrie cried.

"Not as happy as we are to see you!" Faith exclaimed. "We were afraid you would never be back to see us."

Carrie sobered. "I have missed you both terribly. I'm sorry it's been so long."

"Hush, child," Faith said. "The last seven months have been horrible for you. We're just glad you're here now." She pulled Carrie toward the back parlor and then stopped.

Carrie's breath caught when she saw the sadness in Faith's eyes. "Biddy?"

Faith, never one to flinch from the truth, met her eyes. "I doubt our Biddy will reach her hundredth birthday, Carrie."

Carrie took a deep breath. Biddy was to turn one hundred in less than a month. There was a big celebration planned for the woman who was so beloved. She carried a gift for her in her bag. "Faith..." she breathed. As much as she knew she would grieve, she could only imagine the loss Faith would feel. The last year had taught her that grief.

Faith straightened her shoulders. "There is not a one of us who lives forever. I would never willingly let go of Biddy, but I thank God every day that I've had so long with her." She moved forward again. "Biddy is waiting for you, Carrie. She seems to be short on patience these days."

"I may be short on patience, but I'm not short on hearing. Get that girl in here right now."

Carrie grinned as Biddy's demand rang through the house. The voice was a little weaker, but it was still full of life. She jogged down the hallway, remembering how slowly she had moved during her last visit when she was almost seven months pregnant with Bridget. Her steps faltered for a moment, but the lure of her friend pulled her forward. "Biddy!" She surged forward, dropped to her knees, and took the leathery hands in her own. She was appalled at how cold they were, despite the parlor's steamy warmth.

"Carrie," Biddy murmured softly. She freed one of her hands and reached up to touch Carrie's cheek. "You look well, my dear."

"Thanks to you," Carrie replied. She had written Biddy a letter after her trip to Kansas, but there was so much she wanted to say in person. "There is not a day goes by that I don't think of the letter you wrote to me after Robert's death. There were many people who helped me get through those first terrible months, but it was your letter that brought me back to life, and that showed me the way to move forward." She lifted Biddy's hands to her lips and kissed them gently. "I can never thank you enough."

Biddy watched her closely for several long moments. "You're going to be fine, my girly. You're welcome, but I don't be thinking you're done with the grieving quite yet."

"No," Carrie agreed, aware of all the times grief still hit her so hard she felt it would steal her breath and life. "I'm not done, but I'm finding my way through." She paused as she thought of all the times she still believed Robert would walk through the door, telling her his death was nothing more than a disturbing rumor. "I'm finding ways to cope, and I'm moving forward."

"How?" Biddy asked keenly.

Carrie smiled, but her heart ached at the fatigue she saw etched on the old woman's face. Her eyes still glowed with life, but the light was not nearly as bright.

"Don't be looking at me like that," Biddy commanded.

Carrie blinked, searching for what to say.

"Did you think I would be living forever? There is only one end for every person. Your Robert was taken far too soon. I've been here for almost one hundred years. I've seen a lot of grief, but I've seen more than my share of joy, too. I'm ready to go, Carrie."

Carrie gazed into her eyes, struck by the peace she saw there. She knew there were probably hordes of people that insisted on telling Biddy she was going to be fine. She would not be one of them. "I'm going to miss you, Biddy."

"And I'm going to miss you," Biddy said tenderly, her eyes glowing with appreciation. She reached up to push back a strand of Carrie's hair. "I've been waiting for you, you know."

Carrie was speechless for several long moments. "Waiting for me?" she whispered.

"Aye, I was waiting for you." Biddy's Irish brogue lilted through the room, lifted by the heat rising from the fireplace. "I didn't want to go until I saw with me own eyes that you are going to be all right." She smiled. "I see it now."

Carrie remembered Faith's statement that Biddy would not see her hundredth birthday. "You have created a legacy to be proud of, Biddy." She knew the most important thing to the tiny lady was the knowledge that she had made a difference for the Irish people in Moyamensing.

"Aye, Faith and I have done a lot on our own," Biddy agreed, "but it's what you and I have done together that will make the biggest difference."

Carrie knew what she was talking about. "My father and Abby say the factory is doing well."

Biddy nodded with satisfaction. "It's doing more than well. The people there are happy, and they are making enough to support their families for the first time since they set foot on American soil. It has changed everything. My prayer is that, as the Irish begin to change how they see themselves, the country will see them differently, as well."

Carrie watched closely as the fatigue settled more deeply into Biddy's blue eyes. She glanced at Faith, knowing from the concerned look that she recognized the same thing. "What can I do for you, Biddy?" she asked.

"You can carry on for me," Biddy replied weakly. She took a deep breath. Her eyes shone with regret that she didn't have more energy, but her face was determined. There were things she needed to say. "I knew you were special the first day I met you, Carrie Borden. You are going to do important things in this world. Don't let anything stop you."

"I won't," Carrie promised, but her thoughts were on taking care of her friend. "Can I take you up to bed?" She hoped sleep would restore some of Biddy's strength.

"Not right now." Biddy leaned her head back against the chair as Faith moved forward to pull the afghan closer around her frail body, and closed her eyes. "I want you to talk to me, Carrie. I want you to tell me what you are doing now." She blinked her eyes open. "I'm going to close me eyes for a few minutes, but I'm listening. I just want you to talk." Her eyes drifted closed again. "Tell me everything."

Carrie looked to Faith for direction.

Faith nodded her head firmly. "Talk to her, Carrie. I'm going into the kitchen to get those cookies I promised, and some hot tea for Biddy when she feels ready for it."

Carrie gazed at Biddy for several moments, but her even breathing was reassuring. She seemed to truly be resting.

"Talk," Biddy commanded faintly, her eyes still closed.

Carrie began to tell her about the trip to Kansas, the attack on the plantation during the Harvest Festival, and Chooli's arrival. She told her about Susan coming to work on the plantation, and her meeting with Dr. Hobson. "I'm going to New Mexico," she said, praying Biddy was still awake to hear her. "I leave February 2 from Independence, Missouri with Janie, and Matthew, and four other students. We are going to help the Navajo, and we're going to learn as much as we can. We'll be gone through the end of next summer." She paused. "I don't have any idea what comes after that, but I couldn't have imagined this time last year what I would be doing twelve months later. The plans I had made are so totally different from the reality I am living now, but I am finding peace with that."

Carrie had discovered as she talked that she truly had found peace with the life she was living now. There would always be a hole in her life where Robert and Bridget should have been, but every day took her closer to believing she was going to live a good life—the one she knew Robert had sent her back to live.

Faith had stepped into the room sometime during her recital. She stepped forward to hug Carrie exuberantly. "Carrie, you live with one foot ready to step into the next adventure. I am so proud of you."

Biddy's eyes finally fluttered open. "I am proud of you, too," she whispered.

Carrie's heart surged with love for these two women who had become so precious to her.

Biddy beckoned her closer and reached out her other hand for Faith. "I love you both...so...much," she whispered, pausing between words to gather her breath and strength. Faith and Carrie had to lean forward to hear her words.

"You need to rest," Faith said, a frantic note appearing in her voice.

Carrie knew what she was seeing. "I love you too, Biddy," she said softly. She leaned forward to embrace her, and then kissed her on the forehead. "I will always miss you."

"Carrie?" Faith's question was full of pain.

Carrie looked at Faith. "You need to tell her good-bye." Her voice broke on the last word, and her eyes filled with tears.

Faith gasped and knelt in front of the woman who had been her closest friend for decades. "I love you, Biddy. You have meant more to me than any human being in the world. I know you are tired, and that you need to go, but not a day will pass when I don't think about you and miss you." Her voice tightened. "I will see you again one day, but it won't be soon enough. Thank you for all you have meant to me, and to all the people whose lives you have touched. You are a truly magnificent woman."

Biddy locked eyes with Faith. "Thank you," she mouthed. Then her eyes sought Carrie. "Thank you," she repeated. She slumped back against her chair and took a slow, shaky breath, a look of utter peace on her face.

Faith and Carrie were both holding one of her hands when Biddy closed her eyes for the final time.

Chapter Eighteen

Rose stared around her in amazement. "I've never seen anything this huge!"

Felicia nodded. "That's because the Union Station here in Cleveland is the largest building under one roof in the country. It is six hundred three feet long, and one hundred eighty feet wide. It opened last year, after the old one burned three years ago. They built this one out of sandstone, and it is also one of the first buildings in the country to use structural iron."

Rose exchanged a look with Moses. "There is nothing like having a walking encyclopedia with us." She marveled at her daughter's knowledge as she gazed at the cavernous building with eight train tracks running through it.

Felicia grinned. "I believe it is prudent to know about the place where you are moving."

"Prudent?" Moses asked, and then rolled his eyes. "How about you become the lawyer in the family, and I will just keep farming?"

Felicia regarded him soberly. "I think I will have to obtain the right to vote before I can become a lawyer, Daddy."

Rose watched her daughter. "Are you thinking about becoming a lawyer, Felicia?"

Felicia shrugged. "I might, but first I am going to become a businesswoman."

Moses hoisted John to his shoulders so his son could see over the heads of the crowd, and then turned to Felicia. "What kind of businesswoman? You've never talked about this before."

"A successful one," Felicia said with a grin. "Abby told me one of the few things women can do without having so many limitations is business. There are still struggles with men, but hard work can overcome them. If you work hard enough, you can make all the money you want."

"Is that important to you?" Rose asked.

"Certainly," Felicia responded. "Abby has been able to help a lot of people because of her wealth. You and Daddy are going to be able to do more because of the money the plantation is making. If I want to pave the way for black women, it will be easier if I am wealthy." She paused and then answered the question in Rose's eyes. "I don't know yet what I'm going to do, but since I'm only twelve, I believe I have a little time."

Rose bit back her smile, silencing Moses with her glance. "I believe you do, my dear." She cuddled Hope closer to her. The Union Depot was warm, but the cacophony must surely be hurting her little one's ears.

"Look at all the trains!" John shouted.

Moses bounced John on his shoulders, making him laugh with glee. "Which one do you like best, son?"

Rose watched her son scan the locomotives carefully, his serious dark eyes analyzing one before he moved on to the next. All the engines sported gay colors and ornate scrolls. Their brass trimmings gleamed from polishing, and several of the engines had paintings on the wooden engineer boxes and around the headlight.

"I like the red one best!" John hollered as he clapped his hands. "There is a big eagle painted on the side of it."

"How do you know it is an eagle?" Moses asked.

Rose knew the answer before it came.

"Felicia taught me about them."

Felicia shrugged. "There is a magazine in the library at home that has pictures of eagles."

Rose smiled. "I saw a bald eagle on New Year's Day with Carrie."

Felicia turned to her wide-eyed. "You did? A real bald eagle?"

"A real bald eagle," Rose confirmed. As she considered the surprise on Felicia's face, she realized she had never seen one until that day.

"Eagles in Virginia are very rare." Felicia's eyes narrowed. "Do you know what it means, Mama?"

"Means?" Rose remembered the moment the eagle had dived from the sky to pluck a glistening fish from the waters. "I know it was very beautiful."

"The eagle is a powerful symbol. Chooli taught me all about it. When an eagle appears, you are on notice to be courageous and stretch your limits. The eagle is a symbol for great leadership, strength and vision. When you see one, you are being told to become more than you are capable of."

Rose listened carefully, thinking of the conversation she and Carrie had been having when the eagle swooped down to the river. Standing in the midst of a bustling train station, she realized it had been a sacred moment to prepare her for what lay ahead. "Thank you for telling me," she murmured.

"Here comes our train," John yelled. "The *New York Express.*"

Rose stiffened. "What did you say, John?"

"Here comes our train! It's beautiful!"

Rose managed a smile before she turned to meet Moses' eyes. "Isn't that...?" She didn't want to finish her sentence.

"It is the only train that goes to Oberlin," Moses said apologetically.

Felicia gazed at her curiously for several moments before her eyes cleared and then widened. "Isn't that the same train Janie and—"

"Hush," Rose said, glancing at John. Felicia snapped her lips closed, but kept her eyes focused on her mama.

"The engine looks good and strong," Moses stated.

Rose chose not to mention that he didn't know the difference between a strong or weak engine, nor that the engine had nothing to do with the fact that two cars had derailed behind this exact engine only three weeks earlier. She also chose not to mention that there was absolutely no way to determine if the cars that would soon be holding her family were in danger of coming off the tracks. Lake Shore Railway, the train company that owned the *New York Express* had been found not to be at fault for the accident, but that did nothing more than tell her how truly unsafe trains were. Terrible things happened with no apparent way to stop them.

"It's going to be all right, Mama," Felicia whispered.

Rose, marshalling her courage when she saw John's look turn from excitement into apprehension, nodded her head. "It most certainly will be. The train has brought us this far, and we don't have much farther to go. God is going to get us to Oberlin just fine." She forced a bright smile, trying to make herself believe the words her mind told her were true. "John, what car do you want to ride in?"

"The back one!" John cried.

Rose kept the smile pasted on her face, refusing to allow her mind to recall what Matthew had written about the last car bursting into an inferno, burning everyone inside. "That sounds perfect, dear." Moses reached down and took her hand. She read the message of assurance in his eyes, but it was only the sudden peace in her heart that would give her the courage to step onto that train.

*****

It was almost dark when the train rumbled into Oberlin. The station, a simple clapboard building painted stone gray, was deserted except for a ticket collector who looked up and waved when they stepped off the train with their bags.

"Good evening, folks," he called.

"Good evening," Moses called back, pleased to discover the first person they met was friendly, with no look of censure in his eyes.

"Are you new here?"

"We are. My wife and I start school in a few days." Moses decided to accept the friendliness as sincere. "I'm Moses Samuels. This is my wife, Rose, our daughter Felicia, our son John, and the little one is Hope."

"You have a fine family," the ticket collector replied. "My name is Jonathan Maroney. It's good to have you here in Oberlin."

"It's nice to meet you, Mr. Maroney," Rose said. "Might you tell us how to get to the Park Hotel?"

Moses glanced down at Hope. She was snuggled into Rose's chest, but he could tell by the droop of her tiny lips that his daughter was exhausted. All of them were tired, but little Hope had reached the end of her endurance. "I hope it's not far."

"Nothing is far in Oberlin," Mr. Maroney assured them. He pulled out a blank sheet of paper and drew a quick map. "Go right down here to the corner of Main and

College Streets. You've made a fine choice. The hotel is brand new."

"It was built last year," Felicia said. "The old one burned down two years ago."

Mr. Maroney looked at her with surprise. "That's true, little lady. How did you know that?"

"I read it in a magazine," Felicia replied. "The Park Hotel was built by Henry Viets, but not until the college and the town got together to contribute five thousand dollars toward building it."

Maroney's expression went from surprise to admiration. "You must like to read a lot."

"I do," Felicia said promptly. "There isn't much you won't know if you read."

"That's true. How old are you?'

"Almost thirteen," Felicia said proudly.

"I have a daughter who is thirteen," Maroney replied. "She likes to read, too. I'm sure the two of you will meet in school when it starts back up next week."

Moses smiled at the look of delight blooming on his daughter's face. They had been in Oberlin less than ten minutes, and already she was being introduced to a different life. He caught Rose's eyes and knew she was thinking the same thing. He felt the dregs of his apprehension ebbing away as the spirit of the town flowed around them. "It was a pleasure to meet you, Mr. Maroney."

"Jonathan." The balding middle-aged man reached out to grasp his hand, and then shook Rose's. "I can tell already that your family is going to be a fine addition to our town and our college. Welcome to Oberlin."

Moses had questions he wanted to ask, but they would wait. It was time to get his family into a warm, dry room. He glanced down the road, grateful there was a clear path along the sidewalk that wasn't swallowed by the mounds of snow. The wind was blowing, but the buildings and the trees blocked enough of it to make it endurable.

"It's only a few blocks," Jonathan assured him. "I would take you in my wagon, but I have another train coming in soon."

"Not a problem," Moses assured him. "Thank you for the welcome. It's good to be here."

*****

Carrie gazed at the thousand or more people who had gathered for Biddy's funeral. There was not a church in Moyamensing large enough to accommodate them all, so Thomas and Abby had offered the factory. Carrie had overseen the transformation. It had been a herculean effort to clear the factory floor of tables and machines and replace them with chairs, but not one person had complained. The factory and their jobs existed because of the woman who had fought tirelessly for the Irish of Moyamensing.

"She would laugh if she could see the fuss."

Carrie looked at Faith, who was standing next to her, watching as the building filled. "Surely she knew what a huge impact she had on so many lives. There are even more people standing out in the cold. We simply can't fit another body in here."

Faith smiled. "Biddy was never one to care about appearances. She did what she believed was right."

"She changed my life," Carrie murmured.

"And she changed mine," Faith agreed. "She lived by the *Bregdan Principle*. She truly believed every life she touched would cause ripples throughout history. That was what gave her the joy that kept her alive through all she suffered."

"What will you do now?" Carrie had waited to ask the question, but now seemed the time.

"I'm going to stay right here," Faith replied. "I loved Biddy with all my heart. The best years of my life were the ones I spent as her friend." Her eyes softened. "Biddy gave me her house and everything she owned. I'm to pass it on to Arden when I die, but she knew I would use the resources the same way she would have. She knew her time was coming and had already told me what she wants to see happen in Moyamensing. I'm going to make sure it happens. These people are lighter skinned than me, but they have become my family, too."

Carrie grinned, certain she could hear Biddy laughing from heaven.

Faith looked over the hordes of people for several moments and then turned to Carrie. "Biddy wants a homeopathic clinic in Philadelphia. She wants you to run it."

Carrie stared at her, searching for how to communicate that she was greatly honored, but couldn't imagine living in Philadelphia. The last five days, while she was glad to be here to honor Biddy, had drained her.

Faith laughed gently. "Don't worry, Carrie. Biddy knew you wouldn't want to live in the city. She wanted you to set up the clinic and hire homeopathic physicians that will treat the Moyamensing residents the way they should be treated. The money she has left will pay for it. When you get back from New Mexico, of course."

Carrie considered the request and smiled. "I can do that," she promised. If she chose the right people, it wouldn't be hard to oversee. Abby and her father owned the factory, but they were seldom here because they had hired such competent people. She had never really considered doing such a thing, but she had considered very little of what she was doing with her life right now. What did one more unexpected thing matter?

*****

"Biddy would have loved the funeral," Janie said as she scooped hot chicken and dumplings onto Carrie's plate.

"I believe you're right," Carrie replied. "All the people she loved the most were there, and I could hear so many of them saying they had to make Biddy proud of them." She inhaled the succulent aroma wafting up to her nose. "When did you learn how to make this?"

Janie grinned. "Felicia taught me."

Carrie's fork froze in midair. "Felicia? Our Felicia?"

"She made me promise not to tell Rose and Annie."

"Why?"

Janie's grin widened. "Because she doesn't want either of them to know she can cook as well as they do. She wants to stay in the library, not in the kitchen."

Carrie laughed. "Let me guess... She learned how to make chicken and dumplings in a book."

"She did," Janie confirmed. "She heard me talking at Christmas about how I wished I could make something special for Matthew. She suggested chicken and dumplings, but I assured her I was a total failure at dumplings. Two days later, when Annie was visiting June at Blackwell, she took me into the kitchen, pulled out a book, and taught me how to make them."

Carrie took a bite, then closed her eyes in ecstasy. "She definitely needs to hide this ability from Rose and Annie," she murmured. "This is fantastic. You learned well."

Janie's eyes shone with pride. "Matthew thinks so, too."

As if called by her words, they heard the front door open. Matthew had gone out back to put away the carriage that had taken them to Moyamensing for the funeral.

"Do I smell my wife's chicken and dumplings?"

"You'd best hurry before I eat them all," Carrie called.

Matthew strode into the kitchen, waving a magazine. "How about a trade?"

"I hardly think you could have anything more enticing than this," Carrie said before putting another forkful in her mouth.

"How about the very first copy of the *New Revolution*?"

Janie inhaled sharply and reached for the magazine, but Matthew held it out of reach. "The new magazine published by Elizabeth Cody Stanton, Susan B. Anthony, and Parker Pillsbury? Give it to me!"

Matthew continued to hold it high in the air. "I do believe I mentioned a trade," he taunted.

Carrie laughed and quickly filled a plate for him. "Here. Now give us that magazine."

Matthew grinned, handed over the publication, and then started eating. "You have made me a happy man, Janie," he breathed between bites.

"And you've made me a happy woman," Janie replied as she opened the magazine.

Carrie bent over her friend's shoulder so they could read together. "This is the official publication of the National Woman Suffrage Association. They are demanding a federal constitutional amendment to secure the right to vote."

Janie nodded. "The *American* Woman Suffrage Association believes success will be more easily achieved through state-by-state campaigns."

"Actually," Matthew commented between bites, "the women in the American Woman Suffrage Association feel it is necessary to postpone the fight while the country fights for the black vote."

Carrie frowned. "There are now two women's suffrage organizations?"

Janie nodded. "A lot happened last year." She did not need to add that Carrie had been too lost in grief to be aware of political actions in the country. Carrie had joined Abby on the campaign through Kansas, but her stepmother had been careful to not pull her too deeply into all the details of the movement.

Carrie knew she would receive no judgment from her friends for being oblivious in the wake of Robert's murder. She continued to scan the publication. "Elizabeth and Susan obviously disagree that anything less than a federal constitutional amendment will work." She would never forget meeting the two women in New York City a few years earlier. "I can't believe anyone would think they would back down from the fight they started."

"There are women who believe they have to choose the battles they fight with limited resources," Matthew observed. "They are afraid if they push too hard, they will lose the little ground they have gained."

Carrie shrugged. "It's like going onto the battlefield expecting to lose," she retorted. "You see how well that worked in Kansas last year. If you don't fight to win, what is the point of fighting at all?"

Matthew chuckled. "So, I take it you believe in the necessity for a federal constitutional amendment?"

"Of course," Carrie answered. "Don't you?"

"I do," Matthew assured her, "but..."

Carrie looked at him sharply when he hesitated. "But, what?" she demanded.

Matthew met her eyes evenly. "I believe it is going to be a long battle. Perhaps as long as the one it will take to win true equality for blacks. White men tend to demand total power, and they will not relinquish any of it until they are afraid they'd lose power if they *don't*."

"You're different," Janie reminded him.

"Yes, but I am a minority," Matthew answered. "Don't count on other men believing or acting like I do."

Carrie sighed, knowing he was right. "I know action is the only thing that will change the current reality. I read something that Ralph Waldo Emerson said." She paused, wanting to make sure she got it right. "He said that an ounce of action is worth a ton of theory."

Janie nodded. "He's right. No one can afford to sit back when a wrong is being done. I have talked about this with many of my friends at school. Even once we get the vote, we are going to have to fight as hard, or harder, to have any kind of political power because men are going to block us at every step."

"So, we just keep fighting," Carrie said grimly. "I'm sick of living in a country run exclusively by men." Her thoughts flashed to Robert and Bridget. She thought of the anger, fear and hatred fueling the KKK and the other vigilante groups. She thought of the hundreds of thousands of men who had died during the war, and the equal number that would suffer through the rest of their lives with disabilities. "It may take women a very long time to truly have power in America, but we must keep fighting."

"We must try," Janie agreed.

"No," Carrie replied, a little surprised at the intensity in her own voice, but certain she was right. "We can't just try. We have to *do it*." She paused. "Trying sounds as if we'll do everything we can, but we may fail. Failure is not an option, Janie. We have to do it."

Matthew was watching her with something akin to sadness.

"Why are you looking at me that way?" Carrie asked.

Matthew paused, but met her eyes squarely. "Because you are setting yourself up for a battle that will cause you great hurt," he said. "No one who sets out to achieve big change comes out of the battle unscathed."

"I don't expect to," Carrie replied, realizing how little that impacted her decision. "I wanted to go with Robert and Bridget, but I am still here. If I don't make that mean something, then what is the point?"

*****

Carrie was happily full of chicken and dumplings when the first knock came at the door. She had already met individually with all those joining her on the wagon train to Bosque Redondo. They were having their first group meeting tonight, and then she would depart for Richmond the next morning. She longed to be on the plantation for a week before they met in Independence, Missouri.

"Carolyn!" Carrie kissed the older woman's cheek after she shrugged out of her coat.

Carolyn's blue eyes sparkled with excitement. "We're really going to do this, aren't we? It's not some crazy fantasy I'm having?"

"I do believe we are." Carrie also felt that the trip to New Mexico was a surreal hallucination. "The amount of homeopathic remedies and medical supplies we have waiting in boxes seems a sure indicator."

Carolyn grinned, looking far younger than her fifty-three years. "My friends tell me I am certifiably insane, but I tell them I am certifiably happy to have the freedom to do what I want with my life. I believe they are all secretly jealous."

Janie opened the door to their next guest. "Melissa! Welcome."

Melissa Whiteside smiled as she carefully removed her cloak and hung it on the hook. She was a rather plain woman, but the look of warm compassion in her brown eyes attracted everyone to her. She engendered trust in everyone who met her. "Good evening, all. I ran into Dr. Strikener on my way out after my last class. He sends his greetings...and his envy."

Janie laughed. "He's told me he would give almost anything to go on this trip, but he can't miss all the classes he must teach."

"Giving up your career is not such a huge loss," Carrie said teasingly. "He must not want to join us that badly."

Matthew was coming down the stairs when the next knock came. "Randall Bremerton! I'm glad you could make it."

Randall shook snow out of his blond hair and beard. "I've made it here, but I'm not sure any of us will make it home. It started snowing hard just before I got here. The idea of New Mexico sunshine is more appealing all the time."

"I know how you feel," Melissa replied. "I think our classmates didn't really believe this was going to happen. Now that they are watching it come to life, they suddenly realize what they are missing out on."

"Their loss," Carolyn said breezily. "If they think they are jealous now, wait until we get back with all our stories." Her eyes shone with delight.

Another knock announced Nathan Gaffney. Carrie had liked him on sight. Lively blue eyes blazed from under a thick thatch of red hair. He was almost as tall as Moses, but wiry strength replaced Moses' powerful bulk. His strong Irish brogue filled her with delight.

Nathan swept her up into a warm embrace. "Carrie, me love. It's good to be seeing you."

Carrie grinned at him, sure his constant good humor would be a boon during the many months on the trail. "We're all here, so we should get started before the snow gets too deep."

Two hours later, all the details had been hammered out. They all knew their specific jobs before they boarded their train and headed to Independence, Missouri. They would arrive in Missouri on January twenty-eighth, so they would have time to get the wagons loaded before they departed.

"Remember," Carrie reminded them, "whatever you forget can be purchased in Independence. Every wagon train depends on the supplies that can be purchased in the stores there. They will have everything we need, and many things we don't yet know that we'll need. There is plenty of room for everything, as long as you don't decide you need a baby grand piano to serenade us on moonlit nights."

Everyone was still laughing and talking excitedly as they bundled up against the cold and departed. The men would walk the women home before they made their way to their own lodgings.

Janie turned to Carrie when the last guest had left. "We're doing it," she said softly.

"You keep saying that," Carrie teased.

"Doesn't it seem like a dream to you, too?"

"Everything seems like a dream right now," Carrie admitted. The intensity of the trip, dealing with Philadelphia, having Biddy die in front of her, and saying good-bye to Rose and Moses were all swarming in her mind. She caught her breath. "We're walking forward, Janie. Just like when the war started and the first injured soldiers started filling Chimborazo, we have no idea of what we are getting ourselves into, but we got through the war, and we'll get through this."

Janie looked at her curiously. "Is that how you see this trip? Something to get through?"

Carrie considered the question for several long moments. "I suppose I still see every day as something to get through," she responded candidly. "I find glimmers of excitement, and there are times I feel genuinely happy, but then I think about Robert and Bridget, and it all seems so empty." She stopped and stared into the flames crackling in the fireplace. "I think my greatest hope is that we will make a difference, and that somehow, when I return from this trip, I'll feel like a whole person again." She hated admitting it, but she wouldn't deny the truth she was sure Janie saw anyway.

Janie grasped her hands. "I have not experienced the loss you have, Carrie, but I understand the desire to feel like a whole person again. I need to walk away from this life for a while so that I can put the train wreck behind me." She couldn't suppress her shudder. "I can finally sleep through the night, but the nightmares ..."

Carrie gazed into her eyes. "I'm so glad we're doing this together," she murmured. "I have no idea what is going to happen, but it's enough to know I'll be doing it with you and Matthew. You and I got each other through the war, and now we'll get each other through this part of our life." She forced a grin. "And I believe we'll have fun along the way."

Chapter Nineteen

Rose shook snow from her thick coat before she hung it next to the door. She still marveled at the sparkling white clapboard house they were calling home. They didn't live on campus because they had their family with them, but instead rented a house close to classes. At first, she had been afraid they would feel isolated from the rest of the college community, but nothing could have been further from the truth. There was hardly a night that passed when they didn't have other students as company for dinner. It had been only two weeks since their arrival, but she already felt completely at home, and she had never imagined she could feel so secure.

"A penny for your thoughts." Moses appeared from the parlor to wrap his arms around her.

"They are worth far more than that," Rose said loftily as she leaned back against his broad chest. "You are looking at the woman who had the highest grade in her class for the test we took yesterday."

"I'm not surprised," Moses replied, tightening his arms. "You should be *teaching* all the classes you're taking." He leaned down to give her a warm kiss. "Congratulations."

Rose couldn't deny that she hadn't yet been taught anything she didn't already know, but being with other women who had the same passion she had for teaching made sitting in the classes all worthwhile. "It's not their fault I'd read all the textbooks twice before I arrived." She cocked her head. "Are you learning anything?"

"Far more than you are," Moses admitted. "I never got through all the textbooks, and I surely haven't been practicing law for the last four years. I like all my classes, and it is an interesting experience to be using only my brain for a while, but that is not the most important thing I'm learning."

"Oh?" Rose tossed two pieces of wood into the stove, closed the door securely, and started a kettle of water for tea. Then she turned to her husband. She was struck by his serious expression. "What have you learned?"

"I've learned what our country *could* be like for blacks. I've met so many of the black families here." He paused. "Do you know that twenty percent of Oberlin is black?" He shook his head. "Compare that to New York City or Philadelphia, which only have two to three percent of their entire population. The people here feel safe, Rose." He reached for a scone she had made early that morning, slathered it with butter, and took a big bite. "They aren't waiting for the KKK to come here because they never will. There is no fear, and people are free to live their lives."

Rose nodded. "I'm not surprised. Oberlin had more influence on the Abolition Movement than any other town in the country. They fought for abolition before most people ever heard the word. They sent out alumni by the hundreds who started abolition societies in their towns. When other parts of the country were still trying to decide how they felt about it, the people in Oberlin were fighting slavery almost every day. Then, to put more action behind their beliefs, they had thousands come through town on the Underground Railroad."

"We owe this town and this college a lot."

"Does it feel strange?" Rose asked.

Moses understood what she meant. "Strange to not have to always be on guard? Strange to not be waiting for the next attack? Strange to not wonder when your school might be burned down again? Yes, all of those things feel strange."

Rose frowned. "I still worry about everyone on the plantation, but it's so wonderful to send Felicia off to school and not be concerned about what might happen. John will start school next year, even though he already knows more than most of the children." She heard the kettle whistle and turned to pour hot water over her tea. Then she reached in her pocket and pulled out an envelope. "I got a letter from Carrie today."

Moses snatched another scone before he headed for the table. "Read it," he commanded.

Felicia came down the stairs from her bedroom. "Did I hear you say there was a letter from Carrie?"

Rose smiled, handed her daughter the last scone, and carried her tea to the table. She slowly unfolded the thick sheaf of paper. "Most of this is just for me, but there are things both of you will want to hear." She searched for the areas she had underlined, and began to read.

"Your replacement teacher has been hired. All your students miss you, but they are trying to make the best of your absence so you will be proud of them when you return. They are looking forward to the new teacher arriving, and there have been no more threats against the school. I suppose losing several of their men during the Harvest Festival has dampened their spirits for another attack. They know to expect guards. Tell Moses that no one is apathetic, however. The guards are still there every night, and I suspect they will be for years to come."

Moses nodded with satisfaction.

Rose continued.

"Franklin told me to assure Moses everything is running smoothly. He will write soon, but he has been very busy repairing tools for the spring planting. The men are all content working for him. They say he is fair, and they believe they will all continue to do well."

"I knew he was the right choice," Moses stated.

Rose understood the look of yearning in his eyes. He longed every day to be back on the plantation working the tobacco, but her husband had decided to make the most of being in Oberlin. She turned back to the letter.

"There is something else that will make you very happy. June came to see me yesterday, and I was able to give her the happy news that she and Simon are going to have another baby! They have been wanting another child, so they are very excited."

Rose sighed. "I'm so happy to be here, but I hate that I'll miss June's pregnancy."

"You'll not miss all of it," Moses assured her. "They do have breaks around here. There is nothing to keep us from getting on the train and going back to the plantation for part of this summer."

Rose's eyes widened. "I keep forgetting we can afford to do that. It doesn't seem real that we actually have money in the bank."

"And a lot in the box under the floorboards," Felicia added impishly.

"What?" Moses stared at her. "What do you know about that?"

"I know that you took a lot of money out of the bank when we were in Richmond, and you had to hide it somewhere. I just wanted to know where it was. It took me a while, but I finally figured it out."

Rose thought she should probably be angry, but she couldn't stop her chuckle. "Our daughter is far smarter than we are, honey."

Moses tried to look indignant, but he finally laughed too. "Just don't tell anyone, Felicia. That is our emergency money in case we ever need it."

"I promise," Felicia said. "We're rich aren't we, Daddy?"

Moses looked amused. "Rich?"

Felicia nodded. "There is a lot of money under there. I didn't count it, but I could tell it is a thick roll. Are we rich?"

"No," Moses replied. "But as long as we are smart with the money from the plantation, we'll never have to worry."

"You're going to be rich," Felicia said knowingly.

Rose was intrigued by the gleam in her eyes. "What makes you say that?"

"I'm reading a book Abby sent me about business. The plantation is going to continue to grow, and more of the acres are going to be planted each year. The profits will continue to increase. Plus, the value of Cromwell tobacco will go up because everyone will know it is the best quality. The business model you are using, Daddy, means everyone will work hard and give you their best effort. You will make more money every year, which means you will be rich," she finished.

Rose shook her head. "How old are you again?"

Felicia giggled.

"Perhaps we should forget school and return to the plantation so Felicia can handle the business end of things," Moses suggested. "We can all live out the remainder of our lives as wealthy people."

Felicia's smile faded. "We can't do that, Daddy."

"And why not?" Moses asked, amusement still gleaming in his eyes.

"Because the battle isn't over yet," Felicia said.

Rose reached over and took her daughter's hand. "What do you mean?" she asked gently.

"Chooli told me about the hundreds of miles she and her family were forced by the army to walk to get to Bosque Redondo. She said they didn't know where they were going or how long it would take to get there. They just started walking." She drew a troubled breath. "I think it's that way for every black person in America."

"And what makes you feel that?" Moses asked.

Rose was not at all surprised they were taking their daughter so seriously. When it came to keeping a finger on the pulse of the nation, she was far ahead of them.

"There were a lot of people who fought for the slaves to be free," Felicia explained, "but now that we are, most of those people don't know what to do with us. The reality of millions of slaves being turned loose into our economy is more than people had thought about or planned for. They wanted us free, but most of the people who wanted that don't want us to be socially equal. They will fight hard to make sure we stay in our place." She made a face. "Whatever they have decided our place *is*."

"I see," Rose murmured, uncertain what she could say to alleviate her daughter's concerns. In truth, she knew Felicia's assessment was correct. An image of Sojourner Truth flashed in her mind. "I'm not going to tell you it won't be hard," she said. "There were both blacks and whites that fought for our freedom. Many of them fought for decades. I'm sure there were times they never thought we would be emancipated. I've learned right here in Oberlin that the blacks had to make sure slavery stayed at the forefront of people's minds and actions because they were the ones most impacted by it. Most of them were slaves who had run away from the plantations." She gazed into her daughter's intense eyes.

"Do you think things will ever be right for our people in this country?" Felicia demanded.

Rose saw past the anger to the weary fear in her daughter's eyes. She ached that one so young had to ask such a question, but she had asked the same of her own mother, who had been bound by the shackles of slavery and completely helpless to change things for her daughter. That memory gave her strength. "I can't give you an honest answer to that question, Felicia. No one can. Your father and I are both doing all we can to make that answer be yes, but neither of us has any idea whether it will happen in our lifetime." She sipped her tea as she gathered her thoughts. "All I know is I can't stop trying. When I get tired, and when I wonder if it will make any difference at all, I try for you, and for John, and for Hope— and for the grandchildren I will have one day, and the great-grandchildren who will follow in the future. I wonder what *their* lives will be like. I look at the children in my classroom, and I know I must try for them."

"You get real tired don't you, Mama?"

Rose nodded. There was no reason to be anything but honest. "Yes, honey, I get real tired at times."

Felicia turned her eyes to Moses. "And you too, Daddy?"

"Me, too," he agreed. "But your mama is right. There are moments almost every day when I wonder if what we are doing will change things. There are times almost every day when I want to go back to the plantation and farm tobacco." He held up his hand when Felicia opened her mouth to interrupt. "But you are right. The battle is not over yet. There will probably be generations of Americans who believe they have to put us in our place because they are frightened and threatened. I can't do anything about that," he said heavily, "but I can fight with everything I have to change the lives of the people I come in contact with. That's all any of us can do, Felicia. If you look at the way things are for blacks or for women in this country as a whole, then it is too overwhelming. It's far bigger than one person. You find what is *yours* to do, Felicia. Then you do it with all your might. Some people will join you. Others will fight you. It doesn't matter as long as you know you are doing what you are supposed to do."

Felicia nodded thoughtfully as a long silence filled the kitchen. Sounds of children playing outside in the neighborhood floated past the closed windows. Moses stood to add wood to the fireplace. Rose sipped her tea while she watched her daughter. They had just had a very challenging conversation for a thirteen-year-old, but Felicia wasn't a normal teenager. Still, she wanted to protect her from the harsh realities of life as long as she could.

Felicia stood abruptly and walked from the room.

Rose looked at Moses anxiously. "Did we say too much?"

Moses shook his head, watching the stairway up to Felicia's bedroom. "I know that look. She is thinking."

There were some rustling noises, and then Felicia walked back downstairs holding a publication. "Do y'all know who Thomas Carlyle is?"

Rose stared at her blankly, wondering if it was someone she had met in town. "No."

"Me, either," Moses said, his expression expectant as he sat back down at the table.

Felicia held up the pamphlet she had brought downstairs. "It doesn't really matter. He is a Scottish historian and teacher that I read about in Thomas' library. I don't agree with him on some things, but he said something that I remembered while the two of you were talking." She opened the pamphlet and read: "*Permanence, perseverance and persistence, in spite of all obstacles, discouragements, and impossibilities: It is this, that in all things distinguishes the strong soul from the weak.*"

Moses listened. "Will you repeat that, please?"

"Permanence, perseverance and persistence, in spite of all obstacles, discouragements, and impossibilities: It is this, that in all things distinguishes the strong soul from the weak." Felicia closed the pamphlet. "I am joining you in the fight. I know I'm young, but I won't always be. I'm going to use my life to fight. I'm going to persevere, and I'm going to persist."

Rose felt tears of pride welling in her eyes. She held out a hand to Felicia, and one to Moses. "We will fight," she vowed.

"We will fight," Moses echoed.

"We will fight," Felicia said firmly.

*****

Carrie slowed Granite as they started down the trail both of them knew so well. Granite tossed his head, snorted his approval, and then pranced lightly along, kicking up snow as he went. Squirrels chattered from their branches, and a hawk screeched overhead. Carrie took deep breaths of the cold air, knowing it would be a long time before she could return to her sanctuary by the river.

The wagon was packed with hundreds of bottles and packets of herbal remedies that had been carefully wrapped in sturdy wooden crates. She had taken all she felt it was safe to take from her supplies, and then she, Polly and Chooli had made as much as they had time to make. Combined with the large supply of homeopathic medicines ready to be shipped from Philadelphia, they would be able to help many Navajo. She hoped she would also learn even more herbal remedies that she could create once she was in New Mexico. Felicia had carefully copied all the information she had been able to find into the book she had created. Carrie was excited to find the plants she'd read about, and also to learn all she could from the Indians, who would doubtless know far more.

Carrie didn't realize they had reached the end of the trail until Granite came to a stop and stomped one hoof. She laughed and slid from the saddle, making sure to land on the narrow strip of rocks close to the lapping water so as not to sink into the snow. It had been more than a week since the last storm, but the frigid temperatures kept it from melting. She snuggled deeper into Robert's thick winter coat, remembering the many times they had come here together. The feel of his coat brought both comfort and grief. She refused to look at the spot in the clearing where Bridget had been conceived, although she had felt compelled to come here before she left on her trip.

"I'm leaving the plantation for a long while." Carrie spoke the words out loud. She had no way of knowing if Robert could hear her, but it was the only way she knew of to be able to leave. During the long hours of preparation, she had been almost certain she would not actually be able to follow through with her plan. It was as if she were living a fantasy, and just as she stepped off the cliff into bottomless air, she would wake up and discover it was all a dream. She had not woken up. There was a wagon of supplies and packed bags. Evidently, she was leaving the plantation.

She was leaving Robert.

"I have to go, Robert. People need me, but mostly I need to find out who I am without you. I can't do it on the plantation. I remember who I was *with* you when I am here. I want to hold on to that and be nothing more, but my heart tells me that is not right." She fell silent, watching the sun dance across the rippling surface. She had thought coming here would calm her, but it seemed to only agitate her more. She was finally able to face the truth of what she really needed to say. "I don't know why you told me to stay here. There are some days I feel at peace with that, but mostly I wish I was with you and our daughter. Everything I see here reminds me of what I no longer have...What I will *never* have."

A white quartz rock at Carrie's feet caught her attention. The sun glinted off the shining surface as she reached down with her gloved hand to pick it up. She stared at the glimmering stone, the quartz embedded in a large hunk of gray granite that was the perfect foil for its glowing white brilliance. She supposed Chooli would tell her the crystal had special meaning, and that it spoke of beauty in the midst of harshness, but Carrie could feel nothing but sadness and a swelling resentment. It was just a rock.

She wasn't necessarily surprised by the depth of her emotion; Biddy had told her grief was like an onion that peeled back to reveal layers for a long time. So no, she wasn't surprised, but she was tired of the constant battle.

"I'm hoping it will be easier if I'm away from our world," she whispered. "I don't know if that makes me a coward, but I know I have to go. I didn't understand why my father had to leave the plantation when Mother died. I do now."

Will you love again?

Carrie stiffened as the question seemed to float to her on the breeze. She was quite certain she would *never* love again. She knew that Anthony, despite his words to the contrary, would like to court her. The same energy she had felt from Harold had made it easy for her to wave him off after the holidays. They were both fine men, but no one would ever replace Robert in her heart.

Abby found your father.

"Good for her," Carrie said angrily. It felt as if Robert were standing there in the clearing with her. "You told me to stay here," she snapped, ignoring Granite's surprised expression. "I'm here, and I'm trying to make the best of it."

I love you, Carrie.

Carrie choked back a sob, still battling her anger. "I wanted to come with you," she whimpered. "I didn't want to be left here without you and Bridget." The grief felt as raw as the day she had woken to find her husband and daughter were gone from her life forever. In some corner of her mind, she knew it was because she would soon be separated from all that made them real to her. "No one could ever hold my heart like you did," she whispered.

There was no response, only a brisk gust of wind that kicked up tiny whitecaps on the river. As she stared out at the water, she was transported back to seven years earlier. She had been eighteen, struggling with the reality of her life and wanting nothing more than to leave the plantation to escape her mother's, and society's, expectations. Just like that day years ago, dark clouds moved across the sky to blot out most of the sun. Only one bright spot tossed upon the river. Carrie fastened her eyes on the defiant spot. It seemed to be enjoying its moment of rebelliousness. The clouds danced across the sky in a vain attempt to block it out. Just as it seemed they would succeed, the little spot swirled away to light on another tossing wave.

Carrie watched carefully. She vividly remembered the lesson the same dancing spot had taught a rebellious teenager. *If the little spot could have spoken, she was sure it would have laughed and told her of the fun of defying the surrounding sameness. It brought her hope. She may be the only one of her kind, but she didn't want to change. The rest of the world could be clouds, but she wanted to be a bright spot that defied the surrounding sameness. Of that she was sure.*

With the reminder came peace. Her heart had churned with so many questions all those years ago, as it did now. Somehow, she had found her answers, walking forward into what had come. There had been heartbreaking times, but there had also been times of great joy and love. She didn't know what was coming in her new life without Robert and Bridget, but just like she had done years ago, she would live the life she felt she should live. She didn't care about expectations. She didn't care about what other people felt she should do. She didn't believe she could ever love again, but that was not her question to answer today.

"I love you, Robert," she whispered with her eyes tightly closed. "I love you, Bridget. My loves..." She gripped the rock, and then heaved it as far as she could into the river.

As she watched it disappear with a splash, she turned away and mounted Granite.

"I'm going to go find out who I am without you."

Chapter Twenty

Carrie stared around her with astonishment. Richmond and Philadelphia were both very busy cities, but she had never seen anything like the raucous chaos in Independence, Missouri. Throngs of people filled the streets, while what seemed like hundreds of wagons filled the horizon just outside of town. Plumes of smoke rose from fires scattered across the outskirts of town, where people camped before their wagon trains departed. When she looked the other direction, she could see tree-lined streets stretching outward from the downtown area. Glimpses of elegant homes told her Independence had become more than a rough-and-tumble frontier town that was the launching point for wagon trains headed to New Mexico, California and Oregon. A large two-story courthouse graced the town square, with tall columns that extended from the ground to the roof all around the building, and a charming cupola resting on top.

Carrie stepped down from the train platform, wondering if she would be trampled as soon as she left its safety. She gazed around, wondering where her companions were. They had arrived earlier, but her train had been delayed for several hours by an engine malfunction. She wondered how Janie had handled the long trip across the country, but she knew Matthew would have taken good care of her.

"Carrie!"

Carrie's head whipped around as Nathan's voice boomed across the crowd. His red head towered above the rest of the throng, making him easy to spot. "Nathan!" She was glad to see him. The trip had left her tired and drained, and she was looking forward to some rest before they had to meet up with the army unit they would be traveling with. "I'm glad to see you."

"And it's glad I am to be seeing you," Nathan said as he picked up her luggage. "The rest are waiting for us in the dining room at the hotel. We decided to fill our stomachs before we made our way to our camping spot."

Carrie nodded and pointed toward the platform. "The supplies I brought are in that stack of crates."

Nathan motioned to a man who was waiting nearby with a small wagon. "They are right there, Chester," he called. "We need them taken out to the wagons where the other supplies are."

"Sure thing," Chester yelled back. He began to edge the wagon closer to the platform, calling loudly to get people to move out of the way.

Carrie frowned. "Will it all be safe?" She was reluctant to leave it behind.

Nathan nodded. "Your father is paying Chester well, and told him there would be a bonus if everything is well taken care of. There are two men watching the wagons your father bought." He smiled broadly. "I have to admit it is nice to be traveling with people who have money. I've not had that experience before. The Irish in Moyamensing have learned to do without."

Carrie eyed him with curiosity. "You never told me how you got to America."

Nathan nodded. "That would be true."

Carrie waited for him to say more, but he remained silent. "Are you going to tell me? I thought you had just come over with your family." She thought of the couple whose lives she had saved during the cholera epidemic.

"It's not a story to boast about," Nathan muttered. "And the Gaffney's aren't my real parents," he revealed.

Carrie was now certain she wanted to hear it. "Please." She gazed around as she waited for Nathan to make the decision whether he was going to tell her. The heart of Independence was full of wagonmakers, blacksmith shops, gunsmiths, wheelwrights, saloons, and livery stables. When she looked the other direction she saw grocers, tinsmiths, harness makers, mule and oxen sellers, dry goods merchants and hotels. Felicia had been right in saying they would be able to buy everything they needed. Carrie was fascinated by the frantic energy that pulsed in the air, but it also made her a little nervous.

"They were going to kill me," Nathan finally said.

Carrie's attention snapped back to him. "Kill you? Who?"

"Me brothers."

"Why would your brothers want to kill you?" Carrie was struck by the look of anguish in his eyes. She wished she had not started the conversation, but they were in it now.

Nathan took a deep breath. "Me brothers all be Catholic priests," he revealed. "Me parents planned on the same for me." He shook his head. "It wasn't for me. I converted to Protestantism a few years back. They didn't take kindly to my betrayal."

"Betrayal just because you decided you believed something different than they did?"

"The Irish are rather serious about their Catholicism," he responded sardonically. "Me parents were heartbroken and embarrassed to have anyone know. Me brothers decided the way to handle it was to kill me."

"How Christian of them," Carrie muttered.

Nathan shrugged. "God gets blamed for far more than he should, and people use religion to cover up evil far more than they should."

Carrie suddenly saw through the easy good cheer to the true depth Nathan had. She had learned the same truths when she had to deal with her beliefs about slavery years earlier. "How did you escape?"

"I learned of their plans and decided I didn't want to wait around to see if they would succeed or not. I went out on the docks during a dark, rainy night. I dove in and swam out to a merchant ship at anchor. I knew it was meant to leave two days later, but it hadn't taken on crew yet. I snuck onboard by using a ladder dangling from the side, and found a place to hide." He smiled slightly. "I was a wee bit hungry when I finally showed myself two weeks later."

"Two weeks?" Carrie said in disbelief. "You hid for two weeks?"

"Aye," Nathan replied. "I had enough water skins to hold me, but I finished off the meager food I was able to find on board before I hid after three days."

Carrie stared at him. "You didn't eat for eleven days?" She was horrified. "And then you just appeared on board one day?"

"Aye."

"What did they do?"

"They discussed tossing me overboard, but I managed to convince them I would work hard to earn my keep the rest of the way." He dipped his head. "I worked hard."

Carrie could tell by the expression on his face that they probably worked him like a slave for the duration of the trip, but at least he had escaped the fate his brothers had planned for him. She laid a hand on his arm. "So the Gaffney's are not really your parents."

"Aye." Nathan's voice was more uncomfortable, but he had made the decision to tell his story. "The Gaffneys took pity on me when I arrived. Said I looked like a son they had lost. They convinced me I would be safer if I claimed to be their son newly arrived from Ireland. In truth, they are more my parents than me real ones. We agreed I would not talk about my religious beliefs. I know they don't care, but they didn't want me to squander me chance to start over in America."

"Why are you telling me this?" Carrie asked, honored by his trust.

"You asked me to," Nathan said, amusement springing into his eyes again, but then they sobered. "You are a good woman, Carrie Borden. You came into Moyamensing when no one else would. I took a chance you wouldn't care about me background. It feels good to finally tell the truth to someone."

Carrie smiled. "Your story is safe with me," she assured him. "I'm simply glad you're in America, and I'm glad you're with us on this trip." She tucked her hand into the crook of his arm, not missing the look of relief in his eyes. "And now, if you don't mind, I am starving!"

*****

Carrie gazed up at the stars not obscured by campfire smoke, and listened as the voices of dozens of people scattered around her rose on the breeze. She knew the numbers were far higher in the spring months than they were now. Not many wagon trains started their arduous journeys during the winter months. Most of the people surrounding her were the merchants of the Santa Fe Trail who depended on year-round wagons for their trade. She and her friends had thought about sleeping in the hotel that night, but had opted to stay with the wagons. The two men her father had hired were standing guard, but the supplies in the wagon the army had provided were too precious to take a chance with. They wanted to be with them.

"I'm looking for Carrie Borden."

Carrie looked up at the tall, erect man with dark hair who stepped forward into the light of the campfire. His whole bearing spoke military. She saw Matthew open his mouth to say something, but she held up a hand to stop him. It was odd enough for a woman to be heading an expedition, and she was not going to have a man, even one she loved as much as she loved Matthew, talk for her. "I'm Carrie Borden," she said as she stood. "Whom do I have the pleasure of meeting?" Her voice was courteous but firm.

"Captain Jacob Marley."

Carrie waited a moment while his gaze assessed her. She didn't feel any disdain, but there was a large amount of cautious wariness. She didn't suppose she could blame him. "It's nice to meet you, Captain Marley." She turned and quickly introduced the rest of her team. "Thank you for the supply wagon. We have already filled it."

Captain Marley nodded but continued to assess the team. Carrie was certain he was wondering if they would slow him down on the trail. "I can assure you we are all up for the challenge," she said.

"Are you?" His voice was not unkind, but definitely blunt. "Do you folks have any idea of what you are getting into?"

"Assuming of course that medical do-gooders would not have the good sense to research the experience they are going to have?" Carrie asked. It was time to take control of the situation. She had learned the negotiation skills Abby had taught her the year before well.

"I mean no disrespect, Mrs. Borden," Captain Marley said quickly.

Carrie chose to ignore him. "We are aware that close to ten percent of people who start out on this trail don't make it. We are aware traveling in February and March makes it very possible we will have snowstorms and blizzards to contend with, and we can count on being cold for most of the trip. We know to expect mechanical breakdowns. Most importantly, there is a strong possibility of Indian attack by natives trying to defend the homelands white men seem intent on taking from them. Trail traffic has increased greatly, which means our risk has increased greatly."

Captain Marley's assessing look gave way to grudging admiration. "It looks like you have some idea of what to expect over the next months," he conceded. "Being with an army unit won't impact the weather or the chance of mechanical breakdowns, but it will help with the threat of Indian attack."

Carrie met his eyes evenly. "I hope it doesn't come to that, but I can assure you most of my team knows how to shoot."

"You can shoot a gun?" Captain Marley looked amused again.

Carrie knew he figured that the daughter of a wealthy Southerner was going on a reckless adventure to help worthless Indians, and bringing equally helpless people with her. "I can put a hole through the middle of your hat from one hundred paces if I get annoyed enough," she assured him. "I have found that the condition of our country makes marksmanship a valuable talent."

Captain Marley stared at her and then broke into laughter. "I told my men that you and your team weren't going to be any trouble, but they insisted I try to scare you." He walked over to the fire. "Mind if I join you for a little while?"

Carrie's eyes widened before she relaxed. "As long as you are not planning on annoying me any more than you have already."

"I wouldn't think of it. You might decide to miss my hat and aim for my forehead," Captain Marley said with amusement. He settled down next to Matthew. "Are you the journalist?"

"I am," Matthew replied. "And don't worry about being put in your place by Mrs. Borden. You're not the first, and you certainly won't be the last."

Captain Marley nodded. "You've known her a long time?"

"Long enough to know someone like you doesn't have a chance of standing in her way when she wants something."

Carrie watched the exchange, satisfied when she saw the final remnants of suspicion disappear from Captain Marley's eyes. She also remembered the letter Susan had read her just before she left. She settled down across the fire from him. "You're a friend of Captain Mark Jones?"

"I am. Mark told me to not underestimate you."

"That was wise," Carrie murmured sweetly.

Captain Marley laughed again. "Excuse me for being so hard-nosed in the beginning. We don't usually take civilians with us. In fact, we never have. This is very unusual, which makes my unit more than a little concerned that you will slow us down or create problems." He lifted a hand when he saw Carrie open her mouth. "I'm going to assure them they have nothing to worry about."

"Thank you," Carrie replied. "That will certainly make this journey much easier." She already knew she was going to like Captain Marley, but she intended to remain aloof for a while longer. "Do you have information on the current state of affairs at Bosque Redondo?"

Captain Marley scowled. "They are dismal. That is the real reason I let Mark talk me into letting you go with us on this trip. I don't know how much you can do to help those people, but anything will be appreciated." He paused before deciding to speak frankly. "What is happening to the Navajo is wrong. I hate that I have any part in it, but if it provides a way for me to help them, then I suppose I am grateful."

"You are not a fan of Manifest Destiny?" Matthew asked.

"No," Captain Marley snapped. "And I can assure you that if someone was trying to steal my homeland, I would fight, too."

Carrie felt her last resistance fade away. "I think I'm going to like you, Captain Marley."

"That is a supreme relief." His voice was somber, but his eyes danced with laughter in the firelight. "Not all of my men believe the way I do. Despite my assurances, I predict some will give you a hard time. I'll do my best to keep it from happening, but I can't always be available."

"We'll be fine," Carrie assured him. "I don't really care whether anyone likes what we are doing. We are here, we are equipped, and we intend to do what we came to do." She felt as confident as she sounded. There was something about being out on the plains, surrounded by wagons and campfires, that felt completely natural to her. She was surprised to realize she felt as at home here as she did on the plantation. Even with the wagons and people, there was an openness that appealed to her.

She was content to stare into the flames as Captain Marley conversed with the rest of her team. She was aware his eyes rested on her several times during the evening, but she pretended not to notice. Obviously, Mark had not told him about Robert, nor how she had escaped his men by jumping Granite over a fence. She was glad for that. She wanted this experience to be on her terms—not a reflection of the past.

"I understand there are forts along the trail now to provide protection," Carolyn said. "Is that true?"

"Definitely," Captain Marley assured her. "Fort Larned was the first, but there are three more now, spaced out to provide protection for the wagon trains."

Matthew cleared his throat. "What is the Indian attack situation like now?"

Carrie stared at him. She saw Janie lock her eyes on him, as well. Both of them knew his journalistic tone. From the look on Captain Marley's face, he suspected it was more than a casual question, too.

"Are you asking about anything in particular?"

"The name General Winfield Hancock comes to mind," Matthew replied.

Marley sighed. "It was definitely not one of our finest moments," he admitted in a heavy voice. "In fact, it was something the entire army should be ashamed of," he added sharply.

Melissa's voice broke into the silence that followed his statement. "There are those of us who have no idea what you are talking about. We have been buried in books at medical school, not keeping track of Indian affairs. I sense, however, that this is something we should know."

Captain Marley took a deep breath. "I suppose you do have the right to know. I truly don't think there will be attacks on this trip, but I wouldn't have predicted what happened last year either." He stared into the fire for a moment before he began. "General Winfield Scott Hancock is a hero of the Civil War, but he was rather inexperienced at dealing with the Indians. He arrived at Fort Larned last spring with orders to solve the Indian problem because they stand in the way of American expansion."

"American greed," Janie snapped.

"I won't disagree with that," Marley responded. "He had been told the Cheyenne Indians were among the most dangerous on the plains because they are superior warriors. When he arrived, he was legally unable to forge treaties with the tribes so he decided he would intimidate them into compliance. He invited several Cheyenne chiefs to Fort Larned on April twelfth. He told them if they chose to go to war with the white man, they would lose because the United States has many great chiefs with far more men, who have fought many more great battles." He paused. "The chiefs listened and returned home, but not before Hancock told them he wanted to meet with all their chiefs in their village."

Carrie listened, knowing the story wasn't going to end well.

"Two days later, Hancock and his troops went to the village. Before they got there, a large group of Cheyenne warriors rode out to meet them. They had as many warriors as Hancock had troops. Colonel Wynkoop, the agent at the fort, rode out between the lines and asked the warriors to remain calm. They agreed, and the army marched to within one mile of their village. From their vantage point above the valley, they could see how large and magnificent the Cheyenne village was."

Captain Marley's voice grew more somber. "The appearance of so many troops on the hills above them scared the Indians. They were afraid there would be another Sand Creek Massacre, so they fled the village that night. They left most of their lodges and belongings behind."

"The Sand Creek Massacre?" Randall asked, his eyes already glittering with anger.

Matthew was the one to answer. "The Sand Creek Massacre was another fine moment in American history," he said with clipped sarcasm. "The Treaty of Fort Laramie in 1851 gave the Cheyenne and Arapaho Indians extensive territory in Colorado. The discovery of gold around Pikes Peak seven years later persuaded the government to tell the tribes their treaty was no longer any good. In 1861, they took away most of their land, leaving them with a small portion of the original amount."

"That's terrible!" Carolyn cried in a shocked voice.

"It gets worse," Matthew said. "Three years later, seven hundred members of the Colorado Territory militia decided to attack the Indians. The militia was led by Colonel John Chivington, who claimed to be a Methodist preacher. After a night of heavy drinking by the soldiers, Chivington ordered a massacre. Two chiefs, trying to obtain a truce to protect their people, had been advised to camp near Fort Lyon in Colorado, and were told to fly the American flag to establish themselves as friendly." His voice thickened. "In late November, while the majority of the males were out hunting, Chivington and his troops attacked the camp. More than a hundred women and children were murdered. Despite eyewitness accounts from survivors, and even some of the soldiers who were horrified by the event, they were never charged for the heinous attack."

Carrie felt nauseous. The group's shocked silence told her everyone else was feeling the same way. She forced herself to ask the next question. As horrible as it was, they needed to know the truth about the territory they were traveling through. "I understand why the Cheyenne fled Hancock," she growled. "What happened next?"

Captain Marley glanced at her briefly and then turned back to stare into the fire. It was as if the crackle of the flames gave him the courage to continue. "Hancock was too dumb to realize the women and children fled because they were terrified. He took it as a personal offense and demanded they return. Some of the Cheyenne warriors went to look for them, but returned alone. By now, they were afraid of Hancock's anger, so they disappeared into the night, as well. Custer's Seventh Cavalry went after them, but had no success." He rubbed his hands in front of the fire, buying a bit of time before continuing. "Hancock sent troops out for several days, but the Indians had found a good hiding place. He decided their flight meant they were not interested in peaceful negotiation, and that they were in all actuality declaring war." His voice communicated his disdain. "Hancock retaliated by having the entire village burned to the ground."

"No!" Carrie's voice was filled with horror. "What possible good did he think could come from that?"

"His pride had been wounded," Matthew said angrily. "He was not thinking at all!"

Captain Marley nodded. "Matthew is right. Word of the village's destruction spread quickly among the tribes. Battles raged across Kansas all last summer and into the fall. The result was many dead and wounded on both sides. Finally, not wanting to spend more money on the war, the government started looking for alternatives. Hancock was transferred and then replaced by General Sheridan."

"They didn't want to spend more money?" Nathan snapped. "Did the government never acknowledge how wrong it all was?"

"No," Captain Marley admitted, his expression revealing far more than his words. "There was a treaty signed three and a half months ago, but I don't think the Indians really realize the treaty amounts to nothing."

"Nothing?" Carrie was furious.

"The American government is determined to run the Indians out of America, Carrie," Matthew said flatly.

"Where do they propose they go?" Carrie snapped. "Will they run them all the way into the Pacific Ocean where they will drown?" Her voice was shaking. "Why do white men think they can take whatever they want to? First, they enslaved millions of black people. Now they are going to kill off all the Indians? And they dare say it is because God ordains it? I feel sick!"

"It is not something to be proud of," Captain Marley admitted.

Carrie whipped around to stare at him, suddenly not at all sure she could like this man. "Why do you do this?" she demanded. "How can you be part of an army determined to destroy a whole way of life and murder innocent people?"

Captain Marley flinched but didn't look away. "Because it's the only way I know to try and help. I was with Colonel Chivington three years ago at Sand Creek," he said, his voice ragged with torment as his eyes filled with painful memories. "I tried to stop it. The men were too drunk. They wouldn't listen to reason..." His voice trailed off. "I came forward to tell what had happened, but I've already told you nothing was done." He shook his head. "I thought about leaving the army, but that's as good as saying I don't care and turning my back on the Indians. I don't know if I can possibly make a difference, but I have to try."

Carrie gazed into his eyes and realized she was looking a good man. "I'm sorry," she said gently. "Thank you for what you're trying to do."

"And thank you for trying to help the Navajo. There are very few people who care about the Indians. They only think about them when they are standing in the way of what they want, and then their solution is to remove them or kill them."

"I will change that," Matthew said passionately. "When we return, there will be many articles written to give exposure. I can at least bring what is happening to light."

The captain looked at him. "I hope it will help, but America has shown that greed mandates its actions." He shook his head. "It will be a long time before America stops taking all of the West that they want. I suspect they will stop only when there is nothing left to claim."

"The slaves were emancipated," Carrie reminded him, trying to give him hope.

"Yes, but they are far from being free," he said. He stood abruptly. "I'm sorry to put all of this on you on the first night of your journey. You are here to make a difference. I don't know that it will change the Indian situation in this country, but you will certainly help a large number of the Navajo."

"That's reason enough to travel the Santa Fe Trail in the winter," Carrie said, hoping she was right. She was getting ready to take her team across the entire state of Kansas, the scene of horrific battles that had ended just months earlier.

Captain Marley read the expression in her eyes. "I don't believe there will be any raids on this trip," he said. "The Indians settle in for the winter, and they will not want to break the treaty so quickly."

"And on the way home?" Nathan asked astutely. "It will be summer, and more time will have passed."

Captain Marley's silence and grim expression was all the answer they needed.

*****

Carrie watched Independence disappear behind them as the wagon train pulled away. She turned her face toward the open Kansas plains. She had hated the flat expanse when she had traveled it with Abby the year before, but she knew her raw grief had colored everything then. Now she was traveling the same route in a wagon train, but it felt different. It felt right somehow. Her trip through Kansas with Abby had been support for her stepmother, nothing else. Now her purpose for being here was so much more important than that. Nine hundred miles away, thousands of Navajo Indians needed their help.

It had still been dark when they had been rousted from their beds inside the wagons, but the sun had begun teasing the horizon when they pulled out. Carrie, Janie, Melissa and Carolyn shared one wagon. The men occupied the other. Carrie knew it must be very hard for Janie and Matthew to sleep apart, but they didn't have another option.

"Is it all this flat?" Janie asked, her eyes sweeping the horizon.

"No," Carrie assured her. "It gets flatter."

"You're serious?" Janie pulled her coat tightly around her, and then reached for the blankets piled behind the bench.

"Be glad you're not driving," Carrie replied. "At least we have the wagon canvas to break the wind." She could see it buffeting Matthew, and through the back opening, she could see Nathan on the seat of the wagon behind them. His face was almost as red as his hair. He caught her eye and waved cheerfully. She returned the wave and looked back at Janie. "I predict we will soon be bored out of our minds."

"I predict you're right," Janie answered, "but at least I brought books to study."

"How many hours do we travel each day?" Melissa asked, her eyes wide with excitement.

"About seven," Carolyn answered. "I talked to the wagon master last night. The days are short during the winter. No one wants to drive at night, and we need time to set up camp before it gets dark." She held up knitting needles and yarn. "I'm interested to see how many sweaters I can make while we are on the trail."

Carrie looked at Melissa. "What are you going to do to pass the time?"

"Janie and I brought books to share," she answered. "She brought textbooks, but I brought books I have longed to read, but haven't had the time." She pulled out a small crate. "I brought *Walden* by Henry David Thoreau, and Herman Melville's *Moby Dick*. I've heard they both are quite wonderful, though very different. I also brought Nathaniel Hawthorne's *The Scarlett Letter*. I've heard that literary critics praised the book, but religious leaders took issue with the subject matter."

"That is quite true," Carolyn confirmed. "I won't spoil the story for you, but the main character transforms in a way that is quite astounding, becoming quite a free thinker. There are hardly any religious leaders who applaud that," she said. She looked at the box of books with something close to reverence. "I know you have many more books in there. I hope this trip lasts long enough for me to read them all. My life has been far too busy to read. I miss it."

"I think you'll have plenty of time," Carrie assured her with a smile.

"And you?" Carolyn asked. "How are you going to spend your time?"

"I'm looking forward to reading, as well," Carrie answered, "but I'm also going to keep a journal. I'm hoping I will find portions of our journey interesting enough for inclusion in the book on herbs and medicinal plants that will be my final project for my medical degree."

She didn't mention that she also hoped her writing would help her make sense of all the feelings flowing through her mind and heart. Every plodding step the oxen took removed her further from the memories of the plantation, but now that she had what she had wanted, she found herself grasping those memories tightly. It was not going to be easy to separate herself from Robert enough to discover who she was without him.

She searched for a way to distract her thoughts. "Will you teach me how to knit?" she asked Carolyn.

"Knit?" Janie asked in an astonished voice. "I tried to teach you years ago, but you always turned up your nose and said you would learn to knit when you were an old woman."

"That's because I couldn't imagine sitting still that long," Carrie retorted. "Now that I'm going to be stuck in a wagon for months, it's evident I will have the time."

"I'll teach you," Carolyn promised. "I predict we'll need all the warm clothes possible." She stood to place a thick pillow under her bottom, and then pulled a heavy blanket around her. "We may also find it difficult to knit if our hands have frostbite," she said darkly.

Carrie knew she was right. "I don't want anything dangerous to happen on the trail, but I hope there is at least enough activity to keep our trip interesting."

"Stop!" Janie cried.

Carrie stared at her. "What's wrong with you?"

"You forget I've been your friend for a long time. Every time you say something like that we almost die, or something horrible happens."

Carrie laughed. "That is not true," she protested. Janie stared at her silently. "Well," she relented after several moments. "Perhaps a little true."

"Great," Carolyn muttered. "Just great."

Laughter rang through the wagon, pushing back the cold as they rolled forward through the plains.

*****

"I would give anything for a hot bath," Carolyn muttered.

"I might kill you to get to it first," Janie admitted. "I never knew it was possible to feel so dirty." She looked at Carrie. "It's only been two weeks. We won't have a bath for two months?"

"I warned you," Carrie reminded them with a smile.

"Yes, but warning and reality are two totally different things," Janie muttered. "I read some things about wagon train trips before we left. No one said anything about having to be filthy and smelly the entire time."

"That's because most wagon trains leave in late spring," Melissa said wearily, pushing her dirty hair back from her face. "People can bathe in the lakes and rivers along the way. I'm not eager to jump into frigid water in February." She forced a smile. "At least we don't have to worry about the water levels being high for the crossings. There are no rainstorms to cause them to rise, and there is no snowmelt in the mountains."

"I find it hard to be excited about that," Janie replied morosely. "I'm about to decide freezing cold water is better than nothing."

"You'll change your mind quickly," Carrie teased.

"Oh, hush," Janie said. "You know this is bothering you as much as it is bothering us. Why are you being so cheerful?"

Carrie sighed. "Because I feel responsible for your misery. The least I can do is make you feel a little better about it."

"I would much prefer you to be equally miserable," Carolyn retorted, but the gleam of amusement was back in her eyes. "You did warn us."

"I suppose I should be glad Matthew has to sleep in the other wagon," Janie said. "At least he doesn't have to smell me."

Carrie saw her friend's smile, but she also saw the sadness in her eyes. She knew how hard it would be for her if she had been forced to sleep apart from Robert on a trip of this duration. Unfortunately, she didn't know what she could do about it...and she couldn't deny that being dirty was not romantic.

*****

Later that afternoon, Captain Marley rode by their wagon. "Is there anything I can do for you ladies?"

Carrie made her decision quickly. "Yes. I would like to ride one of the horses in your string of extras. I might go quite mad if I have to sit in this wagon for another entire day."

Captain Marley looked at her, obviously trying to figure out how to respond. "We don't have sidesaddles," he said carefully.

"I won't need one," Carrie said. While she had opted for dresses so as to not draw more attention to herself, she had packed her breeches. She was dying to get into clothing that was actually comfortable. As dirty as she was, it hardly mattered what she was wearing, and now that they were on the trail, surely she would not offend anyone.

"Our horses are quite spirited," Captain Marley said evasively.

Carrie knew it was time to play her hand. "Did Captain Jones ever tell you about a woman who managed to escape his troops on a plantation outside Richmond?"

Captain Marley grinned. "As a matter of fact, he did. He was quite impressed with the young lady who thundered across the field on a gray Thoroughbred, and then jumped a tall fence after one of his soldiers put a bullet in her shoulder. And she was bareback!" His eyes narrowed. "How did you know about...?" His eyes widened.

"That was me," Carrie confirmed. "Now, may I ride one of your horses?"

"Most definitely. I'll make sure the men know you can handle any of them."

"I believe I'll prove it myself," Carrie said tartly.

Carrie was dressed in breeches when they stopped for a lunch break of biscuits and cold meat. There was not time to build fires for a hot meal in the middle of the day, but that just made getting into their night camp even more appealing. She pulled on her boots and buttoned Robert's coat securely before she shoved a hat down on her head.

Captain Marley strode up and gazed at her. "Is that how all Southern women dress now?"

"Only the smart ones," Carrie said with a smile. "And only the ones who have spent the last year running a breeding stable."

"I see," Captain Marley muttered. "You know it's not going to go over well with the men if you prove you can outride them."

"Your men's pride is hardly my concern," Carrie retorted, but she relented. "I'll do my best to ride like a commoner."

Captain Marley chuckled, and then beckoned one of his men forward. He was leading a tall chestnut mare with bright, intelligent eyes.

"What a beauty," Carrie murmured, stroking the mare's face gently. "What is her name?"

"Celeste."

Carrie blinked. "Celeste?"

"I'm afraid my daughter was with me the day I picked her up. She insisted on naming her, despite my objections," Captain Marley said with a wince. "I apologize to this mare almost every day."

Carrie grinned. "Hello, Celeste. It's nice to make your acquaintance."

*****

Carrie's feet were cold, but she was grinning when she cantered up next to the captain. "I feel like I have been let out of prison. Thank you."

"You're welcome. You should have said something sooner. I've seen you get out of the wagon and walk long stretches."

"If I had to read one more page, or pretend to enjoy knitting for even one more minute, I was sure I would lose my sanity."

Captain Marley laughed. "Wagon travel is difficult at any time, but it is particularly brutal in winter." He cocked his head. "Why now? Why not wait until spring?"

"You're not the first to ask me," she assured him. Carrie explained her unique situation. "I didn't want to do any other internship, and I didn't want to delay my medical degree longer than necessary."

Captain Marley was watching her closely. "You own a breeding operation *and* you are a doctor? How do you blend the two?"

Carrie had asked herself the same question many times. "I have no idea," she answered honestly. "Right now, Mark Jones' sister is running the stables."

"Susan? That's wonderful! She's quite the horsewoman."

"She is, indeed," Carrie agreed.

"And when you return?" Captain Marley pressed. "What then?"

Carrie sighed. "That is the question I hope I will have the answer for by the time I return. I know I can maintain ownership of the stables, but I also know Susan would love to be partial or full owner of the operation. I am going to be a doctor, but..."

Carrie stared out over the flat sameness. She wished for anything to break the monotony, but perhaps she was simply chafing against the monotony of her thoughts. "My late husband started Cromwell Stables," she revealed.

"Late?"

Carrie acknowledged the captain's ability to draw her out. He was a good listener. She wasn't certain, though, that she wanted to talk about it.

Captain Marley read her face. "Forgive me for prying."

Carrie shook her head. There was something about the vast openness that made it easier to reveal herself "It's all right. My husband, Robert, was murdered last spring by vigilantes from the Ku Klux Klan when they attacked our plantation."

"My God," Captain Marley muttered. "I didn't know. I'm so sorry."

Carrie nodded absently. She was used to people being shocked. "Thank you."

Captain Marley continued to watch her. "You're looking for answers. Many people join wagon trains for the same reason. They want a new beginning, or something different."

"That's true for me, too," Carrie admitted. "My primary motivation is helping the Navajo Indians while I finish my requirements for my degree, but I'm also trying to figure out who I am without Robert."

"You're an extraordinary woman," Captain Marley said. "When I realized you were the woman from Mark's tale about the escaping plantation belle, I remembered everything else he told me."

Carrie couldn't hold back her laugh. "The escaping plantation *belle*? I wish my mother was still alive to hear that. She quite despaired of me ever becoming a belle. To even hear me called one would be balm to her soul."

"Your mother would be very proud of you," Captain Marley insisted. "You're beautiful, even after two weeks on the trail. You are an expert horsewoman, and from all I hear, a brilliant doctor. Not to mention you operated as a surgeon during the war." He paused. "I suspect you were all those things before you fell in love with Robert."

Carrie smiled sadly, though touched by his words. "I was eighteen when I met Robert. We married during the third year of the war when I was working at Chimborazo Hospital. He was my biggest supporter. I miss him," she added softly. She was tired of talking about herself. "And you? You said you have a daughter. Are you married?"

"I am," Captain Marley said. "Sally and I have been married for six years. I have three beautiful daughters. They live in Independence. When Sally realized I was determined to work with the Indians, she insisted on being close enough for us to still be a family as much as possible." He smiled, but his eyes were sad. "I miss them more than I can say. I plan on serving for two more years, and then we're going to return home to Vermont. I don't want to completely miss my girls growing up. I lost so much during the war years," he said.

Carrie understood. "What will you do in Vermont?"

"Run a business," he said. "My father owns a hardware store there. I grew up working with him. I was in the process of taking it over when the war started. He supports what I'm doing, but I know he's more than ready to retire. I've told him and my mother we will he home in two years."

"They will be thrilled to have you back."

"That's true," Captain Marley replied. "It will be good for the girls to have their grandparents, too."

The rest of the afternoon passed quickly as they talked.

Carrie was surprised when he raised his hand to signal it was time to stop and make camp. "I may actually survive this experience if I can ride every day," she said with relief.

"Celeste is yours any time you want her," Captain Marley promised.

Chapter 21

Abby welcomed the blast of warm air when she opened the door to the house after a long day at the factory. The spate of warmer days that teased of spring had been swallowed by a brisk cold wind from the north. All the snow had melted in the last few days, but ominous clouds on the horizon told her there would be more on the ground by morning.

"Ready for some hot tea, Miss Abby?"

Abby smiled broadly. "That sounds wonderful, May. Thank you."

May nodded, a curious light in her eyes. "I'll bring it into the parlor where your guest is waiting."

Abby raised a brow as she picked up the stack of mail on the foyer table. "My guest? I wasn't expecting anyone."

"Which is why I'm hoping you will find me a welcome surprise."

Abby wheeled around as the deep male voice sounded behind her. "Peter Wilcher!" she cried, dropping the mail to clasp his outstretched hands. "You are certainly a welcome surprise! And I see you haven't lost any of that New York accent."

Peter's dark eyes danced with fun under his thick, dark hair. "And here I thought I was beginning to sound like a Southern gentleman. You have quite dashed my hopes."

"It's best to face the truth about things," Abby joked. "It keeps one from false expectations."

Peter laughed. "I just put some more wood on the fire. I'm glad you're home."

"As am I," Abby answered. "Give me a moment to sort through the mail. I am expecting something from a friend up north." She flipped through it quickly. There was no letter from her friend Nancy Stratford, but her eye was caught by handwriting she did not recognize. Her eyes widened when she saw the return address. "This is from Oregon."

Peter stepped closer. "Hobbs?"

"I certainly hope so." Abby hung her coat and stepped into the parlor. It was her favorite room in the rambling three-story brick home on Richmond Hill, and the blazing fire made it cheerful and welcoming. She settled down in a comfortable chair and opened the letter, knowing Peter would be as curious about the contents as she was. A smile split her face. "It is from Hobbs!" She read the single sheet quickly, before reading it aloud.

"I'm not much a one for writing, but I want you to know I made it to Oregon. I was able to join a wagon train because of the money Thomas gave me. There were some real hard times, but we finally made it. It took us six months, but we got here right before snow closed down the last mountain pass."

"He must have gotten there in November," Peter mused.

"It sure enough is pretty out here. I've never seen trees so big in my life. I got hired on at a hardware store here. I miss farming, but this is a good job for me because of my leg. I hope to get a job with the railroad whenever it makes it this far. They are working on connecting it to San Francisco right now. I got me a room over a restaurant, so it always smells good and I don't got to worry about eating."

Peter chuckled. "That sounds like Hobbs."

"I got to tell you I am real glad to be out of the South. Seems like most everyone out here is looking for a new start, so I got a lot of good company. Please give everyone my greetings. Thank you for helping me start a new life out here."

Abby set down the letter with a smile. "I'm so relieved he made it safely."

Peter nodded. "I'm glad he seems to like it out there. I know he made his choices, but walking away from his life in order to help us expose the KKK was a big thing. I'm glad he doesn't know that it didn't seem to have had any impact at all."

Abby sighed. "It's getting worse?"

"It's getting worse," Peter confirmed. "Have there been more attacks on the plantation since the Harvest Festival?"

"Not that I know of," Abby assured him.

"And Matthew is really on a wagon train to Santa Fe?" he asked dubiously. "Never mind that he grew up in the mountains of West Virginia; he's been a city boy for a long time now."

"Yes," Abby said quietly. "Thomas and I received a telegram that was sent the night before they left Independence." She couldn't stop the wave of sadness that engulfed her. "They are on the Santa Fe Trail."

"You miss them," Peter said sympathetically.

"I miss everyone," Abby admitted. "It's hard to believe Carrie, Janie and Matthew are on a wagon train, and that I won't hear from them for months. I got a letter recently from Rose, but I hate knowing she, Moses, and the kids are not on the plantation anymore." She shook her head and managed a rueful laugh. "Ignore my self-pity. I'm afraid I'm not handling this change very well."

"Would you like a distraction?"

"I would love one."

The front door opened, causing the lanterns to cast flickering shadows across the room.

Thomas' voice boomed through the house. "I'm home, dear." He strode into the room, stopping short when he realized she was not alone. "Peter Wilcher! To what do we owe this pleasure?"

Peter stood and clasped his hand. "I thought that with Matthew out rolling across the country in a wagon train, you would appreciate a little inside news on Washington politics."

May appeared in the door with Abby's tea and a plateful of scones. "I'll bring you some tea as well, Mr. Thomas. Dinner will be ready in about an hour." She eyed their guest. "You'll be joining us for dinner won't you, Mr. Peter?"

"If my hosts will have me. I already know that anything you fix will be better than what I can get at my hotel."

"That's a given," May said as she sniffed.

Abby laughed. "There is no false modesty in this house. And, of course, you will stay for dinner. If we're going to pull every piece of information from you that we can, the least we can do is feed you."

Thomas chuckled as he reached for a scone. "From what I can tell, there is never a dull moment in Washington these days."

Abby interrupted before Peter could answer. "Before Peter starts, you should know we received a letter from Hobbs today." She pulled it out of the envelope and read it again, feeling the same joy she had earlier with the realization that Hobbs had been granted a chance to begin anew.

"Good for him," Thomas said. "It would have been quite impossible for him to stay in the South. I'm glad there are still parts of this country where a man can start over."

"Our president may have to think about going to Oregon," Peter said ruefully.

"Impeachment?" Thomas asked keenly.

"Impeachment," Peter agreed. "February twenty-fourth, 1868 is a date that will long be remembered because it is the first time Congress will have voted to impeach an American president."

Abby leaned forward. "Do you believe it will actually happen? Will they actually impeach him?"

Peter shrugged. "The charge they are impeaching him on is rather weak, in my opinion, but that is just the tip of the iceberg. The majority Republican Congress has long wanted him out of office. They may well have the votes to make it reality."

"Do I understand correctly that the grounds for impeachment was the president replacing Secretary of War Stanton with General Grant?" Thomas asked.

"No. Many people believe that, but the grounds are bigger than that. The Radical Republicans wanted Stanton in office because they know he will comply with the Reconstruction policies. To make sure that happened, they passed the Tenure of Office Act last year. Johnson vetoed it, but they overruled him."

"Just like they have with everything else," Thomas muttered. "If I didn't despise the man so much I might actually feel sorry for him. As it is, I can only hope Congress succeeds."

Peter nodded. "I agree. The Tenure of Office Act requires the president to seek the senate's advice and consent before relieving or dismissing any member of his cabinet. In actuality, the act was written specifically with

Stanton in mind." He paused for a sip of his tea. "There was a loophole in the act, though. It permits the president to suspend such officials when Congress is out of session. That's what Johnson did. He asked Stanton to resign, but the secretary declined. That was when he suspended him and replaced him with Ulysses S. Grant."

"But Grant left office last month," Abby said.

"That's true," Peter agreed. "When Congress passed a resolution on January seventh that they were in disagreement with Stanton's dismissal, Grant wrote his resignation letter and left. I suspect he was anticipating that result. Stanton moved back into his office. It got a little crazy, though, because Grant didn't bother to tell Johnson he was leaving." He smiled thinly. "Our president was not pleased."

Thomas chuckled. "I imagine he wasn't."

"What happened next?" Abby asked. "This is as good as a dime-store novel!"

Peter smiled. "It is certainly high drama. President Johnson believes the Tenure of Office Act is unconstitutional so he decided to ignore it. A month ago, he offered the post to Lorenzo Thomas. General Thomas didn't want the job, but somehow Johnson convinced him to take it so he could make a test case against the act. He appointed Thomas Secretary of War on February twenty-first and ordered Stanton's removal from office." He grinned. "This is where it gets really good. General Thomas delivered the notice to Stanton personally, but Stanton refused to accept its legitimacy, and also refused to vacate his position. Instead, he barricaded himself in his office and ordered Thomas arrested for violating the Tenure of Office Act."

"Oh my," Abby murmured.

"Thomas asked if he could be brought to the White House to let President Johnson know he had been placed under arrest. I think Stanton probably realized the arrest would allow the courts to review the law about the Tenure of Office act, and he wasn't sure the courts would uphold it, so he dropped the charges against Thomas and went after Johnson for violating the act." Peter shook his head at the absurdity of it. "Three days later the House of Representatives voted one hundred twenty-six to forty-seven in favor of a resolution to impeach the president for high crimes and misdemeanors."

He reached in his pocket and pulled out a sheet of paper. "This is a quote from Representative Kelly of Philadelphia. *Sir, the bloody and untilled fields of the ten unreconstructed States, the unsheeted ghosts of the two thousand murdered negroes in Texas, cry, if the dead ever evoke vengeance, for the punishment of Andrew Johnson.*"

Thomas shook his head. "I don't think President Johnson ever understood how strongly the country feels about Reconstruction."

Peter grimaced. "Our president has quite an over-inflated ego. Once he sets himself on a course, he is reluctant to let facts or the truth stand in the way. He thinks he has the power to make things happen simply because he is president. I suspect he is finally waking up to just how wrong he is."

"Will the vote be there to actually carry out the impeachment?" Abby asked.

"I don't know," Peter admitted, "but I can guarantee you that whatever dreams Johnson had of running for re-election are dead."

"What happens if Johnson is impeached?" Thomas asked. "Since he replaced Lincoln, there is not a vice-president."

"That's a very good question," Peter responded. "His replacement will be the president pro tempore of the Senate. Traditionally, it is the most senior member of the majority party."

"Benjamin Wade," Thomas said.

"That's right. Wade is one of the most radical Republicans."

"Which means impeachment will be difficult," Thomas mused. "While the entire Congress voted to move forward, surely there are moderate Republicans who are going to have to think about what it means if Benjamin Wade becomes president."

Abby sighed. "It's all just a game, isn't it?"

"Politics?" Peter asked. "I suppose it is, but it is a game with very high stakes. My initial disdain for politics has been tempered by the reality that it mandates the country I live in. That means that in many ways it mandates the life I live. President Johnson's policies have led to the rise of the KKK. I can never forget that because it impacts the lives of so many people I love. Just because I'm not black doesn't mean I shouldn't care as much about the horrors of the KKK." He paused for a moment. "I have learned that if human freedom is denied to anyone in the world, it is therefore denied, indirectly perhaps, to all people."

"Which is why we can't remain silent," Abby said. "The choice to remain silent in the face of evil or violence merely encourages that behavior."

Thomas was watching her carefully. "Something is bothering you, dear. What is it?"

"Isn't the state of our nation enough?" Abby asked evasively. She wasn't sure she was ready to talk about what was bothering her.

"It is," Thomas agreed, "but I suspect it is something more. I understand if you prefer not to talk about it."

Abby sat silently for several long moments. As she stared out the window, she saw the first snowflakes from the approaching storm float down onto the magnolia tree. "Do you believe God put Andrew Johnson into office?"

Thomas sat quietly for a moment, surprised by her question. "Do you?"

"I didn't," Abby replied, "but now I'm not sure." She sighed heavily. "I ran into an old friend today while I was doing some shopping. She is in town from Philadelphia on business for the bank, and I accepted her offer to have lunch."

"And she told you that President Johnson was God's choice for president, and that we should support him no matter what," Peter said.

"Yes," Abby replied. "How did you know? Do you agree with her?" She couldn't imagine that he did, but perhaps he was not being honest about his true feelings.

"No," Peter said bluntly.

"Why?" Abby had been struggling with the issue ever since she had left lunch.

Peter smiled. "Did I ever tell you that I almost became a minister?"

"Really?" Thomas asked. "What happened?"

"Nothing earth-shattering," Peter assured them. "It just wasn't the right fit for me. I did, however, learn a great deal. The issue of Andrew Johnson becoming president is one that many Christians would disagree on."

Abby nodded eagerly. "I've always considered myself Christian, but I find I can't believe that God would put Johnson into office. I've thought about Lord Cromwell, and all the Irish and Scottish he was responsible for killing. How can that be God?" She looked back and forth between Thomas and Peter. "I remember my father telling me about Vlad the Third."

"Who?" Thomas asked with a raised brow.

"He was a prince of the Ottoman Empire in the 1400s."

"You studied the Ottoman Empire when you were growing up?" Peter asked in astonishment.

"No," Abby said, "but my father did. He was quite obsessed with it, actually. My mother hated it when he talked to me about what he was learning, but he did it anyway."

"So I'm assuming Vlad the Third was not someone to be proud of?" Thomas asked

"You would be correct," Abby replied. "He was one of the most tyrannical leaders in history, not only because so many tens of thousands of people were killed during his reign, but also because he delighted in violence and torture."

"I see," Thomas said slowly. "Are you comparing President Johnson to him?"

"No," Abby said. "Although the KKK seems to be quite willing to do the dirty work for him. Since I believe his policies have spawned the organization, I find him responsible in many ways. What I'm saying is that I could never believe God would deliberately put such an evil man in power. It stands to reason that if Vlad was not put in power, then assuming God is responsible for every person in power is wrong."

Peter gazed at her with admiration. "I wish you had been in my seminary classes. You seem to be struggling with your beliefs now, however. Why?"

Abby knew that was the crux of the issue. *Why* was she struggling? "My friend seemed quite certain that the Bible supports her beliefs."

"I certainly believed the Bible supported my beliefs about slavery," Thomas said. "I was wrong."

"That's true," Abby murmured, disturbed that she was so shaken by her earlier encounter.

"It seems rather a denial of responsibility," Peter added.

"What do you mean?" Abby asked.

"God gets blamed for so many things that are done by humans. The Bible gets blamed for so many things...on both sides of the equation. One of the reasons I left the church and became a journalist was that I became so weary of people using God or the Bible to promote their own agendas."

"So, what is the answer?" Abby asked. She held up her hand to silence him when he opened his mouth to answer, suddenly sure she knew. "Love," she said softly.

"Go on," Peter encouraged her.

"Love is the answer." Her certainty grew. "I don't care how many scriptures or beliefs can be used to justify something. If the end result is not love, then it is wrong. God does not tell me to condone something that is wrong simply because someone is in a position of supposed power. I don't have to support the president of the United States if what he is doing is wrong. Johnson has done many harmful things. Blacks are being killed and tortured by the KKK because of things he has said, and things he has done. Our country is in turmoil because of the agendas his ego has mandated, just like slavery existed in this country for so long because of decisions made by people in power."

"And your friend?" Thomas asked.

Abby sighed. "She is wrong. "I know she believes she is right, but if love is not the result of your belief, then it is wrong." All the confusion that had fogged her mind during the afternoon cleared. "I believe the only responsibility we have as humans is to support people and policies that make America a better place—not a place of division and hatred."

Thomas reached over to take her hand. "I agree with you."

"As do I," Peter assured her.

Abby smiled. "I'm glad for that, but it doesn't really matter. I don't even know why this shook me so much. I stood up against politicians and policies for many years while I was involved in the Abolition Society. I didn't care because I knew I was doing the right thing." She shook her head. "I'm not sure where I started to doubt myself, but the doubt is gone."

Peter waited a moment and then said, "You realize President Johnson doesn't act on his own, don't you?"

Abby nodded. "I do. The Democratic Party is responsible for what is happening to our country, but it's also the people who go along with it. Politicians make laws, but people don't have to comply. The government passed laws saying that slaves couldn't escape. The result was that even more slaves found freedom through the Underground Railroad than before." She watched as the snow fell harder outside the window. "There were people who went along with the laws, and then there were those who stood up and acted from love. They did what they believed was right." She smiled. "I believe God applauds those people."

*****

Felicia burst through the door. "Mama! Mama!"

Rose, home only a few minutes since picking up Hope and John from the neighbor who watched them during the day, stiffened with alarm. She tucked Hope close and hurried into the kitchen. "Felicia! What is wrong?"

"Nothing, Mama," Felicia said. "It's good news!"

Rose forced herself to relax. "Could you perhaps not scare me to death the next time you have good news?"

"I'm sorry, Mama. I was just so excited to tell you." Felicia's voice was full of remorse, but her eyes were still sparkling.

Rose shook off the fear that threatened to send her spiraling back to the need for constant awareness on the plantation. She was in Oberlin now, not waiting for the next attack on her school. She took another deep breath and then sat down at the table. "Tell me the good news," she invited.

"I'm going to college!"

Rose wasn't sure she had heard her daughter right. "Excuse me?"

Felicia laughed. "You heard me right. I'm going to college."

"Your father and I plan on that when you are old enough," Rose agreed, not sure where the conversation was going.

"No. I'm going to college now," Felicia said.

"Perhaps you should start at the beginning," Rose said faintly. "Your daddy should be home in a few minutes, and I suspect he will want to hear this. I'm going to fix some tea and make a batch of cookies. Can you manage to contain the news until he gets home?"

"Sure I can," Felicia said, her eyes glowing with happiness. "I'm going up to my room. I'll come back down when Daddy gets home." Humming as she went, she ran up the stairs.

Rose stared after her with a bemused expression, and then began pulling out ingredients for cookies.

Moses sniffed the air when he walked in a short time later. "Nothing smells better than your molasses cookies," he said. He reached for one, took a big bite, and closed his eyes in ecstasy. "Cookies will help me study," he said solemnly.

Rose heard Felicia start down the stairs. "No study until we talk to our daughter. She has news."

"About?"

Rose shrugged. "I made her wait until you got home. All I know is that she said something about going to college."

Moses turned around to smile at Felicia when she entered the kitchen. "Big news?"

"Yes," Felicia said excitedly. She reached for a cookie and sat at the table. "I've been invited to go to college." She waited expectantly for their reaction.

"Perhaps you could expound a little," Rose prompted. She was all for anything that would put a look of such joy on her daughter's face, but she still didn't understand.

"My teacher asked me to stay after class today. She told me she didn't think there was anything else the teachers at my school could teach me that I don't already know."

"I understand that feeling," Rose muttered.

Felicia giggled, sounding much more like an excited little girl than a college student.

"You've only just turned thirteen," Moses said carefully. His expression said he was not thrilled with the announcement.

"Sarah Kinson was very young, too," Felicia said. "She was a captive on the *Amistad*."

Rose was totally confused now. "Felicia, I want you to pretend that your father and I know absolutely nothing about what you are discussing. Now, I want you to explain the situation to us."

"I'm sorry, Mama. I'm very excited." Her eyes grew huge. "I knew life was going to be different here, but I never thought I would be starting college *now*."

"Neither did I," Moses said ruefully. "Could you focus on pretending we know nothing about what you are talking about?"

Felicia grinned. "My teacher told me there is precedence for my starting college because of Sarah Kinson. Actually, Sarah's name was Margru in the beginning. Have either of you heard of the *Amistad*?"

Rose frowned in thought. "Yes," she said slowly. "Wasn't it a slave ship brought over to the United States in the Thirties? I remember reading something about it when your father and I were living with Abby in Philadelphia."

"I remember the name, but I bet you can tell us far more," Moses said as he took another molasses cookie off the plate.

"I can," Felicia agreed. "I made my teacher tell me all about Margru. She was born in Mandingo, a region of West Africa called 'Mende.' She grew up playing with her brothers and sisters, but when she was six years old, her parents sold her to Spanish slave traders to repay a family debt."

Rose stiffened with disbelief. She would never sell one of her children for any reason.

"When there were about fifty people who had been purchased or kidnapped, they forced them all to walk one hundred miles to the coast. They found hundreds of people crammed into slave pens," Felicia said sadly. "They put her in a boat called the *Tecora* with a bunch of adults and three other children." She shook her head. "They were treated very badly."

Rose shuddered, remembering the stories her mother had told of her own ocean crossing. She knew how horrible the slave ships were.

"The boat took them to Havana, Cuba. A bunch of them were sold off to some Spanish men, including Margru and the other children. Their next boat was called *La Amistad*. They were only going to the other side of Cuba, but one of the Mendian men staged a revolt. They killed the captain and the cook, and drove the other two crew members overboard. Then they ordered the two new Cuban slave owners to sail the boat back to Africa."

Rose was both fascinated and horrified. She was also remembering more of the story. "They didn't sail the boat back to Africa. Neither of those Cubans were sailors so I'm sure they had no idea where they were going. They ended up off the coast of New York. The *Amistad* was in such bad shape that people thought it was a pirate ship."

"That's right," Felicia confirmed. "There was a lot of publicity about the captives," she said disdainfully, "and they were treated very badly. A man named Lewis Tappan found out about it."

"Of course!" Moses exclaimed. "Tappan has been a chief benefactor of Oberlin College for years. He is also the man who pressured Oberlin into admitting black men and women into school. I'm remembering more of this story now. When he found out what was happening with the captives, he organized other abolitionists into an Amistad Committee to raise money for their legal defense."

"And that committee became the American Missionary Association that sent me to the contraband camp," Rose added.

Felicia nodded. "Tappan also took Margru under his care. He couldn't set her and the other children free, but he did arrange for them to live with the jailer and his wife." Her expression darkened. "They were better off there, I suppose, but they were servants and not treated very kindly." She turned to Moses. "Daddy, that could have been me," she said. "If you hadn't taken me away from Memphis when my parents were killed, I probably would have ended up as a servant somewhere."

"You might have," Moses agreed. He reached over and took her hand. "But it didn't happen. You will always be our daughter."

"I'm so glad," Felicia said fervently. "Anyway, there was a big court battle about whether the captives still belonged to the Cuban men, or whether they were free and could return to Africa. It lasted two and a half years, and went all the way to the Supreme Court."

Moses nodded. "Where former President John Quincy Adams defended them. I remember now. It was in one of the books I read this winter. It was quite the victory when the Supreme Court declared they were free."

"Thank God they were not sent back to slavery after all they had been through," Rose said, nestling Hope against her chest. She could only pray her own children would never have to face such an ordeal.

Felicia continued. "It took a while for Tappan and his friends to raise enough money to send them back to Africa. One way they raised money was by doing tours up and down the East Coast with Margru and some more of the Mendians. They read from the Bible, they did dramatic enactments, and they sang African songs and Christian hymns. Everyone talked about how smart Margru was. Anyway," she said impatiently, "it's quite a long story how all that happened, but the important thing is that Margru, who Tappan had renamed Sarah, went back on the ship with all the captives and some missionaries. She was ten when she got back home." She pursed her lips.

Rose could tell she was getting tired of telling the story and was ready to get to the point.

"My teacher told me a lot more things, but what matters most is that Sarah wanted to come back to America and go to school. So"—she paused dramatically—"she came back to Oberlin and went to school. She was behind at first, but she caught up quickly with tutors, and then she started college. After she graduated she went back to Africa and taught school!"

Rose shook her head. "That is an amazing story, but the Oberlin policy clearly states now that students have to be at least seventeen years old, and they have to pass an entrance exam."

Felicia nodded. "That's true, Mama, but policies are made to be altered."

"Is that right?" Moses murmured, his eyes shining with amusement and admiration. "You still have to pass the exam."

"I already have," Felicia retorted. "My teacher asked me to take a test the other day. Mrs. Cook didn't tell me what it was for. When she asked me to stay after today she told me I scored very high."

Rose knew they had finally reached the critical moment.

"Mrs. Cook said that if both of you agreed, she would ask the college about me becoming a student."

Rose exchanged a long look with Moses and then turned to her daughter. "Is that what you want?" she asked gently. "I know you are smart, but it will be hard being so young. All the students will be much older than you."

"Mrs. Cook talked to me about that," Felicia admitted. She stared into Rose's eyes. "You've told me many times that I am not a normal little girl. Is that true, or do you just tell me that to make me feel good?"

Rose smiled. "I told you the truth. You are most certainly not a normal thirteen-year-old, Felicia. You are quite extraordinary."

"Then why should I be treated like a normal thirteen-year-old?" Felicia demanded, her eyes blazing with intensity. "The other kids at my school seem so much younger than me—even the ones that are older. I know what I want to do with my life, and I would like to start preparing for that now. When I'm seventeen I will be able to make a difference, rather than just starting college after being bored for four years."

Rose sighed. "She has a point," she told Moses.

Moses was watching his daughter carefully. "I know you are very special, Felicia, but part of my job as your father is to protect you while you are growing up. I know you are smarter than everyone in your school, but it takes more than being smart to be an adult, honey. You have to learn how to be with people."

"I've thought about that too, Daddy."

Moses blinked. "You have?"

"Of course. I walked home very slowly so I could think about all this," she said very seriously.

"And what did you think about?" Moses asked.

"I'm tired of being a child. When I went through the Cocooning Rite I became a woman, didn't I?"

"Yes," Rose assured her, "but you are still a very young woman."

"Yes, but I am a *woman*. One who is not normal. I would still like to have friends my age, and I'm hoping you can both make that happen. I also want to have people over for dinner almost every night so I can learn more about being with all types of people." Her voice sounded uncertain for the first time. "I know I can handle the schoolwork, but I'm going to need both of you to prepare me in the other ways." She hesitated. "Will you do that?"

Rose met Moses' eyes over the top of Felicia's head. She saw what she was expecting. She stood and walked behind Felicia to wrap her arms around her shoulders. "Yes, Felicia, we will do that. We are both so proud of you. We'll do our best to be the parents you need."

"Really?" Felicia's eyes ignited with happiness. "You too, Daddy?"

"Me, too," Moses assured her. "I'm so proud of you I could almost burst."

Rose could barely remember the frightened little girl who had arrived on the plantation two years earlier. Felicia truly had transformed from a caterpillar into a glorious butterfly ready to take flight. She gazed at her proudly, trying to push down the certainty that Felicia's life was going to be one hard challenge after the other.

Tonight they would celebrate.

Chapter Twenty-Two

Carrie trotted Celeste up beside Captain Marley. "Do those clouds mean what I think they do?" They were close to the Colorado border now, but surely the signs of a snowstorm were the same everywhere. After a relatively mild day, the wind had picked up, and dark gray clouds were collecting across the wide horizon.

"That it's going to snow? Yes," Captain Marley said.

Carrie stared at him, hearing something more in his voice, or perhaps reading more in his eyes. Their daily conversations during the long days of riding had turned the captain into a close friend. "You're not telling me everything."

"I've learned the signs for a blizzard," he admitted. "Snow is one thing, but when a blizzard hits, they can be very dangerous. I've seen wagons overturn. Oxen can be lost, and horses killed."

"I've never experienced a blizzard," Carrie admitted, trying to push down the anxiety rising within her. "We have plenty of snowstorms in Virginia, but I don't believe we've ever had a blizzard."

"You would know it if you had," Captain Marley assured her. "A snowstorm qualifies as a blizzard when you have sustained winds of more than thirty-five miles per hour, and the temperatures are below twenty degrees, though here on the plains they can plummet far below zero. You also know you're in a blizzard when the snow is blowing so hard you have visibility less than a quarter mile."

"I see," Carrie murmured, feeling more anxious than before. While it had been cold, the calmness of the last four weeks had led her to believe they would make this trip without any major weather disturbances. She had been wrong.

"They can be very dangerous," Captain Marley said.

Carrie soothed Celeste as the mare pranced away from a strong gust of wind. Her head was high and her ears pricked forward; it was obvious she knew something was coming.

Whether Captain Marley was oblivious to Carrie's fear, or simply determined to make sure she was prepared, he was not done with her education. "A blizzard is formed when cold air from the north meets even larger amounts of warm air and moisture from the south. We don't know where we will be when the two fronts actually meet. If we are on the southern edge of the blizzard, we may have severe thunderstorms and tornadoes, but actually miss the snow." He paused as he eyed the clouds. "My guess is that we are farther north. I won't be surprised if we have more than a foot of snow, but the real danger is how cold it can get with the wind-chills. There are times when the temperature plummets to twenty below."

Carrie shuddered. She thought she had been cold already on this trip. She couldn't imagine cold like that. Even wearing everything she had brought with her, it would be miserable.

"You and your friends might do better sharing a wagon, using each other's body heat for warmth."

Carrie nodded and reached for humor. "Matthew and Janie will be glad to hear that."

Captain Marley smiled slightly, but met her eyes with a steady gaze. "I want you to tie ropes to your wagon on the outside. Once the storm hits, you are not to go outside that wagon without holding onto the rope. For any reason," he said sternly. "The snow can swallow you in seconds, and you'll have no idea how to get back to your wagon. Death comes quickly."

Carrie's eyes scanned the horizon. Blank, flat sameness rolled toward the darkening skies. They had spent two nights at Fort Larned a week earlier, but she knew they were still a week or so out from Fort Dodge. "There is no shelter in sight." She tried to keep the quiver from her voice, but she wasn't sure she succeeded. If Captain Marley was attempting to scare her into compliance, his plan had worked.

"Which is why we aren't stopping yet," Captain Marley said. "There is a thick grove of trees a few miles ahead. I'm hoping we can make it before dark. I don't think the snow will hit until later tonight, but we're going to need the windbreak the trees provide, and we're also going to need the wood. I've sent a group of my men ahead to start gathering firewood."

"I see," Carrie murmured. "Is there anything I need to tell my friends?"

"We will circle the wagons when we reach the grove of trees. All the animals will have to go inside the circle. It's the only way to keep them alive through the storm. As soon as we arrive I want everyone to gather as much wood as they can. That can be hard to come by on the trail so we may have to cut down a tree or two. Whatever is cut, I want it put in the wagons so it stays dry. My men will be doing the same thing, but there's no such thing as too much wood. We'll leave behind any extra for the next wagon train that needs it. If the storm hits before we get there, we'll have to focus on getting dead wood that will burn even if it's wet." He paused. "We have no idea how long the blizzard will last. I've seen them peter out in hours, and I've seen them rage for days. We also don't know how deep the snow will be, or when we will be able to get moving again. We'll have to have enough wood to build fires for heat and cooking once the storm ends."

Carrie nodded, glad to have a focus to diminish some of her fear. "We'll do our part."

"I know you will," Captain Marley agreed. "The last month has proven that. I'm surprised we haven't had a storm before now. I'm hoping this one isn't going to make up for the ones that didn't happen," he said.

"My research said that early spring blizzards can sometimes be the worst." Carrie had read that in the book Felicia had made for her. Somehow, they had gotten through February with nothing but endless frigid days. She had hoped March would signal the advent of spring, but instead, it looked like winter was determined to deal another blow.

"Your research was correct." Captain Marley's smile was more natural this time. "I've scared you on purpose, Carrie, because blizzards are not something to take lightly, but my men have all been through them before. If we do the right things, we'll all be fine." His smile disappeared. "If anyone gets careless, though, someone will die. I don't want that on my watch."

Carrie nodded. "I'll go talk to my team now. I'll make sure everyone knows what needs to be done." Captain Marley nodded and then turned to talk to one of his men who had just ridden up. Carrie cantered over to the wagon Matthew was driving. She was aware he had been watching her and Captain Marley closely.

"News?" Matthew asked casually. His eyes, however, said he knew exactly what was going on.

Carrie smiled. "You've been in a blizzard before?"

"More than one," Matthew replied grimly. "Captain Marley believes one is on the way?"

"He does," Carrie confirmed. She told him everything the captain had told her. She was glad when she saw Nathan and Randall move close enough to hear the conversation.

Matthew couldn't help his grin when she got to the part about all sleeping in one wagon. He and Janie had been given private quarters at Fort Larned for two brief days, but he missed his wife badly. "I suppose I can make that sacrifice. And, as the only married couple in the wagon, we'll make sure the rest of your honor isn't compromised."

Carrie smiled but her heart was pierced by his words. Being on the plains had separated her more from her past, but the pain could still strike easily.

"I'm sorry," Matthew said, instantly realizing the impact of his words.

Carrie managed a smile and then turned to ride up to the women's wagon. Janie, certain she would go crazy if she continued to ride in the back, had insisted she be able to drive the wagon. She was doing a fine job and didn't mind the constant comments from soldiers who rode by. In fact, she had made many friends among the men who were not used to independent women.

Now she was watching the sky anxiously. "Is there a storm coming?"

Carrie beckoned Carolyn and Melissa to come closer before explaining the situation. "Everyone will stay in this wagon tonight because we have more blankets and pillows."

"Do you think we'll make it to the grove of trees?" Janie looked again at the sky that seemed to be stalking them like a famished cougar. "The wind seems to have picked up."

Carrie had noticed the same thing. "I don't know if we'll make it," she said honestly. "Captain Marley believes we have time, but he also admitted it is impossible to predict the weather out here. We're not to let our oxen teams stop until we receive orders." A sudden, sharp gust of wind made her pull her coat tighter and push her hat down more firmly on her head. The temperature was dropping. She patted Celeste's neck as the mare became more agitated. "It's all right, girl. It's all right."

"Will it be?" Melissa asked, her voice high-pitched with fright. "I knew a blizzard was a possibility, but after a month with nothing but cold, I thought we would miss the experience."

"I thought the same thing," Carrie acknowledged. "We were wrong," she said. She hastened to reassure them. "Captain Marley said he and his men have survived blizzards before. If we do what they tell us, we will be fine."

At least she hoped so.

*****

The wind was blowing viciously, but the snow was still clinging to the menacing clouds when the grove of trees appeared in the distance. Carrie drew a deep breath of relief when they reached the trees and maneuvered their wagons into a tight circle on the south side of the wind break. She could hear the sound of axes chopping wood as men swarmed into the woods. Enough men stayed behind to unharness all the teams of oxen and turn the horses loose into the center of the circle. Matthew, Nathan and Randall joined the woodcutters, while Carrie, Janie, Carolyn and Melissa carried the wood back to the wagons. They had been cautioned to move slowly so they would not perspire. Wet clothes would only increase the danger of hypothermia.

There would be no tents set up because the wind would tear them down. Soldiers would have to be jammed into wagons together for safety and warmth. The camp cooks had come ahead to build large fires; now they were hanging huge pots of soup-makings over the flames, hoping to get a good meal into everyone before the storm hit.

The work continued even as the first snowflakes began to fall. Carrie blinked her eyes fast to keep them clear from the driving snow. Her face was covered by a thick scarf, leaving just enough room for her to peer out. Once the men had stopped cutting, they joined her and the rest of the women in loading the wagons. They had left one wagon exclusively for firewood. When it was full, they started loading wood into the other wagons, making sure to leave enough room for the occupants. The wood was stacked around the perimeter of the wagon interior to help cut the wind as much as possible. Once it was stacked, it was covered with tent canvas and then roped securely to the sides of the wagon to create more of a barrier.

Janie asked the question in Carrie's mind. "What happens if the wagons tip over in the wind?"

Carrie looked at her but chose not to answer. Being crushed by a stack of firewood was not something she wanted to contemplate. The wood should weigh the wagons down enough to keep them stable, but she was also aware the tall canvas sides created a large target for the howling wind.

A group of men approached, coils of rope in hand. "We're going to tie your wagon off to some of the trees in the grove," one of them yelled. It was impossible to identify anyone because of the thick clothing and face coverings. "The ropes should keep you from tipping."

Carrie caught the meaning of *should*. There were no guarantees.

"The night is going to be long," another man yelled, "but you're not to light any candles or lanterns. The fire danger is too high if your wagon tips."

Carrie caught the look of terror on Janie's face. She knew her friend was back at the site of the Angola train wreck. "We'll do just as you say," she yelled back to be heard above the wind. She reached into the wagon and pulled out more rope, and then secured it tightly to the outside. It would make sure that anyone who found it necessary to leave the wagon would be able to make their way back. She couldn't imagine any reason that would make her leave their sanctuary once they were allowed to stop working, but she knew they had to be prepared for any contingency.

Captain Marley appeared from the deepening snow. "Are you all set here?"

Carrie smiled up at him before realizing he couldn't see her face. "We are," she called back, nodding her head for emphasis.

Captain Marley nodded back. "Each of you go over to the cook fire and get a big bowl of soup and several biscuits. The cooks will prepare food as long as they can, and then bring more by your wagons. Eat all you can. It will help you stay warm, and I don't know when we can cook again. Wrap your biscuits in a bandana and place them inside your clothing against your body so they don't freeze." He paused. "Once you have your food, get back into your wagon. Don't come out until you hear someone call for you," he added. "We've done all we can. Now we just have to ride it out."

*****

It was possible to pretend for the first few hours of the storm that it was a big adventure. It was fun to all be inside the wagon laughing, talking and exchanging stories of other snowstorms. Even though it was pitch black inside the wagon, the knowledge that they were together held the fear at bay. As the night lengthened and as fatigue from all the hard work cutting and hauling wood set in, conversation petered out and then died.

Carrie hunkered into her cocoon of blankets as the temperature plunged and the frigid air seeped its way through cracks in their wall of wood. The howling of the wind increased. She hated the feeling of alienation that came from no more conversation, but it would have been impossible to talk above the noise now, anyway. She had never experienced wind like this. The wagon shuddered and heaved against the ropes, making sleep an impossibility as she waited for the wagon to overturn and entomb them under an avalanche of firewood.

She tried to reason her way past the fear, but she had seldom felt so alone. She envied Janie in the warm protection of Matthew's presence. Memories of Robert consumed her. She blinked back tears but didn't bother to swallow the moan of pain. No one could hear her over the noise. She had put on Robert's coat over every layer of clothing she could find. She snuggled into it, praying it would be a refuge.

The storm raged on all through the long night. There were a few times when she felt the wind diminish just a little, but within minutes it would start its howling again. She was certain the night would never end.

*****

Janie wrapped herself around Matthew, grateful for his strong arms encircling her. They sat on a nest of pillows, with tented blankets around their bodies. There was not room for everyone to lie down. They all had to content themselves with having outstretched legs as they leaned against the wood. After so many nights of sleeping alone, she was grateful just to have him close.

At first, she thought having him close was going to be enough to hold the fear at bay, but as the wind increased, it sounded more and more like a locomotive barreling down on them, mixed with a shrieking that turned her blood cold. The memories began to swallow her.

She heard the people screaming. She saw the blood. She smelled the flesh burning.

Janie could feel herself trembling and shaking, but she was no longer aware of where she was. As the memories grabbed ahold of her, they blotted out the snowstorm and put her back in the wrecked train car outside Angola. Her breath came in gasps, and she fought the constrictions of the blanket threatening to suffocate her. The wagon swayed and she was once more on the brink of the bridge, teetering into an empty void. She wasn't aware of the scream that ripped from her throat, lifting above the relentless howl of the wind.

As she plunged through nothingness toward her death, she became aware of being shaken, and then felt warm, whiskered kisses landing on her face. She could hear and see nothing, but somehow the love pierced her terror and broke through the memory to land her back in the present. Gradually, the howling and shrieking became a blizzard once again, terrifying in its own right, but it felt good to be aware she was in Matthew's arms. The trembling and shuddering subsided and then gradually stopped. Her husband continued to hold her close and kiss her forehead, eyes and cheeks.

Finally, she slept.

*****

The blizzard had not relented the next morning. The only reason they were aware a new day had dawned was that the darkness abated enough to enable them to see each other's shapes against the gray light filtering in through the logs and cracks in the canvas siding.

Carrie had heard Janie's scream during the night and knew the cause immediately. She didn't know when she had finally drifted off to sleep, but she was exhausted. Every muscle and bone ached, and the continual bellow of the wind made her want to scream. She bit her lip and remained silent. It would hardly be helpful for her to start screaming in time with the wind. The image made her smile just a bit. She pulled back Robert's coat enough to reach under several layers of sweaters to the packet holding four bacon biscuits. She separated one and ate it slowly, not knowing how long the food needed to last. Then she pulled out the water skin she had pressed against her body, grateful to have liquid that was not frozen into ice. She took several swallows and then corked it carefully before replacing it.

She was vaguely aware of Nathan disentangling himself from his blankets, but the continuing darkness and noise made everything slightly surreal. She watched him as he crawled around the wagon, stopping to peer into everyone's face. He would stay in one place for a few moments before he continued on to the next person. When he stopped in front of her, Carrie lowered her face covering long enough to give him a small smile, and then nodded her head to indicate she was all right. She felt far from all right, but she knew all of them were feeling the same fear, boredom and aches. Nathan met her eyes with an encouraging smile and then returned to his mound of blankets.

Moments later, the storm seemed to increase even more in intensity. Carrie wasn't sure it was possible to be colder, but her shivering increased. All of them were in danger of hypothermia and frostbite, but she knew shivering was a good sign because her body was trying to warm itself. If she was hypothermic, the shivering would have stopped because her body would be trying to conserve all the energy it could. Nathan, she realized, had been checking to make sure everyone was responsive. She could only assume that since he had returned to his coverings everyone was, but she knew they needed to take extra measures to stay warm.

Janie and Matthew were safer because they were sharing body heat; the rest of them needed to do the same thing. Now was hardly the time to consider their reputations. None of that would matter if they succumbed to hypothermia. She waited until Nathan turned his head toward her, and then she lowered the blankets enough to wave him over.

Nathan unearthed himself and crawled closer. "We need to share body heat," Carrie yelled. Most of her words were swallowed by the wind, but Nathan understood. He reached back for his blankets and motioned with his hand for Melissa to join them. Moments later Carrie and Melissa were both huddled into Nathan, an even thicker layer of covers holding in the heat they generated.

Randall and Carolyn quickly followed their example.

Carrie breathed a sigh of relief as the shivering slowed. She lay her head on Nathan's broad shoulder and fell into a deep sleep.

*****

The blizzard raged for two entire days. Night became confused with day. Thirst and hunger warred with fatigue and muscle aches. Carrie slept, woke to more of the howling darkness, and counted the moments until she could escape into sleep again. Nathan's solid strength beside her provided the courage she needed.

During what Carrie supposed was the afternoon of the third day, the wind began to taper off. She lay quietly, afraid to hope the end was in sight. An hour later, a blessed silence fell over the plains.

Carolyn was the first to sit up. "Is it over?" she asked.

"I believe it is," Matthew replied.

As if in response to his proclamation, a shaft of brilliant sunshine pierced through a crack in the canvas covering.

Carrie crawled to the back of the wagon, lured by the sunshine but afraid of what she might see if she looked. Had the animals made it through the blizzard, or would they all be dead? She had ached for them as the storm had raged, but there had been nothing she could do. Would all the wagons be standing, or would some have tipped over, trapping their inhabitants inside? She untied the rope holding the cover in place and pulled it back slowly.

"I was just coming to check on all of you!"

Carrie was startled by Captain Marley's voice. She blinked her eyes against the bright light until she could see him clearly. "Hello," she said hoarsely, almost surprised to discover her voice still worked.

"Are all of you all right?"

Carrie considered the question. "Define all right."

Captain Marley chuckled. "I see you haven't lost your sense of humor. That's a good sign."

"A good sign that I have lost my mind?" Carrie countered, relieved beyond words to have human conversation. "Everyone is fine, but I will admit to being hungry."

"My men have tramped down enough of the snow for two cook fires to be built. Hot food will follow shortly. The snow has stopped, but the cold is still brutal. I encourage you to get out and build a roaring fire to warm you up before night falls again."

Carrie glanced down. "Oh, my goodness! That looks like over two feet of snow."

"It is," Captain Marley confirmed. "We won't be going anywhere for a while. The snow is too thick for the wagons to break through, and it's too hard on the animals." He interpreted the look on her face. "All the animals made it through. They are munching on hay and grain right now, and we'll be melting water for them soon."

Carrie smiled. "So it's really over?"

"Well, this one is," Captain Marley said. "You are on the Kansas plains. Anything can happen here. The weather can change in hours. We got advance warning on this one, but there is no way of knowing if the weather has settled into a new pattern."

Melissa stuck her head out. "A new pattern of blizzards?" she asked in horror.

Carrie, certain Captain Marley was teasing, was suddenly struck by the intensity of his gaze. "You're serious, aren't you?"

"I am. We may have clear weather from here to New Mexico. We may also have several more blizzards. We have no way of knowing, so we have to be prepared."

"I see," Carrie murmured, realizing she had to choose not to focus on what *might* happen. She stuck her head back in the wagon. "Let's absorb some sunshine while we have the chance," she called. She didn't mind sinking into two and a half feet of snow. At least she was not entombed in a dark canvas cave.

Captain Marley rode off with a wave. It only took a few minutes for them to push away snow and stomp the remaining powder down to the ground. They started a fire carefully, not wanting to use more of their kindling than they had to, but soon had a roaring blaze. Carrie felt warm for the first time in days, but it also made her realize how dirty and unkempt she was. She had never felt quite so disgusting.

"How far is Fort Dodge?"

Carrie looked up as Janie appeared at her side. "Do you want a bath as badly as I do?"

"I could kill for one," Janie admitted.

Carrie smiled and laid a hand on her friend's arm. "How are you?" The fury of the storm had allowed no time for conversation, yet she knew the experience had been brutal for Janie. Her friend's scream still reverberated through her mind.

"Not something I care to repeat."

Janie's voice was light, but Carrie couldn't miss the haunted expression in her eyes. "I'm sorry," she said quietly.

"It couldn't have been much easier for you," Janie replied. "I had my memories of the train wreck, but I also had Matthew. Two days of being alone with memories and thoughts had to have been hard."

Carrie didn't bother to refute the truth. "It's not something I care to repeat either," she allowed.

"So how far to Fort Dodge?"

"More than a week," Carrie answered, "but that is when we finally are able to start moving again. There's no way of knowing how long it will take for the snow to melt enough to make that possible."

"Oh, joy," Janie muttered.

"We'll heat enough water to at least clean up in the wagon," Carrie promised. It wasn't much, but at this point it held a strong appeal. "At least we have plenty of snow to melt." She wished they could melt enough for baths, but they couldn't afford to waste the wood.

"Mrs. Borden!"

Carrie looked up as a sharp male voice broke into their conversation. "Yes?" she asked, alarmed by the intense expression in the young man's eyes. "What is wrong?"

"You're needed." With no further explanation, his eyes rested on Janie and then settled on Carolyn. "So are you two. Please get your medical bags. I have three horses being saddled for you. I'll explain on the way."

"We will certainly come with you, but you must give us some idea of what we are dealing with so that we bring the right supplies," Carrie said.

"There was a family caught in the blizzard. The cold almost killed them, and their hands and feet..." His voice trailed away as he shook his head.

"Hypothermia and frostbite," Carrie said. She exchanged looks with Janie and Carolyn, and then sprang into action.

Minutes later the three of them were mounted on tall, powerful horses able to break through the snow. They had to move slowly, but at least that would assure Carolyn did not fall off. It was obvious she had never ridden before.

"Lieutenant Ryall?" She thought she remembered a brief introduction two weeks earlier. When the grim-faced soldier nodded, Carrie continued. "Tell us as much as you can. It will help us when we get wherever we are going."

"There was a family caught in the blizzard. The man managed to tell us enough to figure out they had started on the trail with some merchants, but their baby got sick. They decided to return to Fort Larned, but they didn't make it before the storm hit."

"How many?" Janie asked.

"The husband, his wife, and four children. The oldest looks to be about ten."

Carrie caught the strained tone in his voice. "What happened to them?"

The soldier shook his head, not willing to say more. "We will be there soon," he muttered.

Carrie realized they had gotten all the information they were going to get. Trying to take her mind off whatever they would find, she fixed her attention on the remnants of the blizzard. In spite of the fact that she hated whatever had happened to this family, it felt wonderful to be out of the wagon and riding across the plains. She had never seen such a vast expanse of unbroken whiteness. The fields on the plantations were miniscule compared to the sweeping openness she was plowing through. There was nothing to mar the beauty until they caught sight of an overturned wagon in the distance.

"Oh, dear God," Carolyn whispered.

Nothing else was said until they rode closer. The wagon was surrounded by soldiers, but their faces were set with helpless, frustrated expressions. Carrie feared everyone inside was dead, but as they drew closer she could hear quiet sobbing.

"There was no wood for a fire," Lieutenant Ryall said. "All we could do was make sure you could get to them."

Carrie noticed that the snow had been dug out around the wagon, but decided not to mention that anyone with a grain of sense would know these people would need to be warmed. She dismounted and walked closer, kneeling down to look in the wagon. A man and woman looked back at her, their gazes somewhat dreamy and unresponsive; their faces a waxy white. She couldn't see their extremities, but knew they were probably frozen much worse. They had obviously been wounded when the storm overturned their wagon, but she wouldn't know the damage until she could examine them more closely.

Her eyes roamed over the wagon until they settled on the children. Two of them, the youngest girls who looked to be about two and four, were unconscious. They were wrapped together in two blankets, but when the wagon had overturned, the covering had torn in many places. There had been little protection from the wind and the frigid temperatures. Snow was piled high in places, clothing and other articles scattered by the wind that had blown them over. Their faces were waxen and completely unresponsive.

She found the third child quickly. She knew without touching the boy that he was dead. His young face looked to belong to an eight-year-old, but his skin was already a deep blue.

It took longer to find the fourth child. The girl, probably ten, was staring back at her. At first Carrie thought she was seeing a death stare, but her heart quickened when she saw a flicker of life in the eyes that returned her gaze. The girl's body was trapped under two huge sacks of flour that had rolled onto her. She didn't know what damage the sacks had done, but they had likely saved the little girl's life by offering a crude insulation. "Hello," she called softly.

The little girl blinked but remained silent. Carrie read the silent agony in her eyes and backed quickly out of the wagon, grateful for the intense research she had done regarding hypothermia and frostbite before she had left Virginia, as well as all she had learned at Chimborazo during the war years. She had discussed the protocol extensively with her team during the last month.

The first thing she did was bark orders to the soldiers. "These people are going to need a warmer place. I understand a wagon can't be brought in this snow, and theirs is too damaged to offer much protection. A group of you need to return to camp, load up something you can pull behind the horse to carry wood, and bring one of the tents. We have to create a shelter for them until they can be moved. We'll need cots, as many blankets as you can bring, and the tub for hot water. The wood and cots will take some type of sled, but I need the blankets and tent back here as quickly as possible." She took a deep breath. "And I need the rest of my team. I suspect Randall and Nathan were not brought along because you thought they were not needed, but they are. There are five people here that need our help. There should be six of us working on them."

Her demand was met with confused eyes. She could tell the soldiers were not used to taking orders from a woman, but there was no time to lose if these people's lives were going to be saved. "Please leave now, gentlemen," she said firmly. "Their lives are at stake."

"You heard her," Lieutenant Ryall snapped. He barked out several names and waved them off. They went, glancing back over their shoulders.

Carrie knew it would be at least an hour or more before they could return, but there was much that could be done now. She looked at the remaining men. "There is a heavy piece of loose canvas in the wagon. Please pull it out and fashion a lean-to where you have cleared the snow."

She watched as the men went to work, and then turned to Janie and Carolyn. "One of the children is dead, and the two youngest are unconscious. The third, a girl, is extremely hypothermic, but she is at least conscious. We need to check her for internal injuries because two sacks of flour landed on her when the wagon went over. The father and mother may have internal injuries, as well, but we won't know until we have examined them more closely."

She turned back to Lieutenant Ryall. "I need your other men to create a snow wall that will encase the tent."

"A snow wall?"

Carrie was thinking quickly. She had remembered the ground shelters the Navajo had been forced to create when they arrived at Bosque Redondo. "Yes. It will cut the wind and block some of the cold. We've got to start treating the hypothermia and frostbite. We've got to get them out of that wagon so we have room to work on them."

"You've got it," Lieutenant Ryall replied, his eyes full of a grudging admiration. It was obvious he was no more used to taking orders from a woman than his troops were, but just as obviously, Captain Marley had instructed him to follow Carrie's directions. "I'm sorry I didn't tell you more about the situation. You should have your whole team here now."

Carrie nodded her acknowledgement, but there was no time to waste. "I'll take the little girl who is conscious. Carolyn, you take the wife. Janie, you take the husband. We have plenty of treatments to give them, but we need to start slowly warming their extremities."

"How?" Lieutenant Ryall asked. "We won't have firewood back here to heat water for a while."

Carrie answered his question as she moved into the wagon and knelt beside the little girl. "Hello there," she said softly. "My name is Carrie. I'm going to help you, sweetheart." Her heart wrenched at the misery and pain in the little girl's eyes. "I know you've had a terrible time, but you're not alone anymore." The little girl's eyes tried to move, but she seemed to be getting colder and stiffer. "We're helping your parents, and your brother and sisters, as well." She knew now was not the time to tell the little girl that her brother was dead, or that her two youngest siblings were unconscious. She was relieved when the little girl relaxed slightly.

"Now, this may seem strange, but when someone gets as cold as you have gotten, we can't warm you up too quickly because it will only make it worse. We're going to take you out of the wagon and then we're going to put snow on your skin wherever the cold has been too much for you." She understood when the little girl's eyes widened. "I know it sounds crazy, doesn't it? I promise it will start to warm your skin back up. And then we'll build a fire and make you really warm."

Carrie gently probed the girl's body as she talked, relieved when she didn't find any broken bones. "But first we're going to get you freed from these sacks and make you more comfortable."

She could hear Janie and Carolyn talking softly to the mother and father, but her entire focus was on the little girl. She pulled off the girl's gloves, wincing at the gray color of her fingers. Carrie knew without looking that her feet would be the same. The frostbite may be too severe to save all the fingers and toes, but she was going to make every effort to save her feet and hands. She didn't know what had possessed this family to start down the Santa Fe Trail in the winter, but it must have been desperation.

It was only a few minutes before Lieutenant Ryall stuck his head back in. "Your snow shelter has been built. My men will come in and carry everyone out. We'll take their mattress pads and lay them on the snow until the cots get here."

Carrie opened her mouth to add more instructions, but the lieutenant was a step ahead of her.

"We'll come back in for all the blankets. I've already got the men filling some buckets with snow."

"Thank you," Carrie said fervently. She stepped outside with Janie and Carolyn, dimly aware the setting sun was casting a golden hue on the snow. Under other circumstances, she would find it beautiful. Now, it was an ominous sign that nighttime would drop the temperature again. She prayed the men would return quickly with the tents and the wood.

Chapter Twenty-Three

"The man has a broken leg," Janie informed her. "That, and advanced hypothermia and frostbite." She shook her head. "I doubt we can save the fingers on his left hand."

Carrie nodded. Both she and Janie had treated many cases of severe frostbite during the Siege of Richmond. She shuddered as she remembered the huge pile of frozen amputated extremities outside the hospital tents at Chimborazo. She turned to Carolyn with a questioning look. Carrie understood the horror on the older woman's face. Carolyn had probably never seen extreme frostbite like this.

"The woman has a broken arm," Carolyn said evenly. "There is extreme frostbite on all extremities, but her hypothermia is quite advanced. I suspect she tried to reach her children, exposing herself to the cold even more. She is completely disoriented and her heartbeat is very irregular. I don't believe she has much longer if we don't warm her quickly."

Carrie knew she was right. She lowered her voice so the others in the wagon couldn't hear her next words. "The two youngest children are unconscious," she said. "I read, though, that sometimes hypothermia can actually save the lives of young children. It shuts down heart and brain function to limit the oxygen needs. It's possible we will be able to revive them, but first we have to focus on saving the others."

Janie moved over to their medical bags. "I will gather the remedies."

Carrie looked up as several of the soldiers approached. "You must handle these people very carefully," she warned. "They have such severe frostbite that any type of pressure on their frozen body parts can cause a foot or finger to break. There are severe blisters on all their feet that are caused by the frostbite. I don't want those blisters to burst."

"We'll be real careful," one of the men promised. "My little sister died of the cold when she got caught out in a blizzard. I don't want these people to suffer any more than they have already."

Carrie was reassured by the compassionate gleam in the man's eyes. "Thank you," she said. She watched as he and one other man gently lifted the little girl and carried her out to the makeshift bed they had created in the lean-to. Others carried the mother and father out next and then returned for the two unconscious children.

Carrie bent over the little girl. "Can you talk enough to tell me your name?" she asked.

"Frances," the little girl whispered, her voice barely audible.

"It's nice to meet you, Frances," Carrie replied. "The first thing I'm going to do is pack your feet with snow." She motioned Lieutenant Ryall and the soldier who had lost his sister over to assist her. "These nice men are going to do the same thing to your hands."

Carrie worked as she talked, determined not to show her horror at the condition of Frances' hands and feet. She was scared she would not be able to save them, but that was not something you told a terrified child. "We're just going to use the snow until we have restored circulation to your hands and feet. You won't feel anything at first, but as they begin to warm up they may hurt pretty badly. I apologize for that in advance." Frances met her eyes steadily, her expression one of stoic acceptance. Carrie could only imagine what the child had endured during the last forty-eight hours.

Carrie didn't add that the skin may turn black instead of restoring itself to normal. If that happened, gangrene would most likely set in and they would have to amputate. They would deal with whatever they had to deal with as they treated her. She had caught a glimpse of her father's hands. Carolyn had been right about it being unlikely that his fingers could be saved on the left, but they would still do the best they could. It was imperative they get his leg set, as well as his wife's arm.

Carrie looked up at Lieutenant Ryall. "Please have your men get two of the boards from the wagon. I need one the length of the man's leg and another the length of the woman's arm. I also need strips of cloth. There is clothing scattered on the floor of the wagon that can be used."

"You know how to set broken bones?" The lieutenant's voice was skeptical.

"I was a doctor at Chimborazo Hospital in Richmond during the war," she said crisply. "I assure you I have dealt with far worse than this." She met his eyes steadily. "Since you have no one else to help this family, I suggest you trust me and my team, and not hinder us."

"Yes, ma'am, Mrs. Borden," Lieutenant Ryall responded, his eyes once more shining with surprised admiration.

Carrie turned back to Frances, hopeful there would be no more resistance from the soldiers, who had obviously never experienced women doctors. "I'm going to give you a special medicine that will help you feel better," she said soothingly. She reached for the bottle of *Agaricus Muscarius* that Janie had pulled out of her bag. The tincture would begin to restore life to the frozen limbs, and also help with the pain of rewarming. She wished she'd had this remedy during the winters at Chimborazo; it would have greatly diminished the soldier's suffering.

She mixed the tincture in a little cup of water and held it to Frances' lips. "Do your best to swallow this for me, honey." Frances met her gaze and managed one swallow when the liquid went into her mouth. "Good girl! You are being very brave," Carrie said. "It's going to take a little while for the snow to start helping, so I'm going to look after your little sisters and brother." Carrie had watched the girl's eyes try to roam the lean-to, but she had not yet discovered the true condition of her siblings.

"The boards and the cloth are right inside. How else can we help?" Lieutenant Ryall asked.

Carrie's respect for the lieutenant expanded. He may never have experienced female doctors, but he was willing to push beyond his perceptions. "We have to get the youngest children warm as quickly as possible, but we must be very careful. I need two of your men who will undress their top body, get under the blankets, and hold the children against their chests for warmth. I will give the children some medicine, and we'll have to treat them for frostbite, but first we have to make sure they survive the hypothermia. The children are so cold, I'm afraid it won't be a pleasant experience for your men."

Two of the men who were close enough to hear stepped forward immediately.

"I'll do it," one offered. "If it was my daughter, I would want someone to help her."

"Same here," a bearded man with kind eyes added. "I'll take the older one. My daughter is about the same age."

Carrie smiled her gratitude and watched the men crawl under the covers. The children were stripped of their frozen clothing and then passed to them. She saw the men's faces tighten as they embraced the icy forms, but neither murmured a word of complaint.

"I just want you to hold them," she ordered. "Do not massage their bodies, or even rub them. Their skin is too fragile from the frostbite. It will only harm them more." She mixed a quick batch of *Agaricus Muscarius,* praying she could get enough down the tiny throats to do them good. She pulled back the covers to pour a small amount into the children's mouths, thrilled when their throats constricted to accept the liquid. That was a sure sign they were not as deeply hypothermic as she had feared.

"Are you both warm?" she asked the men after they piled more blankets on them. "Relatively speaking, of course," she added lightly. When they both smiled and nodded, she moved over to Janie and Carolyn.

They had followed her lead, packing all extremities in snow. Carrie resisted the urge to check on the results because any movement of the hands and feet could cause eruptions of blisters and make the skin split. All they could do now was wait for the men to appear with the firewood. Once they had the man and woman warm, they would set their broken limbs.

It was only a few minutes before she heard approaching horses. She whispered a silent prayer of thanks as huge piles of blankets were passed inside the lean-to. As she piled them on the victims, she heard the men begin to put up the larger tent that would house the family, and her team, for the night. They would have to stay with the family if there was to be any hope for survival. She could only pray another storm would not sweep across the plains.

Randall and Nathan appeared at the door.

"It's pretty crowded in there," Randall said, his eyes quickly assessing the situation. "We'll make sure the tent is ready, and then I'll set the broken leg while you take care of the arm."

Carrie's smile was genuine this time. Her entire team might be cold and filthy, but they were going to save this family's lives. Warm pride cut through most of the cold.

*****

Carrie sat by Frances' side as the tent was erected. She sighed in relief when she heard more men arrive with the firewood, cook pot and tub. They worked quickly to get the fire blazing as darkness settled in. They hung a big cast iron pot over the flames, filled it with snow to melt, and then erected the second tent that would house the men for the night.

Lieutenant Ryall appeared at the entrance to the lean-to. "The beds are ready," he said quietly. "I had the men cut a hole in the top of the tent to act as a vent so a fire can be built. It's getting warm already."

Carrie stared at him with admiration. "Thank you. That was brilliant."

The lieutenant shrugged, but looked pleased. "I've learned a few things from the Indians," he admitted.

"If your men can build a wall of stones around the fire it will help keep the tent even warmer," Carrie added. "The stones will absorb the heat and radiate it back into the tent."

Lieutenant Ryall eyed her. "You're pretty smart yourself."

"There is a very smart thirteen-year-old girl in Ohio who made sure I had all the information I would need for this trip. I just read what she gave me."

"Thirteen? She much be very special."

"She is," Carrie assured him, feeling a stab of longing for Moses, Rose, Felicia, John and Hope. She pushed aside the thought that they would not be on the plantation when she returned. "I would like a layer of blankets put on the cot before the family lies down. We must create as much insulation between them and the ground as possible. Then at least four blankets on top of them." She gathered several hot water bottles from her team's medical bags. "When the water is hot, but not boiling, please have these bottles filled. It will help keep the family warmer."

"You've got it," Lieutenant Ryall replied. "Randall and Nathan have already given us their bags to be filled. Are you ready for the family to be moved?"

Carrie looked at the two men holding the youngest children under the covers. "Are the girls getting warm?"

"My little one hasn't moved yet, but she doesn't feel like a block of ice anymore," the soldier holding the two-year-old answered gravely. "I'm not sure I would choose the word warm, however."

When Carrie turned to look at the other soldier, she heard a slight whimper from under the covers. She smiled, but the smile faded quickly because she knew the agony the little girl was about to suffer. She turned to the lieutenant. "These girls can be moved as soon as the hot water bottles are filled." She turned back to the men who had volunteered to help. "If you're all right, it will be best if you continue to hold them. Not only for the warmth, but also for the comfort. They are going to wake up to a lot of pain, and they are going to be frightened."

"I've got mine."

"Me, too,"

Carrie smiled her gratitude and then turned to look at Frances. The little girl was staring at her accusingly, but she still didn't seem capable of speech. Carrie understood. "Your little sisters were not doing well, but they are getting warmer." Frances blinked. "I will let you know how your parents are as soon as I get you into the new tent, but first, let me take a look at your hands." Carrie pulled them very gently from the snow that had already melted into slush. She was relieved to see the grayish white color was giving way to a pinker tint. Circulation was being restored. "They are doing better, Frances," she said reassuringly, relieved beyond words that she would not have to remove this little girl's hands to save her life.

Frances whispered a single word. "Danny?"

Carrie sighed, knowing she could no longer avoid the issue. Not telling Frances the truth would be as harmful as telling her. She knelt down next to the mattress, wishing she could hold the little girl's hand, but knowing it was too risky. "Honey, I'm sorry, but Danny died. He got too cold."

The agony twisting Frances' face needed no words for interpretation. When Carrie heard a guttural moan from the mother, she knew her words had been overheard. Carolyn began to soothe the woman, but there were really no words that could assuage the loss of a child. Carrie knew that all too well. Again, she wondered what had brought this family out onto the plains in the winter, but the reason didn't matter. Nothing would change the outcome of the blizzard.

*****

Five days passed before the snow had disappeared enough for Captain Marley to move the wagon train forward.

Carrie stepped outside the tent and raised her face to the warm sunshine, welcoming the breeze that caressed her skin. She knew another blast of winter could still be lurking beyond the horizon, but she was also learning to enjoy the moment in front of her in this wild, unpredictable land.

"Are we leaving today, too? Daddy said we are."

Carrie looked down at the courageous little girl she had learned to love like a daughter in the past days. Frances had made a miraculous recovery and was trying to deal with the grief of losing her little brother, Danny. "You are," Carrie assured her. A merchant wagon train traveling from Santa Fe had arrived the day before, and had agreed to take the recovering family to Fort Larned. The two youngest were still weak, and not out of bed yet, but they would recover. When they were stronger, and when their father's broken leg had healed, they would join another wagon train back to Independence. Frances smiled, but it did not quite reach her eyes. "Aren't you glad to be going back home?"

Frances shrugged. "We left Illinois because Daddy couldn't get a job. There ain't nothing waiting for us back there, but he doesn't want to go on to New Mexico anymore, either. Well, Mama doesn't want to go anymore. She told Daddy last night that this godforsaken land already took one of her babies, and she weren't going to let it take no more."

Carrie understood how the mother felt, but she hoped the family would be able to make a new beginning once they returned home. Finding a job was difficult now that the war was over. After talking to her father, Greg, she understood the desperation that had compelled him to attempt to reach a promised job in Santa Fe. He had fought through the four years of the war, come home to find his family suffering, and had not been able to find a job in the last two years. She had thought the worst part of the suffering was felt by Confederate soldiers; now she understood Union soldiers were suffering, as well. It was going to take a long time for the country to recover.

"That ain't what is bothering me, though," Frances confided.

Carrie brought her thoughts back to the little girl. "What is it?" she asked gently.

Frances dipped her head and then lifted her large hazel eyes up to meet Carrie's. "I'm going to miss you real bad."

Carrie knelt down and wrapped Frances in her arms, feeling a stab of loss. "And I'm going to miss you, Frances. You are very special to me."

"Really?" Frances asked. "You're not just saying that?"

"I'm not just saying that," Carrie assured her. "You have become like a daughter to me. I'm going to miss you so very much."

Frances leaned back in her embrace and gazed at her with piercing eyes. "Why don't you have children, Miss Carrie? You'd be a real good mama."

Carrie caught her breath as the familiar wave of pain threatened to swallow her, but she recovered quickly. "I had a little girl," she said softly. "She died the day she was born."

Frances gasped, her eyes wide as saucers. "The very same day?"

"The very same day."

"I bet you miss her real bad."

"I do," Carrie agreed, not bothering to keep the sadness from her voice. Frances was experiencing her own loss. It was important for her to know it was alright to feel sad.

"Do you miss her every day?"

"Every day," Carrie replied, but she knew it was important to give Frances hope. "It doesn't hurt quite as badly as it used to, though. I will always miss Bridget, but I have learned how to smile and laugh again."

Frances thought about that. "I laughed at something Julia did yesterday. Do you think that would make Danny feel bad?"

Carrie shook her head firmly, remembering the moment when Frances had laughed at her four-year-old little sister. "No, I don't. Danny is happy now in heaven. I believe he wants you to be happy, too. It takes time to get over the missing, but it will get easier to be happy."

Frances nodded slowly. "I reckon I can see that." Then she sighed. "Why doesn't my mama tell me things like this?" she asked. "She doesn't seem to talk at all anymore."

Carrie held her back so she could gaze into Frances' eyes again. "It's real hard for a mama to lose her child, Frances. You miss Danny very badly, but your mama feels she has lost part of her heart. It will take her time to get over it."

She decided not to mention that her mama's grief was compounded by the loss of two of her fingers and three of her toes, as well as her husband losing all the fingers on his left hand. Carrie had not been given any other choice than to amputate the toes and fingers when they turned black and became infected. She was grateful for the surgical experience that had allowed her and Randall to save the couple's life, and had been grateful the youngest ones had not required the same. She knew not having fingers on one hand would make it even more difficult for Greg to get a job, though. He was determined to make the best of things, but her heart ached for him. All he had wanted to do was make life better for his family.

"Do you think Mama will ever get over it?" Frances pressed. "She was already real sad when we left Illinois. Daddy told her we would have a better life down in New Mexico. Now we don't even got that."

Carrie thought quickly. She knew families all over the country were floundering in poverty, but there was no point in living if you couldn't have hope. She couldn't possibly know if Frances was going home to a better life, but she had to give her something to hang onto. "Can I tell you something I have learned in the last year?"

"Yes," Frances whispered as she stared into Carrie's eyes with a penetrating gaze.

"I've learned that life is always going to have pain," Carrie said, "but I've also learned never to give up hope that things will be better. There was a time when I didn't have any hope," she admitted. "I couldn't believe that my life would get better, and I wanted to die." She hesitated, not sure if she was saying more than Frances could possibly understand. Then she remembered all the times Old Sarah had infused her with wisdom that she hadn't understood until years later. The lessons she had not understood as a girl had become lifelines as an adult. "I've learned that hope is the most important thing in the world. Even when I can't see how things can get better, I know that hope will pull me forward into a better future."

"How?" Frances demanded suspiciously.

"Because hope kept me from giving up," Carrie replied. "Honey, I can't tell you if your mama will ever be happy again. I hope so, but I can't promise you that. What I *can* tell you is that you can hold on to hope that things *will* be better for you. In time, they will."

Frances looked unconvinced. "I'm only ten, Miss Carrie. I can't make things different in my family."

"You're right," Carrie agreed. "You can help, but you're still a little girl. I didn't say holding on to hope is easy, Frances. I can promise you, though, that you're going to get older. And when you are older, you are going to have the opportunity to make *your* life different—no matter what anyone else does right now."

Frances cocked her head. "What do I have to do?"

"You've got to take every opportunity that comes your way," Carrie replied, praying her words would lodge firmly enough in Frances' heart to carry her through the challenges waiting for her. "There will be many ways for you to learn new things. When you get older, you'll be able to get a job yourself. You've also got to plan for a different life by studying as hard as you can."

Frances frowned. "I don't get to go to school too much."

"Then you find ways to learn," Carrie replied, wondering if Frances had ever attended school at all. "My best friend wasn't allowed to go to school. She found every book she could and read it. She borrowed books from people so she could learn." She decided not to mention that Rose had borrowed the books from her father's library on the plantation when she had been a slave. "She knew she would get in big trouble if she got caught, but she did it anyway because she wanted a better life."

Frances was watching her with wide eyes. "What is your best friend doing now?"

"She's a teacher, and she is also in college," Carrie said proudly.

"Really?" Frances breathed. "My mama says girls don't need to go to school."

Carrie hesitated, not sure she should dispute the little girl's mother, but she opted for the truth. "That's not true, Frances. I went to school, and now I'm finishing up medical school. Rose, my best friend, is going to school and she is a teacher. I have many female friends who are in college and who are doing things that most women don't believe they can do."

Frances was drinking in everything she was saying. "Do you think I'm smart, Miss Carrie?"

"I do," Carrie said. "Haven't you been helping me take care of your little sisters?"

"I just been doing what you told me," Frances protested. "That's not a big thing."

"You're wrong," Carrie replied. "It's a very big thing because you are only ten. But being smart is only part of what it takes to do something with your life. It also takes courage." She held Frances' face and looked deeply into her eyes. "You are one of the bravest little girls I have ever known." Frances' eyes glowed in response. "The last thing it takes is hope," Carrie reminded her. "You have to hope things can be better. And the hope has to turn into belief," she added.

"Belief?"

"Hope is important, but it's when hope becomes your belief that it makes you able to handle all the challenges that come your way. Things might be hard for your family for a while, but you can believe it will get better."

It was obvious Frances was struggling to believe what Carrie was saying. "Isn't it important for me to do what my mama says? Daddy told me it is."

Carrie considered her response and again opted for honesty. "I did things my mama didn't like," she confessed. "My mother wanted me to be a proper Southern lady, but that was not what I wanted, so I managed to do things my way."

"Didn't it make your mama mad?" Frances' eyes were alive with curiosity.

"All the time," Carrie admitted, "but I could only be what I believed I should be. It was not always easy, but I'm glad I made the decisions I did."

"Did your mama ever quit being mad at you?"

"She did," Carrie assured her, deciding not to reveal it was right before her mother died. There was only so much a ten-year-old could handle. She took Frances' face in her hands again, already dreading the moment when she would tell the girl good-bye. "I'm telling you all these things because you are very special. Life may be hard at times, but you can make it what you want it to be if you want it badly enough...and work hard for it," she added. "It's not enough just to believe something. The belief is good, but the belief is only a good thing if it makes you work hard to make things happen."

Carrie pressed a piece of paper into Frances' hand. "This is my mailing address. You can write me any time you want to." She could only hope there would be enough money to mail the letters.

"Will you write me back?" Frances breathed.

"Every time," Carrie promised.

Frances grinned, but she wasn't done with her questions. "Do you know of any other little girls that have done what you are telling me to do?"

Carrie smiled. Just like she had been as a child, Frances was not content to simply believe what she was being told. "That's a very good question."

Frances sucked in her breath. "You're not mad because I'm asking?" she asked anxiously.

"I'll never be mad at you for asking a question," Carrie assured her. "I think most people don't ask nearly enough questions. If you just go along with what other people tell you, then you'll never know what you truly believe for yourself." She remembered Abby telling her the same thing the summer they had met.

Frances let her breath out. "So, do you know any other little girls like me?"

Carrie smiled. "I do. Her name is Felicia. She just turned thirteen, but she was only ten when she watched her parents be murdered."

Frances gaped at her. "Murdered? Both of them?"

"Yes," Carrie said solemnly. "Remember my best friend who is a teacher? Rose and her husband adopted Felicia. At first she was very frightened of everything, but then she decided to believe things could be better, and she decided to learn everything she could so she could *make* her life better. She is quite wonderful." She paused before adding, "You are so much like her, Frances. You are very special."

"Frances, get on over here, girl. We've got to get going now."

Frances melted closer to Carrie when her father's voice reached them. "You promise you'll write me back?"

"I promise. I won't be at that address until the end of summer, but I promise I'll write you as soon as I get home. You can write me as many letters as you want, and then just mail them all at one time." Carrie thought of all the letters she had written Abby during the war. "Sometimes writing things down helps."

"I don't spell so good," Frances said. "I don't write so good, either."

"Then you'll work on it," Carrie said confidently. "If you want your life to be better, you have to know how to write and spell. And read."

Determination crept into Frances' eyes. "I'll learn. I promise. I won't disappoint you."

Carrie remembered Old Sarah's words. "It's not me you need to worry about disappointing, honey. You need to decide to not disappoint yourself."

"Frances!"

Carrie took a deep breath and held Frances away from her, already feeling the loss. "You've got to go now," she said softly. "I love you, Frances. Don't ever forget that."

Tears swam in Frances' eyes, but she tried to blink them away. "I love you, too, Miss Carrie. I always will." She tore herself away and ran over to her father. Moments later she was in the back of the wagon, waving at Carrie until she was too far away to be seen. Carrie returned the wave as long as she could make out Frances' form, and then dashed away her own tears.

It was time to go to Santa Fe.

*****

Lillian Richardson was more than a little nervous as she rode up to the imposing house that formed the heart of Cromwell Plantation. She had heard about the elegant Southern plantations, but her upbringing in the Michigan woods had not exposed her to anything so grand. She stared at it admiringly, not sure if she appreciated the gleaming white three stories, or the inspiring porch columns the most. When she heard a nicker, and glanced to the right, all thought of the house fled her mind. She pulled her bay mare to a stop and simply gawked at the fields full of the finest horses she had ever seen. "Oh, my," she whispered, not able to tear her eyes away.

Lillian didn't know how long she sat there before she detected movement out of the corner of her eye. Her gaze shifted to the massive barn bordering an edge of the pasture. She caught her breath as she watched a small black girl emerge leading a towering bay Thoroughbred stallion. Her first thought was to call out a warning to be careful, but she snapped her lips shut when she watched the horse dip his head and gently nudge the girl, who just laughed and patted his muzzle. Obviously, she was in no danger.

"Can I help you?"

Lillian tore her eyes away from the stallion as she forced herself to remember why she was here. She recalled Abby's description of the woman running Cromwell Stables. "You must be Susan Jones."

"I am," Susan agreed. "And you seem to have me at a distinct disadvantage because I have absolutely no idea who you are. Should I?"

Lillian liked the humor she saw lurking in the woman's brown eyes. She pulled out the letter she had secured in her pocket. "My name is Lillian Richardson. Rose Samuels sent this letter along with me. I'm the new schoolteacher."

Susan took the letter but looked at her curiously. "I thought the new teacher was Bertha Ogden? We've been wondering why we haven't heard anything."

"Bertha fell seriously ill," Lillian explained. "She was my housemate in Cleveland. When we realized she wasn't going to be able to take the position, the American Missionary Association asked me if I would fill it."

"So you have met Rose?" Susan asked eagerly.

"I have. When I realized she and her family were in Oberlin, I took the train out to meet her. We had quite a wonderful time."

"I'm sure you did," Susan said warmly. "We miss all of them so much."

"They feel the same way," Lillian assured her, "but they are doing well in Oberlin."

The curious expression returned to Susan's face. "You rode your horse out here? I'm surprised Rose didn't send you to meet Thomas and Abby Cromwell."

"Oh, she did. I stayed with them last night after I arrived on the train yesterday morning."

"And they didn't insist on sending you in a carriage with a driver?"

Lillian laughed at Susan's expression. "Oh, they insisted. I turned them down."

Susan looked at her more closely. "You do realize that was probably not your safest option?"

"So I'm told," Lillian agreed. "I decided that if I was too afraid to ride out to the plantation on my own, then I had no business taking this job."

Susan continued to stare at her. "You do realize the Ku Klux Klan does not take lightly to white teachers coming down to teach black students?"

Lillian nodded again. "I've been told. I also know your school has been burned before, and I know the vigilantes keep a regular eye on it." She reached into the waistband of her breeches and pulled out a pistol. "I've also been told most of the teachers sent down to the South don't believe self-protection is an option. I happen to feel differently about it."

Susan threw back her head and laughed loudly. "I think I'm going to like you, Miss Lillian Richardson. Welcome to Cromwell Plantation."

Lillian smiled, certain she had made a wonderful decision when she had decided to take the position Bertha had been offered. "Thank you, Miss Jones."

"Susan. We don't stand on formality around here."

Lillian nodded. "Thank you, Susan."

Susan looked toward the barn. "Let's get your horse some food and water. Surely you didn't bring your own mare all the way from Oberlin."

"No," Lillian agreed. "I purchased her yesterday from a trader Thomas recommended. Misty is a jewel, but..." She turned and let her eyes roam the pasture again. "She can't compare to the fine horses you are raising here."

"You know horses?"

"Enough to recognize Eclipse the minute I laid eyes on him. I saw him race in Chicago at Hawthorne Track."

Susan's eyes widened. "You did? That's amazing. Are you from Chicago?"

"No. I'm from outside Detroit, Michigan. My family moved out there when the Erie Canal made the area more accessible, and started a farm. I was born there. I've had a love affair with horses ever since I was a child. My father took me to the tracks any time he had business in Chicago. My mother was appalled, but Daddy knew how much I loved it."

"Yet you chose to become a teacher. Why?"

Lillian shrugged. "I wish I could run a stables like you do, but I never managed to find a way to do that. Luckily, I love children and teaching as much as I do horses. I'm excited to be here."

"You'll have the best of both worlds here," Susan promised. "We'll go riding together often."

Lillian's grin almost split her face. "I was so hoping you would say that," she murmured. "Did I see a small girl leading Eclipse from the barn?"

"That would be Amber," Susan said. "She and her brother, Clint, train all the foals and yearlings, but she and Eclipse have a special love affair going on. He would do anything for her."

"How old is she?"

"She just turned eleven."

Lillian stared at her. "Eleven?"

"Amber is rather extraordinary," Susan agreed. "I couldn't believe what she was capable of before I saw it with my own eyes. She is truly a prodigy. You should see her ride Eclipse."

Lillian's mouth dropped open. "She *rides* him?"

Susan grinned. "As well as I can," she assured her. "Probably better, because Eclipse seems to adapt his every move to her. I've never seen anything like it."

Lillian continued to watch as Amber walked Eclipse closer to the fenced pasture. Suddenly, a dark bay yearling shot across the pasture and raced up to the pair, prancing to a stop before snorting loudly. "Oh, my..."

"That is All My Heart," Susan said. "She is Amber's filly."

Lillian felt her heart swell. "The one Robert gave her before he was killed."

Susan eyed her. "Rose told you?"

"She thought I should know everything before I came down." Lillian looked back at the horses. "Although she didn't tell me I was coming to horse paradise."

Susan laughed. "Rose rides well, but horses are quite low on her priority list." She looked back at the letter in her hand. "You're going to stay with us in the house."

Lillian shifted uncomfortably. "Just long enough for me to get settled. I'll look for my own housing."

"Good luck with that," Susan replied wryly. "You're welcome here, Lillian. It will be wonderful to have another horsewoman around. Don't feel you have to find another place. We have plenty of room, and you have just become a very valued part of our world by taking the teaching position." She looked up as a clanging bell split the warm spring air. "And we have the best food in the South here. Thank goodness it's time to eat. I'm starving!"

Lillian relaxed even more. Abby had told her to expect a warm welcome, but she had been afraid to have any expectations at all. Evidently, Susan didn't mind that she was dressed casually in breeches and a man's shirt, and she didn't seem put off that her short hair hung freely to her shoulders, instead of being long, and pulled back into a bun like her own. Lillian had been warned about Southern traditions and societal norms. People had sometimes looked at her askance in the North, but yesterday's gawking in Richmond had made her feel like a carnival exhibit. "Thank you. That sounds wonderful."

Twenty minutes later, her mare stabled with a bucket of grain, Lillian sat down in front of a plate piled high with fried chicken, pickled okra, tender baby carrots and fluffy biscuits. She stared at it in disbelief. "You eat like this every day?"

Annie walked into the dining room as she asked her question. "Didn't they feed you where you come from, Miss Lillian?"

"Not like this," Lillian assured her. "I'm afraid this one meal has convinced me I will never leave this house until you throw me out."

*****

Three days later, Lillian saddled Misty and rode to the schoolhouse. Word had been passed around that the new teacher had arrived. Classes would start that day. She had spent the last three days preparing the school room and going over the information Rose had written about all the students, including the adults. It was quite a thick packet of paper, but it had provided invaluable information that would make the transition from their beloved teacher easier.

She took deep breaths of the spring air while she rode, reveling in the fresh smells filling her senses. Warnings of the hot, humid summers had been passed along, but there was no sign of that now. The air was soft and embracing, a welcome change after the long, brutal Ohio winter. Dogwoods filled the woods with their ethereal white blooms, while wildflowers she had no hope of identifying shot color through the greenery. She was in love already.

She had just turned her attention back to the road when two men on horseback, their faces covered with hoods, emerged onto the road in front of her.

Chapter Twenty-Four

Lillian stiffened with surprise, and then lifted her hand casually to her waistband. She was determined not to show any fear. "Well, hello boys," she called cheerfully. "Seems like an awfully nice day to have your faces covered. What can I do for you?" She focused on their eyes because it was the only part of their faces she could see, noticing when they widened with surprise, and then narrowed with anger.

"You can go back to where you came from," one of the men growled in a menacing tone.

"Oh, come on," Lillian retorted. "If your aim is to scare me, that is a poor excuse for intimidation." She was glad the quiver in her stomach was not betrayed by her voice. She had been dealing with bullies all her life. These men were nothing but masked bullies, too cowardly to reveal who they really were. "You know, I heard about you boys." She used the term *boys* deliberately, knowing it would infuriate them because they referred to all black males as boys. "I couldn't believe that grown men would be too scared to reveal their true identity when they go out to threaten someone, but I see now it is true. That's too bad. I thought Southern men had more courage than that." She took a deep breath and decided to go for broke. "I guess I can see why you lost the war."

The man who had spoken to her cursed loudly and reached for his pistol.

Lillian lifted hers faster and fired a round that went through the crown of his hat. She smiled when both the men froze, their eyes filled with stunned hatred. "I hope you realize I could have put that bullet through your heart just as easily. One for each of you," she added as she kept the gun pointed at them, with her finger on the trigger. "I suppose I'll have to write home and tell my friends and family that Southern hospitality is not what they have heard it is."

Her voice hardened. "But I'll just be *writing* my friends and family. I came down here to do a job, and that's what I intend to do. I know you probably have special orders to get rid of all the white teachers, but this one isn't going to go without a fight. You boys already lost several of your own when you tried to trespass on Cromwell Plantation last fall. That didn't go very well for you. I can promise it won't go well for a few of you if you come after me. Oh," she admitted, fighting to keep her voice nonchalant, "you may kill me, but some of you will die in the attempt. You will have to decide who that will be."

"You're treading on dangerous ground." The man who had been silent until that moment had found his voice.

"I would say that, right now, you are the one treading on dangerous ground," Lillian snapped, grateful for all the bullies she had fought in her days. They had taught her to never back down. "And it happens to be ground I need to pass over. Either move in the next few seconds, or I will aim a little lower with my next shot."

"We'll be back," the man called as he cursed and turned his horse. "You can count on it."

"Make sure you know which ones of you are willing to die," Lillian called after them as they cantered away. Once they had rounded the curve and the sound of hoof beats faded in the distance, she slumped into her saddle, limp with relief.

"You handled that right well, Miss Lillian."

Lillian gasped in surprise as a lone horseman emerged from the woods behind her. "Jeb!"

"Yep. It's always been my job to take Miss Rose to school and make sure she got home all right."

"I told you I didn't need anyone," Lillian protested.

"Yep," Jeb agreed. "I see how well that turned out. You handled it right well, but it ain't safe for no woman teacher to be on her own around here. You're right tough, Miss Lillian, but I ain't sure you're real smart."

Lillian laughed, grateful for a way to ease the tension. "You might be right," she admitted.

"Yep," Jeb said again, not hiding his grin this time. "I got me a letter from Miss Rose yesterday. She told me to take you to school, whether you wanted me to or not. You told me not to come with you this morning, but I was following you in the woods on a side trail. It weren't hard to keep you in sight."

"And while I was talking with the men?" Lillian asked curiously.

"I had my gun aimed on the one who didn't have a hole in his hat. I figured you could handle the other one just fine," he answered.

Lillian laughed again and then relented. "So how are we going to do this in the future?"

"I guess you're smart after all," Jeb replied. "I'll ride with you to school every morning. You handle a horse well, so there is no need to take the carriage. I'll keep an eye on the school during the day, and then ride home with you when you're done."

"But aren't you needed in the fields?"

"Yep, but not as much as I'm needed here. All of us got children in your school. And wives who come at night. The men get schooling during the winter, but now everyone is in the fields. They will all work a little harder so I can look after things at the school." He paused and offered her another smile. "We're all real glad you are here. We're sorry Miss Rose ain't here anymore, but she told me in the letter that you are a fine teacher, and that I should take real good care of you. I intend to do that."

"Thank you," Lillian murmured. She turned Misty toward the school. "Now, I would like to get there before my students on the first day."

"Yes, ma'am," Jeb answered as he trotted up beside her.

*****

Lillian leaned against the pasture fencing, watching the yearlings prance through the fields. She knew they would all be picked up next week and taken to their new owners. She could hardly wait for the new crop of colts and fillies to start dropping, but she would be sad to say good-bye to the ones she had already made friends with.

"How was the first day of school?"

Lillian glanced up as Susan rode over on one of the new mares she had just purchased—a beautiful iron gray Thoroughbred with powerful hindquarters and a refined head. "I had a wonderful time with the children," Lillian said enthusiastically. "They all love Miss Rose, but they are willing to give me a chance."

Susan eyed her. "No problems on the way to school?"

Lillian, alerted by the tone of her voice, sighed. "You must have talked to Jeb."

"I did." Susan grinned. "Did you really put a hole through one of the men's hats?"

"Yes. I spent a portion of the day wishing I had gone ahead and aimed lower."

Susan's grin faded. "They are dangerous, Lillian."

"I know," Lillian agreed soberly. "I've agreed to let Jeb ride with me from now on, but I'm afraid I may be putting his life in danger, too."

"If the risk seems to increase, there will be others who will step in for protection."

Lillian nodded. "Some of the white fathers told me they would be taking turns watching the school throughout the day." She shook her head. "I'd heard how hard it is for blacks to get an education in the South, but I didn't realize it is equally hard for white children."

"If you're not white and *rich*," Susan said disdainfully. "Rose did a great thing when she opened the school to all students. Southern men believe people are easier to control if they are uneducated."

"They are right," Lillian said seriously. "Ignorance is the biggest threat to democracy. It's more, though, than being able to read and write. You need to know what is going on in your government and your country if you want to change things. Too many people in power understand that if you limit education, you limit resistance."

Susan was watching her closely. "Your life has been hard," she said perceptively.

Lillian shrugged. "Everyone has something about their life that is hard. I'm not special."

Susan continued to watch her. "You are an ace shot, and Jeb said you stood up to the vigilantes with great courage."

"Vigilantes!" Lillian snorted. "They are nothing but overgrown bullies with hoods. They are not men. They are pathetic little boys who never grew up. I can handle bullies."

"Why?" Susan asked quietly. "Why have you been bullied?"

Lillian sighed. She and Susan had gotten closer in the few days she had been there, spending many hours riding around the plantation. She was going to be nothing but honest with her. "Life is not easy for women who are not beautiful like you are, Susan." She raised a hand when Susan started to protest. "Don't bother telling me it's not true, because I know it is. I don't happen to believe it defines my value or worth as a person, but being homely makes it easy for me to be a target. It always has, and it always will." She stared out at the pasture. "I decided a long time ago to stand up for myself and never back down to bullies. I also decided to become as smart as I possibly could because it was obvious I was going to need to rely on my brain."

"But—" Susan started.

Lillian refused to let her interrupt. "I'm not saying that life is always easy for you, and I already know you are fiercely independent and intelligent. In truth, *every* woman in this country needs to make that choice. No matter how beautiful you are, something can happen to mar your beauty, or old age steals it, and then you are left with nothing." She swung around to look in Susan's eyes. "Have you ever looked at a large group of people and asked yourself how many of them are truly attractive? I have," she said, not giving Susan time to respond. "There aren't that many, Susan. Not many truly *beautiful* people according to the accepted definition. Everyone seems to have something that keeps them from meeting that qualification, but people still seem to value beauty above all else. Too many women believe they have less value because they aren't beautiful. Now that we have magazines that flaunt pictures of women, we all seem to believe we need perfect figures, a beautiful face and the right clothes. I refuse to play into that game!"

"I see," Susan murmured. "Are you going to take a deep enough breath for me to tell you that you're right?"

Lillian chuckled. "I suppose I do become rather defensive."

"Neither of us are responsible for our looks, Lillian. I didn't have any say about how I looked when I came out of my mother's womb. I suppose I'm glad that people think

I'm beautiful, because I'm human enough to appreciate that life is a little easier for me because of it, but if I define myself by my looks then I am no better than the people who define others by the fact they are not as attractive. I prefer to define myself as being independent and intelligent, and as someone who wants to make life better for other people. I have found that is something I am justified to be proud of."

"I—" Lillian began.

Susan was the one who interrupted her this time. "I have only known you a few days, but I already think you are a remarkable woman. And I find it ludicrous that you consider yourself homely."

"People have made sure I am aware of the truth. I'm six feet tall and hardly a beauty," Lillian said flatly.

"Which does not parlay into homely," Susan retorted. "You have beautiful green eyes and a radiant smile. Yes, you are tall, but I suspect people are simply intimidated by that, as well as by the fact that you are strong and confident. I've often wished I was taller. And have you noticed, in spite of how beautiful you believe I am, that I am still single? Most men are simply intimidated by me. I made myself quit caring years ago. Any man would be lucky to have either of us."

Lillian sighed, turning her eyes back to the pasture.

"Did I say something wrong?" Susan asked after a lengthy silence.

"No," Lillian muttered, fighting the resentment bubbling inside her. She wasn't angry at Susan so there was no reason to let her see it. And she certainly wasn't going to talk about what she was feeling. "I could use a long ride after my encounter today, and I think Misty would appreciate it, as well." She took a deep breath. "I think this time I would like to go alone. I need to clear my head."

"Of course," Susan responded, but she laid a hand on Lillian's arm. "I'm sorry if I said something to upset you."

Lillian met her eyes for a moment, wondering if she could share what she was feeling, but she turned away out of habit. "I'm fine," she assured her. "I just need some time to ride off having to almost shoot a man this morning." She kept her voice light, and even managed a smile, before she strode off.

*****

Anthony climbed the steps of Thomas Cromwell's house, glad to be back in Richmond after an extended stay in Philadelphia on business. There was very little to do in the horse industry during the frigid winter months, but now that spring had descended upon the South, it was time to go back to doing what he loved best.

Abby looked up with a glad smile when Anthony entered. "You're back! Welcome."

Anthony set his luggage at the bottom of the stairs. "It's good to be back. I appreciated the opportunities you gave me this winter, but I have discovered I have become quite a Southern man. I hope never to spend another winter north of the Mason-Dixon Line."

"You and me both," Abby agreed. "As much as I complain about the summer heat at times, it is far preferable to endless months of snow and cold. Spring is the very best time to be in Virginia. I'm thrilled to be going with you next week when you get the horses."

"I have such vivid memories of the plantation last summer, and then last fall, but I know neither of those holds a candle to what it must be like in the spring."

"It is paradise," Abby agreed. "I can't help wondering, though, how you are going to move all those yearlings. That is going to be a huge job."

"You're right," Anthony replied. "We arrive on the plantation next Monday, and there will be a team of wagons arriving Friday. We'll tie the horses onto the wagons six at a time and lead them back here. At least to the outskirts. I know Amber and Clint will have them ready to be pulled into town, but they have never seen a train station and never been exposed to the craziness of the city. We'll stop outside town and then take them in two at a time to load them onto the train cars that will deliver them to their destinies."

Abby frowned. "I can't help feeling sorry for them. It will be a terrifying experience for those babies to be yanked away from the plantation and into such chaos."

"You're right," Anthony said in a troubled voice. "I always hate this part of it, but I can assure you that when they reach the stables they are bound for, they will once again have the kind of life they have at Cromwell."

Abby changed the subject to one less troublesome. "Do you think you have buyers for more of the foals coming this year? I suspect the first ones will be born this week."

Anthony grinned. "Your connections up north ended up being advantageous in more than one way. I found I rather enjoyed drumming up business for your factories again, but it was one gentleman in particular who made my winter so profitable."

"Oh? Do tell what happened."

"In late February, I met a gentleman by the name of Percy Antoinette while at dinner with Mark Jones in Philadelphia. Percy has just become owner of a large stables in northern Pennsylvania, and asked Mark if he knew where he could get some good stock." Anthony's eyes twinkled. "Mark happened to tell him he had taken ownership the year before of fifty of the finest yearlings he had ever seen."

Abby started to grin. "And then Mr. Antoinette asked Mark where he got the horses..."

"And Mark happened to mention that I had been the buying agent for all the horses on Cromwell Plantation," Anthony finished with a broad smile. "By the time dinner was finished, Mr. Antoinette had put forth a very impressive offer for all of this year's foals."

Abby gaped at him. "*All* of them? There will be at least seventy foals this year."

"I'm relieved to know I got the number right."

Abby's eyes narrowed. "What is your definition of an impressive offer?"

Anthony threw his head back and laughed loudly. "Do you really believe I would bring anything but an offer that is substantially better than last year's? I am certain you and Carrie have already taught Susan all the techniques you taught your daughter."

"Substantially better?" Abby murmured, obviously trying to sound skeptical, but failing miserably.

Anthony laughed again. "I warned Percy he would be foolish to start negotiations with anything less than his best offer if he wanted to do business with the Cromwell women."

"That was wise," Abby quipped.

Anthony reached into his pocket and pulled out a sheet of paper. "I realize Susan will be the one to make the final decision this year, but I believe you will be interested in seeing Percy's offer."

Abby reached for the paper eagerly, read what was written there, and then closed her eyes for a long moment. When she opened them, they were shining with tears.

"Abby?" Anthony felt a twinge of alarm. Perhaps, in spite of his belief that it was a remarkable offer, she was disappointed. "Is something wrong?"

"No," Abby said. "I just so wish Robert was still alive. He dreamed his entire life of having a breeding operation that would command this type of respect. He accomplished it but will never know it." She shook her head sadly. "It's moments like this that his death hits me particularly hard."

Anthony's lips tightened. "I know. His murder was such a tragedy."

Abby nodded. "I'm glad Carrie was able to get away from the plantation for a while. I don't know what she will decide to do when she returns from New Mexico, but it was important for her to have some distance."

Anthony knew she felt she could talk freely because he had been there for her when her husband, Charles, had died from cholera, and she had supported him when he had lost his wife and child. "Just as you had to move out of the house you shared with Charles."

"Yes," Abby agreed.

Anthony hesitated, not sure if he should ask the next question, but he felt powerless to remain silent. "I know it's not likely, but has there been any word from Carrie, Matthew and Janie?" He thought lumping them all together would make his request a little less obvious. One look at Abby's eyes told him it had been a futile effort.

"Actually, we had the surprise of a letter last week," Abby revealed. She told him briefly about the blizzard, and about the family Carrie and her team had saved. "She asked the father to mail a letter for her when he returned to Independence."

"They are doing well?"

"Besides being unendingly cold and wishing for a bath, they are all fine."

Anthony raised a brow. "Carrie told you that?"

"Of course not," Abby said ruefully. "It is not in her nature to complain, but I did enough research to know what life is like on a wagon train in the winter. All she told me is they are all fine, but missing us. I'm hoping that April has brought warmer weather to the Plains. They should be out of Kansas and approaching New Mexico by now."

"I'm glad to know that, as of six weeks ago, they were all right." He didn't have to wait long for what he suspected was coming.

"Anthony..." Abby began hesitantly.

Anthony raised a hand. "You don't have to tell me Carrie is not over Robert's death, nor that she is certainly not ready or interested in another relationship. I already know that."

"I'm glad you do," Abby replied, her eyes still troubled.

"Don't be concerned for me," Anthony said. "I fell in love with Carrie the moment I laid eyes on her. I assumed at the time she was married, so I'd already told myself nothing could come from it. When I discovered Robert had been murdered, I also knew nothing could come from it. That can't stop me from caring, however."

"That's true," Abby agreed. She opened her mouth to say something, but closed it quickly.

Anthony leaned forward. "What?"

Abby gazed at him for a long moment and then uttered just one word. "Yet."

"Yet?" Anthony was totally confused.

"Nothing can come from your feelings *yet.*"

Anthony sucked in a quick breath. "Is there something you're not telling me?" Wild hope bloomed in him.

"No," Abby said quickly. "Carrie and I have never talked about you, and I know it is far too soon for her to even have thoughts like that. Just as when I met you I could never have imagined loving someone again after Charles. I wasn't ready...*yet.* I encourage you to be willing to give it time."

Anthony sat back and considered what she had said. "I never knew *yet* could be such a beautiful word," he finally said.

*****

Harold Justin swung down from the train car, taking a deep breath of Richmond's spring air. Even with the train and coal smoke, he could feel a difference from Buffalo, New York. Of course, it could have something to do with the almost sixty degree temperature difference. A late spring storm had dumped another foot of snow on Buffalo a few days before he left. He had been eager to leave the cold behind.

It took him only a few minutes to find a hack to carry him up Richmond Hill. He stowed his bags, folded his heavy coat, leaned back in the seat, and watched as the city rolled by. It was certainly busier than Buffalo, but everything about it felt *southern*. They had traveled less than a half mile before he knew he was in love with the dogwoods and azaleas that brought the city to life. He could see evidence of the war years everywhere he looked, but he also felt a burgeoning sense of hope and expectancy in the air that revealed the beleaguered city was coming back to life.

He felt much the same way himself. When he had lost Beth, Martha Ann and Nancy, he had been certain his life was over. He had railed against the cruel fate that had left him behind to live his life in tortured loneliness. His pain had caused him to reach out to Matthew, with no idea it would lead to a new life for him. It had taken him since January to finish up his responsibilities for the *Buffalo Evening Courier* and walk away from the life he had built there since the war. Each mile he put behind him on the train had seemed to unleash his soul a little more.

"We're here, Mr. Justin."

Harold jerked his thoughts back to the present and stared up at the elegant, three-story brick home they had stopped in front of. He thanked the driver, and moments later was standing alone in the street with his baggage. He took a deep breath and approached the door. The Cromwells were expecting him, but with this action he was truly starting into a new life.

It took only minutes for a tall, slender black man to open the door in response to his knock. He was not surprised when the man stared at him for a moment before he found his voice. "Hello, Mr. Justin."

Harold smiled. "It will probably be less confusing if you just call me Harold. That way you won't confuse me with Matthew."

Micah returned the smile. "It might not be quite that easy, sir. The two of you be the spitting image of each other."

Harold knew the man was right. He hadn't been sure he should cut his hair, but he had grown tired of the long locks he had grown during the war for warmth. There was little to tell him apart from Matthew now. They'd had tremendous fun as children when people couldn't tell one from the other. It was a little disconcerting now, but with Matthew on the Santa Fe Trail it might be a little easier.

"I'll let Miss Abby know you are here, sir."

"Fine, but only if you call me Harold. Matthew assured me things were more casual in the Cromwell household."

"Yes, sir, Mr. Harold," Micah replied, his eyes twinkling. "Your room is on the top floor in the right wing. The third door on the left. I'd love to take your bags up, but this old body don't handle that too well anymore."

"Not a problem. This northern boy is not used to being waited on. I prefer to do it myself," Harold said easily.

"Mr. Anthony is in the room next to yours."

"Jeremy and Marietta?"

"Oh no, sir," Micah said hastily. "Not that Mr. Anthony. Anthony be Mr. Jeremy's *last* name. Mr. Anthony is Anthony Wallington. He arrived just a while ago. I think he is unpacking now. Mr. Jeremy and Miss Marietta won't be home until almost dinnertime." He smiled. "Don't you worry none, Mr. Harold. It might be a little confusing at first, but not near as confusing as people seeing you and knowing for certain it is Matthew."

Harold chuckled. "You have a valid point, Micah." He picked up his luggage and moved toward the stairs. "Since Abby is busy, I'll go ahead and take my bags up. I won't be long."

"Take all the time you need," Micah assured him. "May will have dinner ready at six o'clock."

Harold had almost reached his room when the door to the room before his swung open. A tall, lanky man stepped out and stopped short.

"What are you doing here?" He looked totally confused. "I thought you were on the Santa Fe Trail?"

Harold grinned. "You must be Anthony."

Anthony's face cleared as understanding dawned. "You are Matthew's twin brother. I heard about you." He reached out a hand. "It's nice to meet you, Harold."

"The same," Harold replied, appreciating the firm grip. "I met everyone else at Christmas."

"I was with family in Philadelphia, though I admit I would have preferred to be on the plantation."

"It is a special place," Harold agreed. "I hope to get out there while I'm here."

"Are you in Richmond on business?"

"The two of you can get to know each other down here," Abby called, her voice floating up the stairwell. "I have May fixing some lemonade and cookies. Might I entice you to join me?"

Harold dropped his bags in the corridor right where he stood, and turned. "If May's cooking is anything like Annie's, I have no intention of missing it."

"My cookin' be way better than that Annie's!"

Harold grinned. "Does every woman in this house have the hearing of a bat?"

"Did you just call me an old bat?" Abby's indignant response was crystal clear.

"I do believe that was your answer," Anthony whispered. "If I were you, I would stop while you are behind."

Harold groaned. "I'll probably get nothing to eat at all." He hurried down the stairs and rushed to embrace Abby. "You know I would never call you an old bat."

"At least not loud enough for me to hear it while you are hoping to eat in my home," Abby agreed with a warm smile. "I promise you that May does indeed have the ears of a bat. You don't want to say a thing you don't want her to hear."

"I'll hear it anyway," May said with a snort as she pushed open the kitchen door and emerged with a tray full of thick oatmeal cookies and glasses frothy with lemonade. "And I'll know if you even whisper that you like Annie's cookies better than mine." She fixed a steely glaze on Harold. "I don't care if you look just like Mr. Matthew— who I adore. You got to learn how things work around this house."

"I hear and I obey," Harold assured her, trying not to grin.

May stared at him and then nodded. "You'll do." She laid down the tray and then disappeared into the kitchen.

Abby laughed. "And now you know the rules of the house. Thomas and I just pretend we own it. We know who really runs things."

"There's hope for you two!" May sang out from behind the closed door.

Harold laughed, more sure than ever that he was going to have a wonderful time. He turned to Anthony. "You asked if I'm here on business. I have just finished a reporting job with the *Buffalo Evening Courier*. I am now officially my brother's writing partner on his book *Glimmers of Change*, and all the books that will follow."

"I am so thrilled," Abby said. "I know Matthew was hoping you would be here sooner. What held you in Buffalo?"

"I promised Matthew I would do all the follow up articles necessary on the *New York Express* wreck in Angola." His expression became grave. "We both hoped the tragedy would be the tipping point that would mandate change in the railroad industry."

"And has it?" Abby demanded. "I still shudder when I think about what Janie endured."

"It has," Harold assured her. "It will take time to implement it all, but many railroad reforms are being enacted. They are working to replace the stoves with safer forms of heating. They have sped up the creation of iron cars to replace the wooden ones, and are demanding more effective braking systems, as well as insisting on the standardization of track gauges to make sure fewer trains derail. There will be more newspaper coverage, but I felt I had done all I needed to for now."

He didn't mention that he was quite sure he could not have written one more article about the terrible tragedy that still haunted his dreams. What Janie and Matthew were going through, he could only imagine. He knew Matthew's main reason for going on the wagon train was to distance Janie from any memories so she could heal. He hoped that was being accomplished.

"It can't possibly make up for the lost lives and destroyed families, but I'm glad change is coming,"

Anthony responded. "The railroads are experiencing tremendous profits. It's beyond time for them to put those profits into safer travel." He shook his head and turned back to Harold. "Do you have a particular assignment, or are you scouting for stories? I'm fascinated by the book. There is such a need for good stories in the midst of the pain and chaos of this country right now.

"Both," Harold responded. "I'm here to meet with a man Matthew met when he was in Independence. He met him there just before the man moved here to Richmond in early February. When Matthew heard his story, he knew we had to include it in the book."

Abby eyed him expectantly. "Aren't you going to tell us any more?"

"No," Harold said with a grin. "I'm going to meet with him tomorrow."

"You want to eat tonight, Mr. Harold?" May called. "I want to be hearing that story, too!"

"Do you want to hear it *tomorrow*?" Harold retorted. "You'll want to make sure dinner tonight is fabulous!"

May chuckled and went back to slamming pots around.

Abby eyed him thoughtfully. "I believe you're the only person to ever put May in her place," she whispered dramatically. "I do hope you will be here for a while."

Harold sniffed the odors coming from the kitchen. "Me, too," he sighed.

"So we'll be the first to hear the story?" Anthony prompted.

"You'll be the first," Harold promised.

Chapter Twenty-Five

"You're sure this is the right place?" Harold asked. He didn't know what he had been expecting, but the ramshackle cabin on the edge of town was certainly not it.

"This be the place," Spencer assured him, eyeing the cabin doubtfully. "It don't look no worse than most of the black quarter looks. In fact, it looks a heap better than some of it. I don't reckon you're seeing many places like this up in New York, though."

Harold couldn't dispute that fact. He had seen plenty of poverty in the North, but this was a notch above anything he had experienced. He didn't know how he could possibly create a story of hope worth reading about, but Matthew had asked him to interview the man, so he would.

"You want me to wait for you?"

Harold hesitated. His first inclination was to tell Spencer to do just that, but that would be as good as saying he didn't believe there was a story here worth telling. If he was to achieve Matthew's goal of looking for stories of hope in the country, he had to be willing to *look*. "No. How about if you come back in about four hours. That should give me enough time."

Spencer looked dubious. "You can't need that much time to do anything here," he muttered.

"I'll be fine," Harold insisted. He suddenly, and without reason, was sure he should be here. "Come back in four hours."

Spencer waited for him to step out of the carriage, and then drove away, the wagon wheels kicking up dust behind him.

Harold watched him for a moment, hoping he had not made a mistake, but realizing that if there truly wasn't a story here, he could just walk back to town. It was a beautiful day, and the exercise wouldn't kill him. When he turned toward the house, he saw two people watching him. He was surprised when he realized the man was white, and the woman was black.

"Hello," he called, walking forward to discover whether this was a story worth telling.

"Howdy," the man called back. "Who are you?" He frowned as Harold drew closer. "You look like a fellow I met a couple months back in Independence, but I thought he was headed out on the Santa Fe Trail."

Harold sighed but decided to make light of it since he would have to get used to the situation. "You met Matthew Justin," he explained when he drew closer. "My name is Harold Justin. We are twins."

"I'll say," the man said with a whistle. "Do you ever feel like you're looking in a mirror?"

Harold grinned. "All the time," he agreed, and then continued. "Matthew told me where I could find you. Your name is Willard Miller?"

"The last I checked," the young man agreed with an easy smile that lit green eyes beneath a thatch of brown hair that reached his broad shoulders.

Harold liked him instantly.

Willard reached for the hand of the willowy black woman by his side. "This is my wife, Grace." His eyes dared Harold to have a negative reaction.

Harold smiled warmly. Matthew had not told him about a black wife, but he had no reason to care. He had friends in New York that were biracial couples. "Hello, Mrs. Miller. It's a pleasure to meet you." The look of relief in her eyes told him how difficult it must be to live in the South in a mixed-race marriage.

"Hello, Mr. Justin," Grace replied, her voice at once soft and firm.

Harold liked the way she stood erect, the proud tilt of her head saying she would not be an easy woman to intimidate. "I understand you have quite a story, Mr. Miller."

"Call us Willard and Grace," Willard responded. "We weren't expecting anyone, but Grace just pulled some biscuits out of the oven. We would be honored to share them with you."

"And I would be honored to enjoy them," Harold replied, once more warmed by the appreciative glow in Grace's eyes. Within a few minutes, they were seated on the porch enjoying the spring breeze, with a plate of hot biscuits and strawberry preserves in front of them. "There is not a woman in the North who knows how to make biscuits like these," Harold murmured as he slathered butter and preserves on the fluffy mounds. "Thank you, Grace."

"You're welcome, Mr. Justin."

"Harold. If I am to call you Willard and Grace, you must do me the same honor of calling me by my first name."

Grace nodded shyly.

"I'm not sure why Matthew sent you over," Willard said. "After we talked a little while in Independence, he said he would like to hear the whole story, and then asked me if I would talk to you. I don't really know what you are looking for."

"Me either," Harold said lightly. "Why don't we just talk?" He wanted Willard to stay relaxed and comfortable. "From what Matthew told me, your story started when you got captured at the Battle of Lookout Mountain in Alabama. Is that where you are from?"

"Born and raised," Willard agreed, his Alabama twang coming through loud and clear. "I joined up with the Confederate Army in October of sixty-three, after I finally convinced my mama I had to fight. I was the second of twelve children, so I stayed out of the war for a while because my mama needed my help. My father died a few years back before the war started."

"I imagine she would need help," Harold agreed, and then thought about what he had heard. "You couldn't have been in the war very long if you were captured at Lookout Mountain."

"One month," Willard said ruefully. "I spent the rest of the war years at Rock Island Prison in Illinois."

Harold winced. "I'm sorry."

"You know something about Rock Island?"

"Not much," Harold admitted, "but my brother was held here in Libby Prison during the war. He barely survived before he led an escape attempt that freed many of the prisoners. He says he still has nightmares about it."

"Yep, I suspect I will, too," Willard replied, his eyes saying far more than his words. "I've heard a whole lot about how horrible the prisons were in the South, but nobody talks about the prisons in the North. I assure you they were just as bad."

Harold listened carefully. He knew Union soldiers had experienced the end of the war in a very different way than the Confederates had. While there were many hardships for returning soldiers in the North, most of them had gone home to the land of plenty and people who were grateful for their service, as well as pensions to carry them through until they found jobs. People listened when they talked about their horrible experiences in Southern prisons, and articles were written. He had written some of them himself. He tried to remember a single thing published about Northern prisons, but came up blank. Obviously, it was something the North didn't want to acknowledge. If there were ever going to be healing in the country, people should know what Confederate soldiers had gone through. "Will you tell me more?"

"Will you write it?" Willard demanded. "No one else wants to know about it."

"I do," Harold stated. "And, yes, I will write it." Even without hearing all the story, he understood why Matthew had sent him here. People might not like the truth, but that fact alone made the truth even more mandatory if they ever wanted to rebuild America. "I promise."

Willard stared at him and then nodded his head abruptly. "I got to Rock Island in December. There was two feet of snow on the ground, and the temperature was below zero. I don't reckon I've ever felt that kind of cold. Some Yankee soldier took my shoes on the way there, and they weren't handing any out," he said bitterly. "I suppose I was lucky to have a blanket, even though it was a pitiful excuse for one. Some of the fellows who came in after me didn't get one. We were stuck in those buildings like sardines in a jar, but that might have saved some of our lives. The only way to keep from freezing at night was to huddle around one of the two coal stoves in the building. We would take turns getting close enough to keep from freezing to death." He stopped talking and looked off into the distance.

"Tell him about your feet," Grace prompted gently.

Willard took a deep breath. "My feet weren't real good by the end of the war," he admitted, "but there is more to tell you about the prison." He brought his gaze back to

Harold. "I'd only been there a month or so when smallpox broke out. There weren't no hospital buildings, so everyone had to stay together."

Harold sucked in his breath, knowing without being told that the death rate must have been astronomical.

"The smallpox spread like a fire," Willard said. "They made a pitiful attempt to give people a place to be sick, but there weren't enough room, and they made the people who were sick take care of each other. No one else would come close." His eyes shuttered. "I never seen so many people die so fast before it finally petered out." He shook his head heavily. "I reckon I was lucky because I didn't get the smallpox, though there were times when I thought the lucky ones were those being carried out on a stretcher to be thrown into a mass grave."

Willard, obviously trying to regain control of his emotions, reached for another biscuit. After he had chewed for a few moments, he met Harold's eyes again. "I had a chance to go free," he announced.

Harold eyed him. "And you didn't take it?"

"Thousands of us refused to," Willard said proudly. "They wanted us to renounce the South and join the Union Navy. Guess they figured we couldn't escape if we were on a boat, and that we would probably fight if it was the only way to save our life. The offer to join was made in March after they quit burying people from smallpox."

Harold knew nothing about this. "I had no idea," he murmured.

"A few fellows took them up on it, but most of us refused. They hadn't really given me any reason to think I should turn my back on the South," Willard said harshly. "They came back in September and made the same offer, only now we were going to be sent out to the West to fight Indians." He eyed Harold. "I'll tell you something I overheard by mistake, but only if you promise to learn the whole truth."

Harold nodded, both appalled and fascinated by what he was learning. "I promise," he said again.

"When I first got to Rock Island, I was miserable and cold, but they were at least feeding us. That all changed in June of sixty-four. They stopped feeding us much of anything. I figure it was their way of starving us out."

"Starving you out? I don't understand."

"I didn't either until I overhead some people talking. I don't know who they were, but I believe they were telling the truth," Willard said.

"I'm listening." Harold suspected he was about to learn a whole different story than the one he had come to write, but he sensed it was important.

"There was another call to service in September of sixty-four, like I said. I guess they figured after three months of starving us we would be eager to take them up on it this time because they were promising we would eat. There still weren't very many accepting. They kept offering and offering. They even built a special enclosure and left the gates open all night. I reckon they thought if men could go in there without being seen, they would do it."

"But they didn't," Harold observed.

"Not at first...but then it changed real quick. Frontier service became right popular," Willard said. "I watched men who had ridiculed others for joining up turn around and make the same decision. I couldn't understand it until I heard the men talking."

Harold remained silent, knowing Willard would reveal his story in time.

"There was a judge that decided to make himself some money. Judge Petty from the Pennsylvania oil fields. He claimed he had authority from President Lincoln to offer a bounty of one hundred dollars to each man who took them up on the offer to join the Union and go out West. On top of that, if they were rejected because of bad health, they would be released to go home."

Harold leaned forward. One hundred dollars was a lot of money to starving men. Add to it the chance of release, and he could see why more would take it.

"But that ain't the whole story," Willard said. "According to what I heard, every one of the men who enlisted were substitutes for men in the Pennsylvania oil fields. Those fellows had been drafted, but they didn't want to fight, and they were needed in the oil fields. What I heard was that each of them had actually paid three hundred dollars for their substitutes. Judge Petty pocketed the other two hundred bucks for every one of those men who enlisted. I figure he made over three hundred thousand dollars. That's what them fellows said."

Harold whistled and sat back in astonishment, appalled at the realization that men had been starved into submission and then sold off for profit. "My God," he muttered.

Willard stared at him. "You'll find out more?"

"Yes," Harold promised. "I'll do everything I can to discover the truth." He looked at Willard more closely. "You didn't take the deal."

"Not a chance," Willard said darkly. "Being a prisoner was bad enough, but I wasn't going to sell my soul. Me and a bunch others decided death was better than that."

"I'm glad you didn't die," Harold said firmly.

Willard took his wife's hand. "Only because of Grace," he said, love shining from his eyes. "By the time the war ended, I wasn't in such good shape. I wasn't much more than a bag of bones, and my feet were pretty bad. When they told us we could go home in June, there weren't any trains or boats waiting for us."

Harold frowned, realizing he had never thought much about how the Confederate prisoners had gotten home. "What did you do?"

"I walked."

Harold stared at Willard. "You walked?" He did a quick calculation in his head. "It has to be at least seven hundred miles to Alabama."

"Pretty nearly," Willard agreed. "I wasn't really counting miles. I just wanted to go home." He took a deep breath. "I only made it to southern Illinois before I got real sick." He took a deep breath and looked at Grace.

Grace took his hand, and also took over the narrative. "I found Willard on the road near my house sometime in August of that year. I don't remember the exact date. My mama and daddy escaped an Alabama plantation with me and my two brothers right after the war started. I was thirteen when we left, seventeen when Willard showed up." She glanced at him lovingly. "He was passed out on a dirt road and burning up with fever. He kept mumbling things, but I couldn't make any sense of it. He didn't have no shoes on, so I could see his feet were all messed up." She winced as she remembered. "I went home to get my brothers."

"You took him in?" Harold asked.

"Of course," Grace replied serenely. "My parents were nervous at first, but I reminded them of the people who had helped us when we escaped. I didn't know at the time that Willard was a *Rebel* soldier, but it wouldn't have mattered to me. He needed help. My brothers picked him up and carried him back to our house. It took a right long while, but we brought him back to health."

Harold gazed at Willard. "How did you feel when you woke up in a black person's house?"

"I was glad to be alive," Willard responded. "My family was never rich, so we had never had any slaves. I didn't really understand how people could own other people."

"Yet you fought in the war," Harold murmured.

"I wasn't fighting over slavery," Willard replied. "I was fighting to protect my home. At least that is what I believed." He looked thoughtful. "I doubt there were many soldiers who had any real idea why we were fighting. We just were."

"How long did it take before you could get home?" Harold asked, understanding now why Matthew had wanted this story told.

"I left Grace's house in November. It was cold again, but I had shoes and clothes this time, and my feet were a heap better. I walked the rest of those seven hundred miles by the next spring. My mama had given me up for dead," he said with a faint smile. "You'd have thought she saw a ghost when I walked down our road." He took a deep breath. "I stayed home for a few months, but I couldn't stop thinking about Grace. I fell for her real hard, but I didn't believe she would want anything to do with a white Rebel soldier without any money."

Grace stroked his hand. "I fell in love with him, too, but I couldn't believe he would love a former slave girl. I never said a word while I was taking care of him."

"So how did you get together?" Harold breathed, completely caught up in the unfolding drama.

Willard smiled. "I finally decided if I was brave enough to survive eighteen months in a prison camp and walk home seven hundred miles, that I had enough courage to hear for myself that she didn't love me. After living through the war, I wasn't going to spend my whole life wondering what might have happened if I told her how I felt."

Harold grinned. "So you walked back?"

Willard shook his head. "I wasn't that patient. I found work with a company hauling supplies up north. I worked my way up to Illinois and got off the train with my final paycheck. I was mighty scared when I walked up to Grace's house, but I figured the worst they would do was tell me to go back home." He grinned. "They didn't tell me that."

Grace took his hand and squeezed it tightly. "I could hardly believe it when he came back. I had given up hope of ever seeing him again, but I hadn't quit loving him."

Harold watched them, envious of the love that was so evident. The ache of missing Beth almost took his breath. He made himself focus on his assignment. "That is a beautiful story. I have to wonder, though, why you are in Richmond," he said bluntly. "It can't be easy to live as a mixed-race couple here."

"It's not easy anywhere," Willard replied.

"Things are better for blacks in the North," Grace confirmed, "but you shouldn't confuse that to mean they are good. There was a loud cry for the slaves to be freed before and during the war, but now that we are, and now that we are going to have the vote, folks everywhere have decided we have to be taught to remember our place. I don't believe anyone ever considered blacks might have social equality...or might deserve it," she added.

"At least they don't have the Ku Klux Klan," Harold observed. "You realize you have put yourself in more danger down here?"

"I know," Willard conceded, "but it's not easy to find a job in the South right now, and the Union soldiers are getting all the jobs up north. When I found one in Richmond, I figured we should come."

"You found a job here? How?"

Willard looked puzzled. "Matthew didn't tell you?"

Harold shook his head. "Evidently not. I have no idea what you are talking about."

Willard smiled. "After Matthew heard our story, he sent a telegram to Richmond. The next morning, before they pulled out the following day, he came and told me there was a job waiting for me if I wanted it. I'm working for Cromwell Factory," he said proudly.

Harold chuckled. "It that doesn't beat all. I can't wait to tell Abby and Thomas *this* story."

"Abby and Thomas?" Grace asked. "Who are they?"

Harold grinned. "Abby and Thomas *Cromwell*. They own the factory, and they happen to be who I am staying with while I'm here. Abby demanded I tell this story tonight at dinner."

Willard returned the grin. "Well, if that don't beat all," he agreed. "You tell the Cromwells that I'll be working hard, and that pretty soon we won't be stuck out here on the outskirts of town. Seems no one wanted us in the white part of Richmond, and the black quarter wasn't real excited about us either."

Harold felt an idea forming. He waited a few moments before it took shape, and until he was certain it would be well received. "I think you should tell them yourself," he said finally.

"How are we going to do that? I suppose I could go to the office, but I imagine all the Cromwells are real busy."

"You're coming to dinner tonight," Harold announced.

"Dinner?" Grace gasped. "We can't do that!"

"Why?" Harold asked, more sure by the moment that it was exactly what Thomas and Abby would want him to do.

"I ain't got no good clothes, and we're not fancy enough for the Cromwells."

"I think you'll be very surprised," Harold assured them. He glanced at his pocket watch, surprised by how much time had passed. "We've got another hour or so before Spencer returns for me. Do whatever you feel you need to in order to be ready. He'll drive you back home tonight."

Willard and Grace shared a stunned look. Finally, Willard nodded. "If you're sure."

"I'm sure," Harold promised.

*****

Abby smiled when Harold walked through the door with the couple. She had returned home from the factory minutes earlier, and had just sat down in the parlor with some lemonade. She stood and graciously offered a hand. "Hello. Whom do I have the pleasure of meeting?"

"This is Willard and Grace Miller," Harold said. "They will be joining us for dinner tonight."

"I'm pleased to meet both of you," Abby said warmly, noticing the couple was nervous. She knew Harold would explain in time. She had not known him very long, but he was so much like Matthew that she already innately trusted him. "Excuse me a moment," she murmured. "I'll let May know there will be two more for dinner."

"Only if it's not an inconvenience," Grace blurted. "We don't want to impose."

Abby shook her head, immediately impressed with the young lady's proper English. Whatever her story was, it was obvious she was educated. "You are certainly not imposing," she said. "We are always pleased to have company. It makes this big house seem not so empty."

She returned followed by May, who was carrying a tray with iced tea and molasses cookies. "I just pulled these cookies out the oven," May announced. "Taste them and tell me what you think."

Abby understood Grace's startled look. "May prefers to believe she runs things around here. We let her believe it," she said teasingly. "Especially since without her and Micah we would be hopelessly lost. We just pay the bills."

Grace laughed and relaxed a little more. She took a small bite of the cookie and closed her eyes with delight. "May I have the recipe, please?"

Abby watched May carefully. She had never been willing to give out her recipe for the molasses cookies, insisting they were a family secret from generations gone by.

May stared at Grace for a long moment and then turned toward the kitchen. "You come on back here in my kitchen and I'll give it to you."

Abby watched the two disappear with an open mouth, before turning to Harold and Willard. "Your wife is a magician," she said lightly. "I've never known May to share her molasses cookie recipe."

Willard smiled. "She's something, all right. She pretty much always gets her way with me, too. Not that it bothers me. When someone saves your life, it's expected that you would feel indebted."

Abby cocked her head. "Saved your life? That must be quite a story." She caught Harold's smile out of the corner of her eye. "These are the people you interviewed!"

"They are," Harold confirmed. He looked at Willard. "Do you have it in you to repeat your story?"

"Why don't you do it," Willard suggested. "That way I can see how well you listened."

Abby was amused, recognizing the two of them had developed an easy friendship over the course of the last hours. She sat back and listened, completely engrossed in the story. When Harold got to the part about them finding a job in Richmond, she was thrilled. "It's terribly hard to find a job right now. Who are you working for?" she asked Willard.

"Cromwell Factory," Willard responded with twinkling eyes.

Abby sat back against her chair. "You work for *us*? That's wonderful."

Willard nodded and sat forward, fixing his eyes on her. "It's why Grace and I decided to take a risk on imposing for dinner tonight. We wanted to thank you and your husband in person. And Mr. Anthony, as well. I'll probably never get a chance to talk to him, but he is a fine man to work for. I promise you I'll work harder than anyone else at the factory," he said.

"You're welcome," Abby said. "And I believe you. Thomas will be home soon, and so will Jeremy Anthony." Her eyes sparkled. "Jeremy and Thomas happen to be brothers. He and his wife, Marietta, live here with us."

Willard took a deep breath. "When Grace and I got up this morning we never dreamed what we would be doing tonight."

Abby nodded. "I find that most days hold something I never dreamed would happen. It's what keeps life so fascinating for me. Not all the things are pleasant, but I can certainly say they are never boring."

"I would agree with that," Willard replied.

Abby looked up when she heard the door open. "I do believe everyone is here. Thomas and Jeremy were going by to pick up Marietta on the way home."

Abby felt her heart swell as she watched introductions being made. Carrie, Matthew, Janie, Rose, Moses, Felicia, John and Hope might be gone, but new people were coming into her world. She had already fallen in love with Willard and Grace, recognizing a young couple that needed friends in their new city until they found their way. They had shown great courage in choosing to live in Richmond as a mixed-race couple. They would need support, not just a job.

When May called them in for dinner, she grabbed Harold's arm to hold him back. "Thank you," she said softly.

"For?"

"For knowing Willard and Grace would be welcome here," she murmured. "Even though Carrie and the rest don't live here, their absence seems to have left a hole in my heart. I've been feeling lonely. Willard and Grace are a lovely couple. I will enjoy getting to know them better."

Harold smiled broadly. "I'm glad I was correct about how you would react. Matthew has told me so much about you and Thomas, but it's what I've experienced myself that convinced me it would be all right."

*****

Marietta had watched Willard and Grace all through the delicious meal. She was convinced Harold had not told them the truth about her and Jeremy. Neither of them would have been able to hold in their curiosity if they were aware. Now that she knew the story was hers and Jeremy's to tell, she was eager to do so. "It must have been quite a hard decision to move to Virginia," she remarked, holding Grace's eyes. She had watched the lovely young woman relax over dinner as everyone laughed and talked.

Grace shrugged. "When you are choosing between starvation and prejudice, the choice isn't really that hard. Willard had been looking for work for months."

Marietta laughed. "When you put it that way, I suppose you're right."

"Jobs are hard to come by," Jeremy agreed. "I imagine that if employers found out you were a mixed-race couple, they were not eager to hire you."

Marietta watched the confusion appear in their guest's eyes.

It was Willard who responded. "Are you telling us if you had known we were mixed-race, that we wouldn't have been hired at Cromwell Factory?" His words were polite, but his voice was clipped.

"Certainly not," Jeremy answered. "It would only have made us *more* eager to hire you."

Willard raised a brow, clearly skeptical. "Why?"

Marietta was proud of where she knew Jeremy was taking the conversation.

"Because I am mulatto," Jeremy said matter-of-factly.

Quiet fell on the table while Willard and Grace gaped at him. Neither seemed to be able to utter a word.

Marietta smiled gently. "It's true," she assured them. "Jeremy's father is Thomas' father, but they don't share the same mother. Their father had sex with one of their slaves."

"You might as well admit he raped her," Thomas said grimly. "Sarah had no choice in the matter."

"But you're white," Grace argued.

"I look white," Jeremy agreed, "but all the laws in the South say I am as black as you are. My twin sister is darker than you."

Grace gaped at him again. "Your twin sister?"

"Her name is Rose," Marietta answered. "She is a teacher, and is in school at Oberlin College now. Her husband is studying at Oberlin to become a lawyer."

Grace slumped back against her seat, keeping her eyes fixed on Marietta. "You could have a black baby," she murmured.

"I could," Marietta agreed. She never enjoyed talking about the possibility, but she knew it would help Grace to not feel alone, and she wasn't surprised at Grace's response.

Willard was still watching Jeremy. "Do you have much trouble around here?"

"Enough," Jeremy admitted, "but most people haven't figured it out yet. I don't have a problem being half-black, but I find I've been able to be most effective in helping my black friends as a white man. I'm aware, though, that it will become known in time."

"And if you have a black baby?" Grace asked.

Marietta took a deep breath and then opted for honesty because she knew Grace must constantly think about it. "I don't know. It's one thing for Jeremy and me to take the risk. We are adults. It's quite another to ask a defenseless child to deal with the consequences of our decision." She shifted uncomfortably and looked toward Jeremy. He smiled and nodded. "I'll let you know the answer to that in about six months," Marietta added.

"Six months?" Abby breathed. "You're pregnant? You're going to have a baby?"

"That's what the doctor tells me," Marietta said happily, her face wreathed in smiles. "I just found out today."

Abby blinked and then turned on Thomas. "You knew? You've been home for an hour, and you didn't tell me?"

Thomas held up his hands. "They made me promise they could share the news."

Marietta laughed. "We threatened him with bodily harm if he told anyone. I was so excited to tell Jeremy. When Thomas was with him to pick me up from school, I just couldn't wait."

Abby jumped up and hugged both of them. "That is wonderful news! Congratulations!"

May was standing in the door of the kitchen. "Well, if that ain't some grand news." She turned to Micah. "You go get me a bunch of them fresh strawberries out of the garden. I'm going to make us some strawberry biscuit shortcakes to celebrate." She blinked her eyes furiously. "It's about time this house had a baby in it."

Marietta laughed. "I couldn't agree more. And, I would love to have some strawberry shortcake, but only if you and Micah join us to eat it. We keep telling you that you're family. Are you ever going to act like it?"

"I do act like it," May retorted. "I tell all of you what to do to every day, but the kitchen is my place. I'll join you tonight, though," she relented. "This is cause for celebration."

Marietta laughed again, but she had to work to push down the twinge of anxiety. She and Jeremy really didn't know what they would do if their baby were to be born black, or even obviously mixed-race. She couldn't imagine raising her child in the South if it was not white, but she also couldn't imagine leaving the life they had created here. Would racism always dictate their decisions?

Six months...

She would have her answer then.

Chapter Twenty-Six

Thomas looked around with a sense of deep satisfaction as he settled in next to the fireplace. Spring had taken a firm grip on the South, but a cold front that had swept through earlier that day had dropped the temperatures enough to make the crackling flames in the fireplace a welcome addition. Abby had talked Willard and Grace into spending the night with them, so the parlor was full. He settled back with his cup of hot tea, anticipating what the rest of the evening would bring.

Abby was the first to break the contented silence. "I'm almost afraid to bring up the issue of politics, but I find that with a journalist in the house I am quite incapable of leaving it alone. Harold, what can you tell us about the latest happenings in Washington that we might not yet be aware of?"

Harold took a sip of his tea and looked thoughtful. "Are you familiar with the Fourth Reconstruction Act?"

Abby shook her head, but before Harold could respond, Willard cleared his throat. "I find I am comfortable enough with all of you now to declare my complete ignorance. I've done nothing but work and look for jobs ever since I got out of Rock Island Prison. I'm aware that blacks have gained the right to vote, but I know little more than that."

"Black *men*," Grace said disdainfully.

Abby smiled. "You have my full agreement, Grace. It is quite wrong that women don't yet have the vote." She reached out and squeezed her hand. "We'll talk more about that later, but why don't we first enlighten you and Willard on what is happening in our country with Reconstruction."

Grace inclined her head graciously.

Harold looked at Thomas. "Would you like to give our guests a brief history lesson?"

"Of course," Thomas responded. "Even though the war ended, many Americans were starkly aware that the country was not being adequately reconstructed. Slavery had ended, but freedom had not been adequately defined for black Americans. Many also realized that Reconstruction under President Johnson created neither healing nor justice." He thought about the riots that had led to that vivid realization, but decided to keep his explanation simple. "There were things that happened in that first year after the war that resulted in a majority of Republicans being elected to Congress. They had the power to make things change, so they pushed for the passage of the Reconstruction Acts. Our president vetoed all of them, but he was overruled in Congress every time."

"That must have made him very angry," Grace said.

"He made decisions that put himself in that position," Thomas stated. "He seemed to have forgotten that his job was to serve *America*, not himself. When he realized he couldn't veto the Reconstruction Acts, he sought to lessen their effect through the Attorney General. Congress responded with the Third Reconstruction Act. Supreme power has been given to the five Union generals overseeing the Southern military districts. They have been given the power to remove any official, elected or otherwise, from office if they believe the person is impeding the process of Reconstruction."

Willard frowned. "So once again the North is imposing their will on the South."

Thomas eyed him. "Do you have a problem with that?"

"Not anymore," Willard replied quickly, "but none of this is going to change how too much of the South views blacks. It seems like it will most likely only make them angrier." He shook his head. "I don't think there is an easy answer to any of this, but President Johnson seems to have made it worse."

"He did a lot of damage before Congress was able to fight back," Thomas agreed, "but progress is being made. The first thing the Reconstruction Acts did was divide the South into five districts governed by military governors, until acceptable state constitutions could be written and approved by Congress." He paused for a moment to catch his breath. "All males, regardless of race, except for former Confederate leaders, are now permitted to vote for the delegates and participate in the constitutional conventions that are forming our new state governments."

"The Virginia convention is going on right now," Jeremy added, "though our delegates will not be allowed to return to Congress because they refused to ratify the Fourteenth Amendment in January of this year."

"Why didn't they?" Willard asked.

"Because they don't believe blacks should have any rights, and certainly not the right to vote," Grace said.

Thomas nodded. "I'm sorry to say she is right. So far, the Fourteenth Amendment has gone before Texas, Georgia, North Carolina and South Carolina. All of them have failed to ratify it."

Willard leaned forward. "Doesn't that mean all those states can't be readmitted to the Union?"

"That's right," Thomas agreed. "They will remain under military governance until they do."

"That seems rather short-sighted," Willard observed. "They have lost all voice in the government."

"It was the same pig-headedness that produced the Civil War," Harold said ruefully.

Thomas nodded heavily. "I wish I could dispute that fact, but I can't. I discover every day that men's inability to accept equality of all people creates situations I would give almost anything to alter. Even after losing almost twenty percent of all Southern men to the war, there are too many still unwilling to accept that our country has been forever changed. Slavery has been abolished, and it is necessary to accept equal rights for all."

"Including women," Marietta said firmly.

"Yes, including women," Thomas agreed in just as firm a voice.

Abby looked back at Harold. "You said there is now a Fourth Reconstruction Act?"

Harold nodded. "Yes. The main reason it has been so hard to get the Fourteenth Amendment passed in the South is because, as the law stands now, it takes a majority of *registered* voters to ratify the amendment and the constitutions. White registered voters have boycotted elections to keep that from happening." He shrugged. "They are only delaying the inevitable. The Fourth Reconstruction Act changed the law to say only a majority of *actual* voters are necessary. It won't matter if elections are boycotted, except the boycotters will cease to have a voice."

Thomas nodded but remained silent.

"Are you all right, dear?" Abby asked perceptively.

"Yes, but Willard is right that none of this will change how the South views the former slaves. I have to wonder how long this can last. Will Reconstruction truly change things, or will it simply delay new tactics by bigoted whites to enforce their will and beliefs?"

A deep silence fell on the room as all of them tried to look forward into a murky future.

*****

Amber took deep breaths of the early spring air. She was sure she would never get tired of waking before the sun to experience the magic of early mornings. Now that school had started again, she had to make the most of them. She didn't mind school, but she certainly minded spending less hours with the horses.

Susan met her at the door to the barn, a finger held to her lips.

Amber instantly knew why. "Who?" she whispered.

"Sandy Lady and Emerald," Susan whispered back. "I caught them going into labor so I brought them into the stalls in order to keep an eye on them. Horses have been giving birth on their own for a long time, but I feel better if I can check for trouble."

Amber ran quietly to peer over the closest stall door. Sandy Lady, a light chestnut mare, stared back at her, obviously distressed. "It's all right, girl," Amber murmured soothingly, hoping she was right. This would be Sandy Lady's first foal, and the mare was already a little high-strung. They had expected her foal to be born at least two weeks ago, but the mare seemed to have resisted the normal process. It was not uncommon for first-time mothers. "You just go ahead and do things your way," Amber said softly. A quick look confirmed the stall was lined with a thick layer of straw.

"She's doing well," Susan said from behind her. "I don't think it will be long."

Amber's practiced eye determined the same thing. At only eleven, she had seen dozens of births in the last two years. Robert had taught her that it was best not to interfere, but instead let nature take its course. Sandy Lady would probably deliver her foal, clean it and begin bonding without anyone's help.

Amber stepped back and ran over to stare into Emerald's stall. As she looked in, Emerald, a striking coal black mare, dipped her head in acknowledgement and lowered herself to the straw mattress waiting for her. Susan had already wrapped her tail to keep the long strands of hair out of the way.

Amber waved Susan over. "It's time," she whispered when Susan stepped up beside her.

Susan nodded, a broad smile on her face. "I'm eager to see Emerald's foal," she whispered. "I am certain she will be magnificent."

Amber knew she was right. Robert had bought Emerald just weeks before he had been killed, certain she would produce wonderful offspring. Amber caught her breath, wishing with all her heart that Robert was there to witness the birth. She brushed impatiently at the tears filling her eyes. Her mama had told her it was all right to still cry about Robert, but she didn't want to miss the birth. Susan put a comforting arm around her shoulders. Amber allowed herself to lean into her strength, but didn't take her eyes off Emerald.

"Her water broke," Susan whispered.

Amber shivered, wishing the sun would rise a little more. She could see inside the stall, but just barely. "Look! The sac is coming out. Ohhhhh...it just broke open."

"The fluid lubricates the birth canal and the foal," Susan said quietly.

Emerald lifted her head one more time and then lay flat before she began to push. Amber flinched when the sweating mare began to moan, but her mama had explained it was a tough thing to push seventy to ninety pounds of foal through the birth canal. There was plenty of reason to moan.

"Here it comes!" Susan whispered excitedly.

Amber strained her eyes and finally saw the white sac emerge. She breathed a sigh of relief when she saw the foal's front hooves, one slightly ahead of the other. It was not going to be a breech birth. Moments later she saw the nose and head appear. Amber held her breath as the foal slid further out and then stopped.

"It's okay," Susan whispered. "The most difficult part of the delivery is the head and shoulders. Emerald is resting. If she doesn't start pushing again in a few minutes, I'll help her."

Amber glanced at her in admiration. "You know how to do that?" She had seen Robert help a few of the mares, but she hadn't been certain Susan could do the same.

"I've done it many times," Susan promised, "but I don't think Emerald will need my help."

As if to prove her right, the large mare gave another groan and a very hard push.

Amber laughed softly as the rest of the foal slid from the birth canal, landing quietly on the straw bedding as the sac broke free from its head. "Hello, little one," she whispered.

"Emerald and the foal will rest for a few minutes," Susan said. "I'll go check on Sandy Lady. I'll wave you over when she is ready."

Amber nodded, content to remain exactly where she was. She could feel the wonder of a new life force filling the stall, and she understood the look of loving awe in Emerald's eyes when she looked at her baby before lying back to rest and gather her strength for what would follow. Amber knew the rest period was critical because the umbilical cord was still attached, and still transferring a large, vital amount of blood from Emerald to her baby.

Amber pulled out the pocket watch Robert had given her for this very purpose. It was almost fifteen minutes before Emerald stirred, nosed her foal, and then stood. "Good girl," Amber called quietly. Emerald glanced up briefly as she began to lick her foal, cleaning away the rest of the sac. Amber knew it could take anywhere from one to six hours for the foal to stand and begin nursing.

"Amber!" Susan called.

Amber tensed, alerted by something in Susan's voice. She dashed over to the stall door just as Susan opened it and slipped in. "I'm here."

"Good. Sandy Lady is in trouble. It's been too long since the front feet appeared. She is going to need help."

Where Emerald's groaning had seemed normal, Sandy Lady sounded distressed.

"Sandy Lady loves you," Susan said calmly. "I want you to hold her head and talk to her."

"What are we going to do?" Amber asked anxiously, her fear making her forget all Robert had taught her about assisting in births.

Susan reached outside the stall for the lead rope hanging from its hook. "The first thing we're going to do is make her stand up," she said evenly. "Most times this will make the foal slide back into Sandy Lady's womb. I can turn it more easily in there. That should help it come out quicker. You will need to help Sandy Lady stand up."

Amber nodded, grabbed the lead rope and snapped it onto the leather halter. She rubbed Sandy Lady's muzzle before she stood and gave a gentle tug. "Get up," she ordered. The laboring mare stared at her but didn't move. "Get up," Amber commanded, pulling harder on the lead rope. "You can't stay there, Sandy Lady." She suddenly remembered Robert having to do the same thing. Now was not the time to be gentle. Both the mare and foal's life could depend on getting the mare to stand. Amber stepped back, gave a sharp tug, and made her voice stern. "Up, Sandy Lady! Up!"

Sandy Lady's eyes widened, but she folded her front legs obediently and struggled to stand. Amber wanted to cry at the distress in her eyes, but now was not the time to get soft. "Up!" she commanded. "Stand up!" Out of the corner of her eye, she saw Susan roll up the sleeve on her right arm and apply a thick lubricant.

Sandy Lady groaned again as she pushed her way to her feet, swaying slightly when she was upright. Amber wanted to cry with relief, but she simply moved forward to hold the mare's head tightly. "Good girl," she murmured. "Good girl."

Amber watched as Susan slipped her arm into the birth canal. Susan's face tightened with intensity as she worked. Amber tried to imagine what she was feeling inside, praying the day would come when she would be big enough, strong enough, and smart enough to do the same thing.

Susan must have sensed her desire to learn. "I found the protruding leg. I'm following it down to the foal's chest." She paused for a moment. "There is the other leg. And there is the head," she said softly.

Without warning, Sandy Lady began to lay down again. "Sandy Lady! No!" Amber cried.

"It's all right," Susan said. "I believe I've repositioned it enough to make the birth easier." She stepped back just as Sandy Lady collapsed onto the straw and began to push again.

Amber continued to stroke her head and murmur encouraging words, but her eyes never left the foal. "Come on," she whispered. "Come on, little one."

Both the front feet had once more broken free of the birth canal. The nose followed a moment later, but then Sandy Lady groaned loudly and lay still again, her breathing labored.

Susan reached for the towel she had tossed over her shoulder and grasped the front two hooves. "I'm forcing the foal's front feet down toward Sandy Lady's hind hooves in order to rotate the baby's head through the birth canal," she explained as she began to pull gently.

Amber held her breath and prayed. She wanted to cheer when she saw the head and shoulders appear. "Good girl, Sandy Lady. You're doing great!"

"Once the head and shoulders have passed through the birth canal, you pull straight out along the line of the mare's spine," Susan said, demonstrating as she talked. "Sandy Lady is tired, so I'm going to keep helping her." She waited until the hips appeared, and then once again pulled down toward the mare's hooves. "Doing this helps rotate the foal's hips so they can pass through the birth canal."

Amber sucked in a harsh breath of relief when the foal slipped out onto the straw.

Susan smiled and stood. "We're going to leave them right there. Sandy Lady will stand when she is ready. The foal is fine."

"You're sure?" Amber asked anxiously. "The baby isn't moving either."

"The birth was tiring for both of them," Susan said reassuringly. "The foal is breathing normally. If she's not at least looking around in thirty minutes, there will be reason for concern. But," she added quickly, "I already know there is not a reason. This little one is just fine." She nodded her head toward the other stall. "Let's check on Emerald."

Amber cast one last concerned look at Sandy Lady and her foal before she followed Susan. A huge smile bloomed on her face when she looked over the door. "She's sitting up!"

"*He's* sitting up," Susan corrected with a matching smile. "And he is just as beautiful as I thought he would be."

Amber watched as the colt gazed at them for a moment and then, as if inspired by their presence, he folded one front leg under him, and lurched forward slightly. "He's going to stand!" The experience never lost its thrill for her.

The colt pulled one front leg under him, and then the other. He paused for a moment as if questioning whether this was a wise move.

"You can't eat until you get up," Susan murmured. "You can do it."

The foal glanced up at his mother and lurched forward again, pulling his hind legs behind him, and then pushed. He started upward, but teetered precariously. His front legs splayed out to the sides, sending him crashing to the floor again. He shook his head and stared around, obviously startled to find himself still on the ground.

"You can do it," Amber called as she giggled. "The first try is always the hardest."

The colt waited for several moments and then pulled his splayed front legs back into his chest before launching forward again. This time, he gained his feet. He swayed unsteadily but remained upright. He looked completely surprised to discover he was standing now.

"You did it!" Amber cheered quietly. She didn't want to bother Sandy Lady with loud noises.

"Good job!" Susan murmured. "What should we call him?"

Amber was ready. "Eclipse's Ace of Spades."

Susan turned and gazed down at her. "That was quick."

Amber shook her head. "Robert and I named him last spring. Well, if he was a boy...and if he came out black," she added. "Robert wanted him to have a real special name."

"Eclipse's Ace of Spades it is," Susan replied with a delighted smile. "It's the perfect name for him. He's going to be as big as his daddy, and just as black as his mama."

Amber grinned as the colt tottered over to where Emerald was waiting patiently. He leaned against his mama's side for a moment and then began nudging her in search of the meal he knew awaited him. It took only a few minutes before he was latched securely to her teat.

"That's number ten," Susan said contentedly as she watched the pair. "All the mothers should have their babies within the next few weeks. The new foals will make it easier to see the yearlings go."

Amber sighed. "Not that I can tell. I know we are breeding horses for sale, but every time one of them leaves, they seem to take a part of me with them." She watched the colt for a few minutes longer and then peered up at Susan. "Does it ever get easier?"

Susan considered the question. "Not for me," she admitted with a shake of her head. "I wish I could tell you it gets easier, but I feel like I'm losing a part of me every time one leaves, too. I suppose there are people who raise horses just for the money, but I do it out of love. And I fall in love with each one that is born. It never gets easy to see them leave."

Amber nodded thoughtfully. "I'm glad you feel the same way I do." She gazed at the colt suckling his dam. "Anthony is coming today for the yearlings. Did he find real good homes for them?" She had been pushing thoughts of it aside, but since his arrival was only hours away, she could no longer pretend it wasn't going to happen.

"He did," Susan assured her. "He goes to inspect each horse operation before he agrees to represent them as their buyer. His standards are quite high. He loves horses as much as we do."

Amber felt a little better, but she still knew how much it would hurt when the yearlings she had worked with on a daily basis for a year were led away to where she would never see them again. All My Heart took that moment to send a ringing call from the pasture. Her sadness disappeared instantly. "At least I'll never have to say good-bye to All My Heart," she said. When she glanced at Sandy Lady's stall, Susan interpreted her thoughts.

"I'll let you know if I need your help with Sandy Lady. You go on out there with your filly. You have to leave for school soon anyway."

Amber gave Susan a quick hug and then dashed out the door. The sun was hovering over the top of the trees, its rays dancing off the dogwood blooms lacing the woods. The air still held a faint chill, but she knew the sun would chase it away before much longer. She loved spring's soft air. All My Heart was waiting for her outside the barn door that led into the pasture, dancing lightly in place. As soon as Amber appeared, the filly dipped her nose to begin nuzzling her body. Amber laughed softly, standing still as her filly carefully inspected each pocket, finally stopping at the one on the back of her breeches. All My Heart snorted and pawed the ground one time, eying her expectantly.

"Found them again, girl," Amber crooned, reaching in to pull out the carrots All My Heart had discovered. She rested her head against her filly's neck, listening to her crunch the carrots as the sun cut through the low-lying mist over the pastures. She watched the yearlings grazing and playing, knowing they had no idea their whole world was about to change. "You'll miss your friends," she murmured, "but now you're going to be the leader of the pack around here. I expect you to set a good example for all the new foals," she said.

All My Heart bobbed her head obediently and then stepped back to rest it on Amber's shoulder. Amber sighed and stroked the velvety nose, hoping she would never have to leave Cromwell Plantation. She knew there was a big world out there, but everything she wanted, and everything that was important to her, was right here.

"That was a mighty big sigh for a little girl."

Amber gazed up at Miles as he emerged from the stable with a huge yawn. "Did you miss Cromwell Plantation after you escaped before the war, Miles?"

"Every day," he assured her.

"Are you glad you're back?"

"Every day," he repeated.

"Do you ever want to leave again?"

Miles peered at her closely. "No. What is going on in that head of yours?"

Amber shrugged. "Everyone seems to be leaving because they're looking for something else. Maybe something more," she said thoughtfully. "I know Moses and Rose want to make a difference for our people, and

Carrie believes she is supposed to be a doctor. Is it wrong that I don't want to leave? That I just want to stay here and be with the horses?" Now that she had finally had the courage to ask, her emotions swelled within her chest. "Am I bad because I don't want to leave to do things for our people, Miles?" She took a deep breath. "Would Robert be disappointed in me?" she whispered, swallowing back the tears that wanted to come.

Miles stepped closer and laid a wrinkled, leathery hand on her shoulder. "Not all people are the same, Amber. Rose...That woman got a gift for teaching. Moses...He got a gift for speaking and leading. Carrie...She got a gift of healing." He paused. "Each of them gifts mean they gots to leave the plantation to go to school or to use that gift. But you, Amber? You got the gift for horses. You don't got to go nowhere to use that gift but right here."

Amber opened her mouth to interrupt him, but Miles held up his hand.

"Don't say it," he commanded. "I already know what be going on in that head of yours. It ain't up to any of us what gift we got. But it *is* up to us what we do with it. How good we use it. You just got to be the best horsewoman you can be. You got an awesome gift, sho 'nuff. Your gift as special as any other gift, Amber. As long as you use that gift the best you can, you'll be doing exactly what you supposed to be doing for our people," he said. "There be plenty of people who don't think a little black girl can do what you do with horses. Every time someone gets a Cromwell horse they's gonna know just what a little black girl can do, and then they gonna think twice before they say we can't do what we do. As you get older, you just gonna get better and better. That means more people will pay attention."

Amber pondered his words. "I reckon that sounds right," she said, a glad relief blooming in her heart. "I don't ever want to leave here," she confided. "There can't be another place in the world as beautiful as Cromwell Plantation."

"That be right, for sho," Miles agreed. "I'm real glad I escaped so that I could learn how to live free on my own. Leaving here be one of the happiest days of my life. The next happiest be the day I came back home."

Amber wrapped her arms around him in a desperate hug. "You've got to live a long time, Miles."

"I reckon I will," Miles chuckled. "Course, I done lived a long time already."

"I mean it," Amber said fiercely. "I love you, Miles. I don't want to lose you, too." She was surprised when tears clogged her throat once more. She knew she was crying about Robert again, but it didn't lessen her love for Miles.

Miles knelt down and wrapped her in a warm embrace. "I ain't going anywhere right away, Amber," he said gently. "I still got me some things to teach you." Then he chuckled. "And I reckon you got some things you need to teach me."

Amber couldn't clear the tears from her throat. "You have to promise me you're not going to leave me," she said. "Promise me, Miles."

There was a long moment of silence before Miles pushed her back so he could peer into her eyes. "Can't make you that promise, Amber," he said gravely. "I love you. I can promise you that leaving you won't be my choice, but this country is a real crazy place right now. Ain't no black person alive can make that kind of promise."

Chapter Twenty-Seven

"Welcome to New Mexico, Carrie."

Carrie stared at Captain Marley, jolted from her enjoyment of the beautiful terrain they were riding through. Snow-covered peaks surrounded them, their rugged sides painted with pine trees and bare alders. The stream they were following bubbled and danced its way over boulders and rocks. "Really? We are now in New Mexico?"

"We are," Captain Marley assured her. "Of course, you may be cursing that fact by tomorrow."

Carrie thought through what she had read in the book Felicia had prepared for her. "Raton Pass?"

"Raton Pass."

Carrie nodded, choosing to focus her thoughts on the reality that they had successfully traveled through Kansas and Colorado. The choice had been made weeks ago to follow the Mountain Route rather than the Cimarron Route. Captain Marley had explained to her that dry conditions meant there would not be enough water for the animals along the Cimarron Route. They could have carried barrels of water with them, but if a snowstorm were to have blown in and kept them from going forward, most of the animals would have died of thirst. Combine that with the increased danger of Indian attack along the Cimarron Route, and it had been easy to understand why the captain had decided to take the longer route, despite the one hundred miles it added to their trip.

"Is it really so terrible, Captain Marley?" Carolyn asked.

"Raton Pass has quite a history," Captain Marley responded. "When Mexico opened its borders to trade with the United States in 1821, the Santa Fe Trail was born. The biggest problem, however, was how to cross the Sangre de Cristo Mountains. Early explorers and trappers, as well as the Indians, of course, had discovered the path through the mountains, but taking a covered wagon over it was unthinkable."

"Until William Becknell," Carrie interjected, wondering if Carolyn also saw the twinkle in the captain's eyes. Janie and Melissa were reading and knitting in the back of the wagon.

"That's right," Captain Marley replied, being careful not to meet her eyes. "Becknell was a horse and mule trader who was determined to do business with the Mexicans. He was the first to take a wagon through Raton Pass. He proved it could be done, but there were still many that perished in their attempt. The path is narrow, steep and rocky. Some areas of the pass are so tight that only one wagon can go through at a time. It's not unusual for wooden axles to shred and snap on the rough terrain. When the Cimarron Route was developed, it was easy to believe it was the preferable route."

Carrie had already explained to her team why they were traveling the longer route through Colorado, rather than cutting across the relatively flat grasslands and deserts of Oklahoma. "I understand the Raton Pass was used by General Kearny during the war with Mexico," she said, "and then by the Union Army after Kearny improved the trail by having workers remove rocks and debris."

"That's true," Captain Marley said, beaming with admiration before he winked. "Is that in your book?"

"It's in my book," Carrie agreed, but she decided to let him continue to build the drama for Carolyn.

"The trip over the Raton Pass takes five days," Captain Marley went on. "Our teams will have to work hard to make it up the two thousand-foot elevation gain."

"How many miles is it?" Carolyn asked in a tense voice.

Carrie hid her smile.

"Twenty-seven miles to the top of the pass," Captain Marley replied. "There are times the trail is so narrow that it must be propped up by long poles supported by the mountainside below."

Carolyn's face grew white and her eyes widened. "That must be quite dangerous."

"I'm afraid many wagons and animals have been lost."

"People as well?" Carolyn breathed.

Captain Marley's only response was a tightening of his lips as he nodded his head.

"What a relief," Carolyn said brightly.

Carrie looked at her sharply. "What?"

Captain Marley was staring at Carolyn, as well. "Excuse me?"

Carolyn grinned, letting go of her distressed expression. She tossed Carrie a look of haughty disdain. "Do you think you are the only one on this wagon train who knows how to read?"

Carrie laughed. "The book?"

"The book," Carolyn agreed. "It seems it was quite a wise choice for someone to turn the trail over Raton Pass into a toll road when the war ended. It must have taken so much effort to make the trail passible in all seasons. I can only imagine the grading, blasting and clearing that has been done in the last two years. And the bridge building," she cooed. "What a wonderful thing they have done, Captain!"

Captain Marley chuckled. "So you knew all along..."

Carolyn nodded serenely. "You were so caught up in your storytelling that it seemed a shame to cut you off."

Captain Marley chuckled again. "How could I know you had the secret weapon of a thirteen-year-old who was going to give you the information to ruin my fun?"

"Is the toll road profitable?" Carrie asked.

"What does your book tell you?"

"It doesn't cover that," Carrie admitted with a smile. "It seems to me, thought, that it would be wildly profitable."

"It is," Captain Marley responded. "The only ones who rue its creation are the wagon and wheel repair businesses down in Fort Union at the bottom of the pass because they can no longer count on steady business. Of course, it will only be profitable for a limited time."

"Why is that?" Carolyn asked.

"Because of the train. It won't be long before the train follows the same route as the trail. Wagon trains will become obsolete, and the toll road will not be used very much."

Carrie felt sadness swell in her. "I know it will be much faster and easier for people to take the train, but I have fallen in love with wagon travel." She was surprised how much she meant it. The long days of quiet and solitude had settled something deep in her soul. She had also realized just how magnificent the western part of the country was. She had fallen in love with the flat plains, the plateaus, the limestone cliffs and the soaring mountains clothed with great forests. The air was crystal clear, and the skies at night were a miracle. She could only imagine how thrilled Felicia would have been to experience the stars the way she had. There were so many times they seemed close enough to pick them out of the sky the way she picked apples at home.

Captain Marley nodded. "I understand how you feel. There is something special about it, but it will surely become a thing of the past. I'm glad I've been able to experience it. My children will only know it through the stories I tell them."

Carrie looked at him thoughtfully. "Our country is changing so fast."

"Most of it for the good," Captain Marley responded.

"I wonder," Carrie mused. "Oh, I know many of the changes are for the good, but I wonder at the price being paid for progress."

"You're thinking of the Navajo."

Carrie shrugged. "I'm thinking of all the Indian tribes who have been pushed out of their homelands because white men believe it is theirs to take. I'm thinking of millions of slaves who had their lives stolen for profit. The blacks... the Irish... the Indians." She'd had time to do a lot of thinking on the trail. "It saddens me how much is lost in the push to gain."

She shook her head, trying to clear her thoughts. It was a beautiful day, and they were finally in New Mexico. She glanced upward at the pass they were riding toward and stiffened at the sight of dark clouds gathering in the distance. "Am I correct that even with a toll road travel across Raton Pass would be dangerous in the snow?" She fought to keep her voice casual but knew she had failed when Carolyn tensed.

"Snow?" Carolyn echoed, following Carrie's eyes.

Captain Marley looked up as well, his eyes turning grim. "We will not attempt to cross Raton Pass in the snow. We'll go as far as I feel we safely can, and then we will wait for a break in the weather. Nothing may come of this," he added. "Clouds can scatter as quickly as they gather, but I need to communicate with my men." He nodded his head graciously. "Thank you, ladies."

Carrie watched him canter off before she turned to Carolyn. "After we get over the pass, I believe it will be easy for the rest of the way."

"*After* we get over the pass," Carolyn repeated dryly. "I believe *after* is the most important word there," she said, but then she shrugged. "I'm not really worried. We've made it this far. A few more challenges will just add to the stories when we get home."

*****

Carrie sighed with contentment as she watched the flames flickering from campfires all around the circle of wagons. Two huge cooking fires had served up bubbling cauldrons of venison stew and steaming biscuits.

"Venison stew," Matthew murmured, leaning back against the wagon wheel, his long legs stretched out in front of him. His red hair curled from beneath his hat. "Did some of the men go hunting today?"

Carrie shook her head. "A Mexican trader came through. He wanted gun powder and bullets. Captain Marley was going to turn him down until he revealed he had two fresh deer. He decided it would be worth the trade to give everyone venison stew while we are crossing the Pass."

"I thought they couldn't trade gun powder and bullets," Melissa replied. "That it was too dangerous."

"They can't trade with Indians," Nathan said. "Mexicans are all right."

"Even though Mexicans have caused so many of the problems here?" Carrie protested. "They have stolen so many Indians to become their slaves. If I were an Indian, I would fight back, too." She shook her head heavily. Despite the brief afternoon snowstorm, it was obvious spring was coming to New Mexico. Once the snow had stopped, a warm front had melted it as quickly as it had fallen. She knew once they came down the other side of the pass, the temperatures would warm substantially. Her thoughts drifted to Bosque Redondo.

"How far are we from the reservation?" Janie asked.

Carrie took comfort in the knowledge that Janie could still read her thoughts. "Two hundred and fifty miles. The blizzard, and taking the Mountain Route, has added almost a month to our trip, but once we are through the pass we should have no trouble making twelve to fifteen miles a day. We will be there by the end of April." She understood the silence that fell on their campsite as they all tried to imagine what they would find. Their world had become the wagon train, but that would all change when they reached their destination.

"Have any of you ever heard of Frank Aubry?" Matthew asked.

Carrie knew he was trying to change the subject and take their minds off Bosque Redondo. Since thinking about the fort holding the Navajo only distressed her, she realized a new topic would be welcome. "No," she answered. "Who is he?"

"Someone with more endurance than I will ever hope to have," Matthew said lightly. "Frank, whose real name was Francois, was a French Canadian guide and trader on the Santa Fe Trail. He went to Santa Fe early in the spring of 1848 to do some trading. American troops had just taken control of the country so business was booming. Frank sold all his stock for over one hundred percent of his original investment."

"Impressive," Randall commented.

Matthew nodded. "Impressive enough to make him want to see if he could repeat it again that year. He decided to return to St. Louis and bring out another load of stock before the cold weather made it impossible."

Carrie shook her head. "What was *impossible* was believing he could get back to St. Louis in time to make it back down the trail again before winter. He could never have gotten back over the Raton Pass then."

"It was only possible if he could get back over the trail and to St. Louis in eight days," Matthew responded.

"It took us two months to get this far," Carolyn objected. "Even without the blizzard, it's not possible to do it that fast."

"Except that he did," Matthew stated quietly.

Carrie leaned forward. "This is going to be a good story."

"It is," Matthew agreed. "Frank Aubry was not a large man, but he had iron nerves, and he didn't understand the meaning of the word 'quit.' Once he had made his plans, he found four other men willing to attempt it with him, and he carefully selected a small herd of horses."

"I think I already feel bad for the horses," Carrie protested. "How in the world could he ask those animals to do what he was proposing?"

Matthew shrugged. "I agree with you, but I'm just telling the story—not riding the horses."

Carrie smiled slightly. "Go on."

"All the men left at the same time, but Frank outrode all of them. He rode his own mare, Nellie, for the first one hundred and fifty miles, only stopping for food and water. He left her with a settler who agreed to care for her, and then jumped on another horse. By the time he reached the Arkansas River crossing in Kansas, about halfway down the trail, he had left everyone behind. He had also worn out his last horse."

"What did he do?" Carolyn asked.

"He left his horse with someone else and kept going on foot," Matthew answered. "The best anyone can figure, he had to walk about twenty miles to reach Mann's Fort."

"When did he sleep?" Melissa demanded.

"He didn't."

Carrie stared at Matthew. "He did all that without sleep?"

"And apparently without much to eat either," Matthew replied. "Once he got to Mann's Fort he was able to get another horse. He didn't eat hardly anything before he hit the trail again. He was almost to the Pawnee Fork crossing when a band of Indians came after him."

"Oh my," Carolyn exclaimed, but then smiled sheepishly. "I already know he got away from them, or you wouldn't be telling this story."

Matthew chuckled. "You're right, but his escape was very narrow. When he plunged down the twenty-foot bank into the Pawnee River, the Indians left him alone, but probably only because they thought the flooded river would finish him off. Somehow, he and his exhausted horse made it across and on into Independence, Missouri."

"In the eight days?" Nathan asked.

"Nope," Matthew answered with a grin. "He made it in five days and sixteen hours."

"Brutal," Randall grumbled.

"Brutal indeed," Matthew agreed. "It is said that when they helped him out of his saddle it was stained with his blood."

"He made it back with his next load?" Carrie was impressed, in spite of how she felt about the horses being pushed so hard.

Matthew shrugged. "I guess so. No one really talks about that part—they were just impressed with his ride."

Janie cocked her head. "Is that where the idea for the Pony Express came from?"

"I don't know," Matthew answered, "but it's certainly possible."

"The Pony Express?" Carolyn asked.

Carrie stared at her. "Were you so absorbed in city medicine that you don't know about the Pony Express?"

"Evidently," Carolyn retorted. "I make no apologies, but I would very much like to fill in that gap of information." She turned to Matthew. "Will you tell me about it?"

"Oh sure," Carrie scoffed. "Ask the one who can't resist spouting how much he knows."

"Jealousy," Matthew said smugly. "Pure jealousy."

"Nonsense," Carrie answered, tossing her long hair back over her shoulder. "I know as much about the Pony Express as you do."

"Do tell," Matthew invited in a dubious voice.

Carrie was relieved that this time she truly did know what she was talking about. "The Pony Express was only in operation from April, 1860 to October, 1861, but I suspect it will always be talked about. As more people moved to the West, it became obvious there needed to be a faster way to get mail to them. The Pony Express ran from St. Joseph, Missouri to Sacramento, California." She paused for better effect. "The men who rode the Pony Express covered eighteen hundred miles in just ten days."

"What?" Carolyn's eyes were wide with disbelief.

"It was quite the operation," Carrie continued. "There were more than one hundred stopping stations, four to five hundred horses, and enough riders and station agents to make it happen. The Pony Express set it up so there was a new horse every ten to fifteen miles, and a fresh rider every seventy-five to one hundred miles. It required seventy-five horses to make a one way trip, at a speed of about ten miles per hour. Weather was a factor, but it was probably Indian attacks that were the scariest part of the rides."

Matthew raised a brow. "I believe you know more than I do."

Carrie grinned. "Felicia gave me a book about the Pony Express last year. She knew I would be fascinated."

"What happened to it?" Melissa asked

"The telegraph happened to it," Carrie said. "The Pony Express was terribly expensive and very difficult to operate, but as long as it served a purpose, it continued. Just ten weeks after the Pony Express began operations, Congress authorized a bill to build a transcontinental telegraph line to connect the Missouri River and the Pacific Coast. It was finished in October, 1861, during the first year of the war. On October twenty-sixth, San Francisco was in direct contact with New York City through the telegraph. The Pony Express was terminated that day, ending another part of history."

Carolyn smiled. "I bet the riders have great stories to tell their children."

"They do," Matthew agreed. "I remember seeing some of the first ads for Pony Express riders. They called for boys under the age of eighteen who were skinny and wiry. They had to be expert riders, and willing to risk death daily. They preferred orphans."

"No," Melissa protested. "That can't be true. They were just boys! They actually said they wanted orphans?"

"It's true," Matthew assured her. "Orphans didn't have to worry about parental permission. Anybody choosing to be a Pony Express rider was always in grave danger. From a business perspective it made sense to hire orphans. It was dangerous, but probably preferable to donning a uniform and fighting the war."

Carrie was struck by the truth of his statement. If she had been a young man with that choice to make, she would most certainly have chosen the dangers of the Pony Express.

"Was sending mail through the Pony Express expensive?" Nathan asked, obviously fascinated.

"Only if you believe five dollars for a half ounce of mail is expensive," Carrie said wryly.

Nathan whistled. "So mail was only sent by businesses and rich people."

"Most of it," Matthew agreed. "Very few people, especially during the war, could afford that kind of cost. There were many businesses that considered it a justified expense."

Silence fell on the group again. The whispers of the past seemed to lift on the flames and echo through the mountains surrounding them. Carrie was content to lie back in silence, feeling the embrace of the mountains. It was cold, but the air no longer carried the harshness of winter. Just like she could at home, she felt the tender promise of spring swirling in the air. She had always been able to predict the final snowfall.

"What happened to Frank Aubry?" Carolyn asked after a long while.

Matthew frowned. "He was killed in a bar fight in 1854."

"Fame couldn't protect him from death," Carrie mused.

"He was a hard man," Matthew replied. "He lived hard, and he died hard."

"I wonder if he was ready," Carrie said quietly. "I wonder if he knew he was dying." She was aware she was no longer talking about Frank Aubry. She was also aware the rest of her team was watching her carefully. She forced a smile. "I'm all right," she assured them.

"I believe Robert knew he was dying," Matthew said evenly. "I believe he was ready, and I believe if he had to make the choice again to save Amber's life, he would do it."

Carrie stiffened. Would Robert have made the choice to save Amber's life if he had known it would mean leaving Carrie and losing their daughter? She knew it was a pointless question that she had no hope of answering, but she couldn't keep it from spinning through her mind. She wondered if she would ever find peace in the not knowing. One thing was certain; she was glad Robert had not had to make that impossible choice. He had simply acted from his best instincts, saving the little girl who had first saved him...The little girl he loved like a daughter.

Janie reached over and grasped Carrie's hand, squeezing it tightly.

Carrie squeezed it back, letting her mind travel over the last year. She could hardly believe that in just a few weeks it would be one year from the day Robert had been murdered. She could never have imagined she would endure the anniversary on a wagon train in New Mexico. For much of that time, she had not been able to imagine enduring at all. Her prayer for death had been constant. Her anger at being alive had almost consumed her. She was able to embrace life a little more now, and with a little less resentment.

"I bet the plantation is beautiful right now," Janie murmured.

Carrie nodded, knowing she was right. The mares would all be delivering their foals. Anthony would have picked up the yearlings. She wondered if he had buyers for the new ones, but it would be months before she would know. She found a strange solace in the enforced separation. She could not keep the plantation out of her mind, but it had little to do with her life now.

"When we get through the pass we should be able to start collecting plant specimens," Carrie said, determined to take the focus away from her. "I've been studying the information Chooli sent. She drew pictures and had Felicia write down what she knew about the plants. I can't wait to get to Bosque Redondo and meet her family, especially her grandfather." She fell silent again, wondering if the old man had made it through another harsh winter.

Chapter Twenty-Eight

Carrie breathed in the soft, fresh air. The sun glimmered across the plains surrounding them, glinting off the mica, and bringing the red rocks to life. She had fallen in love with the sandstone rocks and cliffs that sometimes towered thousands of feet above them. She knew the red and orange colors were caused by the presence of iron oxide that had rusted in the rain. She seldom missed a sunrise or sunset because the already beautiful formations seemed to explode with life and magic as the sun ignited the colors into dancing flames.

Raton Pass was long behind them, and winter had been swallowed by the warmth of a new season. More regular baths in cold streams had lifted all their spirits, and they had been able to shed their heavy winter coats. The nights were still chilly, but that was the reality of the desert year-round; hot days were always followed by cool nights. She found it far more refreshing than the South's constant cloying heat and humidity.

Carrie was standing near the edge of the wagon circle, watching the red rocks fade into less vibrant color as the sun finished its ascent when Captain Marley walked up beside her. "Hello, Captain," Carrie said quietly. She didn't necessarily want company, but she wouldn't dream of being rude.

"We'll be there today," Captain Marley informed her.

"I knew we were close," Carrie answered, suddenly uncertain how she felt about it.

Captain Marley eyed her. "The Santa Fe Trail can become your home," he said perceptively. "Leaving it means you have to re-enter real life again."

"Yes," Carrie murmured, grateful for his understanding. "I'm reminding myself that the whole reason I am on this wagon train is because of the difference we can make at Bosque Redondo."

"And you will," Captain Marley assured her, "but that doesn't change the reality that the reservation is going to be a rude awakening."

Carrie eyed the captain, hearing something in his voice she could not identify. "There is something you're not telling me," she said. "Out with it."

Captain Marley nodded reluctantly. "I sent a group of my men ahead. They arrived with their report this morning."

Carrie cocked a brow when he quit talking. "And?" she prompted.

"It's bad," Captain Marley finally said in a clipped voice. "The Navajo are starving. They have refused to plant crops because they believe the land has rejected them."

Carrie thought about what she had learned from Chooli over the fall. "The army put them on land incapable of producing crops," she retorted. "They have lost every crop since they were forced into Bosque Redondo. Of course they believe the land has rejected them. Are you saying they are not being fed by our government?"

Captain Marley looked as angry as she felt. "There is not enough food, and disease is sweeping through the compound," he growled.

Carrie gritted her teeth, realizing it would do no good to vent her frustration on him. He felt the same way she did. "We're here to do what we can, but what is our country going to do?" she snapped. "Certainly they will not stand by while all these people starve and die!"

"I sent in reports when I returned from my last trip. Others are exposing the situation. I want to do more, but it seems to be all we can do."

Carrie stared at him. "And you think anyone cares? Enough to do something about it?"

"I have to believe that," Captain Marley said. "Look, I understand how you feel, Carrie. I have felt all the same things. If I could set all the Navajo free and send them back to their homeland, I would."

"Would you?" Carrie demanded. "I heard a group of your men talking about the Navajo. They said they should all be sent up to the Indian territory in Oklahoma like the other tribes. They believe all the tribes should be wiped out or taken where they can't impede the progress of white supremacy." Anger rose in her like a fierce tide.

Captain Marley sighed. "Just like all Southerners did not support slavery, neither do all white males support the policies of the United States right now."

Carrie stared at him, unable to refute the truth in his statement. Tears of fury filled her eyes. She struggled for something to say, but came up empty.

"What's really bothering you, Carrie?"

Carrie narrowed her eyes, wishing she had sent him on his way when he first found her. "What?"

"You've been very tense lately. Today seems to be worse than usual. The Navajo problem is enough reason, but something tells me that is not all." Captain Marley paused, his eyes holding hers. "I haven't wanted to pry, but if it will help to talk..."

Carrie took a deep breath. Janie and Matthew had been walking around on eggshells all day. Janie had offered to talk, but she had cut her off quickly. She just wanted the day to end, but obviously she was not handling her feelings very well. Finally, she met his compassionate eyes and made her decision. "My husband, Robert, was murdered one year ago today."

"My God." Captain Marley stared at her. "I knew he had been murdered, but I had no idea when."

"No." Carrie didn't know how to tell him she was trying to run away from the reality. Most days she could keep her mind on other things. As she had drawn closer to the anniversary it had been impossible.

"What happened?"

Carrie realized talking about it might help her through her feelings. Talking with Captain Marley, because he knew nothing of the situation, was the best course open to her. "The Ku Klux Klan attacked my family's plantation last April. They tried to burn our house, but it was too well protected, so they decided to destroy the barn. No one knew a little girl that Robert loved like a daughter was in there." Carrie sighed. "Her name is Amber. She woke up scared and confused during all the shooting and came out to see what was going on. One of the KKK saw her and decided he would kill her."

"A little girl? Why?"

"Amber is black," Carrie said shortly, relieved when she saw nothing but continued horror in the captain's eyes. "When Robert realized the man's intent, he dove forward to shield Amber." Her voice faltered. "The bullet entered his back, puncturing major organs." She took a deep breath and pushed on. "I was out of town in Philadelphia when it happened. When I got back the next day, I was met at the train station with the news that Robert didn't have long to live. I rode out to the plantation immediately." She faltered again as her throat clogged with hot tears. "At the time, I was almost seven months pregnant. My little girl was stillborn minutes after Robert died in my arms."

Silence surrounded them like a cocoon. Carrie understood there were no words in response to her revelation. It's why she usually stayed silent.

"Carrie..." Captain Marley murmured. He reached out and took her hand, and then pulled her into a warm embrace. "I'm sorry. So sorry..."

The sympathy, stopping short of pity, was Carrie's undoing. She collapsed into his arms, allowing deep sobs to wrack her body. They poured forth from her in unending waves of grief. It felt as if a year had not passed—that Robert had just died in her arms. She could feel his body, hear his tortured voice, see the searing regret in his eyes right before he closed them for the last time.

Captain Marley held her, letting her cry. When the tears finally abated, she found she could breathe again. When she was confident she could stand on her own, Carrie stepped back and wiped the tears from her face. "Thank you," she murmured. "I believe I will survive now."

"I wish I knew more to say."

"There is nothing to say," Carrie assured him. "You handled it perfectly." She couldn't help but smile at the relieved look in his eyes. "I don't break down very much anymore."

"I won't pretend I understand what you are feeling, because I have not gone through what you have. It's easy, though, to *imagine* how I would feel. My whole world would be shattered if something happened to my wife and one of my children. They are my reason for living. I am quite certain I would not handle it as well as you have."

Carrie smiled slightly. "I was a complete disaster for the first three months, but I'm finding my way back to the land of the living. I know that is what Robert would want." She didn't feel it necessary to reveal that Robert had sent her back when she had been so close to death. "Coming on the wagon train has helped. Being able to ride Celeste through such wonderful country has healed my heart so much."

"I'm glad," Captain Marley replied, but there was uncertainty in his voice.

Carrie could see the questions in his eyes. "Go ahead," she invited. "What do you want to know?"

"I've heard bits about the Ku Klux Klan. Are they as bad as I hear?"

"Worse," Carrie said, grateful she could talk about something other than her loss. "But it's not only the KKK. There are many other vigilante groups in the South who are determined to keep blacks from having any rights. They are killing both whites and blacks to achieve their agenda."

"But the South is under military control," Captain Marley protested.

Carrie raised a brow. "So is the West, but it seems like the United States is having quite a challenge handling the Indians," she pointed out.

"It's a huge territory," Captain Marley argued.

"So is the South," Carrie reminded him. "The bigger cities are easier to control, but the rural areas are almost impossible. There are not enough troops in the United States to protect all the blacks."

"So we won the war, but we haven't stopped the problem."

Carrie understood his bitter tone. "It's easier to win a battle than it is to change how people think or believe. The South conceded defeat in the war, but they most certainly have not conceded defeat in their belief that they are far superior to blacks. They will do everything they can to make sure blacks are denied their rights."

"They will lose," Captain Marley said flatly.

"Will they?" Carrie asked.

Captain Marley was the one to raise a brow now. "You don't believe that?"

"I want to," Carrie replied, "but it is going to take a very long time for attitudes and beliefs to change in the South. I am afraid I doubt the determination of our government to provide protection for blacks for as long as that takes."

Captain Marley remained thoughtful. "I hope you are wrong," he finally said.

"I do, too," Carrie answered, but there was no confidence in her voice.

*****

Carrie bit back nausea as the wagon train rolled into Bosque Redondo. She knew she was staring at almost six thousand acres of barren fields stretching for miles down the Pecos River. There were no trees of any kind to block the winds blowing across the unforgiving land, stirring up dirt and swirling dust. The buildings for the military were cared for, but the rest of the reservation was horrifying. Endless numbers of small rustic huts made of mud adobe, covered with stick roofing, were perched in crowded clusters as far as she could see. Stark poverty shouted at her from every direction.

But it was the people...

Hollow-eyed Navajos stared back at her. Their gaunt frames were topped by faces pinched with hunger and sickness, but it was the total despair that ripped at her soul. She didn't know that she had ever seen such hopelessness in a face. She had seen sickness and hunger during the war, but she had never seen someone who looked like their very life-force had been carved from their body and souls. She wondered how in the world her small team could make any difference in the face of such massive need.

"Dear God..." Janie whispered in a shocked voice.

"There is no excuse for this," Matthew snapped angrily. "Every death that has occurred here is the fault of our government. The despair of every person rests solely on the shoulders of the United States."

Carrie nodded, finding a morsel of solace in the fact that Matthew would bring it to light in his articles. She knew, though, that many of the people staring at them would not make it until the wagon train took her team back east at the end of summer. Would Matthew's articles be anything more than a memorial of the destruction of a once proud people? She glanced at Carolyn, Melissa, Randall and Nathan. All of them were staring at the Navajo with sickened, compassionate eyes.

"We will do all we can," Carrie said firmly, hearing a note of desperation in her voice. She straightened on the seat and lifted her head. "Just like during the war, there will be many we can't help, but we will save all we can."

"At least they will know there are white people who care," Melissa murmured, her eyes wide and pained. "What they must think of us..."

Captain Marley rode up. "We will take you to the hospital first, and then we'll get you settled in your quarters."

Carrie had another plan, but now was not the time to reveal it. "Are you as horrified as we are?" she demanded.

"Yes," Captain Marley said curtly.

Carrie saw the pained agony in his eyes and knew he was telling the truth. "Don't some of your men speak Navajo?"

"Yes. I have two soldiers who were here from the beginning. They learned how to speak Navajo for translation purposes."

"May I speak with one of them, please?" Carrie asked, wondering how difficult it would be to find Chooli's parents and grandparents. Were they even still alive?

Captain Marley nodded and rode off. He returned in a few minutes with one of the soldiers. "This is Private Todd Patterson."

"Hello, Private," Carrie said, favoring him with a brilliant smile. "I'm hoping you will be able to assist me."

"I'll do my best, but only if you call me Todd."

Carrie liked the open friendliness in the soldier's blue eyes. She had seen the stocky young man with long blond hair and broad shoulders around the wagon train, but they had not spoken before. "Of course," she agreed. "I am trying to find some people here." She knew how difficult it might be to locate Chooli's family in the midst of nine thousand Indians. Did they even keep record of everyone who was here?

Todd nodded but looked doubtful. "I'll do my best, Mrs. Borden."

"Carrie. If I'm to call you Todd, then we should all dispense with formalities. It seems there are issues here to be far more concerned about."

"I agree," Todd replied. "I don't know if I can help you, but I'll do my best. The military knows how *many* people are here, but I'm certain they know the identities of only a few. How do you know someone here at Bosque Redondo?"

Carrie told him briefly about Chooli, leaving out the part about Franklin disappearing with her and two horses in the middle of the night. She also left out their names. Todd narrowed his eyes, obviously knowing there was more to the story than she was revealing, but he just nodded again. "I don't know the people I am looking for," Carrie finished, "but I do have a letter the woman wrote for when I find them. It is in Navajo."

Todd still looked doubtful, but there was another expression in his eyes she couldn't read. "Do you know her family's names?"

Carrie handed him the letter. "Since I don't speak Navajo, I'm sure I will only slaughter the pronunciation of their names." She realized she was at least going to have to identify Chooli if there was going to be any hope of finding her family. There was no reason to mention Franklin. "I do know Chooli's grandfather is a medicine man."

Todd brightened. "That will certainly make it easier. There are not many medicine men, and they are well known throughout the Navajo Nation." He took the letter she handed him and read it carefully.

Carrie saw his eyes widen slightly as he read, but he didn't look at her.

Todd finished the letter, and then looked at Carrie. "Chooli thinks a lot of you."

Carrie smiled. "And I think a lot of her. We've become good friends." Chooli had not told her what was in the letter; just assured her that her family would welcome her. She wondered if Chooli was enjoying her first spring in the South, or if she was still wracked with homesickness.

"She and Franklin are doing well?"

Carrie stiffened. She had been very careful not to say Franklin's name. She realized Chooli could have talked about him in the letter, but Carrie hadn't noticed his name among the Navajo letters and words. She searched for a response that would not jeopardize their safety. Desertion from the military was not taken lightly.

Todd chuckled. "You can relax. Franklin is a friend. I was the one who told him that if he wanted Chooli and their baby to live, he should disappear. I figured out who you were talking about when you told me the story, but I wasn't going to say anything until I read the letter Chooli wrote. If she says you are all right, then you are all right."

Carrie laughed with relief. "Thank you."

"So, Franklin is doing well?"

Carrie hesitated. She wanted to trust Todd, and her instincts told her she could, but she didn't want to do anything that would put Franklin in jeopardy.

Todd nodded. "You're right to be careful, but Franklin was my friend. I suppose there are people who would like to haul him back into the Buffalo Soldiers, but I am not one of them."

Carrie glanced around and realized there was no one but her team who could hear their conversation. "Franklin is doing well," she confirmed with a smile. "He is managing a tobacco plantation." She chose not to mention it was her family home.

"I'm glad to hear it," Todd said warmly.

Carrie's liking for the soldier grew. It was obvious he was aware she wasn't telling him everything. It was just as obvious that he didn't care. "Chooli had her baby," she added. "Ajei is beautiful."

"My Heart," Todd said. "It's the perfect name for their child. I'm so glad they made it before Chooli gave birth. I knew they would be better off gone from Bosque Redondo, but it was a risk."

Carrie grinned. "I delivered Ajei the night they arrived."

Todd whistled, but turned all-business again when another soldier rode up with a message from Captain Marley. He listened carefully and waited for the soldier to ride off before turning back to Carrie. "I have to go, but I will do everything I can to find Chooli's family. Now that I know Chooli wants you to meet them, it won't be hard. I never knew them before, but I know what part of the reservation to look in. Go ahead and inspect the hospital and get settled. I believe I can take you to them tonight."

Carrie grinned. "Excellent!" As Todd rode off, her attention was caught by a long adobe building that was part of the military compound.

"That's the hospital," Matthew said. "I've been going over the map of Bosque Redondo the captain gave me."

Carrie examined it as they drew closer, impressed with the size. Captain Marley rode up before she could comment.

"That is the hospital," he said.

Carrie stared at it and thought of all the ill, starving people she had seen coming into the compound. "It looks empty. How is that possible? There are nine thousand Indians here!"

Captain Marley scowled. "First of all, there are no longer nine thousand Navajo here. Over a thousand of them have disappeared."

"Disappeared?" Matthew echoed.

Captain Marley's lips tightened. "It would be more accurate to say they left. Groups of several hundred at a time slip away during the night."

"Is the military going after them?" Carolyn asked.

"Not at this point. There are not enough troops."

Carrie found herself glad for the ones who had escaped, but remembering everything Chooli had told her, she wondered if they could possibly make it back to their homeland, and what they would discover when they arrived. Were they leaving one form of starvation only to encounter another? Rage simmered in her over the Navajos' treatment, but she decided to focus on the immediate need. "Why are they not coming to the hospital?"

Captain Marley scowled again. "Syphilis."

Carrie shook her head in disbelief. "A sexually transmitted disease? I don't understand how that has closed the hospital." She understood Captain Marley's surprised look. Though he was more open-minded than most men she knew, it was still considered highly unusual for a woman to know about, much less talk about, sexual diseases. "Pretending sexual diseases don't exist helps no one," she said, her patience growing thin.

"Of course," Captain Marley replied, his surprise giving way to renewed admiration. "The Navajo are used to living scattered throughout their homeland in small groups of a hundred or so. Evidently, putting thousands of them together has unleashed... sexual activity."

Carrie bit back her smile as he produced the information with a very uncomfortable expression on his face. "I still fail to see how that has closed the hospital. It would seem to me that it would make the hospital that much more imperative."

"The hospital became overwhelmed," Captain Marley explained. "Syphilis is not the only issue. They have had mumps ravage Bosque Redondo, but even worse has been the ongoing problem of malaria. There are not many cases right now, but that will change very soon."

"Malaria?" Nathan asked in shocked voice.

Carrie looked toward the river and understood instantly. Right now it was running freely because of snowmelt in the mountains, but it was neither large nor deep. "The Pecos River becomes stagnant in the summer," she observed, "and becomes a haven for mosquitoes."

"Producing malaria, and also dysentery," Nathan finished for her. "And no one deemed it important to know whether the river would run freely year-round before they put nine thousand Navajo here?" His voice was tight with disbelief.

"They were told," Captain Marley responded grimly. "There was a commission that made it quite clear this was a very poor location for a reservation, but General Carleton was determined this was the best place to put it. There was no reasoning with him."

"And so thousands of Navajo are ill and dying," Carrie snapped. She shook her head and took a deep breath, knowing anger would serve no purpose. She had seen the repercussions of male pride throughout the entire war.

"Yes," Captain Marley said. He took a deep breath. "General Carleton decided that the most important thing was to keep the syphilis from spreading. It didn't really matter whether it was being transmitted from Indian to soldier, or vice versa. The soldiers had to stay in good health because they are needed to maintain the peace of the territory."

Carrie stared at him, quickly grasping the situation. "So he decided to isolate the Indians."

Carolyn gasped. "Isolate them?" Understanding dawned on her face. "So the Indians aren't *allowed* to use this hospital?"

"That was General Carleton's solution," Captain Marley agreed. "Two and a half years ago, the Indians were banned from this hospital, and given a small building away from the military compound."

Suddenly, everything Chooli had told Carrie came back to her. It all made sense now. "They were moved to a building next to the Cebolleta Navajos," she said. "They are sworn enemies."

"Felicia?" Captain Marley guessed. "Is that in the book?"

"No." Carrie's mind was spinning. "Chooli told me about it. The Cebolleta Navajo are reviled by the rest of the tribe because they betrayed their people. Which means the rest of the Navajo won't use that hospital because of the proximity. They have been left with nothing." She kept remembering her conversations with Chooli. "They won't go to the hospital, so they are relying completely on the medicine men, who really have no knowledge of how to treat diseases they have never seen."

"Right again," Captain Marley answered.

"Do the medicine men help them?" Randall asked. "Or are they just allowed to die?"

"The Navajo *believe* the medicine men can help," Carrie answered. "Perhaps that is part of it. The Navajo believe that all illnesses are caused supernaturally. They don't take germs or spreading disease through contact into account. Any treatment must be directed toward the cause of the disease, not the disease itself. The medicine man rituals are meant to put everything back in balance so the person can heal."

"Does it work?" Melissa asked.

"Obviously not," Captain Marley snapped.

Carrie's anger was immediate. "How can you say that? The Navajo was the most powerful and wealthy tribe in this area until our government set out to destroy them. They were never exposed to syphilis, malaria, dysentery or the mumps. I hardly think they would have survived for this long if the medicine men were not effective."

"You're right," Captain Marley conceded. "But what about now?"

Carrie sighed. "It's not working," she admitted. "People are dying."

Janie slapped her hand against the side of the wagon in frustration. "So what are we going to do? If the Navajo won't come to either hospital, how are we supposed to help them?"

Carrie was asking herself the same question. She knew their only chance lay with the letter Chooli had written. "We pray Todd can find Chooli's family. I'm hoping her letter will make them trust us."

Matthew looked skeptical. "Do you think the medicine men will let us treat their people?"

"That depends on us," Carrie said. Now that she was here, staring at the horrors all around her, she realized how valuable her conversations with Chooli had been. "If we come in here convinced our way is the only way, they won't let us help them. We have to respect and appreciate their culture."

"Even if their people are dying because of it?" Randall asked.

"*Especially* because their people are dying," Carrie said firmly. "I choose to believe we can contribute to what they are doing. Chooli's grandfather is a revered medicine man. If we tell him what he is doing is wrong, then we close off all communication. Putting people on the defensive is never a way to affect change."

"So what do we do?" Melissa asked in a confused voice. "We have the remedies that will help these people, but only if they take them."

"That's true," Carrie agreed. She stared off into the distance for several moments, and then turned to Captain Marley. "There is no need for us to see the hospital. We will not be using it." Even if the military agreed to allow her team to bring the Indians there, she was certain they would not come.

"I can take you to the other hospital," Captain Marley said, although his face clearly revealed that he did not agree with her course of action.

Carrie appreciated that their friendship was strong enough to produce a certain level of trust. "We won't be using that one, either," she said. Her mind was full of her experiences in Moyamensing. The people there hadn't refused to go to the hospital—there simply hadn't been one available. "We are going to go to the people."

"That is not wise," Captain Marley objected. "I don't have enough men to guard you if you are all over the reservation."

"We won't need your men," Carrie said calmly, praying she was right. She also prayed Todd would find Chooli's family. It was their only chance of creating trust. The Navajo had been betrayed continuously for the last five years. They were not going to easily trust anyone that was white. She knew she wouldn't if she were in their place. "We are here to help these people. We will do it our way, and we will take our chances."

Captain Marley stared at her. "Have you always been this hardheaded?" he growled.

"Yes," Janie replied.

"Always," Matthew said with a smile. "I also happen to believe she is right."

Captain Marley sighed. "Fine. I will take you to your quarters." He turned to look at Carrie. "Will you at least agree with that much?"

"Well, of course, Captain," Carrie said sweetly. "Where else would we stay?"

Captain Marley chuckled and then waved one of his men over. He conferred with him briefly before bidding them farewell. "I must go give my report. I'll check on all of you later this evening."

Carrie reached out and took his hand. "I can't thank you enough for all you've done. It's because of you that we will be able to help these people."

"Thank me when I get you out of here alive," Captain Marley grumbled, but there was a twinkle in his eyes as he said it.

*****

"I am looking for Mrs. Carrie Borden."

Carrie looked up from the trunk where she was putting away her clothes. She recognized Todd's voice instantly. She walked outside into the setting sun, taking a moment to appreciate the golden orb dipping low on the horizon. "Hello, Todd. Do you have good news for me?"

Todd smiled. "I do, Carrie. Chooli's family is looking forward to meeting you."

"They are all alive?" Carrie pressed. "Her parents? Her grandparents?" Todd nodded, but she assumed from his guarded expression that they were not well.

"I'm sorry, but they are only willing to meet with you."

Carrie nodded. "That seems reasonable. We will build their trust slowly. May we go tonight?" Now that they were here, she was eager to begin.

"No," Todd answered. "The Navajo are peaceful for the most part, but the Comanche are known for nighttime raids."

"Tomorrow morning then," Carrie agreed immediately. She might be hardheaded, but she hoped she was less foolish than she used to be.

Todd smiled. "I'll come for you right after sunrise."

"You have Captain Marley's approval?" Carrie asked, remembering his statement that he didn't have enough men to guard their team.

"I am at your disposal during your time here," Todd assured her. He hesitated for a moment before adding, "The Captain must think you're special. He's never done anything like this before."

"He's brought a team of doctors led by a woman before?" Carrie asked lightly.

"He's never done that before either," Todd replied with a grin.

Carrie smiled as she watched him leave.

"He found them?"

Carrie turned when Janie appeared at her side. "He found them." The reality sank in with the words as she spoke them. "I don't think I realized until now how afraid I was that he might not, or that they might have died," she acknowledged.

"And then we would have traveled by wagon train for almost three months, and endured a blizzard for nothing," Janie replied with dancing eyes.

Carrie thought about her words. She watched as the sun set. The sky was beautiful, but everything beneath it was a wretched picture of poverty and despair. She turned her eyes away from the reservation, intent on keeping her focus on the horizon. "Not for nothing," she murmured. "I miss being on the trail," she admitted. "I've seldom felt such peace. Spending hours a day in the saddle...having nothing else to think of except making as many miles as possible each day."

"Eating dinner under the stars," Janie added. "And taking baths in cold streams."

"A person could get used to it," Carrie said. "Being here..." Her voice trailed away.

"Is like having your senses assaulted with everything we dread," Janie finished for her.

Carrie took her hand, grateful for her understanding. "Yes." She took a deep breath. "But this is what we came for," she said firmly. "I have no idea what the next few months will bring, but we'll do everything we can to make a difference."

"And then we have a few months on the Santa Fe Trail going home," Janie said brightly.

"There is that," Carrie responded, glad she had it to look forward to.

Everything they had come for would begin tomorrow.

Chapter Twenty-Nine

Carrie had risen early to unpack the medicines and stack them on shelves inside their quarters. The oil lanterns provided just enough light. She should have been thankful for a room and bed of her own, but she found she missed the wagon's cramped quarters. She would gladly give up space in exchange for the peace of the trail. She shook her head. She was at Bosque Redondo. It was time to quit yearning for what she couldn't have, and settle down to the work she had come to do. She reached for her journal.

I'm here at Bosque Redondo. Finally. I don't know what I was expecting, but the reality is far worse than my expectations. I can feel the despair in the air. I can almost smell the death that awaits so many of the hollow-eyed people I see. I fear I will go home with nothing but bad news for Chooli, but now that we are here, we must do the best we can. I hope the others don't regret their decision to join me. I have never seen such utter destitution. I can't imagine what these people have endured for almost five years. How have they done it?

A noise outside jolted her from her thoughts. Carrie quickly closed her journal and stuffed it under her mattress before she answered the quiet knock on the door. Everyone else was still sleeping, but she had already had coffee and two biscuits. She was tired of nothing but meat and breads, but she had seen no gardens for fresh vegetables, and the produce they had brought on the wagon was long gone.

"Good morning," Todd said. He was leading Celeste. "We'll ride since the spring rains have made it muddy. It should only take a few days for things to dry out, and then you can decide if walking is preferable. Captain Marley said you can have her whenever you want."

Carrie smiled and stroked Celeste's nose. After only a day, she was already missing the mare, though her heart truly ached for Granite. "Hello, girl," she whispered. Celeste bobbed her head twice and nudged her hard as if to say she had missed Carrie, too. Carrie laughed and wrapped her arms around the horse's neck. "We have work to do, girl." Glad no one seemed to mind her breeches, Carrie mounted and followed Todd away from the building.

The reservation did not look any better in the light of a new day. Squalor spread out before her as far as she could see. She smiled and nodded at people who simply stared and looked away. Their faces were not angry, just devoid of all feeling or expression. Carrie swallowed the bile in her throat, wondering how long it had taken a once-proud people to be so totally beaten down. It made her sick to realize this was happening all over the country to other tribes as well, though Felicia had told her the Navajo were suffering the worst because Bosque Redondo was incapable of sustaining them. "Does it bother you?" she asked.

Todd glanced at her. "To see the Navajo like this? Yes."

When he hesitated, Carrie remained silent, knowing he had more to say. Several minutes passed before he continued.

"I didn't care at first. I believed what I was told—that the Indians were a problem that needed to be solved. They needed to be removed from their lands for the safety and the welfare of white Americans. I was told our actions were for the greater good of our country."

Carrie listened closely, hearing the bitterness behind his words. "You don't feel that way anymore?"

Todd shook his head. "I was told to learn their language so I could work as a translator. As I learned Navajo, I also got to know the people. The more I learned about them, and the more people I met, the more I realized just what we are doing to them." His voice was husky. "When Franklin brought Chooli in to clean his place and they fell in love, she became like a little sister to me. I couldn't bear the thought of something happening to her, or to her baby, when I realized she was pregnant."

"What is going to happen?" Carrie demanded. "Surely our government isn't going to stand by while *all* these people die? Is it really true that part of our country's plan is to exterminate all the Indians?"

Todd thinned his lips. "I have heard that," he said. He shook his head. "There are people fighting for things to change. I have to believe something is going to happen."

Carrie looked away and let her eyes sweep the fields. "I heard they are refusing to plant crops this year."

"It's true. They've had crop failures every year they have been here. The first year they didn't have plows or tools so they had to cultivate the fields with their bare hands."

Carrie shuddered as she looked down at the hard, rocky, unforgiving ground. "I can't imagine."

"They worked hard," Todd said. "They had been starved out of their homeland. They wanted to believe the government's promises that Bosque Redondo was a haven for their people so they could eat and be safe," he said harshly. "They walked hundreds of miles to reach a place that is incapable of sustaining their tribe. Every crop has been destroyed by insects or hail. The water is so brackish they get sick from drinking it. The government can't get enough food for them to eat so they are starving." His voice hardened. "I wish I could help *all* of them escape."

Carrie thought back to the year before the war when she had made it possible for every Cromwell slaves to run away through the Underground Railroad. "Is there anywhere for them to go?"

Todd shook his head. "Where they won't be hunted down and forced onto another reservation? No." He forced a note of hope into his voice. "Reports are being sent that show just how bad things are, and at some point the government will decide it can no longer afford the cost. Despite how bad things are, the people are eating *something.* Feeding eight thousand people in the middle of the New Mexico desert is expensive. My hope, now that the war is over, is that someone in the government is paying enough attention to make things change."

"Do you believe that?" Carrie asked.

"I have to," Todd said. "All I have is hope that something will change for the Navajo. I have to hang on to it." He looked across the reservation coming to life with the rising of the sun. "I could have gone back East instead of returning with the wagon train this time. I was going to..."

"Why didn't you?" Carrie asked after the silence had stretched out.

"Because of you and your team," Todd revealed. "I decided that if you were willing to travel for almost six months to try to help the Navajo, the least I could do was be here to translate."

Carrie blinked. "So you were planning this all along? Why didn't you talk to me on the trail?"

"Because I didn't truly believe a group of white people from the East coast really cared about the Navajo," Todd said bluntly. "I was taking a chance, but I thought I was foolish. I also didn't believe you could handle what you would find here."

Carrie nodded. "What changed your mind?" Actually, she wasn't sure he *had* changed his mind. Just because he was helping her this morning didn't mean he believed she and her team could make a difference.

"Chooli's letter," Todd said. "Chooli is an excellent judge of character, and she cares about her people. She loves her family, but she has a passion for the whole Navajo tribe. When I read her letter, it put all my fears to rest. It will do the same for her family." He glanced at Carrie. "There is a tremendous amount of need."

"I know," Carrie replied. "We will do all we can. I am going to need your assistance to make sure I don't offend their culture. I am used to doing things a certain way, but I don't want to do anything that will make them close me out. Will you help me?"

"Certainly," Todd promised. "The first thing you should do is attend some of the medicine men rituals. They may not allow you to be part of them with your homeopathic or herbal remedies at first, but I believe they will soon."

Carrie cocked a brow. "Did Chooli talk about that in the letter?"

Todd grinned. "Chooli didn't tell you what she wrote?"

"No," Carrie admitted. "She just said they would welcome me."

Todd laughed. "She basically told her grandfather to swallow his Navajo pride and let you help. She made it clear how much you helped with Ajei's birth, and told about the men you saved when they attacked the plantation last fall. She made you into a great medicine woman."

"I see," Carrie said faintly as she flushed with warm pleasure. She was flattered but nervous that she might prove inadequate. She took a deep breath to calm her nerves. Just like before, when she had served at Chimborazo, and then helped cholera patients in Moyamensing, all she could do was her best.

She rode abreast with Todd as he wound his way through the reservation. She continued to nod and smile at people. They continued to stare at her with stoic faces before they looked away, but she wanted them to get used to her presence. She had to believe that, in time, they would trust her.

"We're here," Todd announced.

Carrie stared at the primitive adobe hut. At least Chooli's family was no longer living in a pit in the ground with a cover over it, but she knew it was nothing compared to the beautiful home and land they had left behind. She could imagine how she would feel if she were ripped from Cromwell Plantation and forced to live like this.

"Yá'át'ééh," Todd called. When a woman stuck her head out of the door, he greeted her again. "Yá'át'ééh, Haseya."

Carrie recognized the word for hello and that Haseya, which was Chooli's mother's name, meant She Rises, but her knowledge of Navajo ended there. At least for now. She was determined to learn more of the Navajo language and regretted she had lost the opportunity during their three months on the trail.

The woman staring at them looked like a very thin, older version of her daughter. Carrie knew the starvation made her look much older than she actually was. Todd spoke again. The only word Carrie understood was Chooli, but she saw the woman's eyes ignite and turn toward her before she moved all the way out of the hut.

Todd kept talking, gesturing as he spoke. Three more people came out of the hut as he was speaking. Carrie thought they must be Chooli's father and her mother's parents. By the time Todd finished, all of them were staring at Carrie, but their eyes were still wary and guarded.

"Give them the letter," Todd instructed.

Carrie reached into her breeches and produced the envelope she had protected for three months on the trail. The man who she identified as Chooli's father reached for it, his face a mixture of skepticism and eagerness. Moments later the four of them were nodding and smiling as he read the letter aloud to them. She saw Chooli's mother clasp her breast when she heard the word Ajei and learned of her granddaughter's birth. Carrie sat silently while the rest of the letter was read, meeting their eyes with a smile every time they looked at her.

Chooli's father turned to her when he finished the letter, folding it carefully before he handed it to Chooli's mother. "Thank you." His voice was deep and melodic.

Carrie stared at him. "You speak English?"

"Very little. I learn some. Chooli made me."

Carrie smiled. "I could imagine she did." Todd translated what she had said when her father merely stared in confusion. She would have to keep her words very simple.

Chooli's father laughed. "Chooli strong woman."

"Yes," Carrie said warmly. "I like Chooli very much."

The man nodded again. "You call me Shizhe`e."

"Shizhe`e means *My Father*," Todd translated. "He is giving you a great honor."

"Thank you, Shizhe`e," Carrie said, relieved she was being welcomed.

Chooli's father pointed to the rest. "She Shima. Him Shichei. Her Shimasani."

"Father. Grandfather. Grandmother," Todd said.

Carrie smiled. "Yá'át'ééh, Shima. Yá'át'ééh Shichei. Yá'át'ééh Shimasani."

Chooli's father smiled. "Very good."

"Please call me Carrie."

"Very good, Carrie."

Chooli's mother stepped forward and spoke.

"They are inviting you into their hut," Todd told her.

The grandfather began speaking. Again, Carrie looked to Todd, wishing she knew Navajo.

"He wants to know how you are going to help his people."

"Please tell him I would very much like to attend one of his rituals and help anyway he thinks I can. I understand he is a great medicine man." Todd's eyes glowed with approval before he turned to relay her message. Carrie relaxed when she saw Chooli's grandfather look at her with acceptance and nod.

Todd started talking Navajo again as they dismounted and made their way into the hut.

Carrie sank down onto the dirt floor, noting the bed rolls stacked against the wall. It hurt her heart to know these people were sleeping on the floor with only a thin blanket for covering. All four of them were appallingly skinny, with large eyes looking at her from gaunt faces that still managed to hold dignity and pride.

"They want you to know they have nothing to offer you. They are very sorry."

Carrie shook her head. "Please tell them I am happy to be here, and so glad to meet Chooli's family. She misses all of them so much."

The time flew by as Todd translated and spoke. Carrie was happy to be able to report that Chooli and the baby were doing fine. When they asked what Chooli was doing, she explained that she was studying English, and also helping her with medicines for the tribe.

Her grandfather snorted in disbelief and then began speaking rapidly.

Carrie turned to Todd for the translation.

"He wants to know what magic you worked on his granddaughter to make her interested in medicine. She has never cared about the rituals before."

Carrie hesitated, not sure how to say that she did not perform rituals, but had remedies that could help people. She did not want to say anything that would offend. "Once Chooli was away from her family, I believe she realized how much she wished she had learned." Carrie knew herbs were a vital part of the ceremonies. "When she discovered I use herbs in my medicine, she wanted to know more."

"Navajo herbs?" Todd asked, knowing that would be their next question.

"I use herbs known in my part of the country," Carrie said. "It is very different from here. I want so much to learn the herbs and plants of this part of the country." She gazed into Chooli's grandfather's eyes. "Please ask Shichei if he will teach me."

Todd spoke and then listened carefully as Shichei answered. "He will teach you," he reported. "He wants to learn as well."

Carrie glowed with the flush of victory. "Thank you."

The morning passed quickly as the four family members pressed her for information about Chooli, Franklin and Ajei. Carrie saw Todd's eyes widen when she revealed the plantation Franklin was working on belonged to her family.

"She eats?" Chooli's father asked.

"Tell him she eats very well," Carrie told Todd. "Every family on the plantation has gardens, and they all raise animals. She looks wonderful and is very healthy."

More happy smiles followed Todd's translation. Chooli's grandfather had listened very carefully, but Carrie was aware his eyes had never left her face. She prayed he was seeing what he wanted to see. When there was a long moment of silence, he spoke, his deep voice ringing with authority even though his body looked frail and fragile.

Todd turned to Carrie when he finished. "Shichei would like you to join him for a medicine man ritual this afternoon."

Carrie nodded quickly, meeting Shichei's eyes. "I would love to." Then she turned to Todd. "Will you find out more about it for me? I would like to know what he will be treating."

*****

"We're invited, too?" Janie asked excitedly.

Carrie nodded. "Chooli's grandfather was reluctant at first, but I convinced him he would be doing so much to help us accomplish what Chooli asked us to do."

"Nice play," Matthew said admiringly.

"I thought so," Carrie replied smugly, not revealing how nervous she had been to ask the revered medicine man for anything so soon. "I know all of you have read the information Felicia gave us about medicine men, but I learned far more from Todd after we left the hut."

Janie pulled out a chair from the small table in their quarters. "Tell us everything," she commanded. "I don't want to do anything to embarrass us. The more we know, the better prepared we will be."

The rest of the team took their places at the table and looked at her expectantly.

Carrie was happy to teach them all she had learned. "All of you already know medicine men are a dominant factor in Navajo life. They are actually termed 'singers' because of all the songs and chants they do. The Navajo people are intensely religious. The medicine men are expected to become well versed in the mysteries of religion. It is their job to cultivate in the minds of the people the belief that the medicine men are powerful, not only in curing diseases of mind and body, but that they can actually prevent them with their chants and rituals."

She took a sip of water from the pitcher on the table, wondering how long it would be before there was no longer fresh water flowing in the Pecos River. What did the military drink to avoid illness? Carrie forced her thoughts back to the present. "Anyone can decide to become a medicine man or woman, but the rituals take years to learn. The only way to learn is to assist other medicine men. There are three parts to the healing process. Herbalists, who are mostly females, deal with medicinal plants."

"They do?" Melissa asked in surprise. "Are they using them here?"

Carrie shook her head and frowned. "No. They only know the plants in their homeland, and they have not been able to find substitutes here."

"Which means the treatments we brought are going to be even more valuable," Carolyn said.

"It also means it's going to make it difficult for you to write the part of your book that deals with southwestern plants," Janie observed.

"Yes and no," Carrie replied. "I will document everything Shichei tells me, and then…" She let her voice trail off mysteriously.

"Tell us," Nathan demanded. "Or I won't give you any lunch."

Carrie considered. "What are we having?"

Nathan chuckled. "Steak and…"

Carrie eyed him. "You'll have to do better than that if you want information."

Nathan shook his head. "You are a hardhearted woman," he murmured, and then chuckled when she glared at him. "Steak, green beans and peaches," he said triumphantly.

Carrie laughed with delight. "Something other than meat, biscuits or dried beans? When do we eat?"

"*If* you eat would be a more appropriate question for you," Nathan reminded her.

Carrie laughed again. She loved the easy camaraderie they had all developed on the trail. "Fine. Todd knows of a woman healer who lives about five miles from the reservation. He is sure she will teach us the plants from this area." She batted her eyelids. "May I have lunch now, please?"

"Only if you keep talking while I fix it," Nathan said. "I met the head cook and talked him out of some canned supplies."

"I'll do anything for a man who knows how to cook," Carrie said impishly as she watched him begin to move around the tiny kitchen. "Back to the three parts of Navajo healing. There is the herbalist, and there is also a shaman. Their job is to diagnose disease by hand trembling and stargazing."

"Stargazing I can envision, but hand trembling?" Randall asked. "I know I'm not the only one here who has no idea what you are talking about."

"The shaman is actually the most important aspect of Navajo healing," Carrie explained, "though the medicine man gets more attention because the ceremony is so elaborate. The cause of a disease is much more important than the symptoms. The Navajo believe that illness stems from bodily contact with natural elements like lightning, water, wind or animals." She paused. "Disease can also be caused by contact with foreigners, especially enemies." She stopped talking to let her final words sink in.

Janie was the first to comment. "So their letting us come to their ceremony is a really important thing because we are strangers, and because we have the disadvantage of being white. They surely must view us as their enemy."

Carrie nodded. "Which is why we must be respectful of everything that happens."

"Which means it will be helpful if we can learn as much as possible beforehand," Nathan said, turning from where he was putting green beans on to heat. "What is hand trembling?"

"It's rather difficult to explain," Carrie began. Maybe it wasn't difficult to explain, she thought, just difficult to understand. "Hand trembling really is what it sounds like. The shaman, who is usually female, is said to have a *gift* if they experience it. It is not a skill that can be learned." She struggled to put what Todd had told her into words. "The shaman starts out by asking questions. They believe part of the healing process is having the patient talk about what is going on with them, and what they believe has caused it. They make a blessing by drawing a line of corn pollen on the fingers and arm of the patient. They pray to Gila monster for guidance and then go into a mild trance. They believe the Gila monster belongs to one of the Navajo Holy People who will tell the shaman what is wrong with the patient. They know they have the answer when their hands start trembling over the part of the body that is ill. Once they have made the diagnosis, they know what ritual they have to pay the medicine man to do."

"I see," Carolyn murmured, though her confused eyes told a different story.

"Look," Carrie said, "we don't have to understand it. We don't even have to believe it. We just have to respect it."

"All right," Janie said slowly, "but then what?"

Carrie shrugged. "I don't know any more than you do," she admitted. "Todd told me the medicine men ceremonies can last anywhere from one to nine hours. My understanding is that since the patient Shichei is treating seems to have both syphilis and dysentery, he will perform the Mountain Top Way ceremony because it helps with gastrointestinal diseases and skin disorders." She thought about everything Todd had told her. "Shichei will finish the ceremony by preparing a sand painting that represents the Holy People. The patient sits on the painting. They believe the Holy People are drawn into the ceremony through attraction to their own likeness. They merge with the patient who is sitting on the painting." She shrugged. "Healing happens."

Carrie understood the silence that filled the room when she was finished. "There is much about medicine we cannot understand," she said weakly. "I believe there can be real value in having patients talk about their illness, and faith in their Holy People obviously is an important part for the Navajo. They believe medicine is more about healing the person than curing a disease." She found herself understanding more of what Todd had told her as she talked. Verbalizing it was helping it make sense. "There are plenty of doctors who believe that homeopathic doctors are nothing but medical quacks because they can't understand why it works. We've all been told we are not real doctors. I've been accused of fake medicine because I use the herbs Sarah taught me about."

"That's true, but at least what we do works," Janie protested. "There are many so called drugs in traditional medicine that are really nothing but alcohol or opium mixed with honey. We've seen so much of it since the war. It breaks my heart when people actually *can't* get better from the treatment they receive." She paused for a moment in deep thought. "Since none of us truly understands illness, though, it is hardly our place to judge how a society chooses to treat it. I suppose I can see how talking about an illness can help. Finding out everything we can about our patients is one of the key components of homeopathy. I guess everyone does the best they can with trying to understand how to heal the human body. At least the Navajo believe herbs play a role in it." She looked at Carrie. "Is Chooli's grandfather willing for you to bring some of the herbs and treatments we brought?"

Carrie nodded, but she felt no confidence she would get to use them. Shichei had agreed to her request, but his eyes had said something very different.

*****

Carrie and her team had spent the afternoon going over all the information they could find on syphilis and dysentery. The treatment for dysentery, a virulent form of diarrhea, was very similar to the treatment she had used for cholera, so they put more of their focus on syphilis.

Nathan looked up as he put aside a pamphlet Dr. Strikener had sent with them. "Syphilis seems to have been a part of human history since we have been here."

"It makes sense," Carolyn said. "Sex is necessary to create humans to populate the earth. It is easy to pass the infection on."

"It's always been a stigmatized, disgraceful disease," Nathan continued. "Because there was no known treatment, tens of thousands of people throughout a country were infected and then died. Famous people are just as vulnerable as poor people. Every country where there has been an infection blames another country." He whistled softly as he continued to read. "Ludwig van Beethoven, the composer, had syphilis. So did King Henry the Eighth. The list is staggeringly long."

"It's also believed the Irish people of Moyamensing brought syphilis to Philadelphia," Carrie reminded him.

Nathan snorted. "It was there long before they shackled the Irish and brought them to America."

"You're right," Carrie agreed, "but people always need someone to blame."

"Like the military is blaming the Navajo," Melissa observed. "It could well have started with some of the soldiers who forced themselves on their prisoners."

"That's true," Carrie said, "but it is nothing we can do anything about. We have to focus on a cure, or at least a way to treat it." She looked up from what she was reading. "We can also be grateful the military *stopped* treating Navajo syphilis patients," she said angrily. She held up the paper she was reading that outlined military protocol.

Carolyn sighed heavily. "Mercury?"

"Mercury," Carrie agreed.

Nathan looked confused. "I thought we might use *mercurius* on some of the patients. Isn't that mercury?"

Carrie nodded. "It's a very confusing issue. I have spoken at length about it with both Dr. Strikener and Dr. Hobson. Dr. Hobson gave me several books to read this past winter. The primary conclusion is that mercury is a very toxic substance with lethal side effects," she said.

"She's right," Janie added. "Dr. Hahnemann, who we all know developed homeopathy, proved just how deadly mercury was, unless it was prepared as a homeopathic remedy."

Nathan frowned. "I just started school, so may I plead ignorance? I thought mercury was a miracle drug."

Carrie scowled. "Traditional medicine wants you to believe that. Mercury is the heaviest of all known liquids. It weighs fourteen times more than an equal volume of water. I've seen iron and lead float on its surface in an experiment Dr. Hobson did in his office. Mercury is highly toxic. It causes brain damage and nerve degeneration. Patients lose teeth and have muscle tremors. They taste metal in their mouth and have massive abdominal pain with bloody diarrhea. I could go on about symptoms, but the most important thing to know is that more people are probably dying from the mercury treatment than they are from their original illness."

Carolyn nodded. "Carrie is absolutely right. Have you ever heard of the term *mad as a hatter*, Nathan?"

Nathan nodded. "I believe so. Doesn't it have something to do with the hat industry?"

"Yes," Carolyn answered. "Mercury is used to convert animal fur into felt for the hats men and women are so crazy about. Workers in the factory are poisoned."

"What made them think about using mercury?" Nathan asked. He was obviously fascinated.

"The answer is horrible, but it is at least interesting," Carrie said. "I learned about it in one of Dr. Hobson's books. Mercury came into use because in Turkey camel hair was used in felt making. They discovered the felting process was faster if the camel fibers were moistened with camel urine."

"Who in the world thinks to try things like that?" Matthew muttered.

"I agree," Carrie said. "Anyway, when they started making felt hats in France, they didn't have camel urine, so they decided to use their own."

"Disgusting," Melissa said with a groan.

"Quite." Carrie agreed. "As it turned out, one man always produced a superior felt. They discovered the man was being treated with mercury for syphilis, so mercury was in his urine. Testing showed that using straight mercury produced amazing results, so it has become the norm in hat factories." She paused. "It affects the workers' nervous systems and causes them to tremble and appear insane. That's why people say someone is *mad as a hatter*."

"That's terrible," Melissa gasped. "Is that how the military is treating the Navajo?"

"Yes," Carrie answered as she held up the sheet. "But in all fairness, they treat everyone in the military the same way. It's not just the Indians."

"Carrie is correct," Randall said. "The use of mercury is one of the reasons I left traditional medicine and started at the Homeopathic College. I could tell the treatment was killing people," he said angrily, and then looked at Carrie. "Go on."

Carrie nodded, completely understanding how Randall felt. "They are using a cream with mercury in it to treat the syphilis sores. All they are really doing is killing them more quickly. The syphilis goes away, but they die from the treatment."

Janie scowled. "I remember something else I read. There was a mercurial ointment used during the Middle Ages to treat skin diseases like scabies and leprosy. When syphilis struck in Europe in the 1500's, it was believed only mercury could cure it. They took the treatment far beyond a cream, however. The most common technique for administering mercury was fumigation."

"Fumigation?" Nathan asked. "Even the word sounds dangerous."

Janie nodded grimly. "You're right. The patient would sit naked in a large wooden tub above a heated tray spread with a mercurial compound. The fumes would rise to encase them. They would continue the treatment for a month. The side effects were drastic. The syphilis would be gone, but their gums were ulcerated, they lost teeth, and their bones deteriorated."

"My god," Nathan muttered. He looked at Carrie. "And we use mercury in homeopathy?"

"Yes, but it is a very different substance by the time it has gone through potentization. Extracting it in alcohol and water and then diluting it makes it a very effective remedy without any of the side effects. It is extremely effective for both syphilis and dysentery, along with many other illnesses."

"Do we have enough?" Melissa asked.

Carrie shook her head. "Enough for eight thousand people? It really would be best to treat everyone who might remotely have been exposed, but I doubt we have enough for that, and I'm not at all sure the Navajo will take it." She fought a feeling of helplessness.

"They will if we make some people well," Janie said. "You have to find a way to administer the *mercurius* to the patient today."

Carrie knew she was right. She just had no idea how she was going to accomplish it.

*****

Todd arrived to escort all of them to the medicine man ceremony late in the afternoon. This time he was driving a wagon that would transport all of them. Carrie slipped a bottle of *mercurius* into her pocket and made sure they had a jar full of good water. Just like in Moyamensing, it would do no good to treat a patient with tainted water.

When their group arrived at the designated spot for the ceremony, it was already full of wide-eyed Navajo who stared at them suspiciously as they rolled up.

"Yá'át'ééh," Carrie said warmly. No one responded, but their eyes became slightly less hostile.

"Yá'át'ééh," the rest of her team echoed.

Several of the Navajo finally relented enough to return their greeting, but their stoic faces did not change.

Chooli's grandfather stepped forward and lifted his hands. He did not look at Carrie, but she knew he was aware of her presence. She settled on one of the benches placed around the ceremonial circle, intent on learning all she could. The next two hours passed in a haze as Chooli's grandfather chanted, sang and performed endless hand motions. Not understanding the language made it impossible to follow, but she certainly understood why the ritual took years to learn.

There were several times she could feel his eyes on her, but she was focused on the patient. She had known the moment she'd seem him that he was deathly ill from the syphilis. She also suspected he had received mercury treatment before the Navajo had refused to go to the hospital. Combined with dysentery, she knew the young man with limp, long black hair and dull eyes did not have long to live. She wanted to believe the ceremonial ritual could heal him, but all her experience told her it was too late unless there was a dramatic intervention. The bottle of *mercurius* seemed to burn a hole in her pocket, but she remained still. There was nothing she could do but watch, and pray that Chooli's grandfather would let her assist. There was no reason he should trust her enough to allow it, but she was determined to hang on to hope. She had come to Bosque Redondo to make a difference, but she was dependent on their willingness to allow her and her team to help.

Another hour of chanting and singing passed before the sun dipped below the horizon. Carrie was aching and sore, but she was fascinated by the ritual. Although the young man seemed as sick as ever, she saw a measure of peace enter eyes that had been tortured. She suddenly understood the power of a ceremony that surrounded illness with attention and love. If he couldn't be saved, at least he would die knowing he was loved by his family and his neighbors.

"Bitsóóké."

Carrie blinked when Chooli's grandfather stopped in front of her and spoke the one word in his chanting, guttural voice.

Todd leaned closer. "He called you his grandchild."

Carrie smiled and met the medicine man's eyes. "Shichei," she said respectfully as she bowed her head.

Shichei motioned for her to stand and walk to the patient.

Carrie caught Todd's eyes, her heart soaring when he nodded. She reached into her pocket and pulled out the vial that contained the *mercurius*. She handed it to Shichei when he reached for it, watching as he held it high and blessed it with a chant. When he handed it back to her, she pulled out the glass she had secreted in another pocket, poured a cup of water into it from the jug, and then placed several drops of the *mercurius* in it. She glanced at Shichei. When he nodded his approval, she handed it to the young man. He stared at Chooli's grandfather for several long moments before he took it, swallowing it in a single gulp.

Carrie looked steadily at Shichei for several moments and then returned to her place on the bench. Another hour passed while Shichei continued to chant before he had the young Indian sit on the elaborate sand painting he had drawn. When the ceremony drew to a close, illuminated only by the full moon rising on the horizon, Shichei walked over to where they were all seated.

Chooli's grandfather spoke briefly.

"He wants to know what you gave the patient," Todd translated.

"I gave him a remedy called *mercurius*. It is very effective with syphilis and dysentery. He should be better in the morning, but I would like to give him several more treatments for it to work the way it is supposed to." Carrie waited for Todd to make the translation.

Shichei's eyes bored into her before he gave an abrupt nod and spoke again.

"He said that if the patient is better in the morning, he will let you continue the treatment."

Carrie smiled and inclined her head graciously. "Ahéhee' T'áá íiyisíí ahéhee'," she replied, glad she had learned the Navajo phrase for thank you.

Shichei's eyes glowed with approval. "Ahéhee'," he said before he turned away.

Todd led her team to the wagon. When they were all loaded, Todd looked at Carrie. "What now?" he asked.

"Now we hope the patient is better," Carrie replied. She knew they would only have this one chance.

Chapter Thirty

Todd knocked on the door before any of them were up the next morning. Carrie was forcing her tired eyes open when she heard Matthew open the door.

"It's working!" Todd's voice rang through the building.

Carrie jumped from her bed, pulled a robe on, and opened her door. Everyone else appeared almost at the same moment. "Good morning, Todd."

"The medicine is working, Carrie! Chooli's grandfather has sent for you. He wants you to bring more of the treatment."

Carrie's heart leapt, but she had schooled herself to be cautious. "How do they know it was the medicine?"

Todd looked grim, but there was a gleam of satisfaction in his eyes. "Because not one of the people treated for syphilis has ever recovered," he said. "I hope you have a lot of that remedy."

"We have a lot," Carrie answered, "but I don't know that it is enough." She turned to her bedroom so she could dress and then swung around again. "We'll do the best we can, but Todd..."

"Yes?"

"I can't cure starvation, and I can't keep them from getting dysentery because of bad water. We can treat malaria, but we can't stop mosquitoes from hatching. What is going to happen to these people?" The absurdity of the situation made Carrie furious. "Something has to change!"

"I know," Todd agreed. "There are people working on that." He met her eyes evenly. "Can you and your team focus on keeping them alive until then?"

Carrie sighed and nodded, knowing he was right. Permanent decisions would have to be made at a higher level. She could only pray they were made before the entire Navajo Nation was wiped out.

*****

"Yá'át'ééh, Carrie."

"Yá'át'ééh, Janie."

Carrie smiled and returned the greetings coming from the people they passed.

"I can't believe we have been here almost a month," Janie murmured as she waved and returned greetings.

Carrie could hardly believe it either. Every day brought a mixture of such intense feelings. She was thrilled the Navajo had embraced them and trusted them to treat their sick, but it broke her heart to watch them grow thinner and weaker. The food supplies provided by the army were totally inadequate. Parents gave their rations to their children, but Carrie wondered what would happen when the children were left to raise themselves. The water in the Pecos River was running lower, and she knew that soon the mosquitoes that carried malaria would swarm through the camp.

"Yá'át'ééh, Carrie!"

Carrie smiled down at the thin little boy who had raced up to meet her. She swung down from Celeste and gathered him in her arms, trying to not wince as she felt his fragile body. How was it possible that a little boy who had been born in freedom in his homeland was now dying from starvation because of policies her government made? "Yá'át'ééh, Toh Yah." She ruffled his hair, remembering how he had told Todd that his name meant Walking By River. He could remember walking along the San Juan River in his beautiful homeland when he was five and six years old, right before he was ripped away and forced to march three hundred miles with his family. He had turned ten on the reservation a few weeks earlier. Carrie wondered if he would reach eleven. His starvation caused such a weakened condition that any type of disease could easily kill him.

Suddenly, his eyes grew even larger in the pinched face made beautiful by his smile. He said nothing, but pointed to the north.

Carrie turned and watched as a large contingent of troops, the lead wagon flying the American flag, moved toward the reservation. She would find out what it meant later. Right now she was determined to spend her time treating the Indians who needed her. Melissa and Nathan were in another part of the camp. Randall and Carolyn had been taken by Todd to a new area. Now that the Indians had decided to trust them—a trust fostered by Chooli's family—they were eager for their *magic medicine*. The need was endless, but she was certain they had treated at least three thousand people. There were medicine men ceremonies every day, but they also treated people without them because the need was so great. It was a tremendous accomplishment in just four weeks, but all she could think about were the suffering Indians who were still waiting.

She turned back to Toh Yah when he pulled her hand. He had appointed himself as her guide during the last few weeks. He seemed to know everything that was going on, and always knew who needed her most. She thought of Paddy in Moyamensing. She had once felt sorry for the bright-eyed Irish lad who had so little; now she knew he was wealthy in comparison to the little boy gazing up at her with adoration. Her heart clinched with a combination of fury and pity as she smiled and followed him.

The day passed quickly as she and Janie treated close to fifty patients. They dispensed homeopathic remedies, handed out bottles of salve for lesions, burns and cuts, and wrapped wounds when it was needed. Much of their time was spent holding the hands of hopeless women who stared at their children with broken expressions. Carrie had learned enough Navajo to take care of immediate needs, but she didn't have the words to give solace to these women. Of course, even if she knew Navajo, what could she possibly say?

They had saved thousands of lives, but they had been too late for others. Dead bodies accumulated on the outskirts of the reservation.

*****

Carrie was slumped in her chair at the table. The long days in the blazing New Mexico sun sapped all her energy each day. Her only consolation was that all her team had the same depleted expression she had. Except for Matthew. "I don't like you very much," she grumbled.

Matthew grinned. "You say the same thing every day."

"I mean it every day."

"So do the rest of us," Janie assured him. "Though I have to still love you because you're my husband, that does not mean I have to like you."

Matthew chuckled. "None of you seem to appreciate the fatigue of mental strain that comes from being a reporter and writer."

Carolyn rolled her eyes, her face creased with weariness. "I would be happy to trade places with you for a day."

Carrie peered at her, not wanting to express her alarm. Her older friend was showing the strain of the long days. It was hard on all of them to maintain the pace they were setting, but it surely must be harder for Carolyn. "Perhaps you should take a day off," she suggested.

Carolyn snorted. "Nonsense. I wouldn't give up the joy of what we are doing for anything in the world. I'm fine until I see Mr. Bright Eyes over here when we get home."

"I could try to look more tired," Matthew offered, his eyes dancing with fun. Not for long, though. His face sobered as he looked at all of them. "I wish I could be of more help."

Janie shook her head. "Thank you, but what you are doing is as important as what we are doing. We're just giving you a hard time. We are keeping the Navajo alive, but what you are doing will play a part in getting them out of this horrible place. We are dealing with the short-term, but the long-term is even more important."

"Janie is right," Carrie added. "I just wish something could change sooner."

"Well..." Matthew drew out the word and waited for their response.

Janie glared at him. "Building suspense is not an effective strategy with exhausted people. It could get you killed."

Matthew chuckled again. "You're right. I wanted to wait until you eat to tell all of you, but I might as well tell you now."

Carrie remembered what Toh Yah had pointed out earlier. "There was a wagon train that arrived this morning. Was it someone important?"

Matthew raised a brow. "I would say he is *important*, but how you feel about him is probably dependent upon which side you supported during the war."

"No games," Carrie begged. "I can barely sit at this table. My brain is not working well enough for verbal sparring."

"General Sherman arrived this morning," Matthew revealed.

It was Carrie's turn to raise a brow. "I see." She understood Matthew's comment now. Though she had not believed in the Confederate stance that ignited the war, neither had she agreed with General Sherman's utter destruction of Georgia. As she thought of all the horrible stories she had heard, and of all that had happened to Louisa and Perry, her fatigue sparked into anger. "Has he come to finish off the Navajo?" she demanded.

Silence met her furious question. Carrie knew she was the only Southerner at the table, but surely the rest of them couldn't have supported what that monster had done. As she met each of their eyes, she saw nothing but compassion. Slowly, her anger melted away into the same bone-aching fatigue she had felt before. "I'm sorry," she muttered. "It's been a long day."

Randall reached out and covered her hand with his. "No reason to be sorry. There is a part of me that believes General Sherman had to do what he did in Georgia in order for the war to end, but there is another part of me that says his actions are a large part of what has spawned the KKK and other vigilante groups. When you take everything away from a people, and they have no hope to keep them moving forward, the consequences can be disastrous."

Another heavy silence fell on the room as they all contemplated the truth of his statement.

Carrie took a deep breath and turned back to Matthew. "Why is General Sherman here?"

A knock on the door stopped Matthew from answering. Nathan hauled himself up from his chair to fling the door open.

Captain Marley stepped into the room. "All of you look exhausted," he said sympathetically.

Carrie nodded. "Excuse us if we don't get up. Only Nathan has the energy to move."

"Don't forget Mr. Bright Eyes," Carolyn growled.

"Excuse me?" Captain Marley asked, his lips twitching.

"It's a long story," Carrie answered, and one she had no intention of going into. "What can we do for you, Captain?" She pointed toward the one remaining empty chair.

Captain Marley settled down and stretched out his long legs while he pushed his dusty hat further back on his head. "General Sherman is here."

"So we hear," Carrie replied. "Are you going to tell us why?"

Matthew shrugged when Captain Marley looked at him. "I don't know much more than they do. I don't know if the rumors I've heard are even right. I would much prefer to hear whatever you have to tell us."

Captain Marley nodded. "It's a very long, convoluted story so I'll give you the brief version. All the problems at Bosque Redondo, and all the reports they have received, convinced the government that the military was doing a very poor job of handling the situation here."

Randall grunted but said nothing else.

"Last fall, Bosque Redondo was turned over to the Department of the Interior."

"I can hardly see they are doing a better job than the military," Carrie observed in a tight voice.

Captain Marley scowled. "Just like anything in our government, the realities of bureaucracy have made the transition quite difficult. There was some progress made last summer, though. A Peace Commission was organized to carry out the wishes of Congress. It was formed to handle the entire Indian problem throughout the country, not just the Navajo. They came together in an attempt to revolutionize the Indian Service and bring an end to the fighting."

Carrie remained silent, but she had seen nothing that made her believe that had happened.

Captain Marley's expression said he understood what she was feeling. "General Sherman is part of that Peace Commission."

Carrie's eyes narrowed, but she kept her lips clamped shut. How could the man who had ordered Georgia destroyed possibly be part of a Peace Commission?

"The Peace Commission was far more forthright than I believed it would be," Captain Marley continued. "It reported rampant corruption within the service, and recommended massive changes throughout the structure and policies. They actually pushed forward policies that would improve things, but I don't have time to go into all that." He met Carrie's eyes. "The other thing they did was advocate for a treaty with the Navajo."

Carrie straightened. "What does that mean?" she asked cautiously.

Captain Marley shrugged. "I wish I could tell you. General Sherman arrived with Colonel Samuel Tappan."

Matthew smiled. "Tappan is a good man."

"He is," Captain Marley agreed. "He was very active in freeing the slaves, and served in the army during the war. He has been fighting for Indian rights for years, and last year he and his wife adopted a Cherokee orphan girl."

"He is also a journalist," Matthew revealed. "I've read many of his articles. He thinks and communicates intelligently and clearly."

Carrie felt hope for the first time. "What do you believe is going to happen?"

Captain Marley shrugged again. "I've learned not to have too many expectations," he said honestly. "The reports being sent back have convinced the Peace Commission that Bosque Redondo is a failed venture, but I believe General Sherman thinks they should be moved up into Indian Territory in Oklahoma."

Carrie scowled. "They want to go home."

"So does every tribe," Captain Marley reminded her. "You and I both want the same thing, but for now I will settle for the Navajo being removed from this death hole."

Carrie knew he was right. "How long will Sherman and Tappan be here?"

"I don't know. They've been busy all day, observing conditions on the reservation."

"Surely they will see how desperate the Navajo are," Janie said.

"I believe they already know that," Captain Marley replied, "and the government has already decided Bosque Redondo is too expensive to continue. The question that remains, however, is what should be done with the people here."

"Is there anything we can do?" Carrie doubted they could have any impact on the outcome, but she had to ask.

"Just keep as many of the Navajo alive as you can," Captain Marley responded. "My hope is that they will be moved out of here before the Pecos River stops flowing. Wherever they go will be better than here."

"You do realize that many of the Navajo could not endure another long march," Carrie replied. "No matter where they go, if they have to walk there, many of them will die."

"I know," Captain Marley said. "I've already put in a request to be able to accompany them wherever they are going, and have requested enough wagons to transport at least the elderly and the sick."

Carrie smiled slightly. "You are a good man, Captain."

Captain Marley nodded his thanks but did not return her smile. "Let's hope we get them out of here in time. General Sherman is going to be meeting with Navajo leaders during the next few days." He turned to Matthew. "You have been invited to join them."

Matthew's eyes widened with disbelief.

"Evidently, General Sherman knows who you are and is familiar with your work. When he found out you were here, he asked if you would join them to document the proceedings."

Matthew hesitated. "And to also write articles for the newspaper?"

Captain Marley smiled. "Yes. The general already knew you would not do it without that freedom."

"Then I accept with gladness," Matthew said immediately. "When can I join them?"

Captain Marley pulled out his gold pocket watch. "The next meeting starts in twenty minutes."

Matthew gulped some water and then stood. "I'll gather my supplies right away."

Carrie shook her head. "I should have been a journalist," she complained. "You get to have all the fun."

"Like the riots in Memphis and New Orleans?" Janie asked. "Like the explosion on the *Sultana*, or covering the wreck of the *New York Express*?"

"You make a very valid point," Carrie agreed. She smiled up at Matthew. "We'll be waiting for your thorough report on what we are missing. I'm sorry you're going to miss dinner."

Everyone laughed as Matthew glared at her as he followed Captain Marley from their quarters.

*****

Matthew claimed a chair in the back of the meeting room and settled in to watch the proceedings. He was surprised General Sherman had asked for him to attend. No matter what he had told Captain Marley, if the general really knew who Matthew was, and what his articles communicated, he doubted he would have him there. While Matthew had covered Sherman's success in Georgia, he had also questioned the long-term consequences of the general's scorched earth campaign that had so successfully brought the South to its knees. He knew Sherman had been committed to doing whatever it took to end the war, even if it meant destroying his enemy. In one of his articles, he had copied a portion of a letter Sherman had given to the mayor of Atlanta after the city had fallen. The mayor pled for him not to evacuate the city because of all the old and ill residents, but Sherman had been unmovable. His letter had been clear.

You cannot qualify war in harsher terms than I will. War is cruelty, and you cannot refine it; and those who brought war into our country deserve all the curses and maledictions a people can pour out. I know I had no hand in making this war, and I know I will make more sacrifices today than any of you to secure peace. But you cannot have peace and a division of our country. If the United States submits to a division now, it will not stop, but will go on until we reap the fate of Mexico, which is eternal war... I want peace, and believe it can only be reached through union and war, and I will ever conduct war with a view to perfect and early success. But, my dear sirs, when peace does come, you may call on me for anything. Then will I share with you the last cracker, and watch with you to shield your homes and families against danger from every quarter.

Matthew stiffened to attention as a group of men entered the room. General Sherman strode in first. His slim posture was ramrod straight; his hawkish eyes were as piercing as ever beneath his receding dark hair that topped a full beard. Matthew's eyes sharpened as another man followed the general. He had never met Samuel Tappan, but somehow Matthew knew it was him. He was at least a decade younger than the forty-eight-year-old general, but he exuded the same strong confidence. Thick, wavy dark hair topped a moustache and goatee, but it was the compassion in his dark eyes that struck Matthew the most.

Matthew wondered if it was possible for these two men to come to a consensual decision. Tappan was known to be an Indian rights activist. Sherman's negative views on Indians were often strongly expressed. Matthew was certain the general would not hesitate to use the same scorched earth tactics he had displayed in Georgia if he believed it would eliminate Indian hostilities. He also reluctantly believed Sherman's most important agenda was peace. While he disagreed with his means of attaining it, and he questioned the long-term results achieved by Sherman's methods, he also realized the achievement of peace was not an easy goal. There were no simple answers.

"That was a heavy sigh," Captain Marley said as he settled into the chair beside him. "I'm here to identify everyone for you."

"Thanks," Matthew replied.

"The sigh?"

Matthew couldn't help the sigh that escaped him again. "I wish there were easy answers to peace, and I fear there are none," he admitted. He eyed the men at the front of the room. "Do Sherman and Tappan actually work together?"

"They make the appearance of it," Captain Marley said. "This is a tricky situation. Sherman wants to relocate the Navajo further east into the Indian Territory. Tappan seems to be in favor of them staying in the West."

Matthew eyed the group of Navajo clustered on the other side of the room. "And the chiefs?"

"They want only to be returned to their homeland, though I believe they will agree to anything that will bring them freedom and restore a degree of dignity. I've never seen a people so completely demoralized and beaten."

"Hurrah for America," Matthew said bitterly.

Captain Marley nodded. "Government representatives have met with the chiefs before. Every time they have been told that the Navajo want only to return to their homeland. The representatives listen, but obviously nothing has been done."

"And you think something will happen now?"

"It has to. The government can no longer afford to support Bosque Redondo."

Matthew narrowed his eyes. "They could just exterminate them," he said sarcastically. "Isn't that part of their plan?"

"Some of them, certainly," Captain Marley agreed reluctantly. "But not everyone feels that way, Matthew, and now that the war is over there is more public attention on the Indians. They know they can't get away with it."

"Sherman may regret having me at these meetings," Matthew said darkly. "I promise all of America will know what goes on here in the next days and weeks."

"I agree with you, but I suggest you keep it to yourself for now."

Matthew smiled slightly. "Good advice."

Captain Marley nodded his head toward one of the chiefs. "That is Barboncito."

Matthew eyed the slender man with the air of authority. "Tell me more about him."

"He is revered as a spiritual leader. He argued hard for peace and negotiated several treaties, but when Kit Carson invaded their homeland, he reluctantly became a warrior. He was one of the first to surrender, but it didn't take him long to understand the reality of what would happen here. Almost three years ago, he escaped with five hundred other Navajo. He was hunted by New Mexican militia units, but he avoided capture for years."

"What is he doing here?" Matthew asked.

"He was captured early this spring," Captain Marley revealed. "Barboncito and some of the other chiefs were taken to Washington, DC to meet with President Johnson in April. He told everyone who would listen that the Navajo just want to go back to their homeland. President Johnson wouldn't concede to that, but he agreed to send some of the Peace Commission here. The chiefs have been back a few weeks. Barboncito is also a medicine man, so he and the other medicine men have been holding ceremonies in preparation."

Matthew nodded, watching all the men closely. He didn't know if Sherman and Tappan were aware they held an entire people's existence in their hands, but he was quite sure Barboncito and the other chiefs did.

"Barboncito has been chosen to speak tonight," Captain Marley continued. "General Sherman is justifiably horrified by what he has seen today during his tour. He said he doesn't need to see anymore, and he wonders how anybody or anything can live here. Many of the medicine men held a ceremony today, blessing Barboncito and asking that his words be given power to persuade General Sherman."

Matthew's attention was drawn to the front of the room as the meeting was called to order. He tensed, knowing how much depended on the outcome. He agreed with Carrie that most of the Navajo in the reservation would die within the next year if something wasn't done.

General Sherman was the first to speak, asking Barboncito to tell him everything he could about Navajo life at Bosque Redondo.

Barboncito stood straight, his bearing regal and proud. Matthew admired the leader who had escaped the reservation, but who was still fighting for the survival of his people. Barboncito, his voice deep and persuasive, began to talk, his words rolling through the room with passion and strength. Since Matthew could not understand a word of what was being said, he watched Sherman. The general listened politely and intently as the chief spoke, and as the translator interpreted, but Matthew sensed his mind was already made up. He found himself praying for a miracle.

Barboncito, after a lengthy speech, done in segments so the translator could interpret, finally stopped and moved to the side to stand with the other chiefs. His face was stoic, but his eyes flashed with emotion.

Matthew was impressed. Barboncito had made an impassioned plea, telling Sherman how poor, sick, hungry and sad his people were. He had described how many Navajo had died, and how many had disappeared. He explained that Bosque Redondo wasn't meant for his people, and that the Navajo gods expected them to live among their sacred mountains.

When the translator had interpreted the last of the speech, Sherman took out a map of Navajo land, and beckoned Barboncito forward. Matthew listened carefully as Sherman showed the chief boundary lines that had been marked on the map, and then promised that if the Navajo wished it to be so, that all the land inside the boundaries would belong to the Navajo forever. Matthew was beginning to feel the thrill of victory, when Sherman's voice suddenly shifted.

"Barboncito, are you sure the Navajo would not prefer a reservation in Oklahoma Indian Territory? Many Indian tribes live there. The land is good, and you will be safe from your traditional enemies."

Matthew understood the shocked look on Barboncito's face. Hadn't General Sherman heard anything of what he had said? How could he believe the Navajo would want to go anywhere but home?

General Sherman realized the response to his question before Barboncito could open his mouth. "If you wish to go back to your own land, you must live in peace. The army will do the fighting for you. If you promise this, you may return to your own country."

Matthew watched excitement dawn on the chief's faces as the words were translated.

"I hope to God you will not ask me to go back to any other country except my own!" Barboncito replied. "It might turn out to be another Bosque Redondo. When we came, we were told this was a good place, but it is not."

General Sherman nodded, his expression saying he had made his final decision. The Navajo would go home.

Matthew watched Tappan closely, noting the glow of deep satisfaction in his eyes.

General Sherman addressed Barboncito again. "I want you to choose ten headmen for the next two meetings. Together, we will create one last treaty."

*****

June 1, 1868 was a day the Navajo Nation would always remember.

It was a day Carrie knew she would always remember, too. After so much despair and sadness, there was a cautious happiness swirling through Bosque Redondo. The Navajo people were going home soon. General Sherman had called for one final meeting to take place behind the reservation's Indian hospital. Everyone who was not too ill to come would be there.

Captain Marley was with Todd when they arrived by wagon to escort them to the meeting place. Carrie had suggested they all walk over, but Todd had insisted on transporting them.

"I still think this is unnecessary," Carrie protested. "We are used to walking through the reservation now. The people know us."

"And they also revere you," Todd replied. "This is a very special day of ceremony and meaning to them. They are a people who believe in the power of ceremony. They will want their revered healers to do more than just walk among them."

"But that's how we became their friends," Carrie argued. She still thought it was a bad idea.

"Todd is right," Captain Marley said. "You don't want to do anything to diminish the sacredness of the ceremony. Diminishing the ceremony will only diminish the meaning for them."

Carrie considered his words. "This is all about the Navajo today," she conceded. "We'll attend the way you believe we should attend."

Captain Marley grinned. "It's ridiculous how thrilling it feels to win even a small argument with you," he teased.

Carrie laughed along with the rest of her team, and then climbed up into the wagon.

By the time they arrived, there were thousands of Navajo quietly gathered in the fields surrounding the hospital. The sun shimmered high in the sky. Cooper's Hawks and Turkey Vultures soared in the wind currents above them, while a flock of Sandhill Cranes populated the river in search of fish. The temperature hovered close to one hundred degrees, but none of the people seemed to mind.

"Has there been talk of when they will head home?" Carrie asked.

"As soon as possible," Captain Marley answered. "Now that the decision is made, the government wants them back in their homeland. I anticipate them leaving in less than three weeks."

Carrie calculated how many more they could treat before they left to return home.

"You could treat more of them if you came along."

Carrie heard the words, but they didn't make sense. "What?"

"Aren't you sitting there thinking about how many of the Navajo you can treat before they leave?"

Carrie smiled. "You know me well." Only then did his words sink in. "You're saying we could go along when they return home? Really?"

Captain Marley shrugged. "You were planning on staying through July before your team returned to Virginia and Pennsylvania. I calculate it will take about a month for the Navajo to travel home. You and your team can go along with my unit, and then we'll be heading back to Independence."

Carrie, knowing her team was listening to the conversation, turned to look at them. Their wide grins freed the answer resting on her lips. "Yes!"

*****

General Sherman walked forward into the center of the clearing. It was not possible for everyone to hear him, but no one was going to miss the occasion. Thankfully, Carrie and the rest had been reserved a spot next to Chooli's family. As a medicine man, her grandfather had been granted a place of honor close to the Americans, Barboncito and his council of headmen.

"I am going to read each treaty promise out loud." General Sherman made his announcement in a loud voice. It rose and seemed to hang in the air, carrying the hope so needed by a dying nation. "Your leaders will then agree. In agreeing, they speak for all of you." He paused for a long moment as his eyes swept the crowd, and then he began.

"Shall war between the United States and the Navajo Nation end?"

"Aoo'. Yes." Barbancito and his headmen answered in both Navajo and English. Their voices rang strong and clear, their faces and eyes full of hope.

"Shall the Navajo reservation belong to the Navajos forever?"

"Aoo'. Yes."

"Will the Navajos stop raiding their enemies?"

"Aoo'. Yes."

"Shall the Americans build schools and find teachers for Navajo children?"

"Aoo'. Yes."

"Will the Navajo people send their children to school?"

"Aoo'. Yes."

"Shall the Americans buy fifteen thousand sheep, five hundred cattle and one million pounds of corn seed for the Navajo people?"

"Aoo'. Yes."

General Sherman sat down at the table that had been placed there for the occasion, picked up a pen, and signed the document. He then handed the pen to Barboncito with ceremonial flair.

Barboncito signed the paper solemnly, and then passed the pen to Manuelito, who signed, and then passed it on to each of the other headmen.

Carrie watched as twenty-nine Navajo leaders signed the treaty. She could feel the hope and anticipation vibrating in the air. The happiness glowing on the faces of Chooli's family members made her stomach clench with joy. These people who had suffered so much were finally going home.

And she and her team were going with them.

Chapter Thirty-One

June 18, 1868

Carrie could hardly believe the sight that met her eyes when their wagons, driven by Matthew and Nathan, moved into the formation. Covered wagons and people on foot filled the horizon as far as her eyes could see. Everyone capable of walking would walk, but this time they would be protected warring tribes and Mexican kidnappers. Hundreds of soldiers were stationed along the entire line to make sure all the Navajo returned to their part of the country safely. The old and the sick rode in the wagons not being used to house the supplies that would feed everyone. The sheep, cattle and horses, though a paltry amount of what the Indians had arrived with, were also part of the procession.

"I wonder how far back it goes," Carolyn murmured, her eyes filled with both joy and tears.

Captain Marley rode up just then. "Ten miles," he answered, his face filled with satisfaction. He peered into the wagons and nodded his greeting to Chooli's family. Her parents and grandparents nodded back with broad smiles.

Carrie couldn't miss the pain in their eyes, however. She knew they were glad to be going home, but they carried with them the memories of the horrors they had experienced. They carried the losses of all the Navajo who had not lived to see this day. Their hearts carried the scars of losing everything they owned, and of saying good-be to their daughter and as yet unborn grandchild. Her jaw clenched. For what purpose? Simply to return them to where they should never have been taken from? She understood the conflicted emotions on their faces as the wagon started moving. She reached over and took Chooli's parents' hands, but remained silent. She could imagine what they were feeling, but she would never be arrogant enough to pretend she could understand.

Chooli's mother gripped her hand, leaning out of the wagon to peer forward as they slowly began to move. They would head north along the Pecos River to Santa Fe before they dipped south to Albuquerque, where they would cross the Rio Grande River and then head west back to their homeland.

"One month?" Chooli's father asked.

"That's what they tell me, Shizhé'é. It should take a month."

"Home?" Chooli's grandmother asked. "True?"

Carrie nodded. "**Aoo**'. Yes," she said. The Navajo had been betrayed so many times that it was no surprise they were reluctant to trust any promises made to them. "Home," she repeated. She wished she could say so much more, but without Todd to interpret, it was difficult. Her commitment to learn Navajo had faltered under the endless hours of caring for the people who were ill, but she knew she had made the right choice. At least she had the comfort of knowing many of the Indians walking right now had been too ill to do so just a month ago. She and her team had saved many lives.

Janie settled down next to her in the wagon. "I thought you would be riding Celeste."

Carrie shrugged. "I had hoped to, but the military needs every horse for the troops." She frowned as she thought of the stories Chooli had told her about the march that had delivered them to Bosque Redondo. She pushed aside the memories, choosing to believe Captain Marley's assurance that the Indians would be well taken care of. "I am going to work on my journal," she told Janie.

"How is it coming?"

Carrie smiled. "Far better than I would have thought possible when I arrived." She reached for her journal and handed it to Janie, understanding when her friend's eyes widened.

"I didn't know you could draw," Janie murmured, stopping on a page with one particularly beautiful illustration of a Yucca plant.

"That's because I can't."

"Then how...?"

Carrie grinned. "Shima. It turns out she is quite the artist."

Janie studied the book again before she looked at Chooli's mother. "It's beautiful work."

Shima smiled but looked confused.

Carrie searched her mind for the word she needed. "Nizhon," she finally blurted out, and then looked at Janie. "*Nizhon* means beautiful."

Shima smiled. "Beautiful," she said carefully. "Thank you."

Janie continued to flip through the book, exclaiming over the illustrations.

"It has been very helpful that Shima is also an herbalist," Carrie said. "Whenever I have had spare time, Todd has translated what she knows about the plants. I've been able to document far more than I thought I would. I also met a few times with the herbalist who lives near the reservation."

Janie stared at her. "When did you do that? And why didn't I know?"

"The last seven weeks have been crazy," Carrie reminded her. She and Janie had worked together only a few times, and when the team came in at night they usually collapsed onto their beds, only to repeat their actions the next day. Talking had been a rare commodity. "I'm looking forward to being on the trail again."

Janie stared out the back of their wagon at the miles of wagon train following them. "I don't believe it will resemble our trip out here," she muttered.

Carrie chuckled. "Probably not, but we can't do much until the wagons stop every day." She had to admit she was looking forward to some rest.

"Not so fast," Nathan called from his seat on the wagon. "Todd came by earlier. He will be back soon. He said to be ready to visit the wagons that are carrying the sick. He's hoping our team can make many of them well before they arrive home."

Carrie bit back her sigh, knowing that was what they had come for. When she met Janie's eyes, she could tell her friend was thinking the same thing. They would push through their fatigue, just as they had during the war. They were here to make a difference. They would do it with every drop of energy they had.

*****

Life fell into a routine. Carrie and her team worked as hard as ever, but it seemed easier because the Navajo were now full of hope. They weren't being kept alive only to have another disease take its toll. They were going home. The army had at least made certain there was plenty of food for the return journey. Children, even after a long day of walking ten to twelve miles, still had the energy to play games before they crawled under blankets and fell sound asleep. Men could be heard talking long into the night about their plans to reclaim their homesteads, and women talked about rebuilding their homes and replanting their cornfields and peach orchards.

Carrie was standing next to Todd as they watched the sun set below the mountains, turning them into the brilliant red she had come to love so much. There were times she missed the lush green forests and fields of Virginia, but the vast expanses of the West had claimed her heart in a way she had not expected. She shifted slightly so she could watch Janie playing with Toh Yah. Matthew was sitting with one of the headmen, assisted by another interpreter, as he gathered material for the articles he would write when he returned home. She knew he was also planning a book about his experiences. Carolyn and Melissa were helping Chooli's parents build a small fire to ward off the evening chill, while Randall and Nathan were teaching Chooli's father more English.

"I love it out here," Carrie murmured.

"I know just how you feel," Todd replied. "I am eager to see my family in Boston when I return from this trip, but I am not looking forward to the crowds and noise. A man feels he can connect with his soul out here."

Carrie nodded. It was the perfect way to express what she was feeling. Even surrounded by seven thousand Navajo, there was a quiet that spoke to her. She took deep breaths of the air that was tinged with wood smoke, but was still fresh and full. "What elevation do you think we are?"

"Close to six thousand feet," Todd replied. "Is it bothering you?"

"No. I believe all of us have acclimated. It just seems that the higher we go, the purer the air is."

Todd grinned. "Wait until we get to Canyon de Chelly. You will understand why the Navajos' hearts were broken when they were forced to leave. You've never breathed air so pure, nor seen anything so beautiful."

"You've been there?" Carrie asked in surprise. "You weren't with Kit Carson when—"

Todd shook his head before she could finish her sentence. "Thankfully, I was not." He paused for a moment. "Of course, it probably wouldn't have bothered me then. It took time for me to understand that what our country is doing to the Indians is wrong."

Carrie looked out over the vast camp, knowing there were hundreds of troops providing protection. There were pickets on the outskirts of the camp and guards in the mountains. "How many of the soldiers feel as you do?"

Todd sighed. "Not enough," he admitted. "They will protect the Indians because they have received orders, and because they realize getting the Indians back to their homeland will release them from Bosque Redondo as well. I am certain that is the motivation that drives most of them."

"Will the Navajo survive?" Carrie had to ask the question that burned in her mind more and more every day. "Their homeland was destroyed before they left. They surrendered because they couldn't survive. They were going to starve to death. What about now? What makes it better?"

Todd gazed off into the distance for several moments before he replied. "I've asked myself the same question many times. The Navajo were a wealthy, comfortable people before the army destroyed their homeland. They surrendered because they were afraid they could not survive the winter, and because the army was intent on destroying any attempts they made to farm or raise stock. They are coming home in summer so at least they will have time to put in some food crops before winter, but I guess the most important thing is that they have learned what starvation and deprivation truly are. Whatever they have to face when they return home will be far better than what they experienced at Bosque Redondo."

"So it will still be horrible? Just not *as* horrible?" Carrie demanded in an outraged voice. She struggled to control her fury.

Todd cocked his head in thought. "I suppose that is the best way to put it," he said honestly. "But," he said, "I have talked to many of the men, including Chooli's father. They already know it is going to be hard, but they are determined to build a new life. They told me they will never forget the horror of the last five years, but they are not going to let it define their future."

Carrie lapsed into silence as she let his words sink into her heart. *They will never forget the horror of the last five years, but they are not going to let it define their future.*

The sun chose that moment to slip beneath the horizon completely. She watched as the red rocks lost their glow, reverting to the sandstone cliffs that had come to seem somewhat commonplace during the day. Stars began to wink their way onto the cobalt canvas that would soon deepen into the darkest black she had ever seen. She took deep breaths as she watched the quiet activities of the camp surrounding her. As she thought about the future...about the reason she had come on the wagon train...she knew she had been given her answer.

They will never forget the horror of the last five years, but they are not going to let it define their future.

She would not let the horrors of the last years define her future, either. She would not let the years of the war define her future. She would not let Robert and Bridget's deaths define her future. "Thank you," she said softly. She slipped her hand into the crook of Todd's arm and watched the end of another day.

Tomorrow, they would cross the Rio Grande.

*****

Carrie could feel the fear pulsing through the Navajo as the wagon train traveled down into the Albuquerque Basin toward the Rio Grande River. She watched as they caught sight of the great river, their eyes growing wide with terror. Frustration filled her because she was incapable of talking to them to understand why.

The wagons continued moving forward, but the people walking nearly came to a standstill when they realized where they were.

"What is going on?" Janie demanded. "These people are scared to death."

"I know," Carrie replied, "but I have no idea why."

Chooli's father was the first to give her a glimmer of understanding. He walked forward to stand beside her on the bluffs overlooking the river. His eyes were filled with sadness and dread.

"What is wrong?" Carrie asked, praying he would understand her simple question.

"Much death," he responded. "Many die."

Carrie took a deep breath. What had happened here? She scanned the masses of people for someone who could interpret for her. Finally, she saw Todd making his way toward them.

He rode up to Chooli's father and dismounted. "Talk to me, please." His face tightened into a grim mask as he listened. He turned to Carrie when Chooli's father had finished speaking. "Many of the Navajo died in the Rio Grande on the march to Bosque Redondo. They were forced into the river by soldiers on horseback and many washed away and drowned. Some of the women knew they could not cross so they sacrificed themselves and their babies, and simply let the river wash them away."

Carrie imagined the terror the people must have felt then. Of course they would feel the same way now.

"The surviving Navajo pleaded with the soldiers to let them cut down tall cottonwood trees so they could hold the branches as they crossed," Todd continued, "but many of them still drowned."

Carrie looked at the thousands of people who had every reason in the world to expect that they had been brought this far only to die in the river. "How are they getting the people across now?"

"On ferries," Todd answered.

"That will take days!"

"Yes, but it is the only way to do it safely."

Carrie thought quickly. "You have to send messengers to everyone to let them know. They will not cross the river until they are reassured that everything is all right. How many interpreters are there?"

"Ten."

Carrie grimaced but knew what had to happen. "All the interpreters should go to the groups in the front. They have to explain that no one will be forced to swim across the river, and that they are being ferried across on barges instead. They have to know there is no danger."

"You're right," Todd replied. "If I had known about this, I could have explained the situation in the last weeks."

"There's no sense in blaming yourself," Carrie said. "So far we have been lucky that there have been no severe thunderstorms, but Shima tells me they will surely come soon. We have to get everyone over that river before they come."

Captain Marley rode up, his face filled with concern. "What is going on?"

Todd explained it quickly.

"We should have been told," Captain Marley snapped.

"I'm sure no one wanted to confess to murdering Navajo," Carrie retorted. She calmed herself quickly and outlined the plan she and Todd had devised.

Captain Marley listened closely. "Are you sure you don't want to lead this wagon train?" he asked when she was done.

"No, thank you," Carrie assured him, still too angry to appreciate the humor. "I just want to get these people across that river without anyone dying."

Captain Marley hesitated. "Even with ferries, I cannot guarantee that. Especially with seven thousand people and hundreds of wagons."

Carrie took a deep breath. "I believe in you, Captain," she said. Then she nodded to Todd. "I suggest you start talking."

Todd managed a smile before he turned away, riding at a gallop toward the front of the line. It was almost an hour before the line started to move again, and it seemed only to inch forward in spurts, but at least they were making progress.

That night, Carrie watched the glow of campfires on the other side of the river. As predicted, it was going to take days for them to cross the Rio Grande.

*****

Matthew pulled Janie close to his side, watching as a meteor streaked across the sky, seemingly cutting the Milky Way in half. He never tired of watching the night sky here. He thought it had been spectacular on the plantation, far away from all city lights, but in the mountains at six thousand feet, it seemed as if he could reach up and pluck the glimmering orbs from the sky. The heat had been blistering that day, but the cooler temperatures night brought to the desert made the long days bearable.

"You love it out here, don't you?" Janie murmured.

"I do," Matthew admitted. "Now that the Rio Grande is behind us, and we didn't lose a single life, I am able to relax again. Chooli's grandfather told me we are only a few days away from the Navajo Sacred Lands. Being here...experiencing it for myself? I can understand why the Navajo felt their souls had been ripped from them when they were forced to leave."

"What do you love the most?"

Matthew considered the question. "That's a hard one to answer," he finally replied. "I love the mountains. I love the plains with waving green grass. I love the red rocks that seem to swirl with stories and mystery. I love the clear waters of the lakes we pass." He paused for a long moment as the sky once more pulled him into its depths. "I guess, though, that I would have to say I love the quiet the most. It reminds me of the West Virginia mountains when I was a boy. Harold and I would spend days, sometimes weeks, camping out there. We would hunt our own food and forage berries. I loved it because there was nothing to distract me from my thoughts."

"I bet you were writing books in your head, even back then," Janie said as she snuggled closer.

"I was," Matthew admitted. "I have learned to love things about the city, but my heart feels at home when it is quiet like this." The whole camp had bedded down for the night. The only sounds were the coyotes singing in the distance, and the occasional hoot of an owl.

Matthew was content to let the silence wrap around them for a while longer, and then he tipped Janie's face up so he could look into her eyes. There was just enough glow remaining from the fireplace to make her features distinguishable. "How are you?" he asked. There had been so few moments for deep conversation, especially once they had arrived at Bosque Redondo. He worried almost every day that the plight of the Navajo had done nothing but intensify her feelings of trauma after the train wreck.

Janie's smile was genuine. "I'm good."

Matthew gazed at her, searching her face for any attempt to hide her feelings.

"It's true, my love," Janie insisted. "I'm doing well. I'm happy to be here, and I know we have saved so many lives."

"That's true, but hasn't it been hard to deal with so much trauma?" Matthew asked carefully. He didn't want to create problems where there weren't any, but neither did he want to avoid the real issues that had brought them on this wagon train.

"It's certainly been hard," Janie admitted, "but Carrie told me something a few days ago that put it all into perspective. It was something Todd told her the night before we crossed the Rio Grande."

Matthew waited for his wife to continue. He loved the way she thought through everything before she spoke.

"Carrie asked Todd how the Navajo were going to survive returning to their homeland after its destruction had driven them out. She wanted to know how they were going to rebuild, and how they would survive."

Matthew had been wondering the same thing. He certainly understood why they wanted to return home, but how would they live there once they arrived?

"Todd told her that they were determined to put the past behind them. He told her they would never forget the horror of the last five years, but that they are not going to let it define their future."

Janie stopped speaking, but her words penetrated Matthew's heart. *They will never forget the horror of the last five years, but they are not going to let it define their future.* Matthew saw the truth he had denied for months. He would have told anyone that the purpose of the wagon train expedition had been to give Janie a chance to heal from her trauma. Suddenly he realized it was as much for him as it was for her.

"I won't let anything that has happened in the past define my future either, Matthew." Janie's voice was both firm and peaceful.

Matthew's heart swelled with love for his wife, expanding a little more as he heard the courage in her words. "I feel the same way," he said, lowering his mouth to claim her lips in a long kiss. When he lifted his head, his voice was gruff with emotion. "I thought I was coming on this trip for you, but the Navajo have taught me as much as they have taught you. I'm not going to let anything in my past define my future. Nor will I let it define *our* future."

"That's good. Especially since..." Janie's voice trailed off as she lifted her face for another kiss.

Matthew obliged her before holding her back so he could look at her face. "Especially since what?"

"Well," Janie teased, "I wouldn't want our children to be impacted by things from our past."

Matthew stared at her, his heart racing. He finally found words. "Are you telling me... we're going to be parents?"

"I do believe that is the correct term."

Matthew felt a smile spreading on his face. "We're going to have a baby?"

"I believe that is the only way to become parents," Janie answered, a grin bursting forth on her face before she grabbed him into a tight embrace. "We're going to have a baby!"

"Here? On the wagon train?" Matthew knew it was a ridiculous question as soon as it escaped his lips.

Janie laughed softly. "No, silly man. I suspect our child will be born next January or February. I just realized I'm pregnant."

"About time."

Matthew jumped as Carrie's voice sounded above their heads. She was looking down at them from the wagon. He turned back to Janie. "You told Carrie first?" He tried to hide the hurt in his voice.

"Of course not," Carrie retorted. "But don't you think I know how to tell when a woman is pregnant? I may have missed the signs of my own pregnancy, but I never miss the signs of someone else's!"

Janie laughed with delight. "I'm going to be a mother!"

Matthew's heart was pounding with happiness, but he also wondered how Carrie would handle the news after losing Bridget. He heard nothing but happiness in her voice when she answered, however.

"You'll be the best mother in the world," Carrie said joyfully. "And, you, Matthew, will be the best father possible." She smiled down at them for a moment. "And now I'm going back to sleep."

Matthew settled back against the wagon wheel, tucking Janie even closer to him. "It was Fort Larned," he finally muttered.

"That's what I figure," Janie agreed. "It's the only time we were alone together during the three months of the wagon train. Evidently wagon train air did the trick for us."

Matthew chuckled. "You know I'm going to worry about you even more now."

Janie shifted enough to look up at him. "Just figure out a way to make me oatmeal cookies. I find I am craving them."

"That could be rather difficult on a wagon train."

"Yes," Janie agreed. "That's what will make it so spectacular."

"You having our baby is quite spectacular enough." Matthew dipped his head again, smiling against her lips when a wolf howl split the night.

*****

Carrie was in the wagon when she heard the sound begin to swell around her. At first she couldn't identify it, but as she listened, she knew it wasn't a sound of sorrow. She closed her journal and lowered the wick on the oil lantern that provided light for her to write in the early morning darkness. The night before, they had traveled long after the sun went down—the first time they had done so during their journey. The full moon, turning the night into day, had lit the way. She had wanted to ask Captain Marley why, but she had not seen him for a couple days. While it was still dark, Chooli's family had left the wagon without explanation. Engrossed in her writing, Carrie had hardly noticed.

"What is going on?" Melissa mumbled in a sleepy voice.

"They sound happy," Carolyn offered with a yawn.

"They do," Carrie agreed. She tucked her journal away and opened the back flap of the wagon to a glorious dawn. Purple and gold rays shot through the dark blue, dancing off the rocks surrounding them. As the sun crept closer to the horizon the swell of noise increased.

Tsoodził.

Tsoodził.

Tsoodził.

The chant, mixed with cries of joy, rose to meet the rays of the sun. Curious, Carrie climbed down from the wagon and turned in the direction everyone was staring.

And she saw it.

Tsoodził: Mt. Taylor. One of the four Navajo Sacred Mountains that marked the southern boundary of their homeland. The Americans named it Mt. Taylor in 1849 in honor of President Zachary Taylor, but that meant nothing to the Navajo.

Tsoodził.

Tsoodził.

Carrie smiled as she watched young children, probably too young to even remember the mountain, dance with joy as their parents raised their hands in thanksgiving. Tears flowed freely as shouts rang from the people's throats.

The Navajo were home.

There were still miles to travel before they would actually be in their homeland, but their mountain now beckoned them forward. It was proof the Americans were going to keep their promise.

"The peak is more than eleven thousand feet."

Carrie looked up and found Captain Marley at her side. "Look how happy they are," she said in a husky voice.

"They've been through a lot," Captain Marley said, his eyes locked on the Indians as they rejoiced. "Most of them believed they would never see home again."

"What now?" Carrie asked.

"Some will disperse because they don't care about what the army has promised them—they simply want to go back to the land they were driven from. I suspect they will return for the sheep when the army delivers them, but they will not wait." He paused as he watched the people. "Others, those who have become dependent on the government despite the suffering and hardships, will claim the sanctuary of Fort Defiance. They will wait until the sheep and corn have been delivered."

"Do you believe that is bad?" Carrie asked curiously.

Captain Marley hesitated. "General Sherman signed the treaty less than two months ago. The government moves slowly. The sheep will come, but I won't be surprised if the Navajo wait a year before they receive them. If thousands of Navajo descend on Fort Defiance, the conditions there will be very similar to Bosque Redondo."

"So they continue to suffer?" Carrie asked, her anger cutting through the joy surrounding her. As she watched the dancing people, her anger grew. "When does it end?"

"They are free, Carrie," Captain Marley said. "I realize it is not ideal..."

"Not ideal?" Carrie retorted. "They have the choice to risk death in the mountains this winter or to die at Fort Defiance, and you say that is not ideal?" Her heart pounded. "It sounds like murder to me."

"Carrie."

Carrie started when she felt Shima's hand on her arm and heard her musical voice speak her name. She turned to Chooli's mother, once more ashamed of what her government was doing to these proud, wonderful people.

Todd was there as well. "Shima wishes to tell you something."

Carrie nodded, waiting while Shima spoke with great passion for several minutes. The Navajo woman turned several times to gaze at Tsoodził. Carrie didn't have to understand the words to know Shima held great reverence for the mountain, but it did nothing to settle the churning in her spirit.

When she was silent, Todd cleared his throat. "Shima wishes you to know that the Navajo are glad to be back in their homeland. They know there are many hard times ahead, but now that they are home where the Holy People want them, they will once again thrive and become great. The white men tried to destroy them, but they have failed. The Holy People are waiting for them within the sanctuary of their four sacred mountains. They are not afraid of the future now that they are free to live it." Todd's eyes misted. "When they were ripped apart from their home, they were forced to walk into a great darkness. They could not see how anything good could come from it, but they were forced to walk. Now they have returned home. She believes they are a stronger and wiser people, and that they will build an even greater nation."

"But—"

Todd held up his hand to stop Carrie's interruption. "When Chooli left with Franklin, once again they walked into a darkness. Chooli did, too. It broke their heart to see their daughter leave with what would be their first grandchild, but they knew it must be. Chooli sent you, Carrie. You and your friends who have saved so many lives. She told me to tell you that you have done a great thing. You have saved many who would have died. You have saved many who will return and build a stronger Navajo Nation. Not everyone has returned. Many have taken the last journey, but the ones who have come home will survive. They will never forget, and they will never let the generations to come forget what Bosque Redondo was."

Carrie's eyes filled with tears as she turned to embrace Shima.

"Thank you," Shima whispered. "I love you, daughter."

The tears Carrie was trying to control slid down her cheeks. Shima had learned those words just so she could say them to Carrie. She hugged the older woman more tightly, certain she would never forget this moment.

*****

Two weeks later, on a morning full of the glorious sunshine Carrie had come to expect, she said good-bye to Chooli's parents and grandparents. She had said good-bye to many of the Navajo in the past days as they departed the group for their old homesteads, or stopped at Fort Defiance. She forced her mind away from wondering how long they would wait for the promises made by the government to be fulfilled. They would wait— or not—and then they would begin to rebuild the lives they had been robbed of.

The last week had been spent in Canyon de Chelly with Chooli's family and seventy-five others—all that remained of the three hundred people that had started on the Long March from their group. The sheer splendor and beauty of the canyon had stolen Carrie's breath at almost every curve. Never had she seen anything so magnificent. Her peace had grown as she had seen the joy blossom on Chooli's family's faces. They assured her they would replant the cornfields and peach orchards that had been destroyed. The winter would be hard, but they would survive, rebuilding their homes and enjoying the freedom that had been stolen from them. They would grow all they could through the rest of the summer. They also had some supplies from the army, and would gather everything edible they could find.

Their final night, Chooli's grandfather had led a long ceremonial ritual asking the Holy People to bless them and to give them safe journey as they returned home. It had lasted long into the night, but no one had wanted to leave the glowing fire.

"We will be fine," Shizhe`e assured her, his eyes warm with love. "You are our daughter." He looked around the group. "You are our children."

Carrie grabbed Chooli's father into a fierce hug. "Good-bye, Shizhe`e. I love you."

Then she turned to Chooli's mother and pulled her close. "Good-bye, Shima. I love you so much."

"Love you, my daughter," Shima whispered. "Give Chooli love."

Carrie nodded, and then embraced Chooli's grandmother. "Good-bye, Shimasani. I love you."

"Love you," Shimasani replied, her gnarled hands holding Carrie's face gently before she leaned forward to kiss her. "Thank you."

Carrie was weeping openly now. It was so hard to say good-bye to them. How had Chooli done it? Finally, she turned to Chooli's grandfather, the revered medicine man who had taught her so much, and who had trusted them to help his people. "Good-bye, Shichei," she murmured. "I love you. And I will miss you."

Shichei held her close for several moments, and then stepped back enough to look into her eyes. "You great woman, Carrie. Big medicine. I love you."

*****

Carrie was settled in the wagon when Chooli's grandmother stepped up to her.

The old woman, her eyes full of sadness, pressed an envelope in her hands. "For Chooli."

Carrie grasped the envelope tightly. "Yes. For Chooli."

She and her entire team waved until they were out of sight.

It was time to go home.

An Invitation

Before you read the last chapter of *Walking Into The Unknown*, I would like to invite you to join my mailing list so that you are never left wondering what is going to happen next. ☺

Join my Email list so you can:

- Receive notice of all new books & audio releases.
- Be a part of my Launch celebrations. I give away lots of gifts! ☺
- Read my weekly blog while you're waiting for a new book.
- Be part of The Bregdan Chronicles Family!
- Learn about all the other books I write.

Just go to www.BregdanChronicles.net and fill out the form.

I look forward to having you become part of The Bregdan Chronicles Family!

Blessings,
Ginny Dye

Chapter Thirty-Two

Carrie wasn't surprised when no one met them at the train station in Richmond. She had sent a telegraph two days ago when they left Independence, Missouri, but she suspected everyone would already be on the plantation for the Harvest Festival that was taking place today. Part of her was sorry to miss it, but the bigger part was glad for a chance to ease back into the life she had left over eight months ago. "We'll stay at the house tonight and then go out to the plantation in the morning," she told Matthew and Janie.

"Perfect," Janie breathed. "It will be wonderful to see Micah and May, but I'm glad for a chance to take a bath and sleep in a real bed for a night."

"My feelings exactly," Matthew seconded. "I appreciate the speed of train travel, but the last two days have been brutal." He grasped Janie's hand. I can't imagine doing it five months pregnant."

Carrie could not have agreed more. She had savored their return trip on the wagon train, not minding the searing heat of the desert and the Kansas Plains because it made long swims in the lakes and rivers even more wonderful. Following the trail back when it was not covered in snow had been eye-opening. She loved the unending green grasses, and the herds of buffalo and antelope. Thankfully, there had been no trouble with Indians, and her entire team had grown even closer during the months of travel.

Returning to Independence had been an assault on her senses, and the crowded conditions of the train had felt like torture. She was excited to see everyone, but grateful for a day to acclimate.

At least summer had released its grip on the South. Early October had brought cooler temperatures, and was beginning to kiss the leaves with color that would soon be brilliant. New buildings had gone up in Richmond during her absence, and the city was losing the weariness thrust on it by four years of war. Throngs of people bundled in light coats smiled and laughed as they made their way down the streets.

Matthew loaded their bags into the carriage he'd hailed. When he returned, he had a broad smile on his face. "The driver will take us to the plantation tomorrow."

"Perfect!" Carrie exclaimed. She had wondered what they would do; certain Spencer had taken the rest of the family. Then she looked at Janie more closely. "You look exhausted. Are you certain you'll be ready to go out in the morning?" She knew two days of train travel had been taxing on her friend. "Another day of rest might be a good idea." She and Matthew had both learned not to coddle Janie, but she also knew Janie would never do anything to put her baby at risk.

"I'm fine," Janie said. "After we eat, I'll take a bath and go to bed. I'm too excited to see everyone to wait any longer." Her eyes gleamed as she spoke. Pregnancy had indeed given her a glow.

"You just want to tell everyone you're going to have a baby," Carrie teased. She was grateful the reality no longer caused a pang in her heart. She was simply glad for her friends.

"Of course I do!" Janie retorted. "I can't believe it's been eight months since we've seen everyone. I can hardly wait to hear all the news."

Carrie was secretly relieved Janie hadn't chosen to stay in Richmond another day. She would have been happy to stay to protect the little life growing inside her friend, but she was eager to be on the plantation again. Now that they were so close, it was pulling her forward. She thought about the letter waiting for them when they arrived in Independence. Abby, with no knowledge of when they would arrive back in Missouri, and with no communication other than what Carrie had sent back after the blizzard, had sent them a letter more than a month ago. Everyone, including Rose and Moses would be on the plantation for the Harvest Festival. She had hinted at exciting news, but had left them dangling in suspense.

May was standing on the porch, her mouth gaping in surprise, before the carriage rolled to a complete stop. "I been watching every carriage that done come down this road for the last month," she called. "It's about time you folks done get home!" Her eyes widened when Janie stepped from the carriage. "Well, if that don't beat all. Miss Janie, you's gonna have a baby!"

"I am," Janie replied with a laugh. "My little one and I are hungry for some real food, May."

Minutes later, after greetings had been exchanged, they were seated in the parlor with hot tea and hot scones slathered with butter.

Matthew groaned as he bit into one, steam rising from his bite. "I have died and gone to heaven," he moaned. "I'm sure if I had to eat one more rock hard biscuit on the trail, my stomach would have simply refused it."

Carrie smiled but found herself missing everything about the Santa Fe Trail, even the hard biscuits. She had come to cherish quiet above everything else in her life. She pushed aside the uncomfortable question of how she would find it again, and how she would deal with not having it.

May stuck her head out from the kitchen. "You'll have a feast soon. I figure all three of you will appreciate the baths Micah is fixing for you right now. Dinner will be ready when y'all be clean again." She fixed Janie with a stern gaze. "And then you be going to bed, young lady. After all that train riding, you and your baby need to get some rest."

"I couldn't agree more," Janie murmured. She stifled a yawn. "I couldn't agree more."

*****

Rose walked with Lillian through the woods, luxuriating in the fresh morning air. They had been home for a week. She knew it had been good for all of them, but especially for Moses. He missed the plantation so much. When she found him in Oberlin staring out the window, she knew he was thinking of home—watching the tobacco grow in his mind. He had been thrilled to discover another record-breaking crop. He received regular communication from Franklin, but there was nothing like seeing it for himself. He had spent every minute since his arrival with his men in the fields, or in the curing barn. He came in every night smelling of dirt, sweat, rich tobacco and wood smoke.

The only time he could be persuaded to leave the fields was when Simon and June arrived with their four-month-old daughter, Ella Pearl. The precious baby had immediately stolen everyone's hearts. Rose still hated that she had missed the entire pregnancy, but June had understood. She and Moses had planned being on the plantation all summer, but Felicia had been excited to start college when the summer term began. They couldn't bring themselves to disappoint her. It had been pure joy to watch her thrive and grow in an environment that both challenged and supported her.

"Is it good to be back?" Lillian asked.

Rose looked at the woman who had already become a good friend. "Of course."

"But...?"

Rose hadn't realized there was a *but*, though she couldn't deny she felt it once it had been pointed out. She had seen her students and was thrilled to learn they loved Lillian, and that they were learning at a rapid speed. They didn't care that Lillian was white, and she didn't care that half her students were black. She treated them all the same, and she had the same expectations for all of them. "You're quite perceptive," she said lightly, wondering if she could avoid the question.

"Yes." Lillian said nothing else, but she held Rose's eyes.

Rose sighed. "The plantation doesn't feel like home without Carrie," she admitted. "Being apart from her at school was hard, but I am so busy every day that I don't have time to obsess about it. But here?" She shook her head. "Everywhere I look there are memories of Carrie. I wish she were here. I hoped we would see her before we leave, but no one has heard from her, and we have no idea when she will be home." She swallowed the rest of her fears, knowing it would do no good to express them. They would have been informed if something had happened to her or to any of the others. "I can't stand the idea of going back to school without seeing her."

"The two of you are very close," Lillian said.

Rose couldn't miss the envy in her voice. "We've been best friends since we were children. I may have been her slave, but we were friends. When we found out we were related, and then Moses and I became free, it didn't make us any closer, but it gave us more memories. Living here on the plantation together after the war, except for the months Carrie was away at school, was wonderful." Her voice caught. "I miss her."

"Can't she travel to Ohio to visit you when she returns?" Lillian asked.

"Yes," Rose murmured, "but—"

"It's not here, where all your memories are," Lillian finished.

"Yes," Rose said again, grateful for Lillian's understanding.

"You're lucky to have a friend like that."

"I know," Rose agreed. She looked at Lillian more closely. There was something Rose could not identify in her eyes, and something lurking in her voice that seemed like it wanted to stay hidden. Rose told herself she was imagining things, but the feeling would not go away. "Do you have a friend like that, Lillian?"

Lillian hesitated for a long moment, looking off at the horizon. "I did," she admitted.

Rose could almost feel the pain and loneliness rolling off her. "Did something happen to her?" she asked sympathetically.

Lillian stared at Rose. Finally, she shook her head. "No."

Rose knew there was more than she was telling her, but she didn't know Lillian well enough to press her. She tried to think of a way to change the subject, but she couldn't let it go. She knew the look of a woman in pain. "You can talk to me," she murmured, reaching out to take Lillian's hand. "I know we don't know each other well, but if it would help to talk, I will listen."

Lillian stiffened and pulled her hand away. "You will listen, but I promise you will not understand."

Rose was more mystified than ever. "I can try."

"It will do no good," Lillian muttered.

Rose gazed at her new friend, aching for the agony she saw etched into Lillian's eyes. She prayed for her mother's wisdom. "Whatever it is seems to be eating you up inside."

Lillian shook her head. "I can't talk about it."

"Why?" Rose asked. "Not talking about it doesn't seem to be making you feel better."

"Not talking about it won't end up with me having a hole bored through my nose," Lillian snapped, her eyes sparking into anger.

If Rose had been mystified before, now she was totally confused, but her questions were obviously upsetting Lillian. "I'm sorry," she said. "I shouldn't be prying."

Lillian's eyes dropped, along with her entire posture. "I'm the one who is sorry," she said. "There are times I believe I should talk about it, but I'm in the wrong part of the country."

Rose remained silent. She didn't want to push any further. If Lillian wanted to talk, she would.

"President Jefferson recommended that the state of Virginia should either castrate men or punish women by having a hole bored into the nose," Lillian said quietly. "He even authored a bill to that effect."

"Why?" Rose gasped. "I've heard of horrible things being done to blacks, but you're not black."

"I'm a homosexual," Lillian said flatly. Her eyes were defiant but took on a stark shadow of fear.

Rose remained silent as she processed the information. She had never known a homosexual before, but obviously Lillian had suffered greatly for being one. All Rose knew was that she liked Lillian. She had liked her before she knew she was a homosexual. Why should that change now? "I see," she murmured.

"It's against the law, you know. Are you going to report me?" Lillian demanded, her quick anger fading back to fear. She shook her head heavily. "I should have kept my mouth shut."

"Of course I'm not going to report you," Rose said immediately. "I'm sorry, I've never met a homosexual before."

"Oh, I'm sure you have," Lillian retorted. "We've just learned to stay silent and blend in. It's the only way to live when people hate you for being who you are. You wouldn't understand."

Rose smiled slightly. "Really? I live in a world where people hate me because I'm black. I think it would be rather nice to have the opportunity to stay silent and blend in."

Lillian flushed. "You're right. I'm sorry I said that," she replied contritely. "I know your people have gone through horrible times, and are still suffering. One is not harder than the other, though. When you are forced to stay silent and blend in, you start to become invisible. Not just to others, but also to yourself."

Rose nodded. "I can understand that. Look, Lillian, I liked you a few minutes ago before I knew you were homosexual. Why should I like you any less now? I don't pretend to understand it, but it doesn't change who you are." She took a breath, allowing herself a moment to collect her thoughts. "I have a life now because there were people who saw me as something more than just a black woman. When I look at you, I see someone who is a great teacher. I see someone who loves children. I see someone who is wonderful with horses." She paused again, holding Lillian with her eyes. "I see someone I like."

Lillian seemed to sag with relief, but the concern did not leave her eyes. "Not everyone feels the same way you do."

"No," Rose agreed. "The world is full of ignorant people who can't see beyond skin color and labels. You don't need to worry that I will tell anyone. Your secret is safe with me."

"Thank you," Lillian said sincerely.

"So what is her name?" Rose asked, knowing Lillian needed to purge the pain that had started their discussion.

"Roberta," Lillian answered. "We met each other in Cincinnati when I finished school." Her eyes softened. "We lived together for two years. Just as friends, of course. At least that's what everyone thought."

"What happened?" Rose asked gently. She didn't understand homosexuality, but she did understand love, and she understood pain.

"We were careful, but there were people who figured it out." Lillian's voice choked. "There were a group of men who pulled Roberta into an alley when she was on her way home from work. They beat her with a bat." Tears flowed down the woman's cheeks. "When she made her way home, I barely recognized her. I took care of her, but when she was better, she left town to go back to Minnesota. She said she would feel safer there."

Rose gripped her hands. "Why didn't you go with her?"

"I wanted to," Lillian gasped out between her tears. "She wouldn't let me. They scared her so bad that she said she wanted to spend the rest of her life alone."

"They didn't come after you?" Rose asked.

"I got the job offer here the day after Roberta left town." Lillian shook her head. "I still think about her every day."

"Roberta? Or Bertha?" Rose asked gently.

Lillian sighed heavily. "I forgot I told you about Bertha," she finally admitted. She shrugged. "I decided to never say her real name in connection to me because I don't want to increase her risk."

"So she wasn't sick," Rose murmured, completely able to relate to the terror Bertha must have felt when she was pulled into the alley. Just the thought took her back to the day Ike Adams had done the same to her, planning on raping her. Matthew had saved her. "I am so sorry, Lillian."

A long silence stretched between them as they both considered what had been revealed. Rose could tell Lillian was torn between relief and regret. She could also imagine the pain Lillian was in. Being separated from people you love was excruciating.

"Do you hear from her?"

"No. She wouldn't give me an address or even tell me where exactly she was going. I have no way to contact her."

"I'm so sorry."

The mistrust flared in Lillian's eyes. "Are you?" she demanded.

Rose gazed at her for a long moment. "My mother was a slave here on the plantation, and married to John, a man she loved very much. Thomas Cromwell's father raped her one day. She never told anyone, even after she discovered she was pregnant. For all she knew, the baby was her husband's...until she gave birth to twins." Rose paused as she imagined her mother's horror and confusion. "One looked white. I looked black."

Lillian sucked in a breath. "Oh my."

Rose nodded. "Thomas' father sold my brother that day, and he sold her husband a few days later. She didn't see her husband again until I was eighteen. They had less than a year together before he died. My mama never told me about my brother until right before she passed away.

Other than the day he was born, she never saw him again."

"Jeremy?" Lillian asked.

"Yes," Rose said with a tender smile. "He is my twin brother, and the baby who was sold." She gripped Lillian's hands again. "While I might not understand what it is like to be homosexual, I *do* understand what it is like to be judged for something you have no control over."

Lillian stared at her. "You don't believe I'm homosexual just because I'm a terrible sinner?"

Rose shrugged. "I don't believe many would *choose* to be black because it certainly makes life far more challenging than being white. So why would anyone just *choose* to be homosexual? Surely it would be easier to love men."

"You are extraordinary," Lillian said in an awed voice. "And you're not going to tell?"

"I will not tell," Rose promised. "And I believe you are a wonderful teacher. I hope you will be here for a long time."

Lillian smiled. "I do, too, Rose. I do, too."

*****

The porch was lined with people when the carriage pulled up to the house. All three of them had slept through much of the trip, even after a good night's sleep in Richmond. Carrie was glad they were not arriving weary and fatigued. Suddenly, as much as she still missed life on the trail, there was no place she would rather be than Cromwell Plantation.

Crisp air caressed her skin as red and gold leaves rustled above her head. The horses, seeming to know important people were arriving, all stood at attention in the field, their ears pricked forward. Even the foals were standing still beside their mamas. Granite, knowing who had arrived, whinnied loudly and broke away from the group, racing down the fence line, his eyes latched onto his mistress.

"Hello, Granite!" Carrie called. Joy surged through her. Then they were at the house, and she was being pulled from the carriage. The next minutes were a pandemonium of hugs, laughter and tears.

Once her condition was recognized, Janie became the center of attention.

"You're pregnant!" Abby cried.

Janie grinned. "So I am."

"Due in January or February," Matthew said proudly. "We figured it was time for a new baby around here."

Jeremy, who had not been on the porch when they arrived, walked out just then. "We'll beat you to it, my friend."

Carrie looked up as Marietta emerged behind him. "Oh my," she murmured. "Are you due today?" She laughed with delight.

Marietta pulled Carrie as close as she could in a hug. "In a couple weeks. Is it all right to say I'm relieved you're home?"

"It is, but I'm sure Polly could deliver your baby," Carrie assured her. "You won't be in Richmond for the birth?"

Marietta shook her head. "No, we've decided to stay here on the plantation until the baby is born."

Carrie understood instantly. Jeremy and Marietta didn't want the baby in Richmond until they knew what color it would be. "I see," she said. "Then I'm honored to be here to be part of the birth." She could only imagine the strain of not knowing. She was aware, without being told, that their future would be determined by the race of their child.

Matthew turned to Thomas. "Harold was not at the house. Do you know where he is?"

"Right here," Harold called, striding up onto the porch. "I just got back from a ride with Susan. You, my brother, are a sight for sore eyes. I'm glad you didn't get carried off by the Indians."

"Far from it," Matthew said before he pulled his brother into a bear hug. "The Navajo helped me make sense out of the last years of my life."

Abby slipped an arm around both him and Janie. "Congratulations, you two. You'll make marvelous parents, and from the shine in your eyes, I know the wagon train mission was a success."

"We have so much to tell you," Matthew agreed.

"We do," Carrie echoed, "but first I have to go say hello to my horse." She ran to the pasture fence and wrapped her arms around Granite's neck. "I missed you, boy. I promise we'll go out tomorrow." Granite bobbed his head and nuzzled her shoulder, his eyes soft with love.

Talk swirled around the porch late into the afternoon, fueled by copious quantities of fried chicken, potato salad, corn and pie. When the chill chased them inside, they built a roaring fire and continued to share stories and experiences.

The factory was doing well. Harold had enough stories written to finish *Glimmers of Change*, and to start the next one the publisher was demanding. Abby couldn't wait for Carrie to meet Willard and Grace.

Carrie's mind swirled with everything she had learned. President Johnson's impeachment trial had ended with one vote too few to put him out of office. He was still president, but it was certain that Ulysses S. Grant would replace him in the election next month. Surely progress would be made in racial equality then.

*****

Carrie stepped out onto the porch to get some fresh air and still her mind, and Rose stepped out to join her. The two friends grabbed each other tightly. Neither said a word for several long minutes. Time melted away, but both knew there were experiences to share that would stand between them until they had been heard and understood. It was not possible that either of them had remained unchanged during the nine months they had been apart. Just as they had after the war, they would learn who the other person had become, and their friendship would deepen.

"How much longer will you and Moses be here?" Carrie finally asked.

Rose smiled. "We were going to return to Ohio in two days," she revealed, "but we decided to stay another ten days when you arrived. We'll miss a week of classes, but I don't believe there will be a problem. I don't really care, but we are both doing well, and Felicia is so far ahead no one will say a word."

Carrie sagged with relief. She was happy to see everyone, but seeing Rose was like connecting with a part of her soul. Her time with the Navajo had taught her the precious value of that more than ever.

"Am I interrupting?"

Carrie turned to pull Abby into an embrace that encompassed the three of them. "Never," she whispered.

The three women stood silently as their arms encircled each other. No words were needed. Stories would be told, but for this moment it was enough to be together.

Carrie felt the magic of the plantation weave its way into her heart again. She hoped the time would come when she could return to the splendor of the West, but Cromwell Plantation was home. At least for now.

"How long will you be here?" Abby murmured. "I wasn't going to ask because I'm afraid I might not like the answer, but I find I can't help myself."

"I don't know," Carrie admitted. "I haven't asked myself that question yet. It's enough for right now just to be home."

"Who are you now?" Abby asked, stepping back so that the lantern light fell fully on Carrie's face.

Carrie smiled. "Who are we all? It was New Year's Day when the three of us sat on the log by the river and talked about walking into the unknown. I could never have imagined on that day what the decision to go to New Mexico would mean to me."

"I'm so glad the Navajo are back in their homeland," Rose said. "And you and the team saved so many lives."

"Yes," Carrie agreed, but she knew that information was not the answer to Abby's question. She thought back to the conversation with Todd on the bluffs overlooking the Rio Grande. "The Navajo endured so many horrors. They had every reason to be bitter and angry. They had every reason to have lost all hope, and they had every reason to give up on life." She paused, knowing Abby and Rose would give her all the time she needed to communicate her feelings. The knowing made her love them even more. "They didn't, though. When they found out they were being allowed to go back home, they decided they would not let the past define their future." The power of the words hit her again now, standing on her porch in Virginia, as hard as they had back in New Mexico.

"They would not let the past define their future," Abby murmured, "and neither are you."

"That's right," Carrie said. "Whatever I have gone through, it is nothing compared to the terrible things done to the Navajo over the last five years. They have decided it will not define their futures. And, yes, I have decided the same thing." She took a deep breath. "I don't know what my next step is, but I don't need to know right now. I'm home. I intend to ride Granite, sit by the fire, and be with the people I love. I'll know the next step when it is time to take it."

"I don't want to go back to Ohio," Rose cried suddenly. "How can I leave? I've missed you so much."

"You have to," Carrie said. "I don't want you to go away, but you have to finish what you have started. You'll always wonder what you could have accomplished if you had stayed at Oberlin."

Rose stared at her for several long moments, and then looked at Abby in defeat. "She is becoming a wise woman."

"I think it was your mama who told me great wisdom comes from great suffering," Carrie retorted. "It's the only thing that makes the suffering worthwhile." She thought about the things Chooli's mother had told her before she left. "Every experience can give us wisdom if we let it."

The door opened behind them, ending the moment.

"Franklin and Chooli are here," Moses called. "I thought you would want to know."

Carrie smiled and reached for the letter in her pocket. "We're coming."

*****

Carrie, Matthew and Janie had shared parts of their trip to New Mexico, but they had deliberately stalled a full telling until Franklin and Chooli joined them. Franklin had not been able to get away until the last wagons of dried tobacco were ready to depart the plantation for Richmond the next morning.

The parlor was packed full of people. Gabe, Polly, Clint and Amber had arrived. Susan had finished work in the barn, arriving with Miles and Lillian shortly before dark. Annie carried trays of food to the tables before she settled down to join them, her hand clasped firmly in Miles'. John was perched on Moses' lap, his eyes wide with excitement. Hope, who was full of boundless energy, had finally settled down and fallen asleep in Rose's arms. Carrie regretted Simon and June weren't there with Little Simon and Ella, but they had left early that morning after the end of the Harvest Festival the day before.

"I believe everyone is here," Thomas finally said, his eyes full of pride as he looked at his daughter.

Carrie gazed at her father for a long moment, her heart bursting with gratitude for the love they shared, before she stood and moved next to the fireplace. During the long months away, it had become as natural as breathing for her to address groups and assume a leadership role. Talking to her family and friends was something she had so looked forward to.

"I believe I first need to congratulate the young woman who stole my title at the tournament yesterday." She smiled at Amber. "I know you were glad I was away on the wagon train," she teased.

Amber tossed her head. "I'm growing up, Carrie, and I practice a lot," she said confidently. "I would have won even if you were here," she stated. Then she laughed and ran to the front of the room to throw her arms around Carrie. "I love you. I'm so glad you're home! Robert would be real glad, too!"

Carrie blinked back tears and returned the hug. Cromwell Plantation would always carry the memories of her husband, but she could feel his presence urging her into the future while pulling her into the peace of the present. She was no longer fighting it.

"The last nine months have been some of the most amazing months of my life," she began. She told everyone of the long days on the wagon train. She told them about the blizzard, and how the team had learned to work together in that first crisis. She told of first arriving at Bosque Redondo.

"My family?" Chooli whispered.

Carrie walked over to take Chooli's hand. "They are all fine, Chooli. They miss you very much."

Chooli broke out into a musical laugh softened by tears streaming down her face. "All of them? Shizhe`e? Shima? Shichei? Shimasani?"

"Yes. Your father. Your mother. Your grandmother. Your grandfather." Carrie interpreted the Navajo for the others listening. "They send their love to you and to Franklin, and most especially to Ajei." She looked at the beautiful little girl sitting quietly on Chooli's lap. "I can hardly believe Ajei is a year old."

"Yesterday," Chooli said proudly. She looked at Carrie imploringly. "Please tell me more."

Carrie took a deep breath, sharing the horrors of Bosque Redondo. She spoke of the illnesses, the ceremony where Shimasani had allowed her to use her medicine, and of all the people her team had saved. She watched Chooli's face stiffen with agony, but knew it would soon give way to joy.

"I'm glad we saved so many of them," Carrie continued. "They were ready to go when the Navajo went home." She met and held Chooli's eyes as she let silence follow her announcement.

The Navajo woman stared at her, obviously searching for words. "Home?" she finally murmured.

Carrie told everyone of General Sherman's visit to the camp. Chooli's eyes widened with disbelief when she told of the treaty that had been signed. "It took three weeks before the wagon train was ready to take the tribe home." Carrie paused. "We went with them."

Chooli covered her mouth to stifle her cry. "They are home? You went with them to Naabeehó Bináhásdzo?"

"The Navajo homeland," Carrie explained to everyone. "Your people are home, Chooli. They are finally *home*."

Applause rang through the room while many tears were brushed away.

"My family?" Chooli whispered, her look one of dazed joy.

"They are rebuilding your homestead in Canyon de Chelly," Carrie assured her. "Which by the way is the most beautiful place I have ever been."

"Yes," Chooli murmured, her eyes full of both joy and naked homesickness as she envisioned the home she had been ripped from. She turned and looked at Franklin.

He smiled and pulled her close to his side before he turned his eyes to Moses. "I happen to believe Canyon de Chelly is the most beautiful place in the world, too. I will stay here until we find someone to replace me, but then I will take Chooli and Ajei home. I want my wife to be with her people, and I want my daughter to grow up where she is wanted and honored."

"Of course," Moses said immediately. "You came when you were needed. I know there is someone else coming, too."

"We won't leave until next spring," Franklin assured him. "Carrie's stories of the Santa Fe Trail during the winter convinced me I will not take Chooli and Ajei until it is warm again."

Chooli gazed at him with adoration, and then turned back to Carrie. "What did my family say when you left?"

"They sent their love, of course, but they sent something more," Carrie responded as she reached into her pocket and pulled out the letter. "Shimasani sent this to you."

Chooli locked her eyes on the letter and reached for it slowly. "From my grandmother?"

Carrie understood her confusion. "One of the army's interpreters traveled to Canyon de Chelly with us. I believe he wrote it for Shimasani."

Chooli started to put it in her pocket, but Abby's voice stopped her. "Read it now, Chooli. You know you can't wait until later."

Chooli looked up and saw everyone's smiles of approval before she broke the seal on the envelope and opened it eagerly.

The room remained quiet, even the children seeming to understand the sacredness of the moment.

Chooli both laughed and cried as she read the long letter. She finally laid it in her lap and looked up at Carrie. "My family loves you very much." Her eyes traveled to Janie and Matthew. "And both of you. You are loved."

"And we love them," they all chorused together.

"It was so difficult to leave your family," Carrie said. "I hope someday to go back to visit."

"Perhaps you will travel with us in the spring?" Chooli said temptingly.

"Perhaps," Carrie replied with a laugh. "I have no idea what is going to happen next spring, but I'm all right with whatever the future brings." It made her happy to realize how much she meant that.

Chooli's eyes brightened. "My grandmother talked about that in her letter." She picked the letter up from her lap, flipped to the last page, and began to read.

"Your people have gone through a time of great darkness, my beloved granddaughter. The White Man tried to destroy us, but they have failed. The Holy People waited for us here in the sanctuary of our sacred mountains. We are not afraid. We are a stronger and wiser people because we survived the darkness. We are full of hope, and we are ready to walk into the future."

To Be Continued...

Would you be so kind as to leave a Review on Amazon?

Go to www.Amazon.com
Put Walking Into The Unknown, Ginny Dye into the Search Box.

Leave a Review.

I love hearing from my readers!

Thank you!

The Bregdan Principle

Every life that has been lived until today is a part of the woven braid of life.

It takes every person's story to create history.

Your life will help determine the course of history.

You may think you don't have much of an impact.

You do.

Every action you take will reflect in someone else's life.

Someone else's decisions.

Someone else's future.

Both good and bad.

The Bregdan Chronicles

Storm Clouds Rolling In
1860 – 1861

On To Richmond
1861 – 1862

Spring Will Come
1862 – 1863

Dark Chaos
1863 – 1864

The Long Last Night
1864 – 1865

Carried Forward By Hope
April – December 1865

Glimmers of Change
December – August 1866

Shifted By The Winds
August – December 1866

Always Forward
January – October 1867

Walking Into The Unknown
October 1867 – October 1868

***Many more coming... Go to
DiscoverTheBregdanChronicles.com to see how
many are available now!***

Other Books by Ginny Dye

Pepper Crest High Series - Teen Fiction

Time For A Second Change
It's Really A Matter of Trust
A Lost & Found Friend
Time For A Change of Heart

Fly To Your Dreams Series – Allegorical Fantasy

Dream Dragon
Born To Fly
Little Heart
The Miracle of Chinese Bamboo

All titles by Ginny Dye
www.BregdanPublishing.com

Author Biography

Who am I? Just a normal person who happens to love to write. If I could do it all anonymously, I would. In fact, I did the first go round. I wrote under a pen name. On the off chance I would ever become famous - I didn't want to be! I don't like the limelight. I don't like living in a fishbowl. I especially don't like thinking I have to look good everywhere I go, just in case someone recognizes me! I finally decided none of that matters. If you don't like me in overalls and a baseball cap, too bad. If you don't like my haircut or think I should do something different than what I'm doing, too bad. I'll write books that you will hopefully like, and we'll both let that be enough! :) Fair?

But let's see what you might want to know. I spent many years as a Wanderer. My dream when I graduated from college was to experience the United States. I grew up in the South. There are many things I love about it but I wanted to live in other places. So I did. I moved 42 times, traveled extensively in 49 of the 50 states, and had more experiences than I will ever be able to recount. The only state I haven't been in is Alaska, simply because I refuse to visit such a vast, fabulous place until I have at least a month. Along the way I had glorious adventures. I've canoed through the Everglade Swamps, snorkeled in the Florida Keys and windsurfed in the Gulf of Mexico. I've white-water rafted down the New River and Bungee jumped in the Wisconsin Dells. I've visited every National Park (in the off-season when there is more freedom!) and many of the State Parks. I've hiked thousands of miles of mountain trails and biked through Arizona deserts. I've canoed and biked through Upstate New York and Vermont, and polished off as much lobster as possible on the Maine Coast.

I had a glorious time and never thought I would find a place that would hold me until I came to the Pacific Northwest. I'd been here less than 2 weeks, and I knew I would never leave. My heart is so at home here with the towering firs, sparkling waters, soaring mountains and rocky beaches. I love the eagles & whales. In 5 minutes I can be hiking on 150 miles of trails in the mountains around my home, or gliding across the lake in my rowing shell. I love it!

Have you figured out I'm kind of an outdoors gal? If it can be done outdoors, I love it! Hiking, biking, windsurfing, rock-climbing, roller-blading, snow-shoeing, skiing, rowing, canoeing, softball, tennis... the list could go on and on. I love to have fun and I love to stretch my body. This should give you a pretty good idea of what I do in my free time.

When I'm not writing or playing, I'm building I Am A Voice In The World - a fabulous organization I founded in 2001 - along with 60 amazing people who poured their lives into creating resources to empower people to make a difference with their lives.

What else? I love to read, cook, sit for hours in solitude on my mountain, and also hang out with friends. I love barbeques and block parties. Basically - I just love LIFE!

I'm so glad you're part of my world!

Ginny

Join my Email List so you can:

- Receive notice of all new books
- Be a part of my Launch Celebrations. I give away lots of Free gifts!
- Read my weekly BLOG while you're waiting for a new book.
- Be part of The Bregdan Chronicles Family!
- Learn about all the other books I write.

Just go to www.BregdanChronicles.net and fill out the form.

79490858R10272

Made in the USA
Columbia, SC
02 November 2017